Elli

A Second Chance Novel

Tina DeSalvo

This book is dedicated to my soulmate and one true love…my handsome and dear husband, Corey. You have been there in the good times and the bad…always with your amazing sense of humor and unconditional love. I'm a blessed gal.

And

To my dear children…my sons, Hal and Nicholas. You have filled my heart with pride and love and laughter…and palpitations on occasion.

This book is also dedicated to…

My nurses and doctors…You not only cared for me, but truly believed I would beat cancer. Dr. Camille, Dr. Doria, Dr. Stolier, Dr. Gamble, Dr. Long, Dr. King, Jenny, Doe, BJ, Donna and the staff of Mary Bird Perkins Cancer Center (including Sonya who gave the best hugs). You not only administered the medicines and treatments I required but gave me the love and spiritual healing I needed. You all are so very special…My heart is filled with love and gratitude for you each of you.

And, finally…

I dedicate this book to my mother…Ann. An inspiration on how to enjoy each and every day no matter what challenges are in your path. I miss you so very much, Momma. I know you are celebrating the debut of this book in heaven, wearing that pretty blue dress you said you would wear to my first book signing…

ACKNOWLEDGMENTS

This book could not have been written without the support, wisdom, inspiration, love, humor, patience and even the occasional threat from some of the wonderful people in my life. Some of them are recognized on this acknowledgements' page while others are forever remembered in my heart.

A special thanks to those individuals who helped with the local Cajun language, phrases and nuances that I used in this book including: my Cajun husband, Corey; my children, Hal and Nick; my mother-in-law, Gloria Callais; my friends and other family members. They are the true experts. Without them, Tante Izzy and the Bienvenu family could not have spoken with such Cajun spice and flair, Cher.

I acknowledge in a heartfelt way, my sister, Jo Ann DeSalvo Mattison, and my brother, Tom DeSalvo. During a difficult time with our aging mother's failing health, they encouraged me to finish this book. As the three of us took care of Momma, they made sure I had the time and peace-of-mind to write whenever possible. What a gift they gave me! Jo Ann, you gave unconditionally and tirelessly to Momma. Tom, you were dedicated, thoughtful and picked up the burden of practicality. I love you both. Thank you!

Thank you to my mother-in-law, Gloria, for teaching me how to be strong and faithful when life is tough, real tough. To my daughter-in-law, Kristen D Callais, who had amazing babies with my son, Hal. I thank you for teaching me what young, ambitious and noble women of your generation are like. I thank my sweet, wonderful, dear grandchildren, Molly, Trip and Grey, who make my life happier so I can imagine good and fun things to write about.

A special thanks to Stella Barcelona, my cousin, my critique partner, my left brain, my friend...We were not born in the usual way sisters are, but we became sisters through our stories and our passion for the creation of them. I would not have had so much fun or maintained my sanity on the journey to publication without you. I adore you. And, I adore your husband, Bob, too. Thank you, Bob, for never, ever complaining and always encouraging us.

I want to recognize Cherry Adair for her wisdom, encouragement, skills and most of all, friendship. You have made me a better writer and plotter. You get me and totally understand it when I say...if one is good, three is better. You see, I did finish the "Damn Book!". I thank my dear friend, the late, Kate Duffy for putting us together. I also thank her for encouraging me to continue writing for no other reason than ... "you write because you love to write."

I acknowledge the talented booksellers, Molly Bolden and Kay Levine. These ladies started me on my journey to publication oh, so many years ago. Thank you for directing me to my very first writers' conference and to so many amazing authors' books. You have found ways to inspire me over the years. I am grateful for our friendship that has grown beyond the books.

My dear friends, Camille, Denise, Cyd, Nancy Q, Julie S. and Plotters Ink-Eileen Dryer, Deborah Leblanc, Rita Clay Estrada, Cherry Adair and Stella Barcelona, as well as, Deborah Richardson of DRE&MS, my Facebook friends and Fans, my family from all the coasts and in between. You all inspire the words churning in me. I look forward to putting those words into more stories in the years to come.

Prologue

Los Angeles, California
Three Years Ago

"Yes, I understand that dog drool and silk are a fashion disaster."

Elli adjusted the cell phone to her ear with her left hand as she finished a text to the caterer on the second cell phone in her right hand. Francois Joseff was Hollywood's latest fashion sensation and the most sought after red carpet, gown designer of the stars. He was difficult and a bit of a primo-don, but her leading lady had paid Francois handsomely to design a gown for the movie premiere when she hated the one another designer had made for her. Elli had to tread carefully to keep him from abandoning her equally temperamental star the day before the big event.

As she talked and texted, Elli kept walking, her two assistants following quickly behind her into the conference room for the final logistics meeting for the movie premiere. Each of them carried one of Elli's other cellphones; one was in a canary yellow case and one was in a black case with the movie logo printed on it.

Each of Elli's phones was a different color so she could know to whom or at least to what category the incoming and outgoing calls belonged. Elli always kept the blingy, rhinestone phone for her A-list actors and movie investors. The canary yellow phone was for calls dealing with the director, cinematographer, locations director, editor or for anything having to do with the actual movie production. The avocado green phone was the money phone, for accounting, vendors and all money questions. And, the phone with the movie logo cover was for everything else. It was the phone number she gave to people she wanted her staff to screen and hopefully handle so she didn't have to add another person or thing to her very long, detailed, delightfully fun list. As crazy as it might seem to most, she loved the controlled chaos of being one of Hollywood's top producers. She loved owning and using color coded cell phones. She loved wearing designer stilettos and purses that matched those phones on days she felt playful. She loved being followed by assistants, anxious to prove themselves to her. She just loved her life.

"Your gown will be safe and remain perfect. I have assigned someone to each of the dogs for DDC," she told Francois, keeping her voice even and friendly. "They will not so much as shed a teardrop of moisture from their over productive bodies."

"DDC? What in the world is that?" Francois asked annoyed.

"Drool Damage Control. That is a very important and necessary job when your co-stars are Newfoundland dogs with overactive salivary glands." She smiled. "The gown will be protected from the dogs, but I can't promise that I can do anything about the onslaught of fans that will be there drooling over your amazingly fabulous gown." She laughed. "Gotta run. See you tomorrow night." She disconnected the phone, sat at the head of the table and looked around. One of her assistants extended the green phone toward her.

"You need to take this." Elli shook her head. All the current invoices had been paid. The deposits for the premiere were settled. Nothing was outstanding. The green phone could wait until after the meeting.

"It's your doctor with your test results."

"On the green phone?" She shook her head again. "Who gave him that number?" Her assistant shrugged her shoulders. "Tell him I'll call him after the meeting."

"He said you told him you would call him after your morning meetings two hours ago. He said he needs to speak to you now."

"I will talk to him later." Elli's stomach began to knot, the way it had when she heard he was on the office land line earlier. She didn't have time to talk to him now, or hear whatever he wanted to tell her. "Here are the final assignments," she said, handing the clipboards to the dozen staff members around the conference table. She began to discuss limo checkpoints, dog photo stations, and red carpet media positions. She couldn't fully focus on the meeting until her assistant hung up the green phone.

As soon as she did, the yellow phone began to ring.

"Elli, you really have to talk to him," her other assistant told her. "He won't take no for an answer. He said he has all of the numbers of all of the colored phones and he knows where the next meeting is. He also said if you don't take his call now, he has the invitation to the premiere you gave him and will bring a huge megaphone there to talk to you."

Elli shook her head and grabbed the phone. She had no doubt Dr. Doran would do exactly that. "Hold on," she snapped at him as she gazed around the table at her staff. Big eyes, small eyes, brown eyes and blue eyes were all staring at her. They didn't look like people waiting for instructions as she had hoped, they looked like people witnessing an awful traffic accident in the middle of the interstate.

"Lana, please take over. Review the assignments on the clipboards with everyone. See if there are any questions. Get everyone's cell phone numbers. You all make sure your phones are charged and the ringers are on. I'm paying for them, so I expect them to be working."

"Okay, you have 30 seconds," Elli told Dr. Doran as she walked out of the room into her private office. She looked at herself in the mirror that hung behind the door as she closed it. She didn't know why she had, but something told her that it was the face of a woman who would be changed in a matter of moments. In the second that thought rushed through her mind, her face and lips paled lighter than her freshly highlighted long blond hair. Her bright blue eyes dulled. She looked much older than her age. Instead of 31 she could have been 40, her mother's age when she died.

Elli had refused to take a needle biopsy of the lump in her right breast she had found a few days ago, because she couldn't prepare for the premiere with the post procedure limitations of not lifting anything for 48 hours. She had to be at full strength. She agreed to take the one hour PET scan instead.

"You are going to need to take more than 30 seconds for your health, Elli." He began, his British accent smooth, but anger tightened his tone. "We should be meeting face-to-face." He sighed and rushed on, not waiting for her to respond. "I know…no time. If your father were alive he would tell you to make the time." He cleared his throat. "You are a movie producer, Elli. You take on projects from the very beginning and see them to their conclusion. You have to do this now."

Elli held her breath as she walked to her desk on legs she couldn't feel move beneath her. She dropped into her chair, feeling the room turn white and hollow and loose its air. She knew what was coming. Her ears began to burn. Her heart began to ache. She didn't want to hear it.

"Elli, this is the biggest production of your life." He blew out a breath. His voice gentled. "I'm sorry. You have breast cancer."

* * * *

3 Months later

All of Elli's hair had fallen out, except on her legs. She couldn't help wondering with a bit of humor, where the fairness was in that? Her head was shiny and she didn't have a single eyelash to put mascara on, but she had to shave her legs. Make-up couldn't cover her red flushed skin caused from the steroids and other drugs added to her chemotherapy IV, or camouflage the extra puffiness of her face, but since Elli wasn't working on a new project, she figured it didn't really matter. She didn't have to impress or instill confidence in her skills as a producer to investors or A-list actors and directors. All she had to do was focus on fighting the cancer. It was a good thing, too. She couldn't imagine how so many of the other cancer patients maintained their jobs and chased after their children when they felt like they had a bad flu 24-7.

The work required to battle the cancer was hard. Dr. Doran had been right about that. It was the most important production of her life. And, it wasn't the suffering that made it so. The emotional toll, what it did to your soul, was what made getting up and out of bed each day such a chore. Some days were worse than others. Today was one of those days.

Elli thought it may have been the hardest of all the days fighting the cancer. The side effects of chemo were particularly brutal and loneliness was dismally paralyzing. Yet, it was on this day when she didn't want to speak or even make eye contact with another soul because she didn't have the energy to engage another person in any way, that Elli met a wise and very empathetic woman. She was sitting in the chemo infusion lab next to Elli getting what looked like the same red IV cocktail, when she suggested there were other people who felt like Elli did at that very moment. "How would they feel if they knew they weren't alone?" she asked Elli.

Elli looked at this beautiful woman, who was as bald as she was and about the same age. No one had accompanied her to the chemo lab for the three hours she received her IV to play cards with her, gossip or to hold her hand. Elli had always come for treatment alone, too. She had convinced herself she preferred it that way even when the fear and loneliness left her trembling. Was it the same for this woman? Elli felt too sick and tired and weak to talk to her, to ask her if she was also alone, scared. She wondered it, though.

"You know, when I feel sad and woeful," she said, her voice just loud enough for Elli to hear, "I think of the others like me and you, who are attached from med-ports in their chests to their life-saving or death-delaying IVs and I don't feel alone." She smiled, her lips a little blue and dry. "I'm in a weird sort of club." Her eyes settled on Elli's very deliberately. "You're in the club, too and you don't even realize it."

Elli smiled weakly, not wanting to be rude to this woman. "I don't want to be in the club."

"It doesn't matter what you want. Membership doesn't come by choice." She began to cough, struggling to catch her breath. One of the nurses came over to check her, placing a stethoscope to her chest and calling another nurse over. Elli could see by the look on their faces, they were concerned about the woman.

Undeterred, she leaned to the side a little to peer around the nurses and see Elli. "It means something to others that we are going through this," she managed, when she caught her breath. "It's why I write a blog." She began to cough again and handed the nurse something. The nurse gave it to Elli before rushing to the telephone.

Elli looked at the piece of paper. It was a hand written blog address and a password. The woman's blog. She must have written it on the paper before they began speaking.

Seconds later, a medical team came racing through the lab door with a stretcher. One nurse disconnected the IV from the woman's port as another placed an oxygen mask over her mouth and nose. They then lifted and placed her on the stretcher. One of the oncologists came running into the room from the nearby clinic offices pulling his stethoscope off of his neck.

The pretty woman was now as white as the sheet on the stretcher, except for her blue lips. She took the oxygen mask off of her face. The nurses tried stop her but when she insisted, they conceded, telling her she could keep it off, but for only a moment. In a voice that was thin but directed at Elli so she could hear her over the voices of the medical staff, she called her by name. "Elli Morenelli. I give you this blog to shepherd and foster as it was given to me so our words and thoughts can live for another day, even if we do not…"

Elli never learned how the woman knew her name, but her words echoed in Elli's head long after she was taken from the room, so haunting…frightening…and poignant.

Elli discovered that the woman had died three days later. Her name was Daisy Wilkinson.

It was on the day of Daisy's death that Elli wrote her first blog. It was about an insightful, selfless, beautiful woman who had given her a gift like no one else had. As if Daisy had known exactly what Elli needed. Somehow she had looked into her soul.

"I don't know if anyone is reading this. I will trust in the faith of that wondrous woman that someone is, because they need to see my words and I theirs. We should celebrate that we are here today, to write this and read it. Let us be thankful for the people we know, touch, love and hear today…for people like Daisy, who blossom in our lives for but a little while, yet make it so much prettier and better. Let us not worry about tomorrow."

Chapter One

Today is my mother's birthday. Please say a prayer for her. Her name was Mary Grace. I've never told you all this before, my Bosom Blog Buddies, but breast cancer killed her when she was just 40. I miss her so much. I was only 13 at the time, too young to think of things like how awful it had been for her to know she was leaving her only child and beloved husband...I was hurting too much to think of such things. I was aware enough to understand how much my dear, sweet father grieved at the end of my mom's life and in all the years afterwards. As his daughter, I was a salve for his open wound, but it never healed. I could never make him whole again as much as I tried. He loved her so deeply. Thank God, I am single. I will never know that kind of pain. I will always remain single. I hope that doesn't offend any of you with families. If I had a family before cancer, I would probably have a different perspective. I'm sorry to sound so morose. I promised you all to keep this blog real from the beginning...good days and bad and all that fall between. BTW, say a prayer for my dad, too. Today is the two year anniversary of his death. It wasn't cancer that killed him. He had a bad heart. A broken heart. I wish you good health, E.

Bosom Blog Buddies Post

Cane, Louisiana
Present Day

"You know, Elli, you can only eat an elephant one bite at a time," her attorney and friend, Abby McCord, said. Her raspy, familiar voice resonated over the speakers in Elli's parked 550 Mercedes Cabriolet. Her tone was clear: "You aren't getting any pity from me, girlfriend. Toughen up." What she did get from Abby was an eternal and undiluted kinship. It had been that way from the day they met over three years ago in the chemo infusion clinic, each connected to an IV line one month after Daisy passed away. She also got a confidant who understood what it was like living in remission.

Elli gripped the steering wheel. "Yes, I know, you can only eat an elephant one bite at a time. What I don't know is why it always has to be butt first." She stared out the window at the locked gate keeping her from continuing down the narrow country road to salvation, or at least to what would be the foundation's salvation. "When is it my turn to get the easy button?"

"Do you really want me to answer that?"

"Of course not." Elli leaned back into her seat. A lazy breeze wafted into the car, carrying the scent of rich, moist soil and slow-moving water from a canal flowing through the Sugar Mill Plantation. It was a break from the heavy humidity thickening the mid February day. It helped break the cloying gardenia perfume from the tiny dog she rented, who was thankfully sleeping next to her. Right now, the only thing on her mind was getting onto her property, the beautiful Sugar Mill Plantation that she had inherited one month earlier...half inherited, she corrected to herself with a sigh. The other half belonged to a man she'd never met and had only spoken to through his attorney.

Elli closed her eyes a moment and took a deep breath to center herself. Since finishing her breast cancer treatment three years ago, she never let herself forget that life was complicated, fragile, imperfect, unpredictable...wonderful. The wonderful part often came in varying degrees, but there was a life to live. A life she now understood was grand in its imperfection. She had to keep that truth at the heart of each day. She was a blessed woman. Blessed to be alive and blessed to have gotten this inheritance from an aunt she barely knew, at a time when she really needed it.

"I've been on the road for nearly three days with a dog who has a queen-complex and is frustratingly relentless with her demands. I'm tired, anxious, and cranky. I can sort of see and smell the Holy Grail, Abby, but can't touch it. The Gene I.D. Foundation will die if I don't capture it. I want to capture it, hold it up, and hear the chorus of angels sing 'hallelujah' as a brilliant white light shines down on it."

"Really, Elli?" Abby said, sarcasm and humor echoing over the phone. "Don't you think that's a bit over the top? Life isn't played out in movie scenes. Life is a bit more...more..."

"Real."

"Realistic," Abby stated, in her usual solid, stable, logical way.

"I know. I know. I'm being melodramatic." Elli frowned. "I'm just worried about not being able to change the foundation's dire fate. So many people are counting on me to help them."

"We are in this fight together."

"Thank God." Elli smiled, remembering how, over pizza and tears, they came up with the idea. It had been two years after Elli finished cancer treatment that, following Abby's advice, they both decided to take the genetic test for the inherited breast cancer gene. She tested positive but Abby did not. She was happy about her friend's results, but it felt like she had been diagnosed with cancer again; only this time, she wasn't as hopeful she would ever be rid of this awful disease. Cancer was in the very basic foundation of her body, like a poorly set cornerstone inadequately supporting a stone building. It was only a matter of time before it crumbled…before she crumbled. So, working their way through the heartache and fear, Elli and Abby established an agenda, a mission statement, and a timetable for the Gene I.D. Foundation. The foundation would provide financial assistance for patients unable to afford the expensive BRCA genetic test. They soon expanded their goals to include providing financial assistance for families who had negative fallout because of positive test results. This was possible because Abby provided legal and administrative work for free while Elli generously donated her ready cash to start the foundation. Being able to use her healthy movie residual checks to live on made this possible since she no longer had other income.

"You are my rock," Elli told Abby, knowing the words fell short of expressing how much she treasured their friendship.

"And you are my roll," Abby laughed. "Your crazy talk and perspective on a situation are pure joy when they don't get on my nerves." She laughed again. "Seriously, you're not giving yourself credit. You're a big-time producer who can manage multimillion-dollar budgets and flaky stars at the same time. You can do that because you are organized, ambitious, and thorough. Just because there is a drama-queen gremlin living inside you that likes to raise its frazzled head from time to time doesn't make you incompetent."

"I know that. I'm not completely lacking in self-confidence." Elli laughed, looking at the canine diva sleeping next to her without a worry in the world. "And for the record, I'm no longer a producer. I'm a cofounder and chairwoman of the Gene I.D. Foundation that is in major trouble—thanks to me. And we were so close to being financially solvent, Abby. The Griffith Park fundraiser was so amazing, wasn't it? The gowns, the celebrities, the sparkle, the money…" Elli paused, took a deep breath and sighed. "Oh dear, God…the money."

"Don't go there. What's done is done."

Elli again felt the weight of the world on her heart. "It was too perfect. I still can't believe I didn't follow my something-doesn't-feel-right radar that went up during my initial meeting with the FR Group."

"Don't beat yourself up. They were considered one of the top event planners."

Still, she had ignored the warning signs. They had been too anxious, too accommodating. Pride had her reasoning that their red-carpet treatment was a result of them being thrilled to work for her noble project and with her, an Academy Award winning producer. "Have you heard anything from the LAPD?"

"Nothing you want to hear." Elli heard Abby typing on her computer, where she always kept her notes. "The LAPD found that the once-reputable CEO of the FR Group not only stole all of our Griffith Park event donations, but he stole an additional two million from the credit cards our donors used to make their contributions."

"Identity theft?" Elli's heart sank, then constricted.

She clutched her chest, knowing it wasn't a heart attack but unable to imagine it hurting more if it was. "God help us." She forced herself to take a deep breath.

Abby exhaled and Elli imagined seeing her friend lifting her chin and stiffening her spine. "We need the money from the sale of your share of the plantation to have any hope of keeping this foundation operating. That's how we'll rebuild our reputation. Doing good deeds. Good PR." There was more tapping on the computer. "By the way, I had my accountant check the business plan you sent me. He agrees with your figures. The money from the sale will cover the current commitment to our clients and fund operating expenses for a year."

Elli glanced at the tiny, furry, rented dog that would help her save the foundation. "The Gene I.D. Foundation can't die."

Both women remained silent, each left to settle the demons Elli's statement awakened. Elli scanned the locked, pristine, white gate and the eight-foot, vertical slatted fence. Maybe Tom Cruise could scale the fence with his Mission Impossible skills, but she couldn't, despite the fact that she was the fittest she'd ever been. Besides, the fence looked wired. She wasn't willing to find out if it was just a security sensor or an electrified line. Either way, the fence was doing what it was supposed to do. She wouldn't have expected anything less after googling Ben Bienvenu and his highly reputable dog-training facility located on Sugar Mill Plantation. He'd spare no expense keeping the dogs safe at his prized kennel. He'd also spare no expense to keep her out.

"I'd appreciate it if you could do your legal magic and get me onto my property."

"I'll call Mr. Bienvenu's attorney," Abby said, her voice all business.

"I already did. His answering machine message said, and I quote, 'At parade. If you need an attorney, check the telephone book.'"

"You're kidding me!" She laughed. "What parade?"

Elli glanced at the handwritten note stapled to the gate's lock-entry keypad. *At parade. Kennel closed.* "The parade apparently."

She reached out her car window, trying to keep the Louisiana road dust from dirtying the sleeve of her Escada suit. She'd just taken the car through an automatic carwash thirty minutes before, but it was dirtier now than before she washed it. She pressed the call button on the keypad with her short, unpolished fingertip once, then five times more.

"It's Mardi Gras." Abby stated as if it just dawned on her what the parade business was all about.

"Mardi Gras is always on Tuesdays. Today is Friday."

"It's Mardi Gras season. I just read something in the Wall Street Journal about the expected economic impact and trickle-down effect it has on Louisiana." Abby's voice faded on the last words. "Anyway, I've gone off topic. The bottom line is the story indicated that there are weeks of parades and parties."

"Are you telling me that the kennel is shut down for weeks and I won't be able to get on my property until after Mardi Gras?" She hadn't driven three long days with a gardenia-scented dog that had an over inflated ego, only to be defeated before she got a chance to fight. "We don't have that kind of time. Funding will run out by the middle of next month." She thought about that for a few seconds before continuing. "I intend to get the money to continue our work."

"Then," Abby said, "you have to convince Mr. Bienvenu to sell the plantation. It's a hell of a predicament. It was generous for your Aunt Rosa to name you in her will, but it's pretty damn rude of her to have so many strings attached. The worst being that the plantation has to be sold as a whole entity to a nonrelated third party. It would have been simpler if you could have just sold your share of the plantation and kennel to Mr. Bienvenu."

Elli looked past the gate toward an outcropping of buildings 1.4 miles down the road. She knew the distance and the function of each of those buildings after studying the site maps she'd been sent. Some of the buildings were hidden from view by the large trees and evergreen bushes surrounding them. The vegetation hadn't been noted on those maps, but she was pleased to see it there. Landscaping, natural or otherwise, added value to the property.

"I have some third-party investors in mind," Elli said, thinking about the list she'd compiled on her computer. Most of them were venture capitalists with movie industry interest. "First things first. I have to get on my property, survey the place, and put together a sales brochure. I'll make sure I include this Fort Knox fence. It makes a good first impression. The movie cameras will love its long, thick lines and hate its bright, reflective hue. Best of all, producers will love how it offers a layer of security to keep their stars safe."

"Correction. First, you need to convince Mr. Bienvenu to sell the place."

Elli reached under her seat and pulled out the binoculars she found handy to travel with long ago, when she used to scout movie locations. She scanned the area around the buildings, hoping to see signs of someone coming to let her in. Nothing. Nobody. She didn't even see any canine things nearby. The only dog she knew for certain was around was the tiny, designer rent-a-pooch she had the great misfortune as her travel companion. An adorable bundle of champagne fluff that was sleeping in the passenger seat and not giving her one of the perfected, disparaging doggie-looks she was apt to give when she was awake.

"I can't imagine that they'd shut down the kennel for the entire Mardi Gras season," she said, slouching in her seat.

"Mr. Bienvenu's attorney would've told me if it was a problem when I informed him of your plans to see your property."

"As I remember, he did tell you it was a problem. So did the Louisiana lawyer we hired to help us navigate through the state's Napoleonic laws."

"Let me clarify. The problem with you going to Vacherie Parish and Sugar Mill Plantation has nothing to do with Mardi Gras. It has to do with Mr. Bienvenu. He doesn't want to share, nor does he play well with others."

"No problem there. I want to conduct business with him, not play games," Elli said, spotting a five-foot alligator sunning itself on the bank of a wide canal off to the right of the drive. She lifted her binoculars to study it more closely. Two mockingbirds swooped down over the alligator and narrowly escaped a quick thrash of the gator's wide-open mouth. "I've been dropped into Swamp People," she whispered, dropping her binoculars back into the case.

"Okay, movie lady, let's not be too dramatic here. You are on an elegant southern plantation."

"Huh. Just get me the code to the gate or get someone over here to open it. Please." She and Abby ended their conversation with neither one confident about Elli's prospects.

Elli returned the binoculars beneath the seat and picked up her BPA-free bottle of organic grape vitamin water, taking a deep gulp. The tiny fur ball next to her cocked her head prettily and perked her ears. Donna was bred to look adorable. She was equal parts white Bolognese and champagne toy poodle—a Bolonoodle. According to her friend, Blaine, a movie dog handler, he discovered his new talent in a very famous and exclusive dog-breeding salon in Paris. Elli hadn't been charmed by the dog's pedigree, but she'd foolishly been attracted to her sweet-looking button eyes when she'd gone to her friend Blaine's house to rent one of his movie dogs.

She needed a dog to impress the stubborn Ben Bienvenu. Elli figured if he trained search-and-rescue and hunting dogs, he must have a genuine affection for the species. That was what she had learned from observing the dog trainers she'd had around the movie set. They loved the dogs they trained. Elli figured that since she couldn't find any common ground between her and Ben, other than owning the plantation and kennel they had jointly inherited, she'd create a commonality. She would be a dog owner and lover, like Ben. The plan seemed sound until she was two hours east of Los Angeles on I-10 and Donna got carsick. Eww. She realized right then that even designer Bolonoodles were gross. The thought of the episode, and the two after, still made Elli gag. Thank goodness for the doggie carsickness medicine she found at the PETCO just outside of Palm Springs.

She took another swig of water and Donna lightly tapped her high-end paw on Elli's hand that lay on the armrest between them. She poured a little bit of flavored water in the tiny weighted bowl in the drink holder, knowing little Miss Prissy wouldn't be happy with its tepid temperature. It was better to have her reject it than hear her whining, especially when Elli was doing enough of it on her own.

"Now what do we do, Donna?" The dog sneezed at the water and sat, head cocked. "I had hopes that Mr. Bienvenu wasn't as ill-mannered as he presented himself in our dealings over the past month. It seems I may have been too optimistic. He's definitely not the up-on-a-pedestal, honorable genius Aunt Rosa raved about in her will." Donna yawned, looking bored. "Yes, I know. Why did I take what my crazy Aunt Rosa said as gospel when I didn't really know her except for her crazier-than-a-loon reputation? Well, when a person dies and gives you her fourteen hundred plus acre estate, you tend to ignore the bad stuff and think kindly of them. The truth is, it's not her fault Mr. Bienvenu is a coward and a jerk."

Elli looked at the note again, then lifted it and began punching random numbers onto the keypad beneath it. A red light flashed. The gate didn't budge. She tried again. The red light stayed on. Donna looked at her and sniffed. "Well, I have to do something."

A breeze wafted into the car, once again carrying the rich scent of the fertile soil. Donna stood, sneezed, and tinkled on the three-inch stack of newspapers Elli had learned to keep positioned beneath her. The four-legged doggie-diva high-stepped away from the wet spot, looking at Elli as if to tell her to clean up the mess, which, of course, Elli did.

"Don't you worry, Donna," she told the pooch, certain she wasn't worried at all. "I'll get us in." Donna sat back on the remaining newspapers, crossed her dainty paws with their dark pink Chanel polish, and ignored Elli. She decided to ignore Donna, too. She needed to focus on getting onto her property and not being eaten by an alligator in the process.

Elli scanned the freshly painted, white and kelly green sign identifying the place as the Sugar Mill Plantation Kennel and punched the phone button on her steering wheel.

"Number?" the factory-programmed female voice asked.

She read the number off the sign and waited for the call to connect. Once again, she got the answering machine. This time, she didn't leave a message. If no one responded to the six before it, she supposed a seventh wouldn't help. She turned off the car's engine, uncertain how long she should wait, but certain she didn't want to waste fuel in her current financial situation. She was also certain she didn't want to waste money on a hotel room when she owned a perfectly fine, five-bedroom plantation down the drive on the other side of the locked gate.

Elli ran her hand over the soft wool of her favorite powder blue suit. She had selected it to give Ben Bienvenu a first impression of her being a woman of confidence, professionalism, and competence. It was four years old, but the color, a few shades lighter than her eyes, still looked as rich as the day she purchased it at Neiman Marcus. Would he even see it today? Would she be able to initiate her plan to earn his trust and persuade him that she had a profitable solution to their impasse?

Blast. How long did a parade occupy someone's time in Cane, Louisiana?

Elli flipped down the visor and looked into the mirror. Her makeup, which she had applied with a light hand at the gas station down the road, was still good. Her eyes might look a bit brighter with annoyance and her cheeks rosier with frustration, but she didn't think she appeared as anxious as she felt. She snapped the visor up, not bothering to check her unruly, short, caramel curls. Her hair no longer held the importance her once long, flowing, blond, wavy tresses had.

"Ready to find a way in, Donna?" The furry mass of cuteness blinked her perfect, coal-black pooch eyes and yawned. Elli smoothed her skirt and took in a deep, cleansing breath. "I'm coming around to get you. Stay and be good for ten seconds. No tinkling." She knew only one of the three requests would be met. The dog was not going anywhere.

Elli stepped out of her car onto the edge of where the crushed rock and oyster shell drive met dark Louisiana mud. Her Christian Louboutins sank into the ground. "Perfect," she groaned, looking down where she should have seen the Louboutins' red soles. She guessed the soft earth, the color of dark chocolate, was what you got when you built a road a few yards from what the estate maps called a bayou. It was the size of one of the small channels around Balboa Island near Newport Beach. Regardless of what you called it, the result of its ebb and flow was acres of healthy sugarcane, she noted, looking across the bayou at the straight rows of knee-high swaying cane. The land lease for the cane fields was a profitable perk for Sugar Mill Plantation, one she would make note of in the sales brochure she planned to send to prospective buyers.

Elli hobbled to the passenger side of her car to get Donna, who was doing her usual kangaroo imitation. Whenever left alone in the car for two seconds, Donna bounced up and down on the seat as if it was a trampoline. "Can you not be so demanding this one time? I'm struggling here." Elli thought about her comfy running shoes in the trunk. She was ruining a great pair of Laboutins for a man who happily walked in doggie poop.

She opened the door and Donna stopped jumping, lifting her high-class snout. That's what she got for renting a dog that looked like a little girl's toy with one of those cute commercial names like My Lil' Petty. She'd been bred for childless couples with deep pockets or for women who wanted to carry her in a matching Gucci bag. Blaine had dressed this particular model in a fuchsia leather and rhinestone collar to coordinate with the trim on her zebra-patterned kennel.

"Don't get all better-than-thou on me, you little snob. You may be pretty, but you pee like a stray mutt in a dirty alley." Elli lifted the overly excited Donna from the car seat and was promptly rewarded with a pale yellow spot shaped like the state of Idaho on the front of her tailored skirt.

"Of course, you did…" she gasped but her voice was drowned by the blast of an air horn and the whooping of a dozen men. It startled Elli so much she dropped Donna back onto the car seat, causing the princess puppy to begin yapping like a cocaine-addicted auctioneer.

"Happy Mardi Gras!" someone shouted as a decapitated school bus of chaos plowed down the drive toward her. The roof-less old bus was painted in stripes of royal purple, kelly green, and metallic gold. Fat letters proclaiming it The Party Express spread across its side. Ten speakers positioned for maximum coverage blasted "Iko, Iko" at higher decibels than the gospel music in her car. Donna was having no part of this rowdy group. She took off, heading away from the bus and straight for the canal.

"No," Elli shouted, seeing the image of a huge alligator mouth thrashing toward mockingbirds—scratch that—toward Donna! Elli took off after her. "Stop. No. Heel." She managed only four long strides into the field before her shoes were sucked into the Louisiana mud hiding beneath the tall green grass. Her feet jerked out of the shoes and managed a few more steps until they got sucked into the wet pudding earth as well. She fell facedown. Elli heard a splash, then a doggie yipe. "Donna!"

"Well, I'll be damned. I've never seen a dog that can't swim," a deep, masculine voice drawled from somewhere above and behind her. Elli gave no thought to how high her skirt slid up her legs or the fact that her tiny scrap of lace panty might be exposed. Donna was going to be eaten by an alligator!

A flash of neon orange leaped over her as she tried to get up. She watched as the back of a tall man with shoulder-length black hair, wearing a satin, neon-orange costume trimmed in black sequins, raced into the water. An oversized black, red, and white-lighted pirate ship hat flew off his head as he reached for Donna. It bobbed like an amusement park ride with its lights twinkling in the wake created by both man and dog. She heard him shout something in the direction of the alligator on the bank, and her heart stopped.

"Watch out for the alligator," she screamed, knowing it was seconds too late and unnecessary. The man obviously saw it. Still, she warned him again. "Alligator."

Elli got up and raced on bare feet to the bayou's edge, watching as the alligator swam away. It gave her little comfort. The vicious creature was still too close and might return. Elli turned toward Donna who was wet, wide-eyed, and safe in the man's arms. In fact, Donna looked better than safe. If Elli wasn't mistaken, the silly dog was looking all dopey-eyed at her human rescuer. Oddly, Elli understood why. He was a fine specimen of male human. She supposed even a dog would appreciate his dark, rugged, man's man features set against dreamy eyes the color of the emerald sugarcane. He was a beauty, and Donna was appreciating his rescue with smooth, happy licks to his large hands.

"This your dog?" the super gorgeous man asked.

"What? Uh. Yes." Elli's heart seemed to skip when all that male energy was directed at her. She looked away, hoping to reengage her brain, then spotted the twinkling hat. "Your pirate ship is sinking in the canal."

He looked at her a moment, then cocked his head in the confused way she'd seen Donna do when she discussed her plans for the Sugar Mill Plantation. "It's a bayou."

"Whatever." She needed distance from the alligator, the murky water, and the neon pirate. They were sucking all the dense, humid air and she needed to breathe. She turned to walk back to her car and plowed into an army of neon-orange-clad men lined up as if ready to charge into some amusement park battle. Most had the same silly, lighted pirate's hat, except for one man who had a lighted hard hat with cans of beer on both sides and clear tubing extending from it. The ends of the tubes were positioned near his mouth. "Convenient."

"I think so." He laughed and took a big sip.

"Hey, lady," the deep voice behind her rumbled with annoyance. "Your dog."

Elli turned and saw his lifted brows and crooked I'm-not-so-happy grin. "Can you hold her until I get a towel?" She looked down at her skirt with the Idaho-shaped piddle stain, mud, and grass smears around it and sighed. "What's the point?," she muttered in a defeated tone and walked back to the good-looking pirate man standing on the bayou edge and took Donna from him, holding her away from her body at arm's length. The dog whined and began to tinkle.

"Hey, your dog's leaking," one of the pirates shouted, to the hooting laughter of the others.

The jabs and laughter continued until the man with the giant beer-can hat walked up to Elli and scratched Donna under her chin. Donna kicked her hind legs with excitement. "You're a cute thing," he said, sliding his finger under the fuchsia and rhinestone Prada collar. "This, however, is way over the top."

"That said by a man wearing neon-orange satin clothes and a six-pack on his head," Elli countered.

"Hey, it's not a six-pack. It's two tall forties." The men laughed. "Besides, men are supposed to look like this during Mardi Gras. Never should a dog look like a nursery rhyme in drag." He turned to

Donna's rescuer. "Tell her. Real dogs should have drool dripping from their mouths and hunters walking alongside them."

"Mais yeah, Ben," another man shouted in a heavy Cajun accent. "Tell her, a real dawg should fetch a beer from da fridge while da ball game is on. Dat way nobody has to get off da recliner."

Elli's head snapped around to the man they were addressing. She noticed that he had a sexy little scar bisecting his lopsided grin. Ben. Ben Bienvenu? Her partner? Donna's hero. Alligator eliminator.

"A real dog," another man in neon shouted as he swayed a bit drunkenly. "A real dog should be able to protect your woman and lick his…"

"Whoa, I think she's got the picture," Ben said interrupting the rowdy group, all of whom, Elli now realized, were well on their way to having hangovers. The only man seemingly sober was her new partner.

She whirled around to face him, Donna still projecting out from her arms. "So, you are Ben Bienvenu."

He bowed at the waist and waved the dripping pirate hat he'd just retrieved from the bayou. "At your service." He winked, and she noticed another thin scar in the crease of his smiling eyes, causing an unwelcome fluttering in her midsection. Nerves, she reasoned, as his cronies howled and offered a few R-rated suggestions on what kind of services he could render. No doubt about it, his at your service comment was intended more for them than her. The way his eyes crinkled and mouth smirked in boyish humor made that clear. Her odd reaction to him wasn't worth a second thought. It had just been the result of her encounter with the alligator, Donna's near demise, and all that neon.

"Well," Elli said on an exhale, not exactly sure how to introduce herself to her partner. This was not the first impression she'd spent days planning. She stiffened her spine and lifted her chin.

"Uh-oh." The man with the beer cans strapped to his head frowned.

"Mr. Bienvenu." Elli tucked Donna into the crook of her arm, wiped her free hand on her skirt, and extended it to Ben. "I'm Elli Morenelli, I own the Sugar Mill Plantation with you."

Ben Bienvenu shook her hand but looked at the man with the beer cans strapped to his head. His once emerald eyes darkened to the color of army fatigues. Beer man ignored Ben and with a smile, extended his hand to Elli.

"Hi, Elli. I'm Beau Bienvenu, Ben's attorney. We spoke on the phone a few times. Welcome to Cane, Louisiana."

* * * *

The midmorning sun was drying the dew-dampened land of Sugar Mill Plantation just as it had days, years, and centuries before the Bienvenues settled there. It seemed the same, but Ben knew it was different. The humid air felt different against his skin, as did the dark soil beneath his feet. Elli Morenelli arriving on the plantation did that. She disrupted the rhythm of the air and the land. She was here to change what had been there for over two hundred years. Ben didn't want change.

Ben stood next to his truck as he watched Beau drive his sleek, clean, black 520 BMW into the driveway behind the main house. As his cousin got out of the car, Ben climbed into his truck, with his ever present companion, Lucky, a black lab, bull terrier and God knows what else mix. It was an odd looking animal, that mostly looked like a lab but with shorter legs and tail. It was a rescue.

"If you want to talk to me, get in my truck." He started the engine. It was Lucky's signal to lie down on the seat next to Ben where he remained until the engine was turned off. "But I'd think twice about doing it," he growled. "I am not a happy man, Beauregard. Not a happy man at all. And I lay most of the blame for that on you. Your job was to prevent her from showing up to claim her half of my property. Instead, you invited her to spend the night in one of the slave quarter bunks. Here. On my property!"

"Good morning to you, too." Beau opened the passenger door and climbed into the old, dusty, work truck. His voice was hoarse from a night of excessive parade partying. The rest of him, besides a little red spidering in his eyes, didn't show any signs of the hangover that Ben knew Beau had to be suffering. He never understood how Beau managed to always look so fresh and put together. He was like his car. Expensive. High-maintenance. Good-looking. It hadn't always been that way for him. Uncle Ronald found him and his brother, Jack, while responding to a spousal abuse call at a rusty, leaky trailer down the bayou. It wasn't the spousal abuse of the boys' parents that needed the Sheriff's attention. That day he rescued the boys from a life of neglect and hardship and eventually adopted them.

Ben shook his head. "I was really hoping you'd feel like crap this morning, pretty boy." He gunned the engine, jerking Beau into his seat.

"Nope. I'm fresh as a new-sprung daisy." He slipped on his three-hundred-dollar sunglasses and buckled the seat belt. "Now you, cousin, look like the bottom of a chum bucket. And you weren't the one who drank adult beverages until your knees turned to gumbo. Go figure. Was it the little lady that kept you up last night?"

Ben could deny that Elli Morenelli's arrival had robbed him of his sleep, but Beau would know the truth. No one knew him better than his cousin and best friend. There wasn't a childhood memory that didn't include Beau. So he ignored both the question and the fancy Mercedes they had just passed that was parked in front of the slave house where Elli Morenelli had spent the night.

"She's probably on California time and still asleep." Beau said, straining to look back at her car. He loved fast, expensive vehicles. "She'll be looking for you when she wakes. I'm sure you know that. As your attorney, I advise you not to take such an adversarial position with her. You attract more bees with sugar than vinegar."

Ben rolled his eyes. "Give me a break. The only thing you got right in that saying is the bee part. The woman stings my ass." He opened the gate with his remote.

Beau shook his head and petted Lucky on the head. "I know you don't want her here. I know you don't want her to own fifty percent of Sugar Mill and thirty percent of the kennel. The facts are that she is here, and she does have ownership of both. Deal with it."

Ben sneered. "I damn well don't want to deal with the woman, just like I didn't want to have to deal with her aunt after my father died. I can't believe he let his pecker ruin my life. I'm sure we can find a judge who'd agree that just because her aunt screwed my daddy for eleven years, she doesn't have the right to steal what's been in my family for two hundred years."

"Sorry, cuz, you know that's not true. You're getting all emotional here. It's not like you. Think." Beau waited until Ben nodded for him to continue. "We lost when we challenged Rosa's right to inherit when your dad died. Without that being overturned, Rosa has every right to give her property to whomever she wants."

Ben gripped the steering wheel tighter. He didn't bother trying to hide his anger from his voice. "I know. I know. It's all legal. But it's still bullshit."

"Yep. But as unorthodox as the terms of her will are, it's within the confines of the law." Beau strummed his fingers on the dash. "You do have options, you know? It involves negotiating. Maybe some compromise. All within your capacity, big guy. You're a charming fellow." Beau folded his arms over his chest. "Well, you have the potential to be charming. I'm told you are reasonably good-looking." He looked at Ben. "I'm told women like that long hair, messy jeans, and hiking boots look. Me, I think you need a haircut and some khakis."

Ben glanced at the crazy man sitting next to him. Had he made a mistake hiring him as his attorney? "What in the hell are you talking about?"

"I'm talking about making use of your wiles. Make her like you..."

"Like me? As in sliding between the sheets with her? Are you crazy?"

Beau sighed. "No, you dummy. Make her like you as in a 'you can trust me' sort of way. You know, make a good, professional impression on Elli."

"That said by my attorney who was shitfaced and wearing tall forties on his head when he introduced himself to her."

"Yeah, I was, wasn't I?" Beau smiled.

"You're fired."

Beau started laughing. "Come on, Ben. Charming Miss Morenelli isn't a hardship. She's damn nice to look at with her tight, hot body and her sexy, Sophia Loren meets Isabella Rossellini face. You've got to admit, she's got all the right features from her ancestors without that long nose her Aunt Rosa had."

"That long nose didn't stop my daddy from falling into bed with the woman and keeping her there for eleven years," Ben muttered. Not that he was even considering seducing the alluring Miss Morenelli. He thought about her big, light blue eyes, prettier than any Husky pup he'd seen. Her short, café au lait hair was every bit as creamy colored as his first dog, a stray he named Molly. He thought he'd never see that exact combination of tan, blond, and brown caught in the sunlight like he had the morning of his sixth birthday when he found Molly running through the cane fields. To him, the dog looked as if she was surrounded by a halo and was an answer to his prayers. Elli's hair caught the sun that same way; only she wasn't an answer to his prayers, not by any stretch of the imagination.

"She's tall like Rosa," he said, ready to change the subject and not wanting to discuss her features in as much detail as he recalled them. "Speaking of Rosa, I don't think she'd have left Basil, Rosemary, and Tutti to Elli if she knew how her niece treated her dog. Did you see the way she held her?"

"You don't have a say in the matter," Beau reminded him. "She inherited her aunt's dogs. I've got the legal documents that say so."

"I'll see to it that she gets the three dogs." Ben turned into the parking lot of the Vacherie Parish animal shelter.

"What are you up to?" Beau ran his hands through his short black hair. "Tell me you are here on one of your rescue missions to save a stray and train it for some budget-crunching police force somewhere? Tell me you being here has nothing to do with Elli?"

Ben put the truck into park and cut the engine. Lucky sat up and yawned. Ben looked at Beau. The man was a pain in the ass. It had been a big mistake letting him tag along. "Why don't you focus on finding a loophole so one hundred percent of Sugar Mill is mine as it rightfully should be? Let me deal with what I know. Dogs." He rolled down the window and climbed out of the truck, annoyed when Beau followed him inside the shelter. Too bad he didn't stay happily in the truck with his nose stuck out the window like Lucky did.

"There isn't a loophole." Beau grabbed the door that Ben let close in front of him.

"Hi, Ben." The twenty-something petite blonde, who'd recently transformed herself into a mutation of Dolly Parton and Pamela Anderson, eased out of her desk chair. "Hello, Beau," she added with a lot less enthusiasm. Ben wasn't surprised. Beau and Sally had been an item for one of his cousin's usual two-week romantic liaisons. That was about as much time as he gave to any relationship, and the women of Cane knew it. Still, they all hoped to be the one to get past Beau's fourteen-day limit.

"Where are they?" Ben asked, walking to the back of the kennel, which he knew as well as his own place. Beau, watching where he walked, trailed behind them.

"I have them in the yard. Bathed and fed like you asked." Sally smiled. She was a pretty woman with hopeful eyes. Ben liked her, but he wasn't interested, despite her signals. "They are sweet dogs," she told him. "But none of them would ever be considered for Mensa. They'll make nice family pets, though."

"Since when do you rescue dogs for family pets?" Beau demanded. "Oh, hell. These three misfits are for Elli, aren't they? You are going to give her these three dogs pretending they are Rosa's dogs. As your lawyer, I advise you to not…"

"Didn't I just fire you?"

"You can't fire me, I'm your lawyer by transfusion, cuz."

* * * *

Elli heard a strange clacking in the next room as she stepped out of the bunkhouse shower. Her heart began to race at the sound. It sounded like a half dozen alligators scampering around. In full 3-D, the Jurassic Park scene where the velociraptors were chasing the kids in the kitchen flashed in her mind. She was like the kids who didn't know where to hide but knew they had to. Were alligators like the 'raptors? They looked like them in a dwarfed green, toothy, claw-footed kind of way. The most important question was if they had superior intelligence, like the pre-historic predators. They had those short little arms and probably couldn't open the locked bathroom door, but it hadn't stopped the raptors in the movie. Elli didn't intend to stick around to find out what skills they had.

Elli glanced around the room for her cell phone so she could call for help. Darn it. She'd left it charging on the bunk bed. With quick, jerky moves, she wrapped a towel around her body and raced to the only window in the room. "I'm getting out of here. Now."

She tried to unlock the window, the clacking sound getting louder and closer. Her fingers fumbled with the latch, which was locked tight. She banged on the latch with her fist once, twice and a third time before jerking it open. Elli made fast work of wedging the window open. It was then she heard high-pitched barking erupt on the other side of the door, and the clacking stopped. "Donna." Elli looked at the open window and swallowed hard. Donna had her "I'm a tough-girl" bark full on. During the trip, she had done the same short, snappy bark when someone walked near the car wearing unfamiliar department store clothes. She had only been exposed to designer wear so she seemed to perceive any stranger in regular dress as a threat. She also barked like that when she encountered a skunk during a roadside potty break. She acted tough, but Elli knew Donna was frightened. There was little comfort knowing Donna was in her zebra striped dog carrier. It wouldn't be much protection from those sharp-clawed creatures and probably looked like an animal or dinner to them. Elli rushed to the door, but before she opened it, she looked around for a weapon, grabbing the first two things she saw, a mop and a plunger. Elli took a deep breath, made the sign of the cross, and yanked the door open.

"Ha—ha!" she screamed, jabbing her makeshift weapons toward the ground. Donna stopped barking. An ear-splitting howl pierced the silence, followed by barking at every possible octave. Then, out of nowhere, a wet, cold snout slipped under her towel against her thigh. Elli screamed and raced back into the bathroom, slamming the door behind her. Donna was on her own.

Laughter bellowed over the dogs' frenzy from the other side of the door. Male laughter. Oh, she hadn't seen him, but she knew who was laughing. Ben Bienvenu. She could hear his Cajun drawl in his laughter. She could also hear his arrogance and stubbornness.

Willing her heart to stop hammering in her chest, Elli took three cleansing breaths. She had to think clearly. Now was not the time to go full drama, as she was prone to do when she got excited. There would be no winning Ben Bienvenu over in drama-queen mode. She didn't reveal that side of herself very often; she'd learned to manage her overactive imagination and impulsive nature when she entered the world of business. It had always suited her goals to be controlled and conventional. Elli closed her eyes and took one more deep breath. "It's okay. Your dignity wasn't totally destroyed," she assured herself, feeling calmer now. Then she opened her eyes and spotted the red plunger and old-fashioned, hairy mop she held—the germ-ridden, working ends in her hand. "Ewww." She dropped them onto the floor. "Great. Great. I looked like a circus clown." She walked to the sink and scrubbed her hands, imagining she was scrubbing off white clown paint along with the germs. Before she was finished, there was a knock on the door. She ignored it. He knocked again.

She looked at her blotchy, flushed face and closed her eyes, tweaking her nose to make sure a red clown nose wasn't there, just in case.

"You talk to her," she heard Ben say.

"You sure know how to put gasoline on a fire, cousin." There was a light, rhythmic knock on the door. "It's Beau. We sure are sorry for scaring you, cher. Why don't you come on out here and let's start our day over?"

Right. There was no going back now. They'd forever see her as a towel-wearing, plunger-jabbing, swashbuckling clown or the barefoot klutz face down in the mud. Elli sighed. "I'll be out in a minute."

She slipped on the clothes she'd brought in with her. Once again, she dressed as an actor puts on a costume. She had a role to play despite her first disastrous scene. The tailored, tan, A-line dress with cornflower blue cashmere cardigan said she was confident but not arrogant. The narrow, brown leather Coach belt and matching

Stuart Weitzman loafers said she was sophisticated and practical. Except for the red blotches on her face that the light dusting of powder didn't hide, she was the short-haired image of Sandra Bullock in Two Weeks' Notice. "Good morning," she said as she exited the bathroom.

Beau was standing near the door and extended his hand. She shook it. "Good morning, Elli." He smiled. The playful man with beer cans on his head was gone. A charming, stylish gentleman stood before her, apologizing for frightening her and offering reassurances that it wouldn't happen again. As he continued to talk about showing her the property, she glanced at Ben sitting on one of the lower bunk beds with his elbows resting on his knees. He was staring at the floor. Donna sat on the bed next to him with a paw on his thigh. He had taken her out of her carrier and she liked it. A lot. Traitor.

"I'd like to see the plantation house first," she told Beau. Ben didn't say anything; he just got up and walked to the exterior door. He didn't look happy, but it looked like he was going to grant her request. Maybe he was resigned to the idea and would be cooperative. She smiled at him when he opened the door and turned toward her. With his wide shoulders and tall physique, he blocked most of the sunlight from coming into the room, but she could see it was a glorious day outside, a glorious day to tour her property.

Ben whistled and tapped his hand on the side of his leg. How odd, she thought, why was he doing that? Suddenly, the three energetic dogs from earlier bounded into the bunkhouse and ran straight for her. She swallowed a yipe and fought the urge to run. She had to prove to Mr. Bienvenu that she adored dogs, just like he did, especially after having charged at them with the plunger. When the big, drooling, sable bloodhound stuck its snout toward her crotch again, she held her breath and twisted away from it. When the Marley and Me look-alike beige retriever licked her three-hundred-dollar loafers, she gritted her teeth and smiled. When the medium-sized, brown, black, and tan beagle stuck its big, black nose in her suitcase and shoved her clothes around, she fought the urge to chase it away. Instead, she walked toward Donna, who was barking with fury. "Now aren't they cute?" she managed to say, trying not to sound insincere and hoping he'd take them back to his obedience school, which they clearly needed.

"They're yours," Ben said, a glint in his eyes.

She lifted Donna into her arms. "Mine? There must be a mistake." Donna growled at the droopy-eyed hound staring at Elli's crotch. She took a few steps away.

"Tell her, Beau."

"Actually, Elli, the truth is…"

"Your Aunt Rosa left you her three dogs," Ben interrupted, sounding much too pleased about delivering the information. He waved his hands toward the ADD pack of canine chaos running around the room, sniffing everything, climbing on the beds, and occasionally licking something disgusting off the floor. God, she hoped that they came with a prescription of Ritalin. Or Valium.

"I didn't think I'd actually have to take them," she managed to say as the beagle starting baying. "I thought you'd want to keep them here at the kennel. You know, with their friends, the other dogs." Apparently, Donna didn't like the baying any more than Elli did, and she started barking again, which caused her to tinkle down Elli's dress. "Not again." She extended the piddle producer away from her body.

"Your aunt loved these dogs with all her heart. They belonged to her. Unlike the plantation that belonged to my father. You have more right to the dogs than to the property," Ben said, stuffing his hands into his pockets.

"I'll take the dogs." She forced a smile knowing she didn't dare take the time to change her clothes. She was stuck with the wet dress if she wanted to tour the plantation. Ben would use that delay as an excuse to leave her behind for sure. "I love dogs and having them with me." She held Donna at arm's length, walked to the carrier, and put her inside.

"Clearly," he said before turning to Beau. "I've got work to do. Make sure she's out of the house before Joey gets back with Doug around midafternoon."

What a jerk, Elli thought and nearly said to the men who spoke as if she wasn't there. And who in the world was this Joey person he was concerned about? A dog? A girlfriend? She supposed whoever

Joey was, it didn't really matter. Her problem remained the same and Joey couldn't change that.

Warm sunlight spilled into the room and Elli realized Ben no longer blocked the doorway. He had walked away. Beau immediately rushed outside after him. "Oh, no you don't. You're not dumping this on me. I've got a meeting with a client in thirty minutes."

"Cancel it," Elli heard Ben shout. "I'm your client, too."

"No can do." Elli heard a car engine start. "Besides, I thought you fired me," he said, lifting his brows in mischief at Ben. "Remember, don't be a coo-yon. Be a bee-charmer."

Elli walked to the door in time to see Beau drive off in a very nice BMW while Ben kicked the tire of an old, dusty, orange truck. Then he turned and looked at her with eyes that chilled her to the bone. The man was definitely not defined by his name- Bienvenu meant welcome and he was not doing that to her.

Ben must have read her fear and shook his head. "I don't have all day," he said, opening the truck door. She didn't move. She just stood like an expensive boutique mannequin in the bunkhouse doorway for a full five seconds before responding.

"I'll follow in my car." She turned back to get her keys out of her purse and noticed the dogs sniffing and scratching at Donna's carrier, Donna pushed as far back inside as possible. Elli walked out onto the porch and called to Ben, who was sitting in his truck with his window down. "What do I do with the dogs?" When he didn't answer right away, she shouted louder. "Is there a yard where they can play?"

"Put them in the fenced yard on the side of the bunkhouse."

Elli had a hard enough time dealing with Donna; she wasn't sure how she was going to corral three strange dogs, none as civilized as Blaine's Hollywood princess. Her aunt's pets acted like, well, they acted like dogs. She began to slap the side of her leg and whistle. They ignored her. She stepped outside on the porch again.

"Ben, they aren't listening to me. What are their names? In her will, Aunt Rosa only referred to them as her babies." She wasn't about to ask him to secure the dogs for her.

He said something quite rude that she was sure he intended for her to hear, and then got out of his truck.

"If you just tell me their names, I'm sure I can make them listen." She rushed back into the bunkhouse, making every come here sound she had ever heard dog owners make. Ben stepped into the bunkhouse doorway and the room went dark, again. "I'm sure my aunt gave them names," she said, unable to hide her frustration. "Probably something very offbeat, like the names of ancient samurai warriors."

"They're your dogs now. You call them whatever you want." Ben tapped his leg twice and whistled once. The dogs stopped terrorizing Donna and looked at him. He pulled a handful of treats from his pocket and they rushed to him. Without another word, he walked out of the bunkhouse, the three dogs following him to the gated side yard. He communicated with them without uttering a word, albeit he had a bribe.

Elli picked up her purse and looked at her stained dress. Ewww. She had to change. She knew the impatient Ben Bienvenu would be ready to go soon, so she quickly threw on her darkest jeans, nicest sweatshirt, and well-worn running shoes. She looked out the window and didn't see him waiting in his truck, so she took a quick moment to check on Donna, crouching on her elbows and knees to see inside the carrier.

"You okay in there?" Donna was lying on her ever-present newspapers, her pretty little head resting on her crossed paws. "I'm sorry about those rude dogs." Donna gave her one of her pathetic woe-is-me looks. "I'll take you for a nice, hassle-free walk when I get back. I promise. I won't be long. I doubt Mr. Bienvenu will spare very much of his precious time with me, and that's fine by me. I don't want to spend much time with him either. Do you see how cold his beautiful green eyes are when he looks at me? I'm not kidding, Donna. I think he could be a serial killer. Don't go digging any holes in the yard. You might find some bones better left undisturbed. He's a frightening, frightening man."

Elli stood and before she turned, she knew she wasn't alone. The room had gone dark a third time. And, from the cocked brow on the face of the man causing the sun's eclipse, he had been in the doorway long enough to hear what she said.

"Is there anything I can say to help with damage control?" she asked.

"Not a damn thing."

"That's what I figured."

Less than five minutes later, Elli was parking alongside Ben's truck behind the Sugar Mill Plantation home. He stood with his dog next to the truck, but the house grabbed her full attention. None of the pictures and blueprints had prepared her for the actual grandness of the building. It was taller than she expected and she had a physical reaction to seeing it. Her heart was racing so hard in her chest that she had to concentrate on breathing. It was Gone with the Wind, The Skeleton Key, and Interview with a Vampire all rolled into one.

"It's beautiful," she managed, knowing her excitement made her voice breathy and just above a whisper. The cameras would love this place with its three ancient, sprawling oak trees in the backyard and the unpretentious, almost farmhouse-looking back porches on both the lower and upper floors. The oldest part of the house, the center segment that was part of the original home, was of simple construction—white-painted cypress planks under a clay-tiled roof. The additions on both sides of the main home were built about forty years later in the popular Victorian style of the time. It was different from the original home, but the curved walls with large windows under a verdigris copper roof seemed to fit perfectly.

Elli knew from photographs that the simplicity of the back of the plantation home did not mirror the front of the home. She rushed toward the front, anxious to see if the photographs had done the main entrance of the home justice. This was the side meant to awe its visitors. "Slow down. Those bricks are loose on the path. You're on your own if you get hurt," Ben called to her as she raced down the wide walkway. It was February, but the weather was warm, not too humid, and the shrubs and flowers seemed to thrive because of it. Elli wasn't an expert on plants and flowers, but she enjoyed gardening now and again, so she knew some of what she saw. Dark, wax-leaved camellias formed the structure and backdrop on both sides of the path while their white, flamboyant flowers provided the joy. Dotted in the ground, skimming and sometimes overhanging onto the brick path, were narcissuses. Elli was used to seeing the yellow variety in California's mild climate, but never had she seen this soft, white version. Elli found the earthy fragrance of this fertile and blooming land enchanting.

She rounded the corner of the house to an open yard where St. Augustine grass, thick and green, carpeted the lawn while a dark jade turf of liriope swept under the oak and cypress trees' canopy. It spread from the home to the bayou.

"This is perfect." She laughed, feeling a little light-headed. She really did need to remember to breathe. The movie producers and directors would love this place. She'd make a fortune selling it to the right people who'd see it just as she did, a wonderful chameleon movie location. It was so uniquely versatile.

"Perfect for what?" he asked, frowning. "If it's perfect for anything other than my family home and business, I'm not interested."

"As a movie set," Ellie told him, too excited for his mood to bring her down. She could see all the possibilities for movie magic and that would translate to magic for the people who would benefit from the foundation. "You know, keeping this place hidden and not sharing it with people who would appreciate it is a crime."

"Arrest me." He sat on the top of the wide brick steps leading to the front porch, his black dog standing next to him. It was the first time Elli noticed that the dog had looked like a perfectly normal lab when it was sitting in his truck, but when he stood, it looked like it was missing about four inches of its legs. Odd. It had the legs of another breed of dog. "I appreciate it," he told her.

"I'm sure you do." She decided not to tell him the appreciation she spoke of was plural, affecting hundreds, if not thousands. His appreciation was singular.

Elli walked deep into the pathless yard under the heavy, bent limbs of the oaks and the tall, straight cypresses, taking in the place as a camera would with a long shot. The house needed paint, but that might be a good thing if a dark, gothic movie was set here. The coarse gray moss hanging from the trees would certainly add to that kind of mood. It had the potential for much more than a horror or suspense thriller. It could be charming and happy, too. Her years in the movie business told her to look at the bits and parts now. Scenes were filmed in a series of smaller settings, and this place was loaded with them. The bayou running at the front of the property could have the plantation home as a backdrop, or if someone filmed it with their back to the plantation, the short clearing on the other side provided a riverbank. Beyond that was a cypress swamp or medieval forest. The waterway could be a river, a bayou, or a canal.

She saw a small, weathered boat tethered to a huge fallen tree limb along the bank. Later, she'd paddle to the other side of the bayou to take pictures from there, capturing different angles, light, and perspectives she intended to showcase in a real estate brochure.

She walked toward the grand side of the home. "I love how the back is so different from the front, yet it's harmonious," she told Ben. "The bricks on the path, the steps, and the porch were bought around here?"

He shook his head. "They were made in fire pits and ovens here on the property over two hundred years ago."

"Amazing." She could see by his deep frown that he was sorry to share that bit of history with her. Did he think it could make her any more excited about Sugar Mill than she already was?

She stepped onto the porch that spanned the entire home. The columns were different in the front than in the rear. Here they ran uninterrupted from the lower porch up to support the roof above it. The columns were square, unadorned and in the French style, but could be painted with faux details to resemble marble or make them appear round and Italian. The twelve windows lining the front of the home from floor to ceiling were wide enough for two people to walk through side by side, but operated in a traditional up and down way. Props could make it look like the porch of small cottage or what it was—a grand mansion.

There were no stairs, she noticed, to access the top balcony, as there were in the back, but a good computer graphic artist could insert them in postproduction if needed, or a movie carpenter could construct some to suit the director's vision. For a moment, she wished she were producing movies again. Rarely did she miss what she had given up three years ago.

Elli took a deep breath. The scent of camellias, oaks, cypress, and the bayou suffused the warm air that filled her lungs. Yes, she would make a fortune selling this place to the right studio group or venture capitalist. Her foundation would be safe.

She looked at Ben—unhappy, miserable Ben. "There is no place like this anywhere in the world, you know." She smiled and waved her arms as if to take it all in. "Sugar Mill's architecture is so versatile. Plus, the way it's situated on the land is perfect for a long shot to either take in the canopy of ancient trees and lazy bayou or bypass them. The back of the home could be a farmhouse in the Midwest or a modest motel in Savannah with those grand oak trees back there."

"Or it could be a quiet place for a little boy to play with his dogs without a worry in the world, knowing his father and his grandfathers before him played there, too."

Elli wrapped her arms around herself and nodded. "Yes. There is that." Her heart felt heavy and light at the same time. Sugar Mill could save lives by funding genetic testing or it could be home for a father and his little boy. Elli hated taking that dream away from Ben, but it might be a dream he would never realize. He was a widower. She knew that from doing an Internet search of the stranger her aunt cast her into partnership with. His wife had died in a tragic car accident four years ago. She didn't learn much about the woman; there had only been the one article in the local paper about the accident and the funeral arrangements. She hadn't seen any evidence that he'd married again. So this dream of having a son run on the property with a dog might not ever come about. If he did marry, his wife might want to live in New Orleans or Nebraska and not on the plantation. Maybe he'd have a daughter instead of a son. Maybe he wouldn't have any children and remain single his entire life.

Regardless, Ben could still create the utopia he spoke of somewhere else. There were other wonderful places he could have his kennel and his future son playing with dogs. It didn't have to be here. Elli sighed. She'd have to prove that to him. She understood emotional attachment to something, but she also understood what was really important in life, and it wasn't brick and mortar.

She looked at him reclining on the step with his arms folded easily over his chest, his strange looking dog resting next to him. His body might be saying that he was having an easy afternoon, but his bright, narrowed eyes revealed something else. Now was not the time to try to convince him of anything. "Let's go inside," he said, his voice dark and contained. "I don't have all day." He stood and she and Lucky followed him to the front door.

Chapter Two

I have a low-grade fever today! It's one of the things we are cautioned to watch for, and call the doctor immediately about…or go directly to the emergency room. My blood count is down. I'm sick. I'm scared. I hardly have the strength to hold my head up. I'm posting this from my cell phone as I wait in the doctor's office for a wheelchair transport to the hospital bed waiting for me. I'll be spending the night in the hospital…prayers, please. I don't want the blood transfusion the doctor says I may need. I just want to get better fast enough to not miss a chemo treatment. It's irrational but I fear that if I miss a chemo treatment the cancer will go wild. Well, at least tonight I will have someone to take care of me and I will not be alone. I wish you good health, E.

Bosom Blog Buddies Post

Elli understood why Ben loved Sugar Mill Plantation. It was truly amazing. It was beat-up, in need of repair, but had great bones and great history. How in the world would she convince him that he should sell it? Could she have understood how her precious things were just that, things, had she not had cancer? Could she have understood how objects, articles, and stuff didn't define her or really matter, if she hadn't faced death so intimately? How could she or anyone who hadn't lived through that experience? What she had to do with Ben was find that one thing that would make him believe that selling Sugar Mill made sense for him. She had to learn more about him to find that thing. "How long have you lived here?"

"I've lived on the property in one of the slave cottages for the last six years. In here," he gestured to the plantation home, "since Rosa passed. And, for many years before that when I was growing up." He held the door open for her but his dog raced in first. "Look, I'm only showing you around because I have to. Don't think we need to shoot the shit and be social. I don't plan to be your pal or even business partner. All I want to be is the person you used to own Sugar Mill with."

She stepped into the center hall surprised that she had the willpower not to tell him to go to hell. His rudeness and open anger annoyed her. She was used to being light-years apart over issues that needed settling. This was not how differences were resolved.

Elli clasped her hands in front of her and waited for her eyes to adjust to the indoor lighting. When they did, she forgot about Ben smoldering next to her. The inside was just as perfect as the outside. Worn and faded, but perfect. She looked at Ben leaning against the wall with his arms folded over his chest again. "Neither one of us asked for this situation," she began, choosing her words carefully. "I'm sorry it's so complicated and that Aunt Rosa was a flake." He nodded. Finally, they agreed on something. "I didn't set the ground rules and neither did you. Can't we be reasonable enough to find a way through this?"

"Darlin', I have found a way through this. You can go back to Californ-i-ay, let me run the kennel and plantation, and I'll buy you out in a couple of years. Until then, I'll live here and send you a check once a month for half the rent."

"Half?" It didn't escape her that the home was split in half by a wide center hall. It had been a common way to build plantation homes, offering the best ventilation by opening the front and back doors to allow airflow during the sweltering Louisiana summers. Which half was his? Which was hers? She wished it could be that simple.

"Seems fair," he said, looking at his watch.

"Only we can't buy each other out and the plantation can't be divided in a sale to a non-related third party." She quickly took in the details, knowing the watch-looking thing was a warning that time was running out. The ceilings were high and the walls thick. A wide, straight stairwell was on the right, just past the entrance to one of the formal parlors; its match was across the hall on the left. Both rooms were sparsely furnished with old furniture—not antique old, more like 1970s old. The faded velour sofa in the parlor on the right was burnt orange with bold yellow ovals all over it. It was nestled between two dull, antique, walnut end tables. A huge, man-sized, flat screen TV sat on a beautifully carved, antique, French provincial buffet server with a cracked, white marble top. A large beige dog pillow was in front of it, with Ben's dog reclined on it. At a right angle and directly in front of the TV were two mud-brown leather recliners—one adult-sized and one child-sized.

Elli looked at Ben. The man-sized recliner she'd expect in his home, but why was there a child-sized recliner next to it? She'd googled Ben and hadn't read anything about him having a child. In all of Aunt Rosa's long narrative in her will, she mentioned how wonderful Ben was with dogs but never how wonderful he was with a child — his child. Was the smaller recliner for a young cousin? A lover's son or daughter?

She wanted to ask, but decided to see what he volunteered. "Lovely," she said, motioning to the recliners and TV. "Your furniture?"

"Damn straight." They walked past the stairs and down the hall on the first floor.

"What about Aunt Rosa's furniture?"

"Not good enough to donate to St. Vincent's."

She lifted her brows but refrained from asking him to prove how being someone who owned a Me and Mini-Me matching recliners and a Mod Squad sofa qualified him to know good furniture from bad. They walked into the kitchen. It was clean, white, and had the same orange and brown geometric pattern linoleum on the floor as the countertops.

Ben opened the old white refrigerator door and exposed the freezer section above the refrigerator compartment. The door shifted on its hinge and made a thunk sound. He grabbed a bottle of water and lifted it to her. "Want one?"

"No thanks."

He tucked the water under his arm, lifted the door with a bit of effort to realign it back on its hinges, and then closed it.

"What? St. Vincent's didn't want the refrigerator?"

"Didn't offer it to them. It's mine."

"Okay." She absently ran her hand over the old, homemade, scarred, wooden table as she looked around the room. A splinter slid deep into the meaty part of her right hand. The pain was sharp and surprised a gasp out of her. "Oh, no." She looked at the splinter, which felt bigger than it looked. "Damn it." She looked at Ben. "You have a first-aid kit?"

"It's just a splinter. You don't have to look like you just got knifed with a rusty blade on Bourbon Street."

Funny, but that was pretty close to what she conjured in her mind. "I need a first-aid kit," she insisted. "Can you just get it for me?"

"All right, all right." He opened the cabinet under the sink and pulled out a tackle box, dropping it on the table.

Elli sat in the chair. "I hiked on the Inca Trail in Peru and managed to do just fine, but I touch a chewed-up table with two-hundred-year-old germs and may lose my arm because of it."

"I think you're being a bit hysterical."

"The hell I am." She opened the tackle box and took out the peroxide. "Can you hand me some paper towels so I don't get this all over the place? Wait, on second thought, it might help with those two-hundred-year-old germs on this table if I spill some of this on them."

Ben handed her the roll. "You're a bit germ-a-phobic there, cher'."

She glared at him. If he knew how serious this splinter could be, he wouldn't be so sanctimonious. Since her lymph nodes were removed during her lumpectomy and mastectomy, she didn't have a good way to fight off infection in her right arm. She poured the peroxide on the splinter and began trying to take it out with her stubby fingernails.

"You should use a needle."

She glared at him. "Do you mind?"

He walked up to her to take a closer look at the splinter. "Damn. That's big. I bet it hurts."

"Not as much as my fist in your gut would."

For the first time since he realized who she was, he smiled. It was lopsided but genuine and beautiful. Elli's stomach did a little flip.

"You want me to take you to the emergency room?" Sarcasm laced his words, and mischief sparkled in his eyes. Elli had a quick vision of being wheeled in on an old, rusty dog stretcher with her injured arm hanging to the side, banging into the wall as Ben raced down the hall of a veterinarian clinic.

She glared at him a full ten seconds before trying to push the splinter out of her hand.

"Now, don't think you can sue me over this because you're on my property and all." He leaned in to get a closer look, and Elli smelled the clean scent of freshly washed hair. It reminded her of the inexpensive soap of her childhood, but with a masculine, grown-up earthiness. Very nice, she thought, leaning a little closer.

Ben turned his head and nearly bumped noses with her. He looked at her mouth and her heart did a funny jig. Must be the antique germs zipping through my body, she thought, looking away to dig into the tackle box; for what, she wasn't sure yet.

Ben reached for her wrist. "What's this?"

With her heart beating so hard and sending blood flooding into her brain, it took her a minute to register what he was talking about. Her medic alert bracelet. "It's nothing." She tried to pull her arm free, but he gripped her tighter.

"No needles and pressure cuffs in right arm," he read. "Lymphedema. What's that?"

"It's a medical condition."

"Yes, I figured that out with the Red Medic cross symbol and all. I'm smart like that, me," he said with a heavy Cajun accent that thickened with his sarcasm, a far cry from his otherwise gentle, rhythmic, subtle accent.

She yanked her hand free. "I have a compromised lymphatic system. I can potentially not heal properly from injuries in my right arm because of it."

He raised her hand to him for closer inspection. "Hence, the melodrama over a splinter." He pulled out a chair and sat across from her. "Tell me what to do."

"Are you being nice to me?"

"Don't be so difficult. Just tell me what to do."

"Sell the plantation and split the proceeds with me?"

His head jerked up. "Over my dead body."

"Whatever." She looked at her hand. "I can't stick my hand with a needle, so I need to try to wedge this thing out without causing more damage."

Ben washed his hands with the antibacterial lotion from the tackle box, and then poured peroxide on his hands. "I do a lot of doctoring with my dogs," he offered. "Let me try."

Dogs. No surprise there. Why couldn't Aunt Rosa have bequeathed half the plantation to an ugly, smart, generous medical doctor? She gave him her hand. He pressed firmly on the backside of the splinter. "Ouch."

He hesitated, then looked to see how much pain she really was in. It was strange, but she found it kind of sweet that he did that. Did he do the same for his dogs? Probably.

"I think I'm getting somewhere," he said, sweat beading above his lip. Seeing it sent a warm flush over her chest. How odd? "It's poking out a little. Let me get the tweezers." He pulled the tweezers from the tackle box and poured peroxide on them. The liquid spilled onto the table and ran in bubbling rivulets across the wood, onto Elli's nicest, darkest jeans. She began to laugh.

"If Donna's tinkling isn't ruining my clothes, other things are."

Ben frowned and focused on her hand. She wasn't sure he even knew about the spill that was in the process of leaving white spots on her jeans.

"Ah-hah. Mais, I got it, cher." He held up the splinter.

"You sure you didn't leave any in my hand?" She examined her wound closely. "I'd have sworn it was bigger than that."

"Hearing that would make most men unhappy, darlin'."

"Very funny." She applied triple antibiotic ointment and a Band-Aid to her wound, both of which she found in the tackle box. When returning the supplies to the box, she noticed deworming medicine, ear powder, and several syringes. "Is this a first-aid kit for your dogs?"

"Sure is." He closed the box and put it back under the cabinet. "Do you need to take antibiotics or something?"

"Not unless it looks like it isn't healing properly." She shrugged. "It usually does." She stood. "Thank you for your help. I'd like to see the rest of the place now."

Ben's sour mood returned as he led her through tall, double, swinging doors from the kitchen directly into a sunny dining room behind it. The dining room was huge, round, and surrounded on three sides by tall windows. She recognized this room as the Victorian addition. She knew a room mirroring this one was on the opposite side of the house and held the library. As Ben led the way through the dining room toward a huge open archway, Elli made a quick inventory of its sparse contents—a dull, antique, walnut dining table for six; a single, chipped, antique oak sideboard; a brass 1980s chandelier; and two common white plastic folding chairs. Vintage dust was everywhere.

"Don't use this room much, do you?" Elli asked, prompting a sharp look from Ben's hot green eyes. His lips, however, twitched in what she knew was a smile trying to break through.

They quickly passed through an enormous hall and into the library. Books were stacked on the floor, against the windows, almost as high as Elli's five-foot-ten frame, blocking whatever natural light the pulled back, dark red velvet drapes allowed in. The room felt heavy and oppressive. The bookshelves along the back wall were empty and felt equally depressing.

"The drapes have to go," she mumbled.

Ben stopped and turned to face her full on. Elli stared right back at him, expecting him to apologize for the quarter-inch-thick dust on all the surfaces and the frantic disorder of the room. "You can only throw away half the drapes. Leave my half alone." He turned and walked out of the room.

"I'll only remove half the dust too," she shouted after him as he began to climb the creaky stairs to the second floor. His dog appeared from the wind it seemed and raced up the stairs past them and disappeared back into the wind before they reached the landing Elli figured she would see him again.

Elli knew from the property description that the cypress floors continued upstairs, where all of the bedrooms were located. There were five, each with their own white marble bathroom. The first one they walked into was the master—Ben's room. It had a huge, king-size bed and tall boxes for end tables. The bed was made in that sweet, endearing way men made beds; the white sheets and brown blankets were all on the bed but they dragged on one side and were hiked up on the other. The center was a bit lumpy, as if the sheets weren't smoothed beneath it.

Elli smiled, imagining Ben climbing out of the warm, soft bed, wearing plaid boxers and a white rumpled T-shirt. His longish hair would be tucked behind his ear and flopping around his head. She could even see the sexy crease in his cheek where his face had rested against his bunched pillow. He'd turn, bend over, grip the edge of the sheets and blankets together, and shake them out over the bed. Without a second look or thought, he'd toss his pillows at the top of the bed and walk away. Or, maybe, he'd pick up the lint roller that she spotted on the end-table box and roll it across the bed to remove the dog hair that was invariably there.

She heard herself sigh, and then, to her horror, heard Ben grunt. He looked at his watch. "Even if I had the inclination to take you in my bed, cher, I don't have the time."

Elli felt her face ignite, certain it was red and blotchy. No, there was no cute, rosy blush when she was embarrassed. It was pure ugly and rashly looking. "Oh, darlin'," she drawled in a way she imagined Miss Kitty in Gunsmoke might. "If I had the inclination, you'd make the time." She turned and exited stage left.

"Not before you put some calamine lotion on that red, spotty face of yours…darlin'." He chuckled. So much for her acting skills; that's why she produced movies and didn't star in them.

Elli rushed into the bedroom beside the master. "Oh," she gasped as she stumbled over a Star Wars light saber on the floor. She bent down and picked it up. "Yours?"

He took it from her and placed it gently on the single bed. Unlike Ben's bed, this bed was made as neatly and tidily as a military bunk. Its cheerful blue and red quilt with playful black and golden Labrador retriever appliqués stood in contrast to the somber feeling in the room. Elli noticed a bright, royal blue rug where a child could play and Ben's dog now laid on his side. His eyes followed her as they meandered around the room. Colorful toys stacked at the foot of the bed and along the wall were positioned just as orderly as the room was kept. Nonetheless, she still felt heaviness in this room. Not unlike the heaviness she felt in the library with the thick, red drapes blocking the natural sunshine.

On the lone TV tray used as an end table, she spotted a few Newfie Movie figurines. She smiled. She loved making that film and it pleased her to see a child liked it enough to not only buy but play with the toys they'd merchandised for the movie. At one time, that was more important to her than the twice-a-year royalty check she received for the Newfie merchandise sales. Those royalties once made her a very wealthy woman, even though she took a much smaller percentage than industry norm for her position. She had given a portion of her royalties to get the marquis actors she wanted to star in Newfie. Elli was glad she had, because the movie was a huge success due to the great performances by those top actors and she still managed a modest income years after Newfie peaked in popularity.

She picked up the little Newfoundland pup toy. "Bow-Wow." She smiled and lifted it for Ben to see. "He's my favorite."

"Joey's, too."

"Joey is…?"

"My son." He took the toy from Elli, his fingers brushing against hers, causing her heart to skip a beat and her face to heat. She started to turn away, not sure what the hell had happened and why she was reacting to an accidental touch from a man who clearly hated her. He gripped her arm and turned her to face him. "Joey has nothing to do with our problems," he said, looking hard into her eyes.

"I didn't know you had a son." She let out the breath she hadn't realized she was holding. His dream of the little boy playing under the oak tree wasn't a fantasy for a utopian future. It was something he wanted for the son he had now. Elli felt a lump form in her throat. "Joey has everything to do with our problems."

She turned so he wouldn't see the tears stinging her eyes. She felt like a monster. The dog lifted its head and Elli would have sworn he sneered at her. Of course he did.

"No, he doesn't," Ben insisted.

Elli couldn't talk with the emotion clogging her throat. She had a dozen little Joeys counting on her to help their mommies survive breast cancer. Was she supposed to choose between one who played with Bow-Wow and ran barefoot in the cool grass of Sugar Mill Plantation and one who might have the same cancer gene threatening his mother's life? Could she? God, she needed time to think. She needed an easy button. Why wasn't there an easy button? She looked at the dog as she walked out of the room. He seemed to frown at her.

She cleared her tight throat. "Who sleeps here?" she asked, looking into the third bedroom complete with two single beds, a torn, tan leather recliner, and a lamp on another TV tray between the single beds. It was void of any personal items except for a lopsided rawhide dog bone on the floor.

"You are pretty damn nosy." He ran his hands through his hair. "Not that it is any of your business, but this is where aunts or cousins that care for Joey sleep when I'm out of town."

Elli rushed through the final two bedrooms used for storage and a tidy doggie hotel for animals needing to remain under close watch overnight. Then, because the realization of the impossible choice she had to make was so oppressive and heavy on her heart, Elli did what she always did during difficult times, she joked.

"Do you really want me to believe that you brought all of this...uh...exceptional furniture in here on purpose?" she said, closing the last guest room door.

Ben shrugged, then looked at his watch. "I've got an appointment at one. Are you ready to head back to the bunkhouse?"

She smiled and followed him downstairs. "No. Not the bunkhouse. I need to go to a grocery store that sells organic food." She needed supplies and was happy for the distraction of shopping.

"Organic?" He shook his head. "I think your best option for that froufrou stuff is in Californ-i-ay. If you get on the road before dark, you can be at a real fine froufrou store in a couple of days."

She smirked. "Nice try." They walked toward their vehicles. "I'll try my luck in town."

Her stomach chose that moment to echo with a loud bear growl. Elli knew by the way Ben was trying to hide a grin that he heard it, too. If she wasn't mistaken, the entire population of Cane heard it. She needed to feed the bear.

"Cher, it was a real pleasure meeting you," he said with fake sincerity as he stood in front of his truck. "I hope you have a safe trip home."

She waved her arms toward the house and yard. "I did."

His eyes widened and his mouth set in a hard line. Before she saw his heated reaction, she knew she'd made a mistake insult-wrestling with the stubborn Ben Bienvenu. Bad move, she thought, and chastised herself for being so impulsive. She had to be smarter than that.

He walked over to her, standing as close as a person could without touching. His eyes were sharp, piercing, and cold. "Cher, as long as you are on Bienvenu land, you will never be home."

Timing was everything in the movie business as it was in life, so when her cell phone began to ring, she thanked the forces that created this timing gem. Answering her phone gave her something to do other than try to pretend his words hadn't stung.

"Hello, Abby," she said, after retrieving her phone from her jeans pocket and reading the caller ID.

"Elli, your sources were right," she began with an easy laugh.

"Which sources are you talking about?" She looked over her shoulder and watched Ben climb into his truck and drive away.

"Whoever told you that Country Charm is looking for a location to do their exterior shoot."

"That would be the recently fired location director for that sweet romantic comedy." She walked to her car and slid into the driver's seat. As soon as she turned the car on, the Bluetooth took over the control of her phone, and Abby's voice came over the car's speakers.

"Like you told me, most of the movie is set in Chicago, but the opening scenes need to be on a southern country farm. They found a nice farmhouse near Chicago to film the interior scenes before they fired their location director," she continued, "but they haven't found suitable locations for farmhouse exterior shots to set the right tone for the story of a-country-lawyer-moves-to-big-city. They're still looking. One of your pals at the studio came up to me during lunch. He said he recognized me from the fundraiser, didn't believe that we accidentally were dining at the same restaurant on this particular day, and definitely didn't believe in coincidences." Abby laughed. "I thought he was coming on to me with a lousy pickup line."

"Men do tend to do that with you. You are so gorgeous, you make men nervous."

"Well, anyway, he wasn't." She laughed again. "He said you called him a couple of days ago to ask him to let you know if Country Charm found their country location. At the time, he had, but...to make a long story short, now he doesn't."

"He still doesn't have a country location?"

"And according to your pal...God, why didn't I get his name...anyway, he said it was Kismet that he saw me at the exact moment he got off the phone with one of the producers who said the new country location was a no-go. The bottom line—he wants Sugar Mill."

"Perfect. Perfect. Perfect," Elli shouted. She backed out of the driveway and headed toward the bunkhouse; she wanted to check on Donna before going into town. "Sugar Mill is perfect. They were looking for greener and lusher than what's available in the Illinois winter. We got that here."

"Great," Abby laughed. "Make the deal. I've already started preparing the contract. And Elli," she paused and her tone became more serious when she spoke again. "Get the check ASAP. We just got the invoice from the genetic testing lab for January."

"I'll make a few calls and send a few photos to the right people. I think they'll be ecstatic to shoot their exteriors at Sugar Mill. I'm not sure I can say the same about Ben."

"Elli, even though we desperately need the money, as your attorney, I have to advise you to make sure Mr. Bienvenu is on board. We are already dealing with major damage control since the fundraiser, and reneging on a deal because your partner won't sign the contract will be…well…bad."

Elli knew Abby wanted to say final but couldn't. Like Elli, she understood you had to fight final. "I get that. I've got it handled," she said, not really believing her own words. Yet. "When I place a sweet check for ten thousand dollars in his hand for just two days of minimal inconvenience, he'll start seeing things my way. I expect he'll look for a pen to sign the papers to sell the plantation to other movie people who'd have a check with a lot more zeroes on it. Family land is a noble thing, Abby, but the practicality of the almighty buck will win out." She closed her eyes and took a deep breath. "Ben Bienvenu will want to own one hundred percent of his kennel more than he'll want to live on family land."

"If you are right about this," Abby said, picking up on the thread of her reasoning, "with his share of the sale of the plantation, he can buy you out of the kennel business. The will allows him to do that. It will give him a fresh somewhere else."

"It will be a new chapter in the Bienvenu dynasty."

Chapter Three

I thought I had scared a sweet, elderly man in the chemo lab today. It was when I started dancing around with the IV pole I was attached to when another patient played Forget You by Ceelo Green on her iPad. There I was bald, wearing dark sunglasses, black yoga pants, a red Juicy Couture sweatshirt and UGG patent leather rain boots twirling around the room with my IV pole...I was pole dancing! The dear, hunched over tiny man shuffled up to me with his walker and without hesitation stuffed a dollar bill into my waistband. He wasn't frightened of me one bit. It was a great day! I wish you good health, E.

Bosom Blog Buddies Post

"Out!" Ben stormed into the guest room and closed Elli's open suitcase, zipping it shut before speaking again. "You've got some nerve moving into my home, lady." Two hours ago, he thought he'd made it clear to her that she was not welcome anywhere on his land. "Either go back to the bunkhouse for the night or find a hotel...preferably in Kansas!"

She lunged for the suitcase and sat on top of it before he could pick it up. "This is my house, too. I can stay here if I want. You can threaten me all you want, but I have rights. I asked my attorney, and she said I had the legal right to domicile on the plantation if I want...and I want." She folded her arms across her chest as if that made it final. The hell it did.

He gripped the suitcase handle, looking at her a full three seconds to give her ample warning she had better move her West Coast derriere off the suitcase. When she just stared back with that stubborn look he'd seen much too often in the short time he'd known her, he figured they were at an impasse. Again. He shrugged his shoulders and yanked the suitcase off the bed, causing Elli to tumble to the floor. Her little prissy dog, resting on the bed pillow, raised her head and looked at her owner, sniffed, and put her head back down. It was then that Ben realized the dog was lying on a stack of newspapers. What in the hell was that about?

"I'll have you arrested for assault." She stood and sat on the narrow bed. It was old and the springs probably rusty; they squeaked under her unsubstantial weight.

He tossed her his cell phone. "Go ahead, call the law, cher. When you get our sheriff on the phone, tell ole Uncle Ronald that I'm bringing crawfish boudin for the card game tomorrow night."

She had the nerve to pick up his phone and punch in 9-1-1. "I'd like to report an assault," she told the operator. "Uh…yes," She stood and turned her back to Ben, lowering her voice. "Yes, it is Ben Bienvenu's phone. It's him I want to have arrested." Ben could hear the laughter from the operator from where he stood. He'd bet it was his cousin Rachel, who usually worked the afternoon shift. "Here." She handed him the phone, her face bunched in a frown. Damn, if she still wasn't pretty all pinched up.

"Hi darlin'," he drawled. "No, she's not a Yankee. Worse. She's one of those surfer dudettes from Californ-i-ay. No, no kidding. Uh…hold on." He looked at Elli, now sitting on her suitcase on the floor. "She wants to know if you know any movie stars. In particular, she wants to know if you're friends with George Clooney."

"Yes, I know movie stars." She dropped her elbows on her knees and clasped her hands. "But I don't know George Clooney. I am friends with his stylist."

Ben started to repeat what she said, but he had had enough of this silliness. "Rachel, I have to put this conversation on hold. I've got to go. I'm in the middle of tick removal."

"Ha-Ha. Very funny." He hung up and tucked the phone into his back pocket, looking at her all folded over on the suitcase. She slouched in her defeat, but her eyes sparkled with challenge. Damn it if she didn't look like makeup sex with those sexy baby blues goring him like a charging bull.

"Look, I don't want to play tug-a-war with your suitcase," he told her evenly. "And I certainly don't want to carry you out of here over my shoulder." He looked hard into her gorgeous eyes. Instead of being intimidated, she turned her icy eyes on him. Again. Only this time, it felt like a smack right in the gut. "But do understand me, I will physically remove you if you insist on being difficult."

She sighed, and he felt like he was hit in the gut again. What was it about her that got him so damn flustered and took him off task? This woman was hell-bent on messing up his life. Not that he needed any help in that department. The last time he was dealt such a crappy hand, he let a woman deal it. Live and learn. He didn't intend to give Elli a chance to even shuffle the deck. He had to protect Joey.

"We are at an impasse," she began. "Yes, you could physically remove me, but it just wouldn't be right. You know it. I don't want to sleep in that not-so-very-private-bunkhouse when you know good and well that I'd have to move out tomorrow when those New Orleans firemen arrive to pick up their search dogs."

Ben could've asked her how in the hell she knew about his business with the NOFD, but he knew the answer to that. His foreman, Doug Leblanc, was loose-lipped and loose-hipped around the female sex. At fifty-four, he loved women and considered charming them a hobby. Rumor was that he had pretty much been that way since he was eleven. All Ben knew for sure was that women seemed to like him right back. It didn't matter much to Doug if they were tall, short, thick, or narrow as long as they were willing and legal. Ben guessed that Doug rushed over to meet Elli when he saw her hauling her luggage into the cottage next to his. Bragging about their dogs would've been like foreplay to him. He'd talk to Doug about guarding his words around Elli, not that he really expected it to do any good.

"I'm not moving into a hotel when we have five good bedrooms here." She looked around the room. "Mostly good, anyway."

"Four bedrooms," he corrected and wasn't sure why he had. "You can't count the storage room with the hole in the floor the size of a Great Dane."

"Well, I did." She frowned.

He stuffed his hands in his pockets. This conversation was going nowhere. "You can't stay here."

Her shoulders dropped as she exhaled. "Technically, I can stay here, remember?"

He knew she was right, but didn't like it one bit. "You don't actually believe it's a good idea for you to stay here, do you?" He folded his arms across his chest. "Not when you're not welcome and you don't have a female companion to chaperone you around me."

"Ha-ha. Like you would come anywhere near me in that way," she snorted, but when he stared at her with his best "I like sex" smirk, she looked as if she wanted to take her words back. She cleared her throat. "Your son is as good as a sentry guard."

Ben knew she was right on both points. He would never take a woman in his bed with his son in the house, and he certainly wasn't interested in Elli in that way. If she had been anyone else with that tight body, long legs and big baby blues, he'd have her - just not in the house while Joey was there. Not that he didn't think sex with Elli would be hot and satisfying. He shook his head. What a damn stupid thought to pop into his head. "Why do you want to stay here?"

"It's, it's…" she stammered. "I don't have to explain myself to you, Ben. Just know that I've decided to stay."

He took a step closer and stared down at her. She looked pretty pathetic sitting on her suitcase. She looked both like a kid waiting for a scolding in the principal's office and like a bitch ready to protect her litter. Damnedest thing he'd ever seen—vulnerability and courage.

"Stay clear of the other three bedrooms, especially mine and Joey's." What the hell was wrong with him? How could he give in to her so easily? He was willing to concede this battle only because it might be better for him in winning the war. Keep your friends close and your enemies closer. "Stay away from my son. Don't eat my food. And stay the hell away from me."

He turned and walked out the room but not before he heard her say, "Thank you."

Fifteen minutes later, Elli finished hanging her clothes in the armoire serving as a closet. She squeezed next to Donna on the lumpy single bed covered by a faded wedding ring quilt to read her aunt's will again. She was determined to discover a loophole or provision that she and her lawyer had missed. Maybe the will-fairy slipped in something that allowed her to sell her share of Sugar Mill and be free of her partnership with Ben Bienvenu. She absently petted Donna's belly, but as she turned the page, she felt a low growl rumble in Donna's tiny tummy.

"What's wrong?" she asked, still looking at the document. Suddenly, the door swung open and three floppy-tongued dogs raced in. The door closed behind them. "Oh, no."

Donna started yapping so hard she jerked across the bed like a block with springs. The dogs stopped moving, cocked their heads to look at who was barking up a storm, and one by one, their tails started wagging.

"Oh, no. She's not a toy." Elli cuddled Donna into her arms as the Marley and Me dog jumped on the bed and started barking. The small beagle and huge droopy-eared bloodhound started their odd howling. "Enough. Quiet." Elli raced into the hall, closing the door behind her. "Ben," she screamed.

When he didn't come to her aid, she went looking for him with Donna still yapping in her arms. She found him in the kitchen with his head in the refrigerator. Donna wiggled her way out of Elli's arms and ran to him. He picked her up and scratched under her chin.

"Those dogs," she managed to say.

"Your dogs," he corrected.

"Those dogs need to be on Valium."

He opened a cabinet next to the sink and pulled out a jar of dog biscuits. His dog, that she now knew was named Lucky from Ben's foreman, came into the kitchen. He gave a biscuit to Lucky and to Donna, then put her on the floor. Lucky took his treat and left the room.

"She doesn't like dog biscuits unless it's the brie and peanut butter biscotti from Chez Chienne's," Elli said as she watched Donna hold the biscuit between her paws and begin chewing it. "Whatever." She plopped into the kitchen chair. "Those dogs want to eat Donna."

Ben looked at her over his shoulder as he put the container back into the cabinet. "Hardly." He pulled out the fixings for a sandwich and lifted the refrigerator door closed. With his back to her, he began making himself a sandwich without offering her any. She wasn't surprised by his lack of manners, but she was bothered by it.

"You're enjoying my discomfort with my aunt's dogs, aren't you?"

He didn't answer and continued to make his sandwich.

"It's not that I don't like them," she began, weighing each word and using as much sincerity as possible. "I think they are adorable."

He grunted, took a bite of his sandwich, and put the ham and mayo back in the refrigerator.

"The thing is, I don't know where to put them." And I don't know how to stop them from eating Donna, she thought. Standing, she walked to the back door and looked outside. "You don't have a fenced-in yard here."

He hopped onto the small counter and sat, his eyes settling on her bare feet and red toenail polish. He frowned.

"Okay." She crossed her arms over her chest. "If you are going to stare at my feet and not offer any suggestions to help me, I'll assume I can do what I want with them."

"They are your feet." His lips twitched, obviously enjoying his silly little joke.

"You know I'm talking about the dogs." She walked over to stand in front of him, determined to make him pay attention to her. "Could you board them at the kennel for me?"

His eyes slid up her body in a slow and deliberate way. She knew he was not interested in the way his eyes pretended he was. He was trying to unnerve her, plain and simple. In a deep, smooth voice, he said in a Cajun accent so grinding and sexy the Hollywood studios would have gotten into a bidding war to get him on the silver screen, "It'll cost you."

Elli swallowed the sigh sliding in her throat. How in the world could he make a threat sound so hot? She could play that game, too. She batted her eyes in a heavy bedroom flutter as she looked at him with parted lips. He raised his sandwich to his mouth but didn't take a bite. "You wouldn't really charge me, would you?" Her words weren't sexy, but she made sure her voice was. His Adam's apple bobbed in his throat, and he stared into her eyes. Then in one quick move, he took a big, hungry bite out of his sandwich, ending their game.

"Damn straight, I would," he said with a full mouth.

Whatever his fee was, she couldn't afford it. Even if she paid him only his half of the fee. "I assume they're housebroken."

"All but one," he answered while he chewed.

She folded her arms over her chest. "Which one?" When he didn't answer right away, she rushed back upstairs to get the dogs. "Out," she shouted to them when she opened the door. They raced out and down the stairs. She looked around the room at documents scattered and crumpled, but didn't find any other unpleasant surprises.

Ben watched from his perch on the counter as she herded the dogs with a great deal of effort and moved them outside. She rushed back into the kitchen to pick up Donna, who clung to the biscuit in her mouth, then returned outside to deal with her dogs. They weren't in the backyard.

"Here, doggies," she called, worried that they would run into mischief with the wild alligators she figured had to still be in the bayou. "Come. Now. Doggies." She made the immediate decision to name the dogs, since "here doggies" wasn't working. "Come here Jenny, BJ, Doe." She hadn't planned to name them after the three women who had helped through the toughest time of her life, but she could think of no other names. Her nurses were wonderful, caring and had a spark of mischief, too. She just hoped her aunt's dogs proved as much fun. Right now, they weren't.

From a distance, she heard a faint shout. She couldn't make out what was being said, but the angry tone was clear. A woman along the side of the house was not happy, and Elli had a good idea why. Two quick dog barks confirmed it. She took off running with Donna bouncing in her arms, still holding on to the biscuit in her mouth. As Elli rounded the house, she was blinded momentarily by the sun bouncing off of a vintage, Pepto-Bismol pink pickup truck parked in the driveway. No, maybe it wasn't the sun blinding her, but the nearly fluorescent hue of the truck. Who drove something like that, she wondered for a second before the woman's shouts and the dogs' happy barks drew her to the side of the house.

"Fout pas mal," an eighty-something-year-old woman in a long-sleeved, pale pink cotton dress and a hot pink, old-fashioned prairie bonnet shouted from where she sat on a clump of camellia bushes. She was a tiny thing with deep wrinkles in her tanned face and fury in her small, dark brown eyes. Donna started to growl, biscuit in her mouth.

"Oh, no," Elli shouted, as she spotted the only non-pink item on the little old lady: white vinyl, Forrest Gump shrimp boots that two of her dogs were trying to yank off the poor woman's right foot. "Stop, Jenny. BJ," she called, deciding right there that the tan Marley and Me retriever was Jenny and the brown, black, and tan beagle was BJ. With these two animals tugging on the ancient woman's boot, Elli didn't stop to wonder where Doe was. "Heel," she shouted. The dogs ignored her.

"Moodee. Dem dogs for you?" She turned her anger on Elli, who was trying to pull the dogs off the shrimp boot they were fighting over. They thought it was a game and started tugging harder on the boot and shaking their heads. The old lady gripped the camellia bush tighter to keep from tumbling over.

"I'm sorry," Elli cried, grabbing Jenny's collar. BJ took advantage of having Jenny out of the way and jerked on the white boot a final time, pulling it off the old lady's narrow leg. Jenny tugged free from her collar and took off with BJ toward the front of the house with their prize. "Good riddance," Elli mumbled, turning to help the old lady who was still holding on to the bush. "Are you hurt?" Her dress was bunched around her knees so Elli was able to assess the damage — first scanning her skinny, bootless leg, then her other leg, sticking out of her boot like a straight twig.

"Nuttin broke," she said, taking the hand Elli offered. She stood, but didn't let go of Elli's hand. She needed it for support. "Dem dogs should be shot."

Elli gasped. "What an awful thing to say."

"Betta yet, dere owner should be shot." She glared hard at Elli, then let go of her hand and swayed to the side a little. Elli reached to grip her arm, but the old lady swatted her hand away and managed to center her weight. "Get my shotgun in da truck, Nephew."

Ben walked past Elli and picked a tiny leaf from the old lady's short gray hair that curled out from her bonnet. He kissed her on her lined cheek, and she wiped it off with the back of her glove.

"Moodee, rascal," she said, then told him something in Cajun French that had him shaking his head and looking at Elli.

"I'm so sorry, ma'am," she began, but the old lady grunted and waved her glove at her.

"Bring my boot back. I'll be right here." She bent over with her narrow bottom in the air and her adult-sized baby bonnet nearly touching the ground, then began pulling the weeds along the stone path. There weren't many there. From a distance, she heard the howling bark that she recognized as Doe's.

"Now what?" She picked up Jenny's collar from the ground and turned toward the front yard. "I'm really sorry, ma'am."

"Next time, I'll have my gun," she growled, but something softer flickered in her eyes when she looked at Donna and her pretty pink collar. As Elli took off running toward the howling BJ, she realized the collar was the exact same shade of pink as the old lady's truck.

Elli raced to the front of the house and saw the dogs immediately. It wasn't hard to spot them along the bank since BJ and

Doe were still fighting over the boot, and Jenny was swimming in the bayou. Elli slowed her pace and walked to the edge of the water.

"Bad dogs," she scolded as Donna wiggled to get out of her arms. She took her time scanning the area for alligators and when she was confident none were around, she put Donna down. Donna immediately charged into the battle for the white shrimp boot, although the biscuit in her mouth complicated things. Elli stood on the bank, hands on her hips, and Jenny's collar looped around her wrist. She was at a complete loss as to how to restrain this out-of-control bunch. "I'm an intelligent woman who could finesse, negotiate, and navigate dozens of temperamental actors and directors, so why can't I deal with four furry creatures?"

"They don't seem to have any problem finessing, negotiating, and navigating around you," Ben said, standing next to her. "I'd get Tante Izzy's boot back soon or she's going to make a trip to her truck for her shotgun. She won't have any trouble negotiating with your dogs."

Elli looked at him. She could see a contained smile now replaced his usual scowl. "I defer to your expertise in this matter."

"You're not going to dump this on me so easily."

Jenny came out of the bayou with a stick in her mouth and dropped it at Elli's feet. Elli braced for the expected wet dog shake, but it didn't come. She picked up the stick, looked for alligators, and then threw it into the bayou. Jenny dove into the water after it.

"Believe me, there isn't anything easy about any of this."

He looked at her, then at the dogs fighting with the white shrimp boot. "I'll get the boot, only because I hate to see a good dog get shot because of its owner's stupidity."

"Actually, she said she would shoot me." He looked at her as if reconsidering helping her, then went over to the growling pack of dogs and took the boot from them. They bounced around him and looked at him with hope and excitement in their eyes, but not one of them challenged him.

He handed the boot to Elli. It was full of dog slobber. "Eww." Jenny raced out of the water and dropped the stick at Elli's feet. Elli looked down at it and as she was about to pick it up, Doe and BJ gave up on the boot and darted after the stick, knocking her on the ground. Ben began to laugh.

"These dogs have a serious problem with upending women," she said, watching Ben snatch the boot she'd dropped on the ground from Doe as the dog tried to steal it. Donna walked up to him and tapped his calf gently with her tiny paw. He picked her up and scratched her under her chin as she rested her head against his chest.

"My aunt called you the Cajun Dog-Whisperer," Elli said as she stood and wiped the dirt off her jeans. "What's the deal?"

"They just know they have to listen to me." He paused long enough to lock gazes with her. "They know I'll do whatever it takes to get what I want."

"Whatever it takes?" She considered his statement a direct challenge on so many levels. She rolled her eyes. "Yeah, right."

He looked at her with clear, determined eyes before walking away, whistling with the boot and Donna in his hands.

"Hey, you've got my dog." Well, he could keep her. She had enough to handle with the other three—Jenny sitting expectantly with the stick in her mouth, Doe sniffing the edge of the bayou with her ears dragging the ground, and BJ pushing her nose into a moist pile of leaves.

Elli watched for a while, considering various ways to corral them when an idea struck her. They seemed keen on sniffing and retrieving things, so she raced into the house, through the front door, not wanting to run into Tante Izzy and her gun at the side of the house. She trotted into the kitchen, past Ben at the sink filling a glass with water, and opened the kitchen cabinet that held the dog biscuits. She grabbed two handfuls and raced back outside where Jenny, Doe, and BJ were doing dog things around the yard.

"Here girls," she called, tossing a few pieces of biscuits into the yard near them. They sniffed the ground and found the prize. She continued tossing the morsels to them as she took steps backward until they were on the front porch. "Good girls. Good, hungry, girls." She opened the front door and tossed the remaining four biscuits into the house. "Go get it." With what looked like smiles on their muddy faces, the dogs bounded into the house, and Elli slammed the door behind them. "There." She wiped her crumby hands on her pants and walked off the porch toward the kennel. She was going to have a chat with Doug. Ben could deal with whatever mayhem her dogs created. She was going to get some expert advice from the kennel forum on dealing with the girls, and, maybe, some advice on dealing with the big guy, too.

* * * *

Elli was walking back from the kennel with three long dog leashes in her hand when she spotted the hot pink truck coming down the road in her direction. Her heart began to pound in her chest as she stopped in her tracks, looking for any place she could take cover. There really was a gun rack in the old lady's bright truck. She'd spotted it when she'd walked past it on her way to the kennel. There was also an NRA-Proud Member sticker on the rear chrome bumper. Elli sure hoped the little old lady in the bright bonnet had calmed down because there wasn't any place to hide. She was an easy target.

As the truck neared, Elli closed her eyes and said a quick Hail Mary. She held her breath as the truck slid on the gravel road, spraying rocks and dust that pelted her arms and face. "Shoot me in the head," Elli shouted. "I don't want to feel the bullet."

"Moodee, what's wrong wit you?" Tante Izzy said, sounding irritated. "Get in my truck."

Elli opened her eyes and saw that the old lady had stopped two feet short of running her over. "What?" She looked into the truck and noted the shotgun was still secure on the rack. She sucked in a deep breath.

"Are you deaf?"

No way was she getting in the truck with that crazy woman and her rifle. "Thanks for the offer, but I need the exercise."

"You skinnier than a coon with his mouth taped shut. You cain't walk where I wants to bring you. I need to show you somethin' you should have seen right away."

Elli looked into Tante Izzy's faded, chocolate brown eyes. Judging by the determined look and the finality of the old lady's tone, she didn't think she had a choice, so she walked to the passenger side. "I'll come with you, but you better not shoot me," Elli said as she climbed in.

"If I wanted to shoot you, I'd have done did it already." Tante Izzy gripped the wheel with her crooked fingers and punched the gas pedal, which had a three-inch block of wood strapped to it so she could reach it. Elli's head jerked back, and she reached for her seat belt. It wasn't there.

"Didn't have no seat belts when I bought dis beauty in 1956, don't need d'em now."

Elli didn't think they painted trucks neon pink back then either, but that didn't stop Tante Izzy from making that change. "You could retrofit the truck with seat belts, if you wanted."

Tante Izzy snorted. "Why would I waste my hard-earned money on someding like dat?"

"Oh, maybe because it's safer to have them?" Elli gripped the side of her seat, trying to keep from sliding off the slick white vinyl. The seat, she could tell, was original to the truck.

"I've been drivin' since I'm six. Never needed a seat belt all those eighty years—except that one time when I got throwed from the truck when it rolled into da ditch on Bayou Noir road." She waved her hand to dismiss the whole idea of seat belts as they approached the property gate. She reached into her faux zebra print purse, pulled out a remote control, and pointed it at the gate. It opened toward the truck and she quickly put it in reverse to keep it from being hit. When the gate opened completely, she punched the gas and they jerked backward. She'd forgotten to shift into drive. By the time she got going in the right direction, the gate had closed again.

"Moodee, dis newfangled technolgeez." She dug into her purse again for the remote.

"I think you might have to back up a bit again." Tante Izzy ignored Elli and let the gate hit the front of her truck. "I think it might work better if you stay behind that yellow line on the road. I think that's why it's painted there."

"I know dat. Ben put dat down for me lass year." She backed up behind the line, then pointed the remote at the gate a third time. "Dare. Dat wasn't so difficile."

"Piece of cake," Elli said, biting back a smile.

They drove for fifteen minutes until they reached a narrow bridge that, according to Tante Izzy, was built across Bayou Noir when "the peoples liked takin' dare cars more than dare boats to church."

St. Anthony's Catholic Church was not far from the foot of the bridge, a couple of hundred yards from Bayou Noir. Tante Izzy drove into the crushed oyster shell lot and parked the truck. "Even dough your Aunt Rosa was a sinnin' woman, havin' taken up with a married man and all, she still was a good Catholic."

Elli had heard a number of nefarious tales about her Aunt Rosa's gypsy past from her father, but hadn't heard stories of her grand affair with Joseph Bienvenu. Her father had been alive when Aunt Rosa had begun that affair, but he hadn't mentioned it. Elli was just out of college at the time and hadn't thought of the aunt she'd never met. Selfishly, she was wrapped up in her budding career and promising life. Her dad probably wasn't too anxious to talk about his sister, either.

"My father mentioned that she was living in the heart of Cajun country, but not much else," Elli offered, watching the parking lot dust settle around the truck. "It wasn't until I got the call from my aunt's lawyer about her will that I found out how she came to own the plantation—and that was like getting the headlines instead of the full article."

"Well, family is family. Da good, da bad, and da ugly." Tante Izzy shook her head and looked up at the brim of the bonnet on her head as if she'd just noticed it was there. She untied the strings under her chin and pulled it off. "I s'pect Rosa really loved him and he her, but it never sat well wit his family." She patted at a few permed curls on her head, then climbed out of the truck. Elli followed. "Are you Catholic?"

"Yes, I am."

"A church-going Catholic or an Easter and Christmas Catholic?"

Elli wasn't sure where this conversation was going or where they were going, but she tried to follow along. "I go to weekly Mass," she said, wondering if the little old lady was bringing her to meet the parish priest to hear her confession or to reveal her Aunt Rosa's confessions.

"I trust you tellin' me the truth because we'ez on holy ground."

Just when she thought they would go up the steps and into the church, Tante Izzy led her around the side of the old wooden building to the back. She pointed past a pale brick arch to the cemetery. "Youz go on through there, now. Youz aunt's been anxious to see you."

Elli looked at Tante Izzy. "Where is she buried?"

"In one of those drawers on the left. You cain't miss it. Instead of her picture on the drawer, she got a whole mess of dogs engraved on da front." Tante Izzy waved her arthritic hand. "Go on."

Elli walked through the archway and found the wall of "drawers". Aunt Rosa's resting place was on the bottom row at the end. "Rosalina Morenelli," she read, feeling a sudden rush of emotions she hadn't expected to have for a person she didn't know. A brass vase sat empty on the front of the auburn marble marker engraved with five Labrador retriever type dogs. "Hello, Aunt Rosa," Elli began, not certain what to say but knowing she should say something. "Thank you for the plantation—although, I'm not sure why you had to make getting it so complicated." She shook her head and wiped the dust off the front of the marble with her shirtsleeve. "I'm not really sure what you intended for me to do with it, but I know what I intend to do. I think you'd be happy to know it will be in the movies. The plantation will be famous. I don't think Ben will be happy about that, though."

Elli stared at the empty vase, again. It bothered her that no one cared enough to bring her flowers. "I wish I knew how to handle Ben," she confessed. "He seems pretty stubborn." She smiled. "I guess I am, too. That, my mother used to tell me, is a Morenelli trait."

She squatted in front of the marble and began tracing the engraved outlines of the dogs. "I need the money from the sale of the plantation. I've got plans. Grand plans that will help a lot of people, but I've got to see they are completed quickly. Not only because of the importance of making this foundation work, but..." she swallowed past the tightness in her throat, "because I just don't know how much time I have to live. I know it sounds so pathetic and grim, and the doctors aren't giving me any reason to think this way. They say I have every reason to believe I'll live to be an old lady, but I can't help..." She shrugged. "Well, I guess I've said all I have to say." She stood, bowed her head, and said a little prayer for Aunt Rosa to rest in peace. Tante Izzy found her like that.

"I done said a novena fer her," she said before reaching Elli. "God knows, she needed it wit da way she loved on Ben's daddy." She shook her head. "I guess she loved him and made him happy. He needed some happiness."

Elli looked at her. "He must have loved her, too. It would explain why he'd give her what was in his family for so long."

Tante Izzy snorted. "Rosa wanted it. He gave her what she wanted." She harrumphed. "She had him wound around her little finger. She wrote poetry for him. She sung him songs with her beat-up gee-tar. She made him feel like a man."

"How long ago did he die?"

"Six months before Rosa." Tante Izzy made the sign of the cross. "Me, I think she died of a broken heart."

That didn't sound like the Aunt Rosa her father spoke of in censorious tones. The woman her dad spoke of was carefree, rebellious, and eccentric. Enduring love and broken hearts and romantic notions didn't fit her personality. She would have picked up her heels and moved on to the next adventure when this one was done. Still, she had stayed with Joseph Bienvenu for a long time.

"I was told they were together for eleven years. Is that right?" She turned to face Tante Izzy.

"Das right."

"And Mrs. Bienvenu knew about it all that time?"

"Hell, she introduced dem—not dat she thought dey'd be lovers at the time." She shifted on her feet and Elli knew she was getting tired. "She didn't like da public humiliation, but she sure didn't mind him out of her bed. Harrumph. You'll meet her soon enough. She's a Texian, like you," she said as if that explained everything.

"I'm not from Texas," Elli told her. She suspected a Tex-ee-an was the same as a Texan. Tante Izzy had already turned to leave and didn't seem to have heard her.

"Va. Let's go," she called to Elli. "Sun's going down and it's gettin' cold. I'm old and my bones hurt when it's cold. What? You want me to get pneumon-ee-a? I ain't leavin' you no property when I die, you know."

Elli smiled, took a single red carnation from a bunch in a vase from a neighboring crypt, and stuffed it into Aunt Rosa's vase. "I'll bring you some of your own later." She looked at the crypt she'd taken a flower from and shrugged. "I'll get you some too, Miss..." She read the engraved name. "Mr. Joseph Bienvenu." Elli was more than a little surprised that his resting place was next to his mistress. That couldn't have set well with his wife and son. She scanned the other names on the wall as she passed. There were at least two dozen other Bienvenues. "Interesting. Very interesting."

"By da way, young gal," Tante Izzy said, her voice firm. "Dis here is youz church parish. Mass is at eight-thirty and ten-thirty."

Chapter Four

I have discovered I love knitted caps...purple ones...yellow ones...blue ones...white ones...rainbow ones. They feel like a warm hug to my cold, furless head...Like a teddy bear, a blankie, a steaming cup of hot cocoa with marshmallows...all good and cozy things. Oh, it is so much better than a scratchy wig on my sensitive scalp or a floppy scarf that I can only tie into something that looks like a poorly wrapped birthday present. I wish you good health, E.

Bosom Blog Buddies Post

Elli reached for her cell phone on the bedside table with minimal movement, as was her habit to do each morning when she woke. She didn't need to look at the time to know it was six a.m. She always woke up at six, no matter what time she went to bed the night before. Still, she looked anyway. That was her habit, too.

8:00 a.m.

"What?" It didn't take long for her slow-waking brain to figure out that even after two nights at Sugar Mill Plantation, her body was still functioning on Pacific time. Cane, Louisiana, was in the central time zone—two hours later. She should have set the phone alarm. She had a lot to do and this two-hour delay meant she'd have to adjust her rigid morning schedule. Her daily five-mile run would have to be a little shorter. She would not abandon it. Another habit.

Other than the dim glow from her phone, the room remained as dark as night, thanks to the old, heavy, blackout curtains over the large windows. She pointed her phone into the darkness to get her bearings. One by one, dark, black, shadowy figures popped up from her bed. She let out a startled cry. Old plantation. Haunted. Ghosts, she concluded in a single beat of her thumping heart. She cried out again. From somewhere at the foot of her bed came a howling bark.

"Oh, no," she said, half with relief and half with frustration. "Shhhh. Quiet down." She'd forgotten about the dogs she'd put in her room last night after Ben evicted them from the doggie guest room. He had to put a sick, brown-eyed pup in there so he could watch over it. Even if she had remembered the beasts in her room, she certainly wouldn't have figured Aunt Rosa's three pets would be in the impossibly narrow bed with her. "Stop that baying." She kicked her feet from beneath the blanket toward the noisy animal; she knew it was BJ by her ear-splitting howl. The annoying animal snorted, let out another bark, and sat down on her feet. "Lovely."

A whiny yawn sounded from near Elli's head. She pointed her cell phone to her right and found Jenny, resting her head on Elli's pillows in a very human-like repose.

"Pillow hog," she said, at a loss as to when or how Jenny had managed to evict her from the pillows in the tiny bed. "You all need crates to sleep in, like Donna." Doe and BJ stood and stared down at her. Jenny put her thick paw on Elli's arm. Donna probably heard her name and began to whine from inside her kennel at the foot of the bed. Elli recognized the note in Donna's cry. She had to go and there was little time to get her outside.

Using her cell phone to light her path, Elli untangled herself from twisted blankets and excited dogs, scooped Donna from her crate, and raced to the door. She managed only to stub her bare toes twice. Blinking past the sting in her eyes from the sudden burst of light as she rushed out of the room, she darted down the stairs with Donna extended from her body and a trail of yapping dogs behind her. As she raced through the kitchen, she registered in a blur that there were four wide human eyes and a pair of canine eyes looking at her. Of course, there were, she thought, knowing that at least one of the pairs of eyes belonged to Ben Bienvenu. She was destined to show herself at her worst to the man she wanted to impress the most. If holding a leaky dog in a rhinestone collar wasn't bad enough, doing it while wearing pink flannel pajama bottoms; Wal-Mart Clearance Winnie the Pooh, cami; and a worn, homemade, knit cap was scraping the bottom of the barrel. It was only one step above charging out of a bathroom with a towel wrapped around her and spearing a plunger at phantom alligators.

She rushed through the rear, screened porch, tripped down the outside steps, and fell onto the concrete pad, just missing the lush, dew-dampened, grass by two inches. Donna tinkled as she fell.

"Daddy, that lady fell down," she heard a young voice say and her heart sank further. Not only did she humiliate herself in front of Ben but in front of the child he protected like the Terminator protected John and Sarah Connor.

Elli looked at the wet spot on Pooh's head and sighed. Jenny came up to her and licked her face. Doe howled twice, yanked her knit cap off her head, and took off. She had no idea where BJ was and, frankly, didn't care. She hoped the noisy little monster ran away and joined a pack of wild dogs in the swamp. She rolled onto her back and looked up at the bright blue sky for just a moment—she needed a moment, doggone it, so she would take one. She needed for life to level out so she could regain control—control of the doggie chaos. Control over her heart that suddenly felt heavy with guilt when she heard Ben's son's sweet voice. The son who had the mini-man recliner in this grand home. The son who Doug told her was staying with him in the cottage since she moved into the plantation.

Elli sucked in a breath of cool, damp, verdant morning air and absorbed all the good vitamin D-three the warm sunshine offered her. She'd reconcile this problem. She'd help find a home for Ben's son. She could do that. She was a problem solver, right? Maybe she was just crazy and way over her head.

"Daddy, who is that lady on the ground?"

"Come inside. She's a crazy woman waiting for the psycho police to come get her." The little boy slammed the door closed, but not before she heard Ben say, "Stay away from her."

Elli threw her arm over her eyes and groaned. "Crazy? I'll show you crazy!" she shouted after him. She sat up and noticed the torn fabric over her knees. She spotted the small smear of blood before she felt the abrasion from her skinned knees. "Ouwwww."

She wanted to sit nursing her injury, absorbing the sunshine and cool, fresh air, but Doe looked like she was ready to shred her treasured knit cap. Elli jumped up and raced after the floppy-eared beast. She'd had that knit cap and a half dozen others like it since she'd lost her hair from the chemo treatment. She began sleeping with it on her head, then to keep warm, and still wore it to sleep today because it was comforting and cozy. This fuzzy pink, white, and orange one was her favorite. It was the first one she'd knitted.

* * * *

Ben watched Elli through the kitchen window as she chased Doe around the backyard. Her limping didn't hide her agility and grace. She was long, lean, and obviously a runner, but no match for the bloodhound mix. What in the hell did the dog have in her mouth anyway?

As if reading his father's mind, Joey walked to the back door and looked past the screened porch. "The crazy lady looks like she wants her hat back, huh Daddy?"

Hat? Yes, he remembered, she was wearing the knit cap when she ran outside with her fancy poodle mix dangling in front of her like a rotten roast.

"Go on, get your school bag. It's time to go."

"I don't have school, remember?" Joey got his backpack from the kitchen table. "It's Sunday. We're going to eight thirty mass."

Ben nodded. "Yeah, I remember." He smiled at his son, who looked at him as if he expected to hear that he had to go to school anyway. "You still want to help me run the German Shepherds through their drills after Mass, huh?"

"Can I hide the scent box? I know places to put it that aren't easy for them to find."

"I'm counting on it." Before he could tell his son to meet him in the truck, Joey ran outside.

Ben watched as he stopped ten feet in front of the truck, hesitated, and fidgeted with his fingers. He turned abruptly and shouted to Elli. "I hope you get your hat back."

Elli looked at his son, a smile instantly on her face. She waved to him. "Me, too."

His stomach felt like a fist landed dead center. He didn't like the woman who was trying to steal his son's home being so damn chummy with him. "Let's go," he said as he approached the boy.

As they reached the truck, Doe darted around the garage toward them. A limp, fuzzy, pink, white, and orange cap in her mouth. Joey called her over and the dog went right to him. The boy had a way with dogs. He was a natural and it made Ben proud every time he saw him with them. He'd be a great trainer one day. Ben just wished his son could be that comfortable with people. He was shy and timid around both children and adults. There were only three people he was comfortable with—Beau, Tante Izzy, and Doug.

"I know you are just having fun," Joey said to the dog, "but you shouldn't get that crazy lady upset. It isn't right to do that to handicapped people."

Ben began to laugh as he opened the door to the truck. It was then that he noticed Elli standing off to the side. By the red blotches on her cheeks and her gaping mouth, he knew she had heard his son.

Joey carried the cap to Elli. Doe immediately leaped up and tried to take it back. His son laughed as Elli jerked it away. "She don't mean no harm. She's just funning you…"

"I wish she wouldn't do her funning with my favorite cap." She smiled. "I thank you for rescuing it."

She looked down at Joey with a softness in her eyes that made Ben's chest ache. Had she been anyone other than the woman trying to steal his son's home, he would have been grateful for her kindness. Instead, it felt like she was throwing Joey in the middle of a bloody battle. Was she using the son to get to the father? That ploy had been tried on him before, and he wasn't stupid enough to fall for it again.

"Let's go, Joey," he called, controlling his anger. His son stood in front of Elli and didn't move. He acted as if he hadn't heard his father. He was looking down at his dull brown leather church shoes. "What the hell?" Ben mumbled, surprised that his painfully shy son remained standing near Elli even though his body language said he didn't want to be there. He looked like he wanted to say something more. What in the hell was his son doing? "We don't want to be late for Mass. Tante Izzy will have our hides," he said, knowing his voice was rougher than necessary.

"What's your name?" she asked gently.

"Joey." He kicked at the grass. "Joseph Martin Bienvenu, the second. After my Popie." She thought of the man who had loved her aunt and was buried next to her.

"I'm Elli. Elli Morenelli, and I like your recliner." She extended her hand and he looked up at it. "I won't bite. Jenny might, but I promise I won't."

Ben stormed over to them, but not before his son shook her hand and raced to the truck.

"Thank you for your help, Joey," she called to him as Ben reached her. He stood in front of her with his feet spread, hands on his hips. He put his body between her and his vulnerable son.

"Stay away from him." She folded her arms over her chest. "Don't drag him in the middle of our problems. You go near him again, and I'll toss you in a feed sack and send you back to California so fast you won't know what happened."

"You don't scare me, Ben Bienvenu," she said, staring right into his eyes with her big baby blues as if she meant it. "I've faced worse things than you."

"No," he gritted his teeth, "you haven't. Don't try to pretend to be someone you're not, Miss Crocifissa Morenelli." Her eyes widened at the use of her legal name. "Yeah, cher, I know who you really are."

He turned, his ears burning, his fists clenched. Damn if he didn't want to do what he threatened and ship her back to California in a dusty feed sack. He climbed in the truck and backed out of the driveway. Before he shifted into drive, he looked at her one last time. She stood where he'd left her. Her eyes were bright with anger. No, Miss Morenelli didn't like being threatened, but she was smart enough not to let her emotions get the best of her. He'd have to keep his guard up with her. She was going to try to outwit him to get what she wanted. He could see her already calculating his demise in those bright blue eyes. Ben suspected she was good at it, too. Well, he was good at getting what he wanted. Handling the pretty, long-legged Miss Morenelli would be as easy as training a stubborn shepherd. She'd figure out soon enough who was the pack leader.

* * * *

Thirty minutes later, she was still angry. "Crocifissa Morenelli," Elli grumbled, shoving her legs into her black spandex running shorts. "Nobody calls me by my given name, not even my doctors." She stuffed her feet into her running shoes and laced them with sharp jerking movements. "The last time someone used that tone, saying my name the way Ben did, was when my third-grade teacher thought I intentionally put poison sumac leaves with the railroad daisies I'd picked for her from the field near the school. I did nothing wrong then and I didn't do anything wrong now."

Jenny, whom Elli had quickly realized was as sweet and nurturing as Aunt Bea in the Andy Griffith Show, came over and put her paw on Elli's foot.

"Thank you, Jenny." She scratched the retriever's soft neck and gave her a quick hug. "You know, he tossed my name at me like he was swinging a sledgehammer through a stone wall." She petted Doe, who came over to get some of the attention Jenny was enjoying. "It's a good name. It's an old family name passed on from generation to generation. I choose to use my nickname because, it's…it's…well, it's better." She sighed. "Who am I kidding? I like Crocifissa in a family tradition kind of way, but not at all in the living with it kind of way." She shrugged. "I have got to not let his petty taunts get to me." She nodded. "Sticks and stones and all that." She stood and the dogs started bouncing and circling around her. "Keep your eye on the finish line, Elli."

She looked at the dogs in perpetual motion. "Who's ready for a run?" She got the leashes for Jenny, Doe, and BJ. "You need a lot of exercise and calming energy to behave," she said, quoting the Dog Whisperer whose shows she found online right after she logged onto Ben's wireless Wi-Fi the night before. It wasn't hard to figure out his password either, she remembered with a smile. It was D-O-G-S. The man was certainly not worried about internet security.

"I aim to follow the Dog Whisperers advice for all of you," she said, feeling her spirits lighten. "Even you, Donna. We'll walk this afternoon." She looked at the pretty bundle of fluff resting in her kennel. There was no way her tiny legs could keep up with the bigger animals. Besides, they'd trample her for certain.

Yes, this dog exercising thing was a trifecta, Elli thought. The dogs got exercise, she got exercise, and she got to scout the grounds for photo locations for the real estate portfolio she was putting together. She'd picked a course through the areas she thought two specific venture-capitalist groups would be interested in seeing. They both were looking to build a "Hollywood South" studio. With Louisiana's special, tax-free incentives for movies filming in the state, she understood how appealing Sugar Mill Plantation would be to them.

Jenny, Doe, and BJ were remarkably well behaved as she started running from the front of the house, toward the bayou. Doe, the most energetic of the three, took the lead, followed by BJ. Jenny ran at her right side in what seemed to be a protective position between Elli and the water's edge. She guessed that if an alligator or opossum darted out of the water, she'd defend her. Or not. Maybe her active imagination was just making all of that up.

"Good girls," Elli said and the dogs' heads lifted higher with pride. "This is fun." She smiled, deciding Doug's instruction on using the leashes was very good advice. She'd have to ask him on techniques to housebreak BJ, whom she discovered had left her a surprise on the bathroom floor.

She gazed around the bayou, feeling content and making mental notes of a twisted cypress tree, a thick palmetto plant, and a smooth, flowing bayou bend that she'd photograph later for the portfolio. She was feeling hopeful and full of good, calming energy, and the dogs were feeding off of it—or so she thought until she turned at a small road to her left that led into a cane field. Doe wanted to keep going straight, BJ wanted to turn onto the road, and Jenny wanted to stop running altogether.

Elli stumbled before stopping in the middle of the road. BJ tried to keep running. "Whoa, girl." She tugged on her leash and BJ jumped up, shoving her paws against Elli's hips and nearly knocking her over. "Hey, cut that out." Elli looked at the pedometer on her wristwatch. She'd only gone a half a mile.

"You don't know who you're messing with. I'm tougher than I look." She laughed and started running down the road where, on this warm February day, the new crop of cane was more brown than green, and was as high as her knees. It actually looked more like beach grass or bamboo than sugarcane. Each season, she thought, would bring a different look to the fields. There would be the lush, towering, emerald cane in the summer; the bare, just harvested fields of fall; the tan stalks of winter; and the fresh, new green sprouts of spring. Each was beautiful in its own way, she realized, inhaling the sweet, earthy scent she imagined would also change with the season, making it sweeter, heavier, and richer.

She stopped in the middle of the road, and for a moment, she took it all in—not worrying about the tangle of dogs or the perfect photos she would take. She simply appreciated the hushing quiet of the sugarcane stalks swooshing in the wind. This was pure. Unpretentious. Elemental. Healthy. The sky was a perfect, fresh shade of blue. The road was a dry, rich, earthy brown. The cane stalks were a crisp, robust tan with new green shoots starting to stand up around it. All Elli could think was wow, and she felt the word whisper over her lips. She thanked God for giving her this exact, perfect, wonderful moment. Life was, after all, made up of remarkable moments. She never wanted to skim over them, because you never knew if one would be your last.

Without thought, she tugged on the leashes and turned to walk into a narrow row of the cane fields. She wanted to be part of this basic, natural thing. She wanted to let it seep into her skin, her blood, her bones. She wanted to be in harmony with it.

The dogs must have sensed her need for quiet and peace. They followed her unobtrusively, sniffing and high-stepping, doing things dogs do. Elli didn't pay attention to how far she walked until she wandered into a straight line of towering cedar trees that smelled sweet, heavy, and familiar. In the home she'd grown up in near Santa Clarita, they'd had a cedar-paneled storage closet upstairs where they kept ski clothes, her old baby clothes, and other items they didn't often use. Smelling the familiar scent of her carefree childhood made her feel good. The dogs must have sensed her happy mood and came over to her, wagging their tails.

"Aren't you all an intuitive bunch," she said, petting each of them. As she was scratching Jenny under the chin, something behind the cedars caught her eye. It was gray and its texture was very different from the scaly, sienna brown bark of the cedars. Elli moved forward, past the man-sized trunks and low branches, until she was in a clearing where a small, ten-by-ten, weathered shack stood on the edge of a moss-draped bayou. The moss and the weathered cypress building were just about the same color. The dogs pulled on their leashes, trying to get closer to the water.

"Stay," she said, sensing they shouldn't go any further. She felt like she was trespassing, so she checked her pedometer to see how far she actually had traveled. One-point-six miles. With the twists and turns she made, she knew that meant she was still on Sugar Mill land. It was odd that this bayou-side shack wasn't noted on the maps she'd received in her documents nor listed in the property descriptions.

What did it matter? She had found it now. She'd come back here to take pictures. This would definitely have to be included in the real estate packet. "Charming fishing camp or country cottage," she said, thinking of the angles from which the movie camera could film the tiny building with its four single-paned windows and lone rusty-hinged door. "Definitely charming." She smiled, looking at the small, half-collapsed, wooden dock leading from the narrow porch into the bayou.

Jenny sat next to Elli and began to whine.

"What's wrong, girl. Are you tired?"

Doe began to bark her odd bloodhound bark, pulling on the leash as if she wanted to take off toward the shack to their left. Elli looked in the direction she was barking pulling on her leash to keep her from rushing forward. "What do you hear? An animal?" she asked, not seeing anything that would make Doe so upset. "There's got to be raccoons and snakes and other creatures in there." She didn't know Doe very well or understand why dogs barked, but the way Doe was acting made the hair stand on her scalp. It was such a primal response that Elli knew something had to be wrong. A chill raced down Elli's spine and she knew she couldn't excuse it away.

She began to back out of the clearing, using the same path by which she had come. BJ and Jenny were now barking and lunging toward this unknown thing or things. Elli just wanted to get the blazes out of there. She had to use all of her strength to pull them back to the road. Once she got there, they settled down and forgot about the cabin. Elli hadn't. She took off running as fast as she could down the road, the dogs followed her for a while, then Doe and BJ raced in front of her. Jenny tugged on the leash and trailed behind her. She was stuck in the middle. How in the world had she let this happen?

"Stop. Heel," she shouted as Doe and BJ huffed and coughed from the choking pull of the leash against their throats. Elli tried to run faster to keep them from strangling. Jenny would have none of it. She pulled and reared up on her hind legs behind Elli, twisting to try to get out of her collar.

"Oh, no you don't."

Without missing a stride, Elli lowered the leash close to the ground behind her to keep Jenny from slipping out of the collar. It worked, but Elli had to run in an odd lunging fashion. Her thighs began to burn as they reached a wide crossroad about a mile and half down from where they had started this bizarre tug-of-war dash. BJ and Doe darted to the left.

"I planned to go that way anyway," she shouted to them, a bit breathy from the fast-paced, lunging run. Now her shins were beginning to ache. She leaned back to try to slow them down, but it only made them strain more against the leashes and made Elli work harder. Jenny tried to sit down behind her for the hundredth time. "Move it. Now."

The lead dogs pulled her like she'd seen runaway horses do in a hundred different westerns while Jenny moseyed along like a drunken cowboy stumbling out of a saloon. Elli was tugged sideways in the battle of speed and lethargy.

"Stop. Halt. No. Slow," she called to the dogs in front. "Move. Faster. No. Go," she shouted to Jenny behind her. She was certain her limbs would rip out of their sockets. "Hey, you're supposed to be feeling my calm, assertive energy."

She spotted the pretty, white, slatted fence surrounding the dog kennel ahead of them. Maybe that's where Doe and BJ were heading. They would have to slow down when they got near the fence, she thought. She'd get control of them there. Or not, she realized, as the dogs led her into the kennel through a small open gate she hadn't noticed before. To make matters worse, the two young men whom she had seen working at the kennel with Ben and Doug, had witnessed her dog handling ineptness. In fact, by their laughter, they seemed to find quite a bit of humor in her running sideways and being ripped in half by three miserable dogs. The only consoling thing about this humiliating scene was that Ben wasn't there to witness it. He was at Mass. She looked down at her watch. Nine-fifty. Mass had been over for twenty minutes.

Maybe luck would be on her side this time, she thought, but was immediately relieved of that hope as Ben stepped out of the first cottage and leaned against a post on the front porch. He crossed his booted ankle and folded his arms over his denim-clad chest. "Arrogant jerk," she mumbled.

"You look like you're trying to herd wild lions instead of housebroke dogs," one of the men shouted as she ran past him. She recognized him as one of the costume-wearing pirates from a few days ago.

"Only two are housebroke," she smiled, trying to pretend she meant to run like this.

"Is that how they walk dogs in Cali-forn-ee," another man said, chuckling.

"Not all of Cali-forn-ee," the first pirate-guy said. "Just in Holly-la-de-la-wood."

Elli saw Doug get out of his red pickup truck near his cottage. "Hi Doug," she shouted, lifting the leash as high as the dogs would allow to let him know she was using them as he suggested. But instead of waving back or smiling his usual quick smile, Ben's foreman, her one ally, just shook his head. Her heart sank. The look of disappointment on his face made her want to cry. So what if she didn't know how to walk dogs and was trotting through the kennel in front of his peers like an inebriated chicken?

She smiled and gave the three men her best I'm not comic Lucille Ball; I'm alluring Scarlett Johansson wave as she continued down the road toward the plantation house.

Blessedly, she saw the curve in the road ahead where she knew that once she got around it, Ben and his staff wouldn't be able to see her struggles. She tried to hurry Jenny toward the Holy Grail, and just as she reached it, she spotted a truck speeding toward her. A bright pink truck with a tiny, gray-haired lady barely visible behind the wheel. "God help me."

Tante Izzy slammed on the brakes a few feet from Elli. "Youz goin' to be late," she shouted out of her window, her mouth barely clearing the opening.

Elli lifted her tired arms in a shrug. "Late for what?" she asked, not really wanting to know the answer. She just wanted to get back to the house and save her limbs from the relentless dogs.

Tante Izzy made a strange half snort, half hissing sound. Her disappointment was clear in her cloudy eyes. "Mass. Get in right, now. Youz soul will be as black as youz Aunt Rosa's if you don't go."

Elli was too tired to argue. She climbed into the truck and dragged the dogs in with her.

"Father Étienne won't be happy havin' dem in church." She shoved Jenny out of her way, jerked the truck into drive, and sped off. "You better just keep dem out da baptismal fountain."

* * * *

"I think they were all very good girls in church," Elli said, more to the dogs than to Tante Izzy as they left the St. Anthony Church parking lot. "I can't believe I actually brought a pack of dogs to church. I'm grateful the cry room was empty and we could bring them in there."

"E'sept for da howlin' when Elridge sang 'Ave Maria,' day waz quiet."

Elli laughed. "BJ sure can't carry a tune." She scratched Jenny under the chin as she remembered Ben had with Donna. "And thank you, Miss Izzy, for warning me about the baptismal fountain. Jenny surely would have dived in if I didn't have a good hold on her leash. She loves the water."

"Tante Izzy, not Miss." She slammed on her brakes and skidded to a stop at the traffic light. "Humph. Look at all dat traffic." She pointed to the three cars on the other side of the intersection.

"That's not traffic," Elli smiled. "If you want to see traffic, you should drive on the Four between five and six."

"Four, five, and six? What's dat? A kindergarten lesson?"

"No, a highway in Los Angeles and the time when it's at its worst."

"I drove in the city one time, me." Tante Izzy nodded her head once with pride. "Yep. Went to New Orling for a pa'rade. Wanted to see if it was better than what we got here on da bayou."

Elli turned to face Tante Izzy. She really liked her and pretended for a moment that Tante Izzy was the grandmother she had never known. "And, was the parade better?"

"Mon dieu, child. What kind a question is dat?" She shook her head and nearly drove off the road when the light turned green. "Of course not."

"Well, how was I supposed to know? I've never been to a Mardi Gras before. I've seen it on TV."

"TV?" Tante Izzy looked at her as if she was crazy.

"Red light!" Elli shouted, grabbing Jenny and Doe. She braced her feet against the floorboard to keep them all from flying through the front windshield when Tante Izzy slammed on the brakes. "That's it." Elli opened her door. "I'm driving." She walked around to the driver's side and opened Tante Izzy's door. "I want to live another day." She looked at the startled little lady behind the steering wheel, and her heart softened. "Do you mind? I really would prefer driving." Elli understood pride and independence. She had more than her share of those traits, and she was learning that Tante Izzy did, too. "It's not that I think you're a bad driver, it's just that I'm a terrible passenger. I'm what everyone refers to as a 'backseat driver,' no matter where I sit."

"Harrumph." Tante Izzy slowly eased out of the truck and walked to the passenger side. "I'm only lettin' you drive because of all dis traffic," she told Elli after she climbed back in. "I hate traffic."

"Thank you." Elli slid into the seat and her knees hit the dashboard as the steering wheel rested against her chest. "I've got to adjust the seat, or I won't be able to make a right turn much less breathe." She found the lever and scooted the seat as far back as she could. The light turned green before she had the mirrors adjusted, so she remained stopped in the middle of the road and ignored the car horn blowing behind her.

"Is dat you, young Marcel Arceneaux? I'm goin' to call your momma and tell her how youz is disrespectin' your elders." The kid behind them looked suitably embarrassed. "I'm gonna teach him some manners, me."

Elli took off through the intersection just as the light was changing from yellow to red. "I saw it, so you don't have to say a word." She glanced at Tante Izzy, who was hiding a smile behind her hand. Her bright, crinkled eyes gave her away, though.

"I'm gonna teach youz some manners, too."

"Whatever," Elli said with a huge smile as she pushed Doe away from her thighs before her sniffing nose hit her favorite target. "Where to, Tante Izzy? I'm your chauffeur for the day."

"To the pa'rade, of course. Cain't have no Texian come to Vacherie Parish and not see a Mardi Gras pa'rade."

Elli smiled. "I'm not from Texas."

In her heavy, Cajun accent, Tante Izzy looked at Elli with narrowed eyes. "Whatever."

Elli burst out laughing and passed through an intersection, not noticing the stop sign.

* * * *

"So what are you going to do about your houseguest?" Doug asked, walking into the grooming room where Ben was washing the last of the three New Orleans Police Department German Shepherds. The three canine officers were about to arrive, and he wanted to make sure the dogs looked their best.

Ben finished rinsing the unhappy shepherd not certain how to answer the man. What in the hell was he going to do about Elli? He knew he wanted her to go away, but how to make that happen was a damn mystery to him.

"I can't say that I don't like the lady," Doug continued, running his hand through his thick salt-and-pepper hair. He was always doing that, although Ben had never seen a single hair out of place. It was the same thing with his clothes, always neat, clean, and perfect. "You know she came to me for advice on how to control her dogs?"

"I figured it was you who gave her the leashes." Ben towel- dried the dog, lifted it out of the large sink, and put it on the counter. He plugged in the blow-dryer and turned it on. The dog whined but didn't move.

"She is totally clueless about how to handle those animals. Seems to me they are handling her. I guess that's what you wanted when you gave them to her." He shook his head and smiled. The smile did not reach his eyes. Ben had known Doug long enough to understand that he was worried about what Elli would do, even though he was trying to act as if he wasn't. Doug had it easy at the kennel. He pretty much set his own hours. Ben didn't mind because Joey really liked having him around. He supposed, if he was honest with himself, he liked having Doug help with Joey, too. It was a win-win to have Joey's only grandfather around.

"I know I have a few decades on her," Doug continued when Ben didn't say anything. "But I do find her...intriguing. Damn intriguing. Maybe I can help you by keeping a close eye on her. See what she's up to, if you know what I mean."

"I don't need any help," Ben snapped, not happy with the idea of Doug romancing Elli. Not that he cared if she warmed the man's bed. He just didn't want to give her any more excuses to stick around. "I think you should stay away from her."

"Why? Are you interested?"

"Hell, no." He turned off the dryer.

"Hmm. Sounds like thou protest too strongly." Doug turned and walked out of the cottage through a back door in the room.

"Sleep with the damn Texian if you want," he called after him.

"What Texian?" Elli said, walking into room way too cheery with her froufrou Hollywood dog in her arms. Like someone hit a switch, her smile faded, and her face blushed pink.

"What do you want?" he snapped, causing her tiny ball of fur to jump and let out a girly bark.

"Uh...were you talking about me?" she asked, then shook her head, causing her dark blond waves to bounce around her face. "Don't answer that." She cleared her throat and tossed her shoulders back. If there were ever a picture in the dictionary describing the word uncomfortable, it would be the way Elli looked standing in the middle of the room in her dark blue jeans and silver running shoes. "Oh, isn't he pretty?" she said, her eyes falling on the shepherd. With much too much enthusiasm, she moved toward the dog to pet him.

The shepherd wanted no part of it and lunged at Elli, barking, growling, and showing his sharp teeth. Ben tightened his hold on the leash, jerking him to a halt as Elli ran into the corner furthest from the dog. Donna stuffed her nose into Elli's armpit, and Elli secured her hold on the tiny dog. She immediately dropped one of her arms and stood up as tall and broad as her thin body would expand. Elli looked down at the shepherd and stared right into his eyes. His lips lifted in a snarl that was all teeth and intimidation.

"What the hell are you doing? Are you trying to make him bite you?"

"I'm doing like one of those books from your library says." She kept her eyes wide and steady on the shepherd's. "Make yourself bigger and look him in the eyes like you are meaner and tougher than him."

"Cher, trust me. You will never be meaner or tougher than he is and he knows it." Ben gave the shepherd a silent signal to sit, with a twist of his hand. Then he pointed to Elli and commanded her to do the same. "Stay."

Elli started to laugh. Donna pulled her long snout from Elli's armpit and looked up at her. Ben couldn't help it; he laughed, too.

The shepherd didn't find anything humorous about Elli. He had decided she was the bad guy and began to bark and lunge at her.

"He wants to eat me," she cried.

Ben silenced him by jerking on his leash.

"Isn't it his nap time or something?" she asked. Her voice was light, but Ben could see by her dilated pupils that she was frightened. She didn't move out of her corner.

Ben carried the dog off the table and secured his leash to a pole at its base. He grabbed Elli by the arm to lead her out of the room, but she didn't want to step an inch closer to the shepherd, so she awkwardly turned into him instead, her body rubbing against him in the process. "Damn it." He wasn't happy about his physical reaction to her, but couldn't say it was unexpected either. She was a beautiful, sexy woman who was now poured over him like hot sex. He tried to step back. She grabbed the front of his denim shirt and held on. "He's not going to attack you."

"Sure looks like it from my point of view. I've seen how well those tiny collars hold a dog." She sighed, looking up at him with her big, bright, baby blues. Hell if that didn't make him even harder.

He took in a fortifying breath and immediately knew it was a mistake. Wildflowers, he thought, she smelled like a freakin' spring meadow of wildflowers. "Let go of me," he said through clenched teeth. Donna whined between them. Neither he nor Elli seemed to notice.

Elli just kept her eyes glued to his, as if she was afraid she'd be eaten by the shepherd if she looked away. The vulnerability Ben saw in her eyes nearly undid him. Then, her gaze slid down to his mouth, and he felt like he had been sucker-punched. Elli began to breathe more deeply, like she was struggling for air, too. Her perky, round breasts lifted more firmly against him, and his thin, navy polo shirt did nothing to separate them. She might as well have been naked, he thought, and immediately regretted thinking of her standing next to him in only her skin. "Damn."

As if by a will of its own, his mouth moved closer to hers, but before he could taste those sweet, plump lips, an alarm went off in his head. He started to back away, but not soon enough, for Elli leaned in and captured his mouth with hers. A sigh vibrated in her chest, and he pulled her tighter against him, changing the angle. Elli trembled in his arms. Damn, but he had to taste more of her, he thought as his tongue took a slow slide around her plump lips. He felt the sigh slip like a hot caress across his mouth. Then, she slipped her tongue into his mouth, and her desire poured from her into him, or was it from him into her?

He slid his hands up her body until his thumbs rested on the sides of her breasts. A moan echoed from deep in his chest and just as quickly as this kiss ignited, it was extinguished. Elli shoved him back with so much force he nearly tumbled onto the dog behind him.

"What are you doing?" she shouted. The shepherd didn't like her tone any more than Ben did, and he lunged toward her again, straining against the leash. Elli grabbed Ben's shirt and jerked him in front of her. "Do something about that vicious beast."

"Are you talking about the dog or yourself?"

"Ha-ha." She let go of his shirt, took a deep breath, tossed back her shoulders and lifted her chin. It only took a couple of seconds but when she spoke again, her tone was much calmer. "Please, Ben. I think Donna has completely emptied her bladder because of him."

He took the shepherd outside, happy to be away from Elli so he could clear his head and cool down from whatever it was about her that got him riled as much as the shepherd. He put the dog in the kennel behind the building, hoping Elli would be gone when he got back. She wasn't.

"Wow, you got quite a canine book collection here," she said, looking at the books on the shelves near the door. Like he'd seen before, her cheeks were bright pink and blotchy, and she refused to look at him. However much she wanted to pretend nothing had just happened between them, though, her swollen lips gave it away. "Can I borrow this one?" She lifted Be the Pack Leader.

Ben grabbed another book off the shelf and handed it to her. "I think this one will be better for you."

"An Idiot's Guide to Dog Behavior." To Ben's surprise, she burst out laughing. It was such an unguarded, natural, sweet sound that he found himself smiling. It irritated him that he was and he wiped it off his face on a forceful exhale. "I do like your sense of humor, Mr. Bienvenu, as much as seeing your cute crooked smile. It's so much better than this unpleasant scowl of yours."

"I don't really care what you like, Miss Crocifissa."

She shook her head. "Please don't call me that."

"It's your name, isn't it?" He grabbed Donna from her arms and walked into the veterinary clinic to the left of the grooming room. Elli followed him.

"Yes and no." He looked at her. "Legally, yes. It's on my birth certificate, driver's license, and medical records. But no one ever calls me by that name anymore." A deep sadness seemed to sweep into her eyes and cast her light baby blues a half dozen shades darker.

He put Donna on the examining table.

"What are you doing? She's up-to-date on her shots. You can check the tags on her collar."

"I think she's got a UTI," he told her as he took out a digital thermometer and slipped the plastic sleeve over the tip.

"A urinary tract infection? You do?" Elli patted Donna on her head. "Oh, you poor thing," she said, not questioning his diagnosis. Oddly, it pleased him that she trusted him on this.

"It would explain her lack of bladder control and the way she sometimes whimpers when she goes on her own." He put petroleum jelly on the tip of the thermometer and lifted Donna's tail.

"Eww, can't you take her temperature under her tongue or somewhere less invasive?" Without his asking, Elli moved to hold Donna when she tried to sidestep away.

"You can take a reading from their ears, but it's usually harder to get a dog to cooperate."

"It's okay, sweetheart," she said in soft tones next to Donna's ear. "It'll be over in a minute. This is for your own good."

The thermometer beeped and he read the display. "One-oh-three." He tossed the plastic cover into the trash.

"Oh, Ben. That's high. Should we give her an ice bath or bring her to the veterinary emergency room?" She picked up Donna and hugged her against her chest. She put her lips to her forehead as a mother might do to her child.

"You can feel the pads of her paws to see if she's warm, not her forehead," he told her, knowing he sounded annoyed. "She's okay. Normal range for dogs is ninety-nine point five to one hundred and two point five. I'll call our vet and see if he can take a look at her in the morning. No ice bath. If you want, you can put a cool towel on the hairless areas of her body—the pads of her paws, under her belly—but if this temperature is from an infection, it won't help a whole lot."

"Can we start her on antibiotics in the meantime?" Her eyes were their usual pale blue again.

"It's best we get a culture first so we don't give her the wrong medicine and disrupt her system and cause other problems." He leaned his hip on the examining table and folded his arms across his chest when he wanted to take her hand and reassure her. "We'll increase her water intake, make sure she's eating quality meat-based food to assure a good PH balance, and check her temp every four hours to see if there's any change."

"Did I do this to her?" Tears filled her eyes but didn't flow. Without realizing that he was doing it, he took her hand into his and squeezed it gently.

"She'll be fine." He knew he hadn't answered her question, and by the look on Elli's face, she understood why. Diet could cause UTIs, which meant it probably was her fault.

"Ben, I fed her organic food and gave her the pure mineral water she's used to having." She sniffed, but still held the tears back.

"There are plenty of reasons a dog gets a UTI. Diet is one of them. Sometimes you can do everything right and animals still get sick. Some are more sensitive than others. My guess is she has a PH imbalance from her organic food. It's probably grain-based and she needs a meat-based food."

Elli shook her head. "She's been incontinent since we began our trip, so it must have been..." She didn't finish her thought. "Where do I buy the right food?"

"I've got some in the pantry at the training gym." He went to the cabinet and got some alcohol to clean the thermometer. He handed it to Elli with a box of protective covers. "You can handle taking her temp?"

"Sure," she said too easily. Ben wasn't convinced. "Every four hours."

He cleaned the stainless examining table with disinfectant and led her to the main kennel training building across the street. On the way over, the pseudo truce they had because of their mutual concern for Donna ended. The single-minded woman saw to that.

"Do you think we can have a meeting tonight to discuss our situation?" she asked, in a tone filled with a confidence Ben knew she had because of the cozy little scene in the clinic.

"I already know everything I need to know about our situation, Miss Crocifissa." He pulled the gym door open and walked in first. She rushed in behind him to keep the door from hitting her on her backside.

"Actually, you don't." He stopped and gave her a hard look. She had the nerve to stare right back at him, sliding her big eyes over his mouth again. Damn.

"Considering you can't do anything without me agreeing to it, I can't see how that is possible. Unless we're talking about the way you molested me with your hot little body and sexy mouth, earlier." He turned and walked into the food storage room at the end of the hall.

She followed him. "I didn't molest you," she said, her voice not as confident as it was just minutes before. "I...I...I'm sorry for kissing you the way I did. I don't know what came over me. I didn't get a good night's sleep." Ben glared at her. "Okay, I have no excuse for my behavior. It was totally inappropriate and unprofessional."

"Depends on your profession." He let out the breath he didn't know he was holding and filled a box with a few plastic bags of dry dog food. The sooner he was away from her the better. More importantly, the sooner she left Sugar Mill and was out of his life, the sooner things would be back to normal. "It's best to feed all of your dogs this food. You add water to it. Follow the instructions on the bag." He handed her the box, and after a few awkward seconds of her repositioning it in her arms, she put Donna inside it.

"After dinner would be a good time for us to meet," she said, pasting a smile on her deceivingly sweet face. "We can meet in the dining room. I'll see you then." She turned and walked away, and Ben's eyes fell to her well-shaped ass.

Before she reached the door, it swung open and three super-fit New Orleans Police officers, wearing tight black T-shirts and uniform pants, came inside. They stopped in front of Elli, huge grins on their faces as they spoke to her. "Ma'am."

"Hello, beautiful."

"Hi, honey."

She looked at Ben, then smiled a flirty smile at New Orleans's finest. "Welcome to Sugar Mill Plantation," she said. "My name is Elli Morenelli." She extended her hand while balancing the box with Donna and the dog food with the other. She shook their hands.

"Pleasure to meet you," the tallest and most muscular of the three said. "Please tell me we'll be working with you while we're here."

She laughed that womanly kind of laugh that always grabbed a man by his balls. "Oh, no, I don't work here. I'm just part owner of the kennel and plantation." She looked Ben directly in the eyes. "See you after dinner tonight, Mr. Bienvenu."

* * * *

Elli heard Ben and Joey talking downstairs and decided she wouldn't push her luck by joining them in the kitchen. She didn't want to anger Ben before their meeting by hanging out with his sweet little boy. She needed to have him in the best possible mood when she told him that a movie crew was coming to shoot a few scenes on

Tuesday and Wednesday. Not interfering in what she figured was routine father-son time would allow Ben to feel that his life hadn't been turned completely upside down. Which she knew it was. Elli remembered how much she loved the quiet talks she had with her father over dinner. She missed the times when she would seek his advice, tell him about her day, or just sit near him in silence and absorb his love. She imagined it was the same for Ben and Joey. At least, it seemed that way when she managed to spy on them a few times. Ben's entire body looked fluid and relaxed when he was with his son. There was a peace in his voice, his eyes, and his smile. Elli envied that honest, unconditional love they shared.

She looked at the dogs sleeping on the bed next to her and smiled. "Do you love me unconditionally?" Only Jenny responded with a single wag of her tail. Elli supposed her newfound relationship with these crazy creatures was kind of like that. They seemed to accept her as-is, she supposed, until she didn't feed them.

Elli walked into the en suite bathroom, carrying the sandwich she had made from the small stash of food she had in an ice chest in her room. She turned on the water in the dull, claw-foot tub and added the organic lavender bath foam and salts she had brought with her from California. She would take a long, hot, relaxing bath and review what she wanted to say and how she intended to say it to Ben at tonight's meeting. That is, if he showed up. Elli stripped off her clothes and tossed them in a rumpled heap in the corner. She placed one bath towel on the floor and another on the edge of the pink porcelain sink before climbing into the tub.

"Ahh." She closed her eyes as she sank deeper into the almost too hot water. The frothy foam hissed as it floated around her. "Relax and find your center," she murmured, before filling her lungs with the clean, floral-scented air produced by the massaging bubbles. This was good, she thought. Therapeutic. This allowed her time to focus on her plan and make the adjustments needed to reach her goal. Yes, staying focused on the goal was everything. Get the money needed to save the foundation so the services they offered would continue to help save lives. Well, actually, achieving the goal was everything.

Elli sighed. It sounded simple, but reaching it was much more complicated than anticipated. She had expected Ben to be difficult to persuade, but she hadn't counted on facing so many distractions. The families the foundation helped deserved better from her. They needed the financial, educational, and spiritual support in their journey for early detection. That kind of support saved lives by leading them to proactive medical surveillance for their families.

Elli lifted a handful of bubbles and blew them into the air. There was no doubt that if there had been an organization like Gene I.D. Foundation to guide her mother or even Elli prior to their diagnosis with cancer, they would have been fighting the clandestine enemy before it wounded them with its deadly force. Her mother didn't know the full power of the enemy she was battling. Elli met it head-on. She prayed the foundation would be an effective early-warning system for others.

"Okay, Elli, you can do this." She closed her eyes and took a moment to center herself. "God, I wish there was another funding source other than the sale of the plantation." She would gladly turn over all of her personal money today if she had something to give. Still, no matter how much the foundation needed the money, she didn't regret using most of her personal savings to pay her medical bills and live an unencumbered life. It was what she had to do. From the moment she realized she wasn't immortal, she decided to live as if the next hour or day would be her last. She spent the huge pile of money she had earned being one of the best in her field, without regard for tomorrow. She supposed it was foolish for her to blast through her savings, even with giving some of it to charitable causes, because in just three years, the money was gone and she wasn't. As crazy as it was, she knew she would have done it all over again if she were given a do-over.

It was her journey, and Abby's, too. Yes, she remembered as if it was yesterday how it took them both a few years to come to terms with life after breast cancer, but they had. They knew they would live another day and had to pay their good fortune forward. That's when they got serious about starting the foundation. Abby was broke, but Elli was able to use most of the savings she had left as start-up money. She was happy her successful career allowed her to do that. She downsized her life and had enough to survive on a modest portion of her annual Newfies royalties while the rest of that money was dedicated to a trust she established in the early months after her diagnosis and before Gene I.D. She came to Louisiana knowing that selling the plantation was her only option financially. No matter how much she wished for crisp, thousand-dollar bills to rain from a bright blue rainbow-edged sky into the foundation's expanding bank account, it wasn't going to happen. "The bottom line is that I have to convince Ben Bienvenu to sell the plantation, when he is determined to keep the status quo."

Elli lathered the washcloth with fragrant lavender soap as she thought of ways to convince Ben it made sense and was good for both him and his son to sell the plantation. Selling it to a movie company to use as a studio didn't mean he wouldn't be allowed access to the property. He wouldn't own it, but he could come on the land and share stories with Joey about their ancestors. It would still be part of his world. She could make sure the sale's contract included a stipulation allowing him access to the Sugar Mill property when he wanted. Elli smiled. That was reasonable.

Tonight, at their meeting, she'd suggest he let this film crew on the property as a sort of trial. They'd pay him a ridiculous amount of money for little use of the house and property. He'd see that they were respectful and professional stewards of Sugar Mill Plantation. Elli's heart raced with a hopeful excitement. She'd have to take baby steps in a hurry with Ben. She'd have to stay focused, a bit of a problem since meeting the stubborn man. Why was that? It wasn't like her to lose sight of her goal. Maybe it was because she hadn't planned for all the possible scenarios and hadn't reacted well to the unexpected. That, too, wasn't like her. She had a reputation for being like a block of concrete under pressure. At least she was when she was producing, before the breast cancer.

"I guess my skills haven't been challenged in the last three years," she murmured, slipping her head under the water to wet her hair. Breast cancer had changed everything about her life. She took her washcloth and ran it over chest, taking a moment to look at the four-inch scar on the side of her right breast. It was just a thin, pale line now, but it might as well be a huge, electronic billboard with bright, colorful lights advertising how fragile life was. If that scar didn't remind her of her mortality, the mastectomy reconstruction scars that were now vertical lines beneath both of her nipples and the horizontal scar slashing across her hip would. When she looked at all those scars, including the two-inch scar from her chemo port, near her left collarbone, she was very grateful for her life.

Elli slapped the water with her hand, sending foam flying over the side of the tub. "A woman with a noble cause must be fearless. She must put on her armor, mount her steed, and charge into battle with her sword drawn," she said, affirming aloud what her mind was trying to reason. "I will not feel guilty or remorseful for selling the plantation. Ben and Joey will be happy with a fat nest egg in the bank. That kind of security is much better for them than romantic sentiment about family legacy."

She reached for her sandwich and took a bite, but before she could put it back on the paper plate on the floor, a blur of tan fur flew in front of her and landed in the tub. She let out a scream. "Jenny! No!"

The big Lab-mix wagged her tail, sending water and foam flying across the room. She turned to face Elli with a big smile on her goofy doggie face. "Out!"

Elli heard the patter of dog claws running on wood floors, and before she could get out of the way, Doe was in the tub with her, too. "Nooo." She thought it was a game and started her god-awful happy baying. "Out!"

Donna and BJ came running, barking and howling the whole way. They were slipping on the wet floor and tugging on the towel she had hanging on the sink.

The door to her bedroom flew open, and from where she was huddled in the tub, she saw Ben and Joey race in. "What the hell is going on? It sounds like someone is getting murdered in here," Ben shouted.

"Out, or there will be a murder!" she cried, trying to cover all her naked bits with what foam was left in the tub. She looked at little Joey who was laughing at the top of his lungs. "Cover your eyes, young man!" He threw his hands over his eyes and slipped onto the floor. He rolled onto his side and continued laughing. BJ jumped on top of him and began licking his hands covering his face.

Ben's beautiful, scared mouth lifted in a full smile. "Cher, if you wanted company for your bath, all you had to do was ask."

"Ben!" She gave him a proper insulted look, nodded toward Joey, and mouthed the words—watch what you say in front of him.

He reached into the tub and pulled Jenny out first. He grabbed the towel from Donna's mouth and began to dry her drenched, beige coat. His eyes, however, weren't on his task. They were on Elli's naked body, or what she hoped he couldn't see of it. She had her knees tucked under her chin, and the slices of sandwich bread positioned like a bikini top over her breasts.

"Joey, without looking, can you throw me a towel?" she asked, knowing by the mischievous spark in Ben's eyes that if she asked him to do it he would refuse.

"Sure thing." Joey opened the linen cabinet against the wall and in one swift movement, tossed a small, thin washcloth over his shoulder.

Ben laughed. "That's my boy."

"Can you toss me a bigger towel," she called to him, and for some reason, Doe thought Elli was calling her. She plodded thru the bathwater to where Elli sat tucked in the corner and licked her face with her big slobbering tongue. "Ewwww." She grabbed the washcloth and wiped her face with it. Doe spotted the sandwich bread and snapped one of the slices into her mouth in one big, hungry bite. "Doe!"

Elli was mortified. The surgeons had done a beautiful job reconstructing her breasts, but now the scars were there for Ben to see. She twisted in the tub, giving him her backside instead.

"Everybody, out!" she shrieked, "Now."

"I think she's going to cry," Joey said, grabbing Jenny by her collar and pulling her to the door.

"I'm not going to cry," she said over her shoulder. "I'm just…just…embarrassed. Mortified, really."

Ben reached into the tub and lifted Doe out. He leaned close to Elli's ear. "You have nothing to be embarrassed about, cher. It's not like you have a lumpy ass." She splashed him with a handful of water.

"Out!"

He ran his fingertips down her spine, and as much as she tried to prevent it, she shivered right there in front of him. She knew the arrogant man saw it and was gloating over his power to affect her that way. And as unwanted as it was, he did have some kind of power over her body. She didn't know what in the world was going on between them, but something was. It was most likely pure, simple lust and sexual chemistry. How that fit into their adversarial partnership, she didn't know. It certainly complicated things. She didn't think she had the emotional fortitude to keep the two things separate. Nothing could come of this…thing…between them. So what if the man was ridiculously sexy. He was off limits. To be intimate with him would make her feel even more vulnerable than she already felt. He'd see her scars and her imperfect body and know she was damaged. Your opponent shouldn't know your weakness. Besides, she just couldn't stomach the idea that he might feel sorry for her.

"Don't forget our meeting," she told Ben as he was walking out the door with Doe and Donna. "I'll see you in the dining room at seven." That is, if she could crawl out of the hole she wanted to bury herself in.

* * * *

The heavy brass and amber crystal chandelier was on when Elli walked into the dining room promptly at seven. The light cast golden prisms on the faded green and cream magnolia wallpaper and matching silk drapery while blending with the inlet edging the round, mahogany table. Elli's theatrical eye appreciated the scene set before her by one of Ben's relatives from long ago. She was disappointed that Ben wasn't in it. She knew, however, that he had been there. His smooth, earthy scent, which reminded her of a warm, fall day in the woods, lingered in the room. He probably just walked away for a moment, she figured.

She sat on one of the ornately carved dining chairs, pushed against the wall, and folded her arms over the soft blue cardigan sweater set she had spent so much time deciding to wear. It was casual, yet sophisticated. Like her black wool slacks and black Jimmy Choo pumps. She listened for Ben's footsteps or voice. All she heard was the distant sound of the TV in the main parlor. Was he there? She waited another minute, then stood and looked at her watch. It had been seven minutes since she came into the dining room. Was he standing her up for the latest episode of The Simpsons? Would he be that rude? That defiant? Elli sighed. He might be, she thought, looking more closely at the dining room table, hoping to find a note.

There, in the center of the table, was a small piece of torn paper bag with her name on it. It was no wonder she'd missed it, with the way he tucked it under the brass candelabra centerpiece. It was printed in all caps.

"Going to see a man about a dog—literally. B."

She smiled. It wasn't a rejection. That was good. Great, really. Her mood lifted to a place it hadn't been since she arrived. He had intended to meet with her. She clutched the crumpled note to her chest. There was hope. He didn't hate her, she sighed, having a Sally Field at the Academy Awards moment. "He likes me," she shouted, twirling in a circle.

The image of the sexy white scar slashed over his lip, wet from their kiss, came to her and her heart beat faster. Her spine tingled with the memory of his fingers stroking her with a whispered touch. "Stop it." She willed her crazed mind not to provoke her womanly bits so much. It was dangerous. She had to stay focused on the goal. Ben wasn't the goal, selling the plantation was.

Elli left the dining room and headed to the parlor where she heard Joey's laughter mingle with the sounds of the TV and what she now realized was Sponge Bob, not Lisa Simpson. There was also the sound of commentary from a female voice she didn't recognize. She peaked around the side of the arched entrance and spotted Joey in his recliner with three of her dogs sitting on the floor at full alert near him. He held a big bowl of popcorn that the dogs were clearly hoping to get a taste of. On the sofa, speaking in a gentle, rhythmic tone was a gorgeous, petite woman with coal-black hair and deep blue eyes.

She looked like Snow White in faded jeans and a Tulane University sweatshirt. Her running shoes had been tossed askew on the floor, and her sock-clad feet stretched out on the sofa.

"Elli," Joey shouted, spotting her. He lifted the remote from his chest and muted the TV.

"Hey, kiddo." She walked into the room and extended her hand to the fairy-tale princess. "Hi, I'm Elli Morenelli."

The woman accepted her hand with a firm handshake and a nod. It was clear in her intelligent eyes she had recognized Elli's name. "I'm Camille Comeaux."

"She's a doctor," Joey offered.

"A vet?" Elli wondered if she was the person who was supposed to examine Donna, who was looking comfy, tucked on the doc's very trim lap.

She smiled a pretty smile with perfectly straight, white teeth. "No. I'm a primary care physician."

"She's my doctor and my dad's," Joey offered.

Elli sat on Ben's recliner and looked at Joey. "Are you ill?"

He laughed. "No. She's our friend, too. She's here to keep me company while my dad does an invention."

"He means an intervention," Dr. Snow White corrected. "Apparently, one of the dogs he trained a few years back has gone rogue."

"I hate when that happens," Elli said, looking at her Aunt Rosa's pets.

"Want some?" Joey extended the bowl of popcorn to Elli, and Jenny thought he was offering it to her, so she stuck her snout in it. Joey snapped his finger and pointed at Jenny. She sat.

"How do you do that? That was amazing."

"I don't know." Joey slid out of his recliner and walked to the kitchen carrying the popcorn bowl. The dogs followed him.

"He takes after his father. They have a gift." Snow White sounded totally smitten. Elli's stomach pinched. "I heard you went to the Krewe of Terrenians parade with Tante Izzy today." She sat up and Elli noticed she had pretty, full breasts that looked impossibly perfect—in the I have great genetics, not a great surgeon kind of way.

Elli crossed her arms over her chest. "Uh...the parade was fun. Tante Izzy is fun." Elli smiled and Camille did, too. She wanted to hate this very smart, perfectly built, petite woman, but she couldn't. She had a nice, genuine smile, and her eyes reflected that she was kind. "I have a huge sack of beads upstairs that I don't know what to do with."

"And you'll get more. There are many more parades to come." She petted Donna with long, easy strokes. "You could donate them to the Parish Center for the mentally and physically challenged clients. They have a work program where they take the beads, wash them, and repackage them to sell to Mardi Gras Krewes."

"I love that idea." Elli was thinking of how it gave her the incentive to fight harder for the plastic necklaces at the next parade she attended. "Thank you."

"So, Ben tells me you're a movie producer."

"Used to be." Elli didn't realize she had rested her hand over her chemo port scar that wasn't hidden by the sweater, until she saw Camille's eyes shift to her hand. She dropped her hands in her lap.

"Produced any movies I might know?"

Joey walked into the room carrying a bag of potato chips. Jenny, BJ, and Doe were close behind. He climbed into his recliner and laid the remote on his chest.

"My best friend in college wrote Desert Heat. Because I was too young, naïve, and arrogant to know better, I asked her to let me produce it."

"Oh my God, that won an Academy Award," Camille said, sitting up. "I loved it. It was poignant and the characters were so endearing."

"We got lucky," Elli admitted. "If I had been smart, I would have tried to pitch it to one of the big studios and let them do it. Instead, we took it on—not knowing how Hollywood really operated. It's scary to imagine that we could have killed her wonderful story because of our ignorance."

"Instead, you did something remarkable. I remember reading an article about how two college friends beat the odds and did something rarely done. As I recall, a critic called you stubborn, tenacious, loyal, and focused."

"You remember that? We did the movie almost ten years ago!"

Camille tapped her index finger to her head. "Memory like a steel trap. Comes in handy with my job." Elli laughed. "What else did you produce?"

"Tug of War, With a Dash of Salt, Newfie..."

"Newfie," Joey interrupted. He climbed out of his chair and opened a drawer in the cabinet under the TV. He pulled out a DVD of the movie. "I like watched it a bazillion times. It was while my dad was watching the movie that he figured out he wanted to train Newfies. We're getting two in tomorrow. You want to watch it now?"

"Sure." Elli smiled, finding pleasure in knowing she had done something that affected Ben's kennel—as small as it was. "I loved making that movie. The dogs were so well trained. They listened better than the actors."

"Speaking of the actors," Camille said, wiggling her pretty, arched brows. "Some of the hunkiest men in Hollywood were in that movie."

"It wasn't hard to cast them. Their agents were chomping on the bit to have their superstar bodies exposed in that movie. It was a two-for."

"A two-for?" Camille asked.

"Yeah, they were cast in the heroic role as lifeguards with their adorable Newfoundland lifeguard rescue dogs while spending almost all of their screen time in a bathing suit." Elli laughed, remembering the number of phone calls she received. "In the end, we made a really good movie the cast was happy they could show to their children."

"My favorite in the movie is Mark Collin. He's so handsome and…well, you know." She wiggled her brows again. "Tall, dark, and dreamy. He reminds me of Ben. Especially without his shirt."

Joey started the movie and saved Elli from having to respond to Camille's revelation. It was a revelation that Elli had the distinct impression had been said to let her know that the doctor and Ben were more than friends.

The credits were rolling on the screen, and when her name came up, Joey shouted and clapped. "I never knowed anyone whose name was in the movies before."

* * * *

Elli woke to her alarm the next morning. She felt rested, having gone to bed when Joey did, around nine, right after the movie ended. She knew she had a long, busy, and stressful day ahead, and frankly, she wasn't in the mood to see Doctor Snow White and Ben together when he returned. Elli wondered if she had gone home after he did or if she spent the night. As much as she could imagine Ben and Camille together, she knew in her soul that Ben wouldn't take a lover to his bed with Joey in the house and she knew Joey had slept in his own bed last night. He was back in his own bed. Still, the idea of them being lovers weighed heavy on her chest. Feeling that really bothered Elli. She had no right. They were business partners. Nothing more. The kiss didn't cast them in the category of being involved.

"I'm glad I got that settled in my muddled brain. Let's go out," she called to the dogs crowded in her bed, noticing BJ had already done her business on the floor. After cleaning the doggy mess, Elli slipped on black Capri running pants and threw a pink hoodie over her Winnie the Pooh shirt before getting Donna out of her crate. She tossed the knit cap from her head onto the bed and grabbed the thermometer. She still wasn't very good at using it on the difficult Bolonoodle but it had to be done and she intended to get Donna's temperature as the other dogs did their business outside. Elli headed to the stairs. This time she let Aunt Rosa's energetic pack go down the stairs ahead of her. When she got to the bottom of the stairs, she was glad to see the lights off in the kitchen. Only the dim light of the breaking morning lifted the darkness.

"Good morning," a pretty, feminine voice called to her as she passed the kitchen.

Elli jumped and clasped her chest. "Oh, I didn't see you there. Good morning, Camille." She paused in front of the doorway just long enough to be polite. She looked at Ben sitting across from Camille at the table with a cup of coffee in his hands. "Gotta let the dogs out." She rushed outside.

So, Camille did spend the night. None of her business, she reminded herself. Still, she couldn't help feeling a little angry about it. Ben was a player. He had kissed her until her insides felt like a gooey brownie and made her naked flesh feel like sunshine while he had a pretty girlfriend on the side. That was despicable. Or, maybe it was part of his plan to get what he wanted from her with Sugar Mill. Was his scheming so different from hers? Heck, yes it was. She wasn't using sex to lure him into seeing things her way. She was trying to show him that she was a professional, smart businesswoman who had a great plan for their inherited property.

Elli sat on the back steps. Despite seeing the doc here so early in the morning, her instincts remained rock solid on the point that Ben wouldn't allow any hanky-panky under the roof while Joey was there. He was too protective of the child. The cozy scene in the kitchen was intended for her to see either by Ben or Camille or both. Joey had referred to Camille as his doctor and friend, not his dad's girlfriend. Even little boys knew the difference between girlfriends and girl friends. It was something she'd have to think about. How far would Ben go to get his way, she wondered? She thought for a long time. The only logical responses to any number of scenarios were for her to stay on course and on guard against his advances.

The back door opened and Ben and Camille stepped out onto the screened porch. "Thanks for breakfast," she told him. "Tell Joey I'll see him later." Elli moved off the step so she could pass. "It was nice meeting you, Elli."

"Likewise."

Camille's eyes fell to Elli's chest, then to her collarbone. Elli grabbed the two ends of the hoodie and zippered it up. Those blue eyes were much too intelligent for comfort. If she saw the med-port scar, she would know what made it.

"I'll see you tonight?" Camille asked Ben, then leaned in and kissed him on the cheek. He smiled. Elli had been in the business of storytelling long enough to know that they were telling her a story. She just wondered whose point of view she needed to consider. She suspected Camille had more to say. She also knew that whatever her story was, the kiss she and Ben shared was chaste, not a kiss between lovers.

"I'll pick you up around seven thirty. Thanks for last night."

"Anytime." She fluttered her fingers in farewell to Elli and walked to her Volvo. Scene exit. If Elli had to pick a car that suited the doc for a movie scene intended to show her personality, that would be it. It was the kind of car a person thought about in a smart, logical way. It wasn't the kind of car a person bought with crazy emotions because a salesman said the overpriced, pretty Mercedes matched the color of your eyes. That was the car she'd cast for herself. Heck, she bought that car for herself the day her first movie went from the red to the black.

"How's the man and his dog?" Elli asked once Camille drove away.

He took Donna from Elli and felt the pads of her paws. "The man was fine once I brought the dog back here. Seems he needs a refresher course."

"Who? The man or the dog?"

"The man." He sat on the top step. "You've been taking her temp?"

"Yes." She lifted the thermometer, already covered in the sleeve. "I was about to get a morning temp." She sat next to him. "It's been about the same, a few points lower at times. Never higher than at the clinic."

He took the thermometer from her, and she handed him the small packet of petroleum jelly she had in her pocket. Without saying a word, he took Donna's temperature and showed her the digital reading.

"I'm glad it isn't getting worse." She scratched Donna behind the ears. "What time will the vet be here?"

"Around eight."

"You know, I thought Camille was the vet when Joey told me she was a doctor."

Ben smiled. "She has helped take care of my dogs a time or two when I couldn't get Dr. Danos here fast enough." They sat companionably silent for a while, watching BJ and Doe sniff around the backyard.

"I guess I should go find Jenny. She's probably in the bayou or playing in a puddle somewhere."

"She's a Lab. Labs love water. She's fine." He stood and stretched his arms over his head with a big yawn. His button-down cotton shirt lifted just enough to give Elli a peek at his tan, flat belly. Just that little bit of skin showing convinced her that he would have looked just as good as any of the actors in Newfie.

Ellie started to ask him about setting up another meeting, but Ben spoke first. "I don't think we are going to ever agree on what to do with Sugar Mill." He ran his hand through his wavy hair. It was the first time Elli had ever seen him without his usual stubby ponytail, and loose, his hair went just past his collar. "Why don't you give me a couple of months to see if I can work up something? Maybe, I can get Beau to buy the place and put it in trust for Joey."

Elli shook her head. "I wouldn't mind doing that, but we can't sell it to a relative."

"I know that." Ben blew out a breath. "I'm just making a point that there has got to be a way to zigzag to get to the right resolution. I just need some time to figure it out. Give me some time."

How could she tell him that she didn't have time, that the Gene I.D. Foundation was on the brink of bankruptcy, she had no liquid capital, and what residual money she had coming in a few months wasn't going to be enough to solve the problem? She needed the money now. To tell him all that would completely negate her efforts to prove to him that she was a good businesswoman who knew how to best deal with Sugar Mill. "I don't know."

Ben looked at her, his green eyes darkening to the shade of magnolia leaves. The muscle in his jaw tightened from clenching his teeth. "Think about it," he said, his tone controlled but angry. She nodded and he walked back into the house.

* * * *

An hour after her upsetting conversation with Ben, Elli prepared for a run with all the dogs except Donna, who remained in her crate in the bedroom. Elli slipped her camera into the small pack she strapped to her back. She was excited about capturing the scenes she had scouted for the sales brochure during her earlier run and was certain there were others she had yet to discover. She thought of how the overcast sky would diffuse the morning light and sharpen the greens, browns, and grays of the plantation landscape. It was a perfect time to get the shots she needed, she thought as she secured the dogs to the leashes she shortened by wrapping them around her hand a few times. Giving them less of a lead seemed to work better. Having them run in front of her, albeit pulling her along, also worked until they turned onto the road through the sugarcane fields and neared the area where she had found the rustic shed. Once again, the dogs went on alert and started pulling her into the cane field. The force of their powerful movements painfully tightened the leashes around her left hand.

"Stop it," she shouted. "Heel." As expected, they ignored her. So, to keep them from choking themselves or dismembering her, Elli didn't fight them. "I'm going to stop taking you with me on my morning runs if you keep this up," she threatened. They didn't seem to hear, understand, or care what she was saying. They kept straining against their collars and coughing from their efforts.

Elli grabbed the straining leashes and fought to unwrap them from her hand. "This was a bad idea," she shouted, managing to free herself. The dogs must have sensed their opportunity and lunged forward. The leashes flew from Elli's abused hand.

They took off running into the field; barking, howling, and baying. Elli stopped chasing them. She wasn't keen on meeting up with whatever animal had gotten them this excited. Hadn't she read somewhere that there were bobcats in the area? Her heart sank a little. God help her, but she couldn't leave those animals vulnerable to whatever wildlife was out there. Even if it meant she would be vulnerable, too.

She retrieved her camera from the backpack and powered it on. She wasn't sure why she had, but she felt a little more armed because of it. She headed off toward the dogs, stomping through the field with loud, heavy steps, hoping to scare away any wild animals. Old, dried cane crunched under her running shoes. She took a quick picture of the cane under her feet as she moved forward. It was crazy, but she wanted to document what might be her last minutes on earth. God if she videoed her last seconds on earth, it would make it onto YouTube for sure. It would go viral. That was not a way she wanted to be remembered, she thought, and kept it in camera mode. Elli snapped another shot of the dry stalks as they bit into her ankles, and then pointed the camera ahead of her. Without checking the framing through the viewfinder and took one photo after another. She could have taken a dozen or two hundred photos. She had no clue. All she did know was that she was scared and the fear was escalating with each step she took toward the barking dogs. It was like riding in a clacking rollercoaster as it slowly climbed the first steep rise. She knew once she reached the crest she would take that awful, frightening plunge.

The dogs' barks grew louder and more frantic as she neared them. The scent of her fear and the earthy sweetness of the cane filled her nostrils. Her heart beat harder. Her eyes scanned the area, praying she didn't come face-to-face with a bear or bobcat. She flipped the camera to the video mode as she took a few steps more and spotted the rustic shed she had seen yesterday. It was to her right, twenty or so yards through the cane. She turned toward it, knowing there was cleared land around it and hoping there might be a real weapon inside the shed if she needed one. The closer she came to the clearing, the more she could see what the dogs were doing. They were scratching at the weathered, gray cypress door—Jenny on her two hind legs, BJ with her nose on the ground, and Doe with her snout pressed along the seam. Elli didn't see any bears or bobcats, so she snapped a quick photo, fumbling awkwardly with the buttons as she raced toward the animals.

"Come here," she demanded, grabbing the leashes trailing on the ground. The dogs growled deeper, louder. "What's wrong? I don't see a problem here."

Elli started to pull the dogs away from the shed when an odd feeling swept over her. She felt as if someone or something was watching her. The hair stood on the back of her neck. She looked at the single, dirty window at the front of the shed, and from the black void inside, she saw two dark eyes staring back at her. She yelped, and with strength that her burst of adrenaline gave her, she picked up Jenny, who was giving her the most trouble, and took off running out of the field. She dragged BJ and Doe behind her.

She didn't stop running until she was through the gate at the kennel. There, she dropped to the ground, leaned against the fence, and gasped for air. Ben, who was in the training field behind the gym, spotted her. She didn't have an ounce of energy left to pretend everything was okay. She saw him put a leash on two black, longhaired puppies and walk over to her in huge strides; the puppies had to run to keep up with him.

"What's wrong? You're as white as a sheet. Are you hurt?" He squatted next to her. The puppies started jumping on her, licking her arms and face. "Heel," he said, tugging the leash in one smooth motion, forcing the dogs to obey. They whimpered but stretched out on their bellies. Doe and BJ started sniffing them. The puppies thought it was a game and began tugging on the older dogs' ears. Jenny, however, remained in her arms. She hadn't realized it, but she still held her in a death grip.

"Elli?" He brushed a curl, wet from perspiration, clinging to her cheek. "Did someone hurt you?" His eyes slid over her body, looking for injuries.

She shook her head. "I...okay...uh..." she stammered. "Eyes. Eyes...shed." Her heart wouldn't stop pounding. She grabbed his forearm and somehow found strength in the warm, solid, masculine feel of it. "I can't...catch...my breath. Heart attack."

"Let me take her." He took Jenny from her arms, and Elli noticed him checking her for injuries, too. With Jenny's weight off her, the pressure in her chest immediately lessened. Ben grabbed her wrist and felt for her pulse. "Take deep breaths, Elli." She gripped his wrists as if they were anchors as she tried to suck in air. She knew she wasn't in danger, but the certainty that she had been only minutes before overpowered her.

"I'm such a wimp," she said, her chest rising and falling with the effort of speaking. "Never so scared in my life—well, almost never." She rested her hand on her chest.

He sat on the ground next to her, and the puppies crawled on and off his lap. "Can you tell me what happened?"

"I was running when the dogs took off into the cane field," she began, leaning closer to him to pet the adorable puppies. "They were barking and howling, really determined to charge after…whatever it was they were charging after. They got away from me." She swallowed and looked up at Ben who was staring into her eyes. "I followed them."

"Of course, you did." He shook his head. "Stupid move, Texian."

"Yeah, well, I did it." Her hand brushed against Ben's hand, and she looked away, pulling her hands into her lap. Jenny put her paw on Elli's leg. "Anyway, I found them at this old, weathered cabin, scratching at the door, trying to get in. That's when I saw someone looking at me from inside. At least, I think it was a human someone." She shook her head. "Yes. Yes, I'm certain of it."

"No one usually works the fields this time of year." He grabbed her chin and turned her toward him to look in his eyes. She knew he was trying to figure out if she was lying, being a drama queen, or telling the truth. "What cabin? Where is it?"

She stood on legs still wobbly from the exertion and fear. She pointed to the right. "Over there. Not too far from where the dirt road runs into the bayou."

Ben stood and leaned on the fence. "I know that area. I haven't been there in about a year, but the last time I was in that area, I saw only the skeleton of an old hunting cabin. I'm surprised it's still standing."

"It's standing," she said, her voice coming out in short breathy puffs. "And, it looks old, but sturdy. Maybe, we aren't talking about the same cabin. This one is next to a small bayou."

"No bayous around there. Just a big ditch."

"Bayou, canal, ditch. I can't keep them straight." She shook her head. "Anyway, I was going to take pictures of the cabin—shed yesterday before Tante Izzy kidnapped me."

"Kidnapped?" He lifted a brow.

"Will you just listen to my story instead of getting hung up on my word choices," she snapped. "Okay? I'm exaggerating a little about being kidnapped, but I'm not about what happened at the cabin." Ben nodded, and she looked in the direction of the cabin. It had to be a mile away, maybe a half mile as the crow flies. "Look, Ben," she shouted "There's smoke."

"What the hell? It can't be the cane fields burning—wrong season for the controlled burns." He climbed onto the fence to get a better look. "I don't see flames, but something sure as hell is burning."

"Should we call nine-one-one?"

He picked up the puppies, took the leashes for her three dogs, and took off running to the main kennel office. Elli followed him. He shouted to one of his workers coming out of the gym to take the dogs. The young man did as he was told. A few seconds later, Elli was in Ben's truck, and they were driving toward the black billowing smoke.

"Do you think it's the cabin?" she asked as they turned onto the dirt farm road.

"Hell if I know." As they neared the plume of smoke, they saw bright orange flames. Ben took his phone from its holder on his hip and called 9-1-1. "There's a field on fire at Sugar Mill Plantation," he told the operator, then gave her directions to the blaze.

"Ben, I smell gasoline," Elli said, looking at her clothes and shoes. "I don't see anything on my clothes. Do you smell it?"

Ben sniffed and looked around where he was sitting. "Yeah, I smell it." He looked at Elli and then her clothes.

"It's not on me," she shouted. "I didn't start the fire, if that's what you're thinking. I swear I didn't."

Ben nodded once and she could see he believed her. She wasn't really sure why he did, but was relieved about it.

A minute later, Ben parked the truck and ran toward the fire. Elli followed. When they got near the clearing, they could see the shed completely engulfed in flames, the smell of charred wood and grass filling their lungs. The dry grass in the clearing was starting to burn, and the light breeze was pushing the flames into the cane field bordering the ditch.

"What's going on?" Doug said from behind them, climbing out of his truck. He was with the man Elli now recognized as one of men she had seen working with the dogs at the kennel the day her dogs had dragged her on their first walk.

"I was just here at this cabin and it was fine, now it's on fire," Elli told him.

Doug stepped into the clearing, staying safely away from the blaze. "Looks like cypress wood, the way it's burning," he said.

The other man nodded. "If it is, it's old," he added. "Built maybe fifty years ago or more."

"Haven't had rain in a while and the humidity's been low." Doug said. "It'll probably have to burn itself out. Wind's pushing the fire to the ditch. It should be okay."

"The wildfires in California don't usually burn themselves out," Elli said. "They often leap over water and start up on the other side. I hope the fire department gets here quickly."

"It's a volunteer department, but they get moving pretty fast," Doug said a moment before they heard the sound of a distant siren. "They'll have to pump water from the ditch to put the fire out—

probably not enough water in the truck reservoir," Doug said. "The ditch water is low, but it should be enough."

"Well, at least it'll be enough to mitigate the damage," Elli reasoned. Then she realized that not one of the three men asked how the fire started. She looked at Ben. Why hadn't any of these men asked? It would be a natural thing to do. Did they assume she had started the fire because she said she was just at the cabin?

Two dozen firefighters, wearing full protective gear, dragged hoses into the clearing and began putting out the blaze. Living in the dry west had taught her that even small fires could turn into big problems. It must have been the same for south Louisiana. Either way, this fire seemed to be under control. Doug had been wrong about not having enough water in the fire engine reservoir to put out the blaze. Maybe if only one truck had showed up that would have been true. Having five there took care of it.

After an hour, everyone left the scene except for two firemen who remained to watch for hot spots with one of the engine trucks. Even the fire chief didn't stick around after he took Ben and Elli's statements. It seemed like a nonevent except for the way everyone, including Ben, kept looking at her as the firefighters raced around the field. What was it they weren't saying?

She and Ben rode back in silence to the kennel. As they parked in front of the main office, she turned to face him. "I didn't start that fire."

"I didn't say you did."

"I think the person in the cabin started it."

Ben didn't answer. She could see he was thinking about what she said.

"But why?" She sighed. "Why destroy the cabin? Do you think a hunter or a homeless person was there?"

"Could be." He shrugged.

"I'm grateful the firefighters didn't find a body in the rubble. I was really afraid they might."

Ben nodded and opened his door, but hadn't made it out of his truck when Tante Izzy pulled up next to them. She got out faster than Elli imagined her old bones could move.

"What's dis I hear? You started a wildfire?" She opened Elli's door.

A big Cadillac El Dorado pulled up on the other side of Ben's truck. A grizzly-sized man, wearing faded denim overalls, red T-shirt, and LSU baseball cap rolled out of it. He went straight to Ben, who was still sitting in the truck. "I heard Rosa's niece started one of those California-sized forest fires on the plantation?"

A petite but squarely built redhead with three-inch-high and hot-rolled hair, got out of the other side of the Cadillac. She waddled to Ben, stumbling on pebbles on the ground beneath very bright orange, patent leather pumps with four-inch heels. She wore a matching rhinestone-studded, knit pantsuit and she clutched a People Magazine in her well costume jeweled fingers. "I think we need to start a Smokey the Bear Prevent Fires campaign before this wildfire thing becomes an epidemic. We could hold a charity dance right here on the plantation, where the fire started. Do you think Joseph Boudreaux's band would play for the dance?"

Ben turned to Elli. "This is your fault."

An attractive woman in her late fifties drove up in a black Lexus and got out. She was wearing pressed jeans, crisp yellow button-down shirt, and elegant gold jewelry. Hers was not costume. She poked her head into the truck next to Tante Izzy. "So she did start the wildfire? Have they issued a warrant?"

Ben rolled his eyes.

"I hadn't heard that," the redheaded woman said, sounding disgusted she hadn't gotten the news earlier. "I don't see her in handcuffs." She looked at the man in overalls. "Jed, did you hear if there's a warrant out on her?"

"Ruby, you should know that the bayou-grapevine news always gets ahead of itself." The stunning looking, middle-aged brunette whom everyone seemed to know said, speaking to the redhead. Then, she turned to Elli. Her sophisticated bob swished prettily. "And, sometimes it just isn't fully accurate."

"It's mostly true," Tante Izzy interrupted.

"The news passes over the fence and on scratchy phones," the brunette continued. "Besides, the news might have been embellished a bit. I heard it was old man Theriot who started spreading the story when he heard what happened while listening to his scanner." She shook her head and tsked. "We all know he can't even hear Tante Izzy at full holler when he's standing next to her and the wind is blowing in his direction."

"I got my news from one of the Bayou Cane firemen," the big burly man said. "He can hear just fine. He said the Texian started the fire and looked real guilty as she stood by, twisting her hands as she watched them put out the fire."

"I did not..." Elli stammered, but the brunette lady patted her on the shoulder and gave her a sympathetic look.

"I came out here because I was bored and thought it might be fun to see the Bienvenues in full force," she said with a smile. The redheaded woman snorted. "I was right." She extended her narrow hand to Elli. "By the way, I'm Helen Bienvenu. Ben's mother. I don't know if you did this deed..."

"She did," the big man in overalls mumbled.

"Or, if you didn't," she continued. "But if you need an attorney, you should call Ben's cousin, Beau. I think you've met him before."

"She's met me," Beau said, walking up to Elli's side of the truck. "So, has this lynch mob read you the Miranda rights, yet?" He winked at her.

Elli opened her mouth to defend herself but nothing came out.

"Youz look like a trout ready to get hooked on a fishin' line," Tante Izzy said. "Close youz mouth, Texian. The rest of youz, step back and let da girl breathe. I don't think youz gonna do too well in prison with da way you reactin' to dis small group. I hear dere's a lot of overcrowdin' in da state prison in Angola."

"She won't have to go to Angola," Ruby said. "She'd have to go to St. Gabriel. That's where Cousin Sylvia went when she stole the lunch money from the safe at the Piccadilly." She looked at Elli and frowned. "She had a gambling problem."

Elli felt as if she was in a scene from It's A Mad, Mad, Mad, Mad World. "Wait a minute." She held up her hand and silenced the Grizzly Bear man, who was telling everyone exactly which slot machine Cousin Sylvia preferred and how if she had played Sand Blast Seven, she wouldn't have gotten into trouble because Sand Blast Seven always paid out.

"As your attorney, I want to warn you to be careful of what you say, Elli," Beau said, his tone light and teasing. "If these people are called to testify, no telling what they'll say they thought you said."

"You can't be her attorney, you're mine," Ben snapped. "Never mind. Be hers. You're fired."

"My word, he sounds just like The Donald when he says that," Ruby pointed out. "It would work better if you jabbed your fingers forward while you said it." She pointed at Beau. "You're fired."

"As I was saying," Elli said, talking over the sound of another car driving up. "I didn't start the fire. It was someone else."

Ben's mother leaned in closer. "That's what they all say, honey."

Elli looked at Ben, pleading with her eyes for help. "Are all these people related to you?"

"'Fraid so."

Doctor Snow White joined the large crowd huddled around Ben's truck. "Don't you worry about this little lady, Camille," Grizzly Bear told her. "He'll no more take up with a criminal than he would a Texian." He laughed. "And she's both."

"No, I'm not." Elli pushed her way out of the truck. "I'm not from Texas and I am not a criminal." A sheriff's car pulled up behind Ben's truck. A hush fell over the crowd.

"Youz got your handcuffs, Ronald?" Tante Izzy called to the uniformed lawman getting out of his car. "I bet she resists arrest. Youz might want to draw your weapon."

Ronald. Ben's uncle. The sheriff. The man whose name had been flaunted at her as if he was a Golden Globe when she had called 9-1-1. Of course, he was the lawman here to deal with her alleged pyromania. "I think I'm being framed," she told him. "I'm like Ashley Judd being framed for the murder of her not-so-dead-husband in Double Jeopardy."

"Did she just say she was Ashley Judd?" Ruby shouted. "She's too tall to be Ashley Judd. She's as pretty as she is, though. What do you think, Camille? Could she be Ashley Judd?"

"Oh for goodness' sake, you are missing the point, Ruby," Ben's mother said. "She didn't say she was Ashley Judd. She was just making a movie reference about how she thought she was being framed like Ashley Judd was in Double Jeopardy."

"Don't think I saw that movie," the man in the overalls said. "Is Ashley Judd related to Wynonna? I sure like her voice."

"They're sisters," Ruby said and rolled her eyes. "And, she don't look like neither one." She rolled her eyes again. "But, maybe she knows her." She smiled a hopeful smile. "Do you know Ashley Judd?"

Elli's head was spinning. What were these people talking about? "Excuse me." She walked away from the mass of Bienvenues and their crazy talk with as much pride and dignity as her hammering heart and watery knees allowed. She walked into the office and slammed the door, but before she did, she heard Tante Izzy ask Ben if he kept any loaded guns inside.

Elli leaned against the door and dropped her head into her hands. What in the hell had just happened? Lucky, who was resting near Ben's desk, let out a soft bark. She didn't bother looking at him since she hadn't been worth his effort for a full bark.

"Got trouble, little lady?" She jerked her head up. What now? "Doug." He was sitting in an office chair with his feet propped up on a paper-strewn metal desk.

"Yeah, I've got troubles."

"By the sound of the mob outside, I'd say it was Bienvenu trouble." He twisted a paperclip in his hand. "Best advice I have is to step back and regroup. Come back later when you've got a plan." He shook his head. "In your case, stay one step ahead of that mob outside. They are an opinionated and clannish group."

"Oh, I've got a plan." She stood, walked to the sofa, and plopped down. "It's obviously a lousy one."

"Get yourself another one." He stood, walked to the sofa, and sat close to her. "I'm a good listener if you have a mind to talk."

"Over the past four years, I've managed to simplify my life," she said with a shake of her head. "Somehow, in the last few days here, I've managed to completely complicate it. I've taken a wrong turn somewhere."

Doug took her hand into his and squeezed. It was gesture of support, but his soft, dilated eyes didn't match what she thought was a sign of friendship. He had been the only person who seemed to be her ally at Sugar Mill. Elli's stomach knotted. She lived in the top zip code where older men acted on their attraction to younger women, so she recognized the dark, inviting look in his eyes. She certainly didn't need to deal with this now. He put his arm over her shoulder. Yeah, life was hugely complicated.

The door swung open and Ben walked inside. Doug grasped Elli's hand tighter as she tried to pull away. Lucky got up from where he was resting and greeted Ben.

"Well, this is cozy." Ben petted Lucky, then walked past them into his office. He turned around and came right back out. His face was red, his jaws clenched. "Where are the Newfies?"

"I put the puppies in the runner and Elli's dogs in my yard." Doug looked at her, and Elli got the distinct impression he was trying to stake claim on her. "Your dogs seem happy there, darlin'." Elli jumped up, finally managing to pull her hand from his. She wasn't sure where to put herself. Lucky barked his soft bark at her again, then made a circle and settled on the floor to take a nap.

Joey rushed into the office, dropping his book bag on the floor and leaving the door open. He looked at Elli with wide eyes. "Everybody at school is talking about how you started a forest fire."

Elli couldn't say why the events of the day came bubbling to the surface then, but they did. She burst out laughing. Joey grabbed her hands and jumped up and down in front of her. He laughed, too. Lucky came running over and joined in the play. Elli saw Ben stuff his hands in his pocket and scowl at Doug. His body was tight and contained as tears streamed down her face. Tante Izzy and the rest of the Bienvenu clan peered through the open door.

"I think she done lost her mind," Tante Izzy said. "Might need to get da coroner here to have her declared."

Joey leaped onto the sofa and onto Doug's lap. He laughed as only a child can laugh with abandon and hugged Doug around the neck. "I don't think she started a forest fire," he said with total conviction. "She's too nice to do that."

Elli smiled at Joey, a sob caught in her throat.

He bounced on Doug's lap. Lucky bumped his nose against Joey's leg and Joey automatically pet him. "I bet you don't think she did it either, huh, Grandpa?"

Elli's eyes widened. Grandpa! Doug was Joey's grandfather? The father of Ben's beloved wife. Sugar Mill Plantation was a virtual Peyton Place of family.

"Step back," a commanding male voice demanded from somewhere on the porch. "Let me pass or I'll toss all of you in jail for obstruction."

"Back up, let da law through," Tante Izzy shouted, and the sea of Bienvenues and a Snow White princess doctor parted.

"Ben. I'd like to speak with Miss Morenelli," he said addressing his nephew and ignoring her.

Ben nodded. "Should Beau be here?"

Elli's heart thudded, not so much from the fear of being wrongfully arrested, but because Ben's simple question touched her. It had been a very long time since someone other than Abby, or someone she'd hired, was concerned for her welfare.

"Despite what the consensus is outside, no one is accusing her of anything," Ronald said.

Ben nodded, then looked at Elli. Did she just want someone to care for her so much that she imagined seeing honest concern in his beautiful green eyes or was it really there? She swallowed past the lump in her throat, hating how wanting someone to care made her feel exposed and needy. She looked away, afraid Ben would see the vulnerability in her eyes.

"Doug, would you mind taking Joey to the house and getting him something to eat?" Ben asked. He looked at Elli a few seconds longer before turning to Joey, who was complaining about not wanting to leave. "Why don't you get the Newfies and take them with you to the house," he told his son. That was all the enticement the child needed.

"You want me to take your dogs, too?" Joey asked Elli.

"I'd like that very much." She smiled. "Thank you."

Joey raced out of the office. Doug patted Elli on the shoulder and followed his grandson.

Ben walked to the door and turned to his uncle. "Just the same, I think we should have Beau sit in on this." Ben called Beau inside, then closed the door. Lucky seemed bored with the energy in the room and went back to his spot and settled in for another nap.

Elli heard Tante Izzy shouting to everyone. "Ya'll go on home, now. I'll call youz and let youz know what happens." The sounds of cars leaving followed.

Ben leaned against the desk, Beau pulled the office chair next to Elli, who now sat on the sofa, and the sheriff walked over to Elli. He extended his hand to her. "I'm Ronald Bienvenu. Sheriff of Vacherie Parish."

Elli shook his hand. "I didn't start the fire."

"No one is accusing you," Ronald said and smiled.

"Except everyone at Joey's school and the entire Bienvenu family."

Ronald laughed. "That wasn't even a fourth of the Bienvenu family. You'll get to meet the rest of them after the parade on Mardi

Gras." He looked at Ben. "She's coming to the crawfish boil, isn't she?"

Ben shrugged.

"Of course, she is," Beau interjected. "And she's riding in the parade on the family float, too."

Ben's brows lifted, and Elli knew he didn't approve of the announcement, but he kept his opinion to himself.

"Good. You'll have fun." Ronald sat next to Elli and pulled out a small spiral notebook and stubby pencil from his shirt pocket. "I've got the field report from the Fire Chief. Because he thinks it was deliberately set, I have to file a report. So why don't you just tell me what happened in the cane field."

Elli told him the story of her jogging, the dogs racing into the field as if they were chasing something, the eyes staring back at her from the shed, frightening her and causing her to run to the kennel and Ben.

"That's when we saw the smoke," Ben interjected.

Ronald sat in silence, making notations. After a few minutes, he stood. "Would you recognize the person from the shed if you saw him?"

"No." She sighed. "All I saw were eyes. Dark eyes, through a dirty window. It was like looking through a smudged camera lens. Sorry." Elli's heart pounded in her chest. "Oh. My camera. I forgot about my camera. I had it with me. I must have dropped it somewhere in the field or near the cabin. Did anyone find it?"

"No. Not yet." The sheriff leaned back in his seat. "Can you be more specific about where you dropped it?"

Elli closed her eyes, trying to recall when she last had it in her hands. "I took some pictures of the dried cane on the ground and then whatever was in front of the lens. I just snapped pictures and at some point I flipped the camera to video. I was too scared and worried about the dogs to frame the shots." She shrugged her shoulders. "It's kind of embarrassing to admit, but I had thought that if something bad happened, like an animal attacking me, there would be evidence of my death. Not that you wouldn't have figured it out from the claw marks on my mauled body."

"Do you think you got video of the cabin?"

Elli shrugged. "I don't know. I was so frightened of wild animals attacking the dogs and me, that I don't know where I pointed the lens when I got close."

"Could you have been so scared that you don't remember tripping over or knocking over something that started the fire?"

Had she? Elli felt the eyes of the sheriff, Ben, and Beau on her. Could she have started the fire and not known it? "I don't think so," she said, but knew her voice didn't hold much conviction.

"I think we've covered everything," Ronald stood. Lucky raised his head to look at him but didn't move from his spot. "If I have more questions, I'll call you."

"Call me, Dad." Beau said. "I'm representing Elli in this matter."

"Dad? Why am I not surprised?" She looked at Beau and didn't see any obvious resemblances to the sheriff other than similar mannerisms. "Thank you for your offer to represent me," she said, her heart growing two sizes larger with his offer to help. "But I think I can handle this. I didn't do anything wrong." Besides, she couldn't afford to pay him. She was broke and the money she'd get from the movie filming at the plantation had to be used for the foundation, not legal bills.

Ronald shook her hand and nodded to Ben. "See you on Mardi Gras, if not sooner." Beau walked out with him, closing the door behind them.

Elli looked down at her hands. "Thank you. I appreciate you being here."

"I don't like someone starting fires on my property," he said, his voice quiet and steady. "That fire, cher, was definitely not started by natural causes. I look out for what is mine."

Elli knew that didn't include her, but she couldn't help but think how nice it would be if it did. She knew such fanciful thoughts were useless. She didn't want, hope, or need to be cared for, protected by, or committed to a man or to anyone. She didn't want intimate, close relationships. If the cancer returned, the ugly, awful, destructive beast would rip into the world of someone she cared about. Why would she ever want that?

She stood. Lucky stood and walked to Ben and sat near his feet. "I know I have complicated your life since I got here," she began, fidgeting with her hands. "That wasn't my intent." She clasped her hands in front of her and looked at him. She was about to tell him about her ideas of selling the plantation to solid venture capitalists and how that would resolve their problem, but every fiber in her body stopped her. This was not the time. She shouldn't mix her expressing gratitude with her desire to leave the plantation. They were two separate things—or were they? Oh, she was so confused. Her mind was too muddled. She needed a nap. "I've got to go," she said, noticing a contained smile on his face. "What's so amusing?"

"You." He walked up to her and lifted her chin so she'd look into his eyes. "You're right. You do have a knack for complicating things—intent or not." This time when he smiled, it was a full-force, sexy, crooked grin.

Elli lifted her hand to his beautiful, scarred lips and touched them lightly with her fingertips.

He exhaled hard. "What am I going to do with you?" He swallowed. "One minute, I want to toss you over my shoulder and put you on the first plane to California and the next—" He hesitated, wet his smooth lips, and leaned in so close she felt his breath on her lips. "The next minute, I want to toss you on the cool grass and have my way with you."

Elli's heart pounded so hard in her chest that she knew it would explode if he didn't kiss her in the next instant. It was wrong. They hardly knew one another. They didn't even like each other. Yet, here it was. She wanted his mouth on hers so desperately she could feel it in the marrow of her bones. "Kiss me." She gripped his shoulders and pulled him to her.

"Oh, hell." He grabbed her bottom and pressed her intimately against him. He swore, his words riper than before and with more heat. She understood that he didn't want this any more than she did and just as much as she did. He closed his mouth over hers.

The room tilted and the floor seemed to slip from under her. She gripped his shoulders tighter, and Ben must have realized her bones had turned to liquid. He lifted her into his arms as his warm, wet mouth and tongue continued their hot exploration of hers.

Fire and lust heated Elli's flesh, blood, and all the places identifying her as a woman. She trembled as feelings too big for her body to control swamped her. Her fingers played with his ever-present ponytail, feeling like cool silk. His scent wrapped around her, mixing with the hint of smoke from their bodies. His mouth left hers, and he scraped his teeth over her chin and down the column of her neck.

"Oh," she gasped, tilting her head back.

She heard him suck in a breath as her fingers traced the outline of his ear, following it with her mouth and tongue. His back muscles bunched beneath her hands. Ben sat on the sofa, put Elli on his lap, and found her mouth again. He fed off her like a starved man in an isolated desert as she took his tongue into her mouth and suckled. Ben growled from deep in his throat and lifted his hips to press more firmly against her bottom. She shifted and slid closer to him.

Ben swore again. The word sounded both angry and sexy. Elli trembled. He slid his hands along her sides and over her breasts, his thumbs rubbing firm circles over her nipples. Surgeries had left them numb, but she felt the pressure of his touch and the intimacy. Sounds she didn't know she could make, slid over her lips as Ben dipped his head and took her left breast into his mouth through her T-shirt. Her legs parted a little, and her hot center pressed tighter against his hard erection. He sucked in a deep breath and pulled her shirt off, leaving her in a sports bra. His mouth claimed her left breast as his hand slipped under the tight bra to claim her right. Elli bolted off his lap and nearly tripped on Lucky who had managed to wedge himself next to Ben.

He looked at her with dark, heavy eyes. His hair was tousled and he was breathing hard. He had to be the sexiest man she had ever seen. Just looking at him made her want to climb back onto his lap—

but she couldn't. She shouldn't. She mustn't. This was wrong. He hated her. She didn't like him. Most of all, she already felt so ridiculously vulnerable around him. She couldn't stand the idea of him seeing her scars, her damaged breasts, and finding her lacking. Why in the world did she care what he thought about her?

"I...I...can't," she managed, a tear sliding down her cheek. She turned her back to him and wiped it with the heel of her hand. She pleaded to God to not let her cry and humiliate herself more than she had already.

She heard him exhale hard, and the sofa seemed to moan from him moving. She knew without looking that he'd leaned back on the sofa and probably folded his arms over his chest. She owed him an explanation, but couldn't think of anything to say other than the truth. She couldn't tell him the truth.

"I'm sorry. I should have stopped this sooner...I'm just..."

"A tease? Using sex to get your way?"

She jerked around to face him, her arms covering her breasts already hidden behind a sports bra. "No! You've got it wrong. I was drawn by your eyes," she admitted, "and your kiss made me. . ." How much should she tell him? Why did it matter?

"Save your breath, Miss Crocifissa." He picked up her T-shirt and balled it in his hands. "I have a good idea what happened, and you should know I'm not like my dogs that get crazed and stupid when I'm around a bitch in heat."

"I'm not trying to manipulate you," she snapped. "You are culpable in this too, you know. I wasn't the only one doing the kissing."

"No, but you were the one who asked for it."

Before she could answer, the door opened and Beau walked in.

"The state fire marshal is coming tomorrow to investigate the..." Beau stopped in midsentence when Ben jumped up from the sofa and blocked him from looking at Elli in her sports bra. Beau smiled at Ben. "I see you took my advice."

Ben scowled at his cousin and pointed to the door. "Get out."

Beau grinned, saluted Ben, and turned to leave. "Elli, you should know this guy's bark is worse than his bite." He walked out, and a few seconds later, they heard him drive off.

Ben tossed Elli her shirt and walked out the door with Lucky.

Chapter Five

Why do people call the doxorubicin chemo drug the red devil? I say we should call it the RED ANGEL for the good it does destroying the cancer. Think of that, my Bosom Blog Buddies, when the nausea and fatigue knocks you back into bed and your bones ache like a horrific flu that won't abate—the RED ANGEL is working her blessings through you…not the devil. Keep the faith and positive spirit; you will not be receiving chemo and radiation forever! It is finite…stay focused on the end-goal. I wish you good health, E.

Bosom Blog Buddies Post

Tante Izzy walked into the Sugar Mill kitchen dressed in a royal purple T-shirt, kelly green Capri pants, canary yellow tube socks, and matching yellow sequined Keds. "Get dressed," the old lady said, looking at Elli's clothes.

Elli paused in mid-bite of her organic yogurt, but didn't get up from the table. "For what?" She shoved the spoonful of yogurt in her mouth and closed the book she was reading.

"We are goin' shoppin'." She looked at the yogurt and the book, then frowned. Elli suspected the yogurt was more distasteful to her than the book, which was titled You and Your Neurotic Dog. "Then we'z is goin' to have lunch with Ruby."

"And who is Ruby?" She tossed her yogurt carton into the small can she had found to use for recycling.

Tante Izzy harrumphed. "You met her yesterday."

"Let me guess. She's the lady with the ruby red hair who kept accusing me of starting a forest fire." Elli washed and dried the spoon before putting it in the drawer.

"Seems to me she wasn't da only one pointin' a finger at you."

"I didn't set the fire."

Tante Izzy waved her hand. "Tell it to da judge." She looked at Elli from head to toe. She smiled. "I know youz didn't do it, child. Now, go get out of da pajamas and get dressed."

Elli smiled, pleased that Tante Izzy believed she hadn't started the fire. "This," she waved her hand over her clothes, "is the very fashion forward, nautical blue, Juicy Couture track suit."

"You ain't goin' ta run on no track. Youz is goin' shoppin' wit me. Besides, why would youz want to be seen in public in that thing? It's got patches on it. Juicy Cooter, huh? Sounds like a porn star name if youz ask me."

Elli burst out laughing and gave Tante Izzy a big hug. This old lady dressed in bright Mardi Gras colors had appointed herself the fashion police. "I adore you." She looked into the old lady's faded eyes. "That is the only reason I'm going shopping with you." She turned to go change her clothes. "By the way, why and where are we going shopping?"

"Ronald tells me youz are ridin on the family float. We need to get you some Mardi Gras throws."

Elli stopped. "The sheriff?" She shook her head, thinking that avoiding face time with the law might be a better idea. "I appreciate the invitation to be on your family float, but I can't afford to buy the trinkets to throw off it."

"Pshhha. I can afford it. I've got me an oil well drillin' on my land. I don't own it, but it keeps me flush."

Elli smiled. "And dressed well." Tante Izzy, an oil tycoon? That was something her brain couldn't compute. She had said she didn't own the oil well, hadn't she? Either way, pride wouldn't allow her to accept her generosity. "It's kind of you to offer to buy my trinkets, but I can't accept..."

She waved Elli on. "No arguin' with me, now. I want to do dis. Besides, I'll never spend all da money I got tucked under my mattress."

"I'll pay you back," Elli said. She really was excited to be in a Mardi Gras parade. If she had a bucket list, riding on a Mardi Gras float would be on it. It ranked near the top of her mental list with a trek up Mount Elbrus in Russia, which she had done. "We need to drop off the girls to Doug on our way out. Donna's still with Ben, and I need to bring her to Doug, too." She smiled. "Did you hear? The vet said Donna's going to be fine. Changing her diet should get her on track again." Tante Izzy looked at the nonexistent watch on her wrist. "Anyway, I don't want to leave the girls here to tear up my clothes and do their business on the floor."

"Looks like dey done got to youz Juicy track suit. Hurry up, now."

* * * *

It took Tante Izzy and Elli almost two hours to shop for colorful stuffed animals, plastic swords, giant toothbrushes, and necklaces of different themes, colors, and lengths. She knew Mardi Gras riders tossed cheap beads and things off the floats to revelers, but she'd never considered that all the stuff had to be purchased somewhere. As it turned out, there were huge warehouse stores filled with things any float rider could want, including bubble gum, potato chips, and yummy MoonPies.

"…and she ate bout a half dozen of dem MoonPies, while waitin' in da checkout line," Tante Izzy told Ruby as they sat at a small, round table in a cozy diner in the center of the old downtown. This part of Cane, with its neat, two-story structures and large window fronts, was nestled along the banks of a wide, river-like bayou. It looked like hundreds of other American towns that had once been commerce centers but had faded with the introduction of malls and interstate highways. "She ate so much, I'm bettin' she has a hollow leg."

Elli narrowed her eyes. "You're a rat."

"MoonPies? I thought you said she was an organic?" Ruby asked, settling her napkin on her lap. "That's why I picked Café Breaux. You can get a big salad with no meat or a vegetable plate."

"Oh, I'm not a vegetarian," Elli said, only to receive a disapproving look from Ruby. "I eat meat. I just don't eat anything that has been sprayed with pesticides or injected with hormones."

"I get injected with hormones once a month," Ruby informed her.

"That's why I'll never eat you." Elli smiled.

"I don't see anything wrong with hormones," Ruby insisted. "Without them, I'd have hot flashes and grow a mustache."

Tante Izzy pointed her crooked finger at Ruby. "Harrumph. Without dat waxin' you get every couple of weeks at Margie's Beauty Shop, you'd have a mustache."

"Tante Izzy!" Ruby turned as red as her name. "I'm just saying, hormones are good for a person."

"There are some instances when hormone supplements aren't good," Elli offered. "If you've had breast cancer that's estrogen receptive, you're often put on hormone suppressant drugs for five years to help reduce your chance of recurrence." Elli wanted to tell the ladies how she knew this and that she still had to take the medicine for one more year, but she didn't. When she was receiving her chemo and radiation treatments, she and the other women discussed their medicines, prognosis, and side effects with each other like they were new moms discussing their babies' sleeping patterns. Sometimes, she still talked to her best friend about meds and side effects from her treatments. Most of the time, she just kept her thoughts to herself. In her experience, people really didn't want to know the details of cancer treatment or discuss it at all. She supposed that was because talking about cancer to someone who had it was hard. People just didn't know what to say to you.

"I know'd someone who was on dat her-mone suppress drug," Tante Izzy said. "She was only forty-two and the drugs made her go through her change. She had hot flashes and all."

"Did she grow a mustache?" Ruby asked.

"Hello, ladies." Helen Bienvenu walked up, dragged a nearby chair to the table, and sat down. "You don't mind if I join you? I do hate eating alone."

"Cain't stop you," Tante Izzy said, sounding annoyed.

"Hello, Elli. I'm glad to see my son and his family haven't chased you out of town. They can be very territorial."

Ruby rolled her eyes.

"She ain't scared of him." Tante Izzy stated. "In fact, I think shez kinda sweet on him."

Elli picked up the water the waitress just placed on the table and took a big sip.

Helen smiled. "Is that so?"

"No." Elli croaked. "We are business partners. That's all."

"So, it's true that Rosa left you and Ben the plantation?" Ruby asked. "That woman had no shame. You'd think she wanted you to live in sin like she did." She made the sign of the cross.

Helen smoothed the front of her crisp, burgundy Liz Claiborne blouse. The gesture was subtle, but Elli knew Ben's mother didn't like being reminded of her husband's infidelity.

"Well, the single women of Cane won't be happy to hear their most desirable bachelor shares a plantation with a pretty Hollywood executive." Ruby frowned.

"But I'm sure you will be more than happy to tell them," Helen said, bitterness and a hint of sadness in her voice

The waitress saved them from further discussion on the subject when she took their order.

"So, Elli, I understand you're a movie producer," Helen said, starting a new conversation. The woman was beautiful, graceful, and her dark brown eyes were intelligent. Elli wondered why Helen had stayed with her husband, knowing he had a mistress. She didn't look like the kind of woman who would have trouble finding a faithful man.

She returned her empty water glass to the table. "I was until three years ago."

"According to People Magazine," Ruby said hefting her large red, vinyl purse and rummaging through it. "You did some of my favorite movies. She pulled out the same People Magazine she had with her at the kennel the first day she met her. It was the one with a picture of her at the Griffin Park fundraiser in a small inset on the cover. "What movies did you produce, again? I forgot to take my memory pill and I'm a little sluggish today," Ruby said.

Helen rolled her eyes.

Elli wanted to rip the magazine from Ruby's hands and shred it into a million pieces. "I produced Desert Heat, Tug of the Heart, With a Dash of Salt, Newfie. . ."

"I loved Desert Heat," Ruby gushed. "I have it on Blu-ray."

"I saw Newfie with Joey," Tante Izzy interrupted. "About ten times. Dat boy loves dat movie."

Elli smiled, remembering how excited Joey had been when he found out she worked on that movie. "I'm glad." She sensed Helen's eyes on her and met her gaze. She felt like she was being evaluated by an editor examining the frames of film for a crucial scene. Elli instinctively wanted to fix her hair or fidget in her seat under the intense scrutiny, but then it came to her what was happening. She wasn't sure how she knew, but Elli was certain Helen hadn't just accidentally met up with them in the restaurant. She was there because she was interested in Elli. What was it she wanted to know? Did she hope to learn more about her husband's mistress by meeting Rosa's niece? Did she want to determine Elli's character because she was a stranger tossed into the lives of her son and grandson? Maybe it was something else. Elli couldn't read the woman. She was cool and kept her emotions hidden. Just like her son.

"How exciting it must be to work with movie stars," Ruby gushed, . "Do you know George Clooney?"

Elli laughed. "That seems to be the question."

"And what is the answer?" Ruby insisted.

"No. I don't know him. Sorry." She shrugged. "I know his stylist."

"Do you think you can get her to ask Mr. Clooney to come to Cane for our Prevent Forest Fires benefit?"

"Oh, for goodness' sake, Ruby." Helen shook her head, and her perfect bob moved as it was supposed to move. "Leave the girl alone. She said she used to be a producer." She looked at Elli with sharp, determined eyes. "Why is it you said you weren't producing anymore?"

"I didn't say." Elli took a sip of her water. Yes, Helen was as smooth as she was sly. She was steering the conversation exactly where she wanted it to be. So was Ruby—without a sliver of Helen's poise.

"What about Ben Affleck? Do you know him?" Ruby asked.

Elli shook her head.

"I told you it waz a waste of yur time to come to lunch," Tante Izzy told Ruby. "She cain't help you bring in a famous star."

Elli had to bite her lip to keep from telling them that she'd just gotten a call that morning from the location director of the movie scheduled to shoot at the plantation tomorrow. He'd informed her that Academy Award–winning heartthrob Sam Cooper was added to their shoot schedule to do a couple of nonspeaking close-ups on the front porch and along the bayou. He'd also told her that they needed to have the front of the plantation painted. If she got it done for them, they'd pay her an additional five thousand. She had the paint color number in her purse and planned to ask Tante Izzy to stop at the hardware store on the way out. Should she tell Ben the movie crew was coming before or after she painted the front of the house? Either way, she knew he wasn't going to be happy.

Ruby huffed. "What good is it to know a movie producer if she can't get a movie star to come to Cane."

Elli covered her smile with her hand. It hadn't gone unnoticed by Helen, who raised a brow much as Elli had seen Ben do.

The waitress brought their food and Elli watched Ruby automatically place the magazine back in her purse to make room for her lunch plate. She hadn't mentioned Elli's photo on the cover or the embarrassing article on page 36. Maybe she had forgotten to mention it because she was indeed sluggish for missing her dose of the memory pill. Tante Izzy looked at Elli's salad. "That's rabbit food." She took a big bite of her dark beef stew.

"She's an organic," Ruby informed Helen. "But she does eat meat."

"You mean, she's a vegetarian." Helen corrected. Ruby rolled her eyes.

"I'm not a vegetarian. I eat organic food," Elli laughed. "Except for MoonPies."

"Youz got dat right," Tante Izzy said, shaking her head. "A half a dozen of dem."

"I had three," Elli laughed. "And a half."

"It would have been four if'n youz hadn't given the LeBouef child some."

"It's one of Ben's favorites too," Helen said, sounding distant and a bit sad. "At least, it was when he was a child, about Joey's age." She wiped the corner of her mouth with her napkin. "Well," she began, her voice steady again. "You know, crawfish are organic," Helen informed Elli. "You will be joining the Bienvenu clan for the annual pre-Ash Wednesday, Fat Tuesday crawfish boil, won't you?"

Before Elli could answer, Tante Izzy did. "She'z not only comin' to the boil, she'z riding on the family float." Helen raised her brow again but didn't say anything. "We done got her throws," Tante Izzy continued. "Might have to get more with the way she ate those MoonPies. She'z ready to ride…"

"Unless she's in jail," Ruby interrupted. When everyone sat silent and just stared at her, she rushed on. "Have ya'll forgotten how she set that forest fire?"

"You seem to have, Ruby," Helen insisted. "Wasn't it you who invited Elli to lunch…and after you called her, what was the word…oh, yes, a pyromaniac."

Ruby dropped her fork and turned to Tante Izzy. "You see. This is why I didn't want to invite her."

"Thatz enough sass, Ruby." Tante Izzy waved her napkin. "You talkin' stupid, and Helen is just pointin' it out. There'z no way Elli will be in jail for Mardi Gras. She won't even have a trial by then."

Elli jerked around to face Tante Izzy. "I thought you said you believed I didn't start the fire."

"Don't matter what I think, now doez it?" Tante Izzy leaned back in her chair and sighed.

Elli looked at Helen. She had been the only woman here who defended her, even though Elli wasn't sure what the woman really thought about her. Still, she had experience dealing with this crazy clan. God, she hoped Ben's mother would be with her the next time the Bienvenues ganged up on her. "Helen, will you be riding on the Bienvenu float?"

Tante Izzy grumbled but Helen ignored her. "No honey, I'm not." She smiled a half smile. "I'm not a Bienvenu. My son and grandson are, but not me."

Ruby gasped. Tante Izzy exhaled a heavy sigh.

"Never really was," Helen replied, her tone even. Elli knew there must have been a lot of history attached to that statement. Her tone made it clear there was a lot of pain, too. She wanted to ask Ben's mother why such a beautiful, intelligent woman never divorced her husband and moved on with her life. What reason could she have had to tolerate her husband's long-term, public affair with Aunt Rosa? None of those things, however, were any of her business— unless you considered that the long-term affair resulted in Elli eventually owning half of Sugar Mill Plantation and thirty percent of the Sugar Mill Kennel.

"That waz your choice, Helen," Tante Izzy stated.

Helen lifted her iced tea glass in salute to Izzy. "You are absolutely correct."

"Holy cow," Ruby hissed. "If I had known y'all would be talking about old, family scandals, I wouldn't have come to lunch. I thought we were going to talk about the Prevent Forest Fires Benefit."

"Moodee, Ruby. I tole youz I didn't think it waz a good idea." Tante Izzy turned to Elli. "I got myself indigestion. I want to go home and take a nap."

A nap sounded good to Elli, too, but she had painting to do before the end of the day. "Would you mind stopping at the hardware store on our way back to the plantation?"

"As long as it don't take too long," Tante Izzy said. "I needs my beauty rest."

"Elli, I want you to know, I didn't mean any offense about my comment of you going to jail," Ruby said, her cheeks blushing bright pink. She looked at her short fingers, unable to meet Elli's eyes. Elli knew the woman was sincere. Ruby might think she started the fire, but she hadn't meant to offend her, especially when it didn't help her cause. "No hard feelings?" She extended her hand to Elli. Helen rolled her eyes, but didn't say anything. "I'm sorry."

Elli shook her hand. "Apology accepted."

Ruby smiled. "Are you sure?"

She looked at Ruby, who not only looked remorseful but like her blood pressure had shot through the roof. Elli felt sorry for her. Letting her heart rule her head, she made a ridiculous offer to Ruby that satisfied neither the woman nor herself. "I'll help you with your Prevent Forest Fire event." When Ruby started to speak, Elli held up her hand. "I will help you decorate, serve punch, and collect tickets at the door, but I cannot get a celebrity for the event." She definitely was not in a position to ask a favor from any star on her e-mail list. Anyway, they had probably changed their e-mail addresses since their identities were stolen.

Ruby looked disappointed. "Would you consider letting me borrow your cell phone for a little while?" Elli shook her head. No way. "I won't make any long-distance calls or nothing. I just want to look at your contact list for, oh, about an hour.

"No."

"Ten minutes?" Oh geez, what had she gotten herself into?

Elli stood. "This was an…an interesting lunch. Thank you for inviting me." She placed the money for her share and a generous tip on the table. "I have a very busy afternoon scheduled."

Tante Izzy stood and started to dig money from her purse but stopped. She picked up Elli's money and handed it back to her. "It's Ruby's treat." She pointed to Ruby. "Youz give our waitress a good tip, now, youz hear?" Ruby nodded and rolled her eyes at the same time.

"I'll see that she does." Helen smiled.

"You ladies are so insulting," Ruby grumbled. She stood and reached for her orange purse. "I'm not going to stand around and take this abuse."

"Sit down, Ruby," Helen told her. "That bluster won't get you out of paying the bill."

"Helen, you are such a b-i-t-c-h." Ruby sat back in her chair.

"Yes, my dear, I am."

Chapter Six

Abby and I went wig shopping with a lovely, good-humored woman who started the post-second chemo treatment shedding. She is losing her beautiful wavy, gray hair...Guess which celebrity we saw in the women's wig store in Santa Monica. I will give you a hint...it's a man!! I wish you good health, E.

Bosom Blog Buddies Post

Ben was waist-deep in the chilly bayou in front of the plantation training the two Newfie puppies with Lucky, when he saw Tante Izzy's truck pull into the driveway and Elli get out. He had to shade his eyes with his hands to watch her walk along the side of the house in the bright afternoon sunshine. He wasn't wearing sunglasses, so the pups could see his eyes while he was training them. He noticed she was carrying two one-gallon paint cans, one in each hand, as she walked toward the bayou side of the house. Ben hoped the paint didn't mean she was planning to paint or decorate the house. If that was her intent, then she planned to stick around awhile. Like hell, he'd let her do that.

Elli reached the porch, put the cans down, and turned to where she heard one of the puppies playfully barking at Lucky. She shaded her eyes with her hand and looked toward the bayou. "Hello," she called and walked toward Ben. "Aren't you afraid of alligators," she asked when she got to the edge of the bayou.

"Nah. Not with these tough guys." One of the puppies paddled to the edge of the bayou, raced to Elli, and turned in silly circles at her feet.

"Oh, I can see how he would frighten any gator who dared come near him." She laughed, and the wet puppy jumped on Elli's cream-colored, expensive-looking pants. She didn't seem to notice that there were wide puppy prints on them. He suspected she wouldn't be happy when she did. "How's Donna?"

"Temp's down and she seems to like her new food," he said, looking at his mischievous pup playing with Elli. "She's in her kennel in your room. She seems to be having fewer accidents already."

"That's great news." She smiled, and her eyes twinkled with it.

Those eyes were damn alluring, he thought, as he watched them slowly slide down to look at his naked chest. He instantly went hard. Oh, no. He wasn't playing this game with her again. He had no idea why this woman made him think about hot sex and cool sheets when he should have been thinking about her packed bags and backside leaving. He had to stay focused on seeing that happen. "What's up with the paint cans?" He nodded to the porch before refocusing on putting the retrieving float in front of the puppies for them to scent. He tossed it across the bayou. Lucky darted after it, and the puppies swam after him.

She stabbed her fancy, pointed shoe into a patch of grass, looked at him for a few seconds, then tossed her shoulders back and jabbed her fists against her hips. She went from timid and awkward to bold and challenging in a few blinks of the eye. Ben knew he wasn't going to like her answer.

"It's for the shoot tomorrow," she said, her tone firm. "I tried to tell you about it. It's what I wanted to meet with you to discuss last night."

"I suppose we aren't talking about a turkey shoot or a skeet competition, are we?" She shook her head no. Ben felt his ears begin to burn. "Elli, what in the hell have you done?" Lucky paddled up to him with the float in his mouth, giving Ben a moment to get hold of his anger. He took the float and automatically repeated the routine of having the puppies scent it before tossing it into the middle of the bayou. All three dogs swam after it. Ben thought for a moment about tossing Elli into the bayou as he had the float.

"I'm making us a lot of money." She stepped closer to the bayou's edge. "It's only for a couple of days, Ben. The film was in a pinch and needed a country location for their exterior shoots. The place they had scheduled didn't work out. Sugar Mill did. It's perfect for what they need, so I negotiated a rate that's eighteen percent higher than the industry standard. We couldn't seem to meet about it, so I took the initiative and hired out the plantation for the filming. It's really a no-brainer. They'll be in and out of here before you even notice them. Your wallet will be fatter, and you won't be bothered at all."

"I'm already bothered, Elli." He shook his head. "You had no damn right to do this. You overstepped, big-time. Who the hell do you think you are?"

She squatted to look him straight in the eyes. As pissed as he was, he had to give it to her: She had the balls to look at him straight in the eyes. "I get it. I didn't have the right to make a business decision for both of us. I admit that. I probably would be upset if the tables were turned. But I did." She bit her lower lip and pointed to the dogs that he hadn't noticed were swimming around him and whimpering, waiting for him to toss the float again. When he did, she continued. "The bottom line is this: I did it for the money. If I hadn't given them an answer straightaway, we wouldn't have gotten the deal."

"Then we shouldn't have gotten the deal." He shook his head. He felt the muscles in jaws cramp. "There isn't a 'we' here, Elli. You and I aren't real business partners. We are some kind of temporary, awful anomaly. We should just be me, making decisions and owning Sugar Mill. Don't fool yourself into thinking this thing is permanent."

"I'm not the one who is delusional." She stood. "The film crew is coming tomorrow at eight a.m. Unless you want to get a court order to stop them, or if you want to turn your back on enough money to build that air-conditioned kennel Doug said you wanted to add near the training gym, then get over yourself."

"Get over myself?" Ben wanted to wring her neck. He wanted to laugh at her, too. The woman's backbone and fight surprised him and seemed oddly out of character for her. She acted smarter than he figured her to be. Her standing up to him made him want to smile. So did her goofy word choice. He was angry and amused at the same time. Damn, crazy, confusing woman. "Get over myself. What in the hell does that mean?" He grabbed the float from Lucky, let the

Newfies scent it, and tossed it onto the bank near Elli's feet. He knew they would come charging out of the water and wet everything within four feet of them. "How much money?"

Elli shouted a crazy number at him as she darted away from the leaping, waterlogged dogs. The puppies thought it was a game and chased after her.

"Tell me about the paint?" he called out to her, and she immediately stopped running. She turned and walked in five quick strides to the bayou. Her eyes bright and hopeful, her cheeks flushed with excitement.

"We...I just need to paint the front exterior of the main house." She smiled, ignoring the puppies who were tugging on her pant legs. "Even with just one coat to even out the chipping paint and to fit the scene as the director wants, I'm sure it will be an improvement to the place." She bent down to pet the excited, wet Newfies and wipe her soiled pants. "It needs painting anyway."

"And who's going to do the painting?" Ben took the float from his dog.

"I am." She shrugged again and the bad feeling that hadn't quite left deepened in Ben's gut. "I'm just going to put a single gloss over the imperfections for tomorrow's shoot. We can change it back after that, if we decide it isn't a market improvement."

"Not we, cher. You will change it if I decide it needs changing."

She chuckled and stood. "I personally will paint it on both ends. We'll get to keep more of the money if we don't hire painters." When she looked at him, he knew she saw the doubt in his eyes. "I can do this, you know. I've got skills. It's not like I'm a virgin at it, you know?"

Ben lifted his brows. Had her choice of words been meant to tease him? Was she playing him? Had she played him to get him to agree to the filming on the plantation? What in the hell was going on? Had he lost his mind? No, he didn't like her hiring out the plantation without his approval, but he wasn't going to cut off his nose to spite his face. He could use the ready cash to add the new kennels and expand his business. He wasn't illogical and hot-headed enough not to see she was right. Still, how she got him to agree so quickly had him questioning his fortitude with this woman. He had to make sure he kept his guard up with her. He wasn't about to be manipulated into doing something he didn't want to do because of the temptation of great sex.

Huh, great sex? Where did that thought come from? Shit. Why in the hell did he know with certainty that he and Elli would have great sex together? Probably because the woman didn't do things by halves. Shit. No. No sex with Elli, great or otherwise. He wouldn't let his pecker get in the way of sound reasoning. Been there, done that. He was older and wiser now. No woman, especially one who was a heat-seeking missile, searching for big bucks, was going to toss his life around again. He had a son and a business to protect.

One of the puppies, who chased after Lucky as he was retrieving the float, ran out of the water to Elli. She bent down to pet him and Ben noticed that she handled the puppy a hell of lot better than she'd handled her designer dog when it wandered into the bayou the day Elli arrived.

"I love these webbed paws," she said, lifting the puppy's soggy paw and spreading its pads. "It's amazing, really. Where in the evolutionary process did this happen?" She patted him on his head. "And this fur. It's crazy how it doesn't absorb water."

"Actually, he has double coats. Both are flat, oily, and water-resistant. His breed's coats, webbed paws, strong muscles, and natural swimming abilities make them excellent water rescue dogs." He started to walk out of the bayou. "Of course, you know that from producing Newfies."

"And the adult dogs are excellent droolers," she laughed. "I had hand towels sent in for all of our Newfie crew. I had Drool Here embroidered on all of them. The crew wore their towels tucked in their waistbands in case they encountered one of the larger slobberers." She smiled, looking at the black, button-nose pup. "You adorable thing. Are you going to grow to have a leaky mouth?"

She stood and her eyes went right to Ben's abdomen. He wasn't a conceited man, but he was confident in the knowledge that he wasn't soft and fleshy. In fact, Beau always said, with a thump on both of their abs, that they each had good six-pack genes. Of course, that was usually when they were sharing a six-pack of beer.

"Go play with your paint, Elli," he said, feeling himself getting hard with the way she was looking at him, like she wanted to slide over his naked skin. "Keep the film crew the hell away from my dogs and kennel. I don't want to know they are here. And, Elli, don't you ever negotiate a deal for the use of my plantation again. Understood?" She nodded, but he didn't see a lot of conviction in her eyes. He whistled once for the dogs to follow as he walked away. The Newfies sniffed around a bit but didn't take long to bounce after him and his loyal dog.

* * * *

"I appreciate you telling Envision Investments about Sugar Mill," Elli told Abby as she sat on the third rung of the ladder to talk on her cell phone. She had carried the ladder and all of her supplies up to the second floor balcony, planning to start painting there. "But I'm not ready for them to come here, yet. More accurately, Ben isn't ready for them to come here. Yet. I'll e-mail you a real estate sales prospectus tomorrow night. You can show them that to keep them interested."

"Send it to me tonight," Abby insisted. "I don't know if they'll be interested the day after tomorrow."

"I have the narrative I did before coming here, but I need to change it up a bit since seeing the place." She swatted a fly buzzing around her. "I also need to take some more pictures. The pictures from the appraisal that were included with Aunt Rosa's will doesn't do the place justice. And the ones I took with my camera were lost in the fire. I bought a camera when I went into town for the paint. I'll take whatever pictures I can before sunset, add graphics, and slick it up." She pulled the cell phone away from her ear to look at the time. "I'll get you what I can tonight, Abby. Right now, I have to paint the front of this huge plantation house."

"Make it a priority." Abby cleared her throat. "Our financial situation is worse than we thought. The bank called to tell me the foundation account is overdrawn."

Elli's stomach pinched. She felt bile rising in her throat. "How? We had enough to cover the next two months."

"Our evil fundraiser planner has stolen from us, too. It looks like he altered the check we cut him for the event and gave himself a raise."

"Oh, God." Elli sighed. "We have to have that money. We have clients counting on us helping them pay their bills." She inhaled deeply. "I'll sell my car. It could maybe get us through a week. The money from the filming here will help a little bit, but it isn't enough to carry us over."

"I've put some of my personal money into the account to cover this week," Abby said, her tone as defeated as Elli felt. "I don't have a huge savings stash to draw from, so I can't do more. I'm afraid we might be tumbling into a black hole. We can take care of our commitments, sort of, for the next few weeks, but Elli, it looks bad. I also got a call from the caterer for the Griffith Park event. She is threatening to sue us if we don't pay what is owed her."

"I did pay what was owed," Elli said, her voice growing louder. "With a check to our planner. I suppose we'll be getting calls from the florist, valet service, musicians…everyone we thought we already paid."

"I expect we will. We need a plan B, Elli. What if you can't get the plantation sold and at least some of the money in the bank within three weeks? We may have to declare bankruptcy."

Elli's throat tightened. "That would protect the foundation from creditors but do nothing to help the people we've asked to trust us to help them. Failure isn't an option." She ran her hand absently over her chest. She remembered another time in her life when failure wasn't an option. "I need you to talk to Veronica. We hired her because she was the most creative, empathetic, and effective social worker around. See if she can start researching possible programs available for our clients who can't be without our help if the worst happens."

"Okay, but you should know that Veronica came to me in tears this morning. She informed me that it's killing her, but she can't stay on if we can't pay her. She is the sole earner taking care of her grandmother and niece. She did offer to take a pay cut for a month, if that helps." Abby sighed. "I hate this."

"Me, too." Elli shifted on the ladder, making it wobble, but she ignored it. "I hate all this pressure. I wish we had a long-term plan that had time to mature and unfurl. We don't. We have an impossible deadline to sell a multimillion-dollar plantation in a state with Napoleonic laws, to capitalists I've yet to meet. Not to mention," she said, knowing she was almost shouting now, "that I have to do this with a partner who doesn't want me to do it."

"Elli, I need to know. Is this task impossible? Will the sale happen?"

"Impossible? Yes, it's impossible," she shouted, dropping the long paint roller extension to the ground. "It can't be impossible. I will make this possible. Oh, God, Abby, Walt Disney was so wrong."

"What are you talking about?" Abby snapped. "What does Walt Disney have to do with our problems? Another movie reference, Elli? Really? Do you have to do this now?"

"I'm sorry. I can't help it. They pop into my head." She was now feeling overstressed and short-tempered. "I just thought of the quote by Walt Disney: It's kind of fun to do the impossible. I don't think this is fun. Not one little bit." Her voice started to rise. "I've got to paint the front of a nine-thousand-square-foot shingled plantation house, put together a professional-looking prospectus, walk a pack of hyperactive dogs, and nurse a prissy Bolonoodle with an UTI, all before sunrise tomorrow." She threw her shoulders back.

Elli turned and spotted Ben looking at her through his open floor-to-ceiling bedroom window. Great. She hung up her phone without telling Abby good-bye. How much of her conversation had he heard?

"You also have to meet with the fire marshal at seven," Ben said, leaning halfway through the window. When she glared at him with eyes that spoke of the fire burning in her gut, he raised his hands in surrender. "Don't kill the messenger. Beau called and asked me to tell you."

"Perfect," She mumbled in a control voice when she wanted to scream. She turned and spread the drop cloth on the wooden balcony floor. By the smug look on his face, she figured he hadn't heard the part of her conversation about selling the plantation or he would have blown a gasket. Thank God for small favors.

"Beau will be here at six thirty." He stepped through his window onto the balcony, looking too blasted happy about her rotten mood. Yeah, no doubt about it, he was there to gloat about her overextending herself with this painting project. "Nice shirt." He motioned to the tattered, New Orleans Saints Super Bowl Champions T-shirt she wore over her running shorts like a mini dress.

"I found it in the rag pile in the laundry room." She picked up the long-handled paint roller and leaned it against the ladder.

"Rag pile?" He shook his head and walked to the balcony railing with casual ease. "That's my favorite, Sunday afternoon football watching shirt." He turned to face Elli, resting his bottom on the railing. "It was in the wash pile, not the rag pile."

She shrugged. "Who knew?"

"I hate when you do that."

"What?"

"That." He shrugged his shoulders. "It's a sign you have more to say but decided not to say it."

"Oh." She shrugged her shoulders with intentional exaggeration and pasted a fake grin on her face.

"Very funny."

She smiled, surprised she had one in her after hearing the awful news from Abby. As frustrating as the situation was between her and Ben, she enjoyed his intelligent humor and easy manner. It was an odd thing, she thought, considering how desperate and stressed she felt about saving the foundation. Who knew there could be something akin to a near-functioning release valve for her overstressed boiler brain? She settled onto her knees and looked at

Ben. "You might not want to hear this, but I don't think you are a jerk all the time."

He burst out laughing. "Too bad."

She leaned back onto her heels and started to open the paint can with the opener from the hardware store. She glanced at his worn Saints jersey and pushed the fabric away from the paint can. "I'll try not to get paint on it."

"On the house? Good." He smiled.

"On your shirt." She laughed.

He shrugged.

"Now who has more to say but decided not to?" Elli wedged the lid loose. To keep things tidy, she reached for the roll of paper towels instead of the other shirt she had taken from the laundry room to use as a rag. It was probably his favorite watching agility dog shows shirt.

"You don't want to know what I was about to say about my shirt," he said, in a deep, slow voice. Elli looked up at his dark, hooded eyes and knew what he threatened to say about the shirt would involve words that would stroke, caress, and heat. Like it or not, the man had skills.

She shook her head. "You're right." She started to pull the lid off the paint, but something told her not to and she hesitated. She looked down at the paper towel in her hand and saw it smeared with a bright, candy-colored pink. Oh my God. Her head jerked up to Ben. He was looking across the lawn and hadn't noticed the obnoxious pink paint, which had to be a mistake. Elli jumped up, knowing she had to make Ben leave so that she could call the production manager to get the correct paint color before the hardware store closed. She had no idea how she was going to do that.

Ben's cell phone began to ring. When he reached into his pocket to answer it, she yanked a handful of paper towels and laid it on top of the paint cans. She got her cell phone and texted a quick note to the production manager.

Wrong paint color. This looks like an offspring of The Pink Panther and a pink flamingo. Send corrected color number, ASAP. The hardware store closes in a couple of hours.

Elli sent the text message and went to the task of sealing the paint lid back onto the can. She didn't have a hammer or mallet so she took off her tennis shoe and used it to bang the lid shut. She looked over her shoulder at Ben who was still on the phone and quickly wiped the pink paint that remained in the lid crease, and then she stacked an unopened can on top of it. Satisfied, she turned around and sat on the ground to put her shoe back on. Ben was staring at her, in the way Helen had earlier that day. He was trying to figure out what in the hell she was about while he still had the phone pressed against his ear.

"What?" she mouthed, then slipped on the shoe and began to tie it.

"I'll be there," he said, speaking into the phone. "I'll have to rearrange a few things." He paused as the other person on the line spoke. "Camille will understand. I'll have her meet me at the Krewe of Hyacinthians ball instead of picking her up." He disconnected the phone and stuffed it in his pocket.

"Problem?" Ben's eyes lingered on her legs, which she'd folded up in front of her to tie her shoe. "You need to see a man about a dog, again?"

"A woman. Camille's cousin. Mating problem."

"Hers or her dog's?"

Ben stepped closer to Elli, and when she struggled to stand, he grabbed her by the elbow to help her. Heat seemed to pour through him and into her. By the way his eyes darkened, she knew he felt it, too. It offended and thrilled her at the same time. He had just mentioned a date he had tonight with another woman a few seconds before he looked at her as if he would jump her bones right there on the balcony.

"I'm not sure what's going on between us," she offered, taking a step back. "It's got to stop."

"Or we have to get it out of our system." He ran his hand through his long hair. "Shit. I can't believe I said that."

"Me either. Now I think you are a jerk, again." She shoved both her hands against his chest to push him away. He gripped her wrists and pulled her against him. He was definitely aroused. "You may not have a problem with starring in Cheaters, but I do."

"Cheaters?" He lifted her chin so she was looking into his darkening emerald eyes. He brushed the pad of his thumb over her lips. It was rough and gentle at the same time. She could smell the sweet, tempting scent of his breath.

She swallowed hard and fought the urge to kiss his hand.

"Dr. Snow White?" she said and was immediately sorry she let her private nickname for the beautiful doctor be known.

Ben smiled his sexy half smile. "Jealous?"

Elli looked away and made hissing noises to dismiss what she knew was the truth. "No."

"You need a starring role in the show Liars."

"I don't lie." Her throat was dry and her brain muddled. The man did that to her and she didn't like it. "No, Ben Bienvenu, I'm not jealous of you and Camille. I think the beautiful doctor and you are perfect for each other." Then, because she couldn't stop her inner troublemaker, she shrugged her shoulders in a huge, overdramatic movement. Ben burst out laughing.

"I can only imagine what you left unsaid, cher." His eyes were brighter, softer, and friendlier than she'd ever seen before.

"No, cher…trust me, you have no idea what I've left unsaid." It was perfect timing to exit scene stage left, but he held on to her when she tried to turn away.

"I know you better than you think, Crocifissa." He released her, stepped back, and stuffed his hands in his jean pockets. "I have made a career out of reading people and their dogs."

"You've only read the opening scenes of the latest release. You have no idea what's in the prequel."

He stood stock-still and stared at her. Elli knew she had him on that one. No one really knew the totality of who she was—the lonely child, the ambitious overachieving producer, the grieving daughter, the frightened cancer patient, the inspired re-inventor of her life.

"I live in the present." He ran his fingers through his hair again, leaving a few waves sticking up and looking crazy sexy.

"Our past dictates where we are in the present." She smoothed his disheveled hair in a friendly gesture before clasping her hands behind her. "Unless you're a dog." She smiled. "The Dog Whisperer says dogs can only live in the present."

Ben smiled a warm, genuine smile and nodded. "Touché." He looked at his watch and shrugged his shoulders. Whether the move was intentional or not, it cracked her up and Elli burst out laughing. Ben laughed too and took a step toward her, but stopped and shook his head. "I don't know what it is about you that has my blood running hot as sunshine one minute, then cold as shaved ice the next."

"I'm sure it'll be revealed in the prequel." Elli smiled. "Go on, you're going to be late for the ball if you don't get going." And I'll be too late to exchange the paint at the hardware store. "You can't keep the princess waiting."

Ben nodded. "Remember to keep those film people away from the kennel and my dogs." He waited for her to indicate she had heard him before leaving. Elli quickly gathered the paint cans and headed down the stairs toward her car. While the urgency of what needed to do loomed over her, she wondered what would be in the prequel of Ben Bienvenu's life. She knew a large part of it would have to be about growing up with parents who had an odd relationship based on infidelity. Another important part would be about him falling in love with his wife, then suffering the heartbreak of losing her. Before she could delve into that thought, Elli's phone dinged that she had a text. It was from the location director, giving her the paint color number.

"Are you sure?" she texted him back.

"Yes." He texted the paint number again. "It's pink popsicle."

"WTH," she responded. It was the pink atrocity she already had.

"LOL." He returned. "It's a statement pink. Heroine who owns the house is an eccentric artist."

"Can't you add the color in post?" she typed.

"No. Budget too tight for that in post. Paint cheaper. You should understand that."

"K." She sighed and turned the car around to head back to the house. Her phone dinged again.

"BTW. Heather Harley will be coming with Sam Cooper tomorrow for a few scenes. Both actors have personal security. Expect calls from them."

Elli sighed. Great. A simple shoot was going to look like a freaking presidential visit.

"No problem." She lied. She didn't know how she would keep the visit of two of Hollywood's hottest actors from turning into another Mardi Gras. If the speed and veracity with which the news spread about the cottage fire was any indication of what she was to expect, she was in trouble. She'd have to talk to Ben about changing the code on the gate to keep looky-Lous out. Even if they were his family. Oh, geez. This was not going to be good. Maybe she should post Helen at the gate to deal with the Bienvenues.

Fifteen minutes later, Elli had managed to roll enough paint on the front of the house to give her an upset stomach. Maybe, it was because it reminded her of Pepto-Bismol. God help her when Ben saw this Alice in Wonderland color on his amazing historical home. He'd toss her off the property and probably out of the parish, regardless of her legal rights to be there. She'd bet no one would try to stop him, not even Beau and Doug who had befriended her. Heck, she wouldn't blame them for forming a lynch mob for turning the magnificent Sugar Mill Plantation into a giant blob of cotton candy.

"Ah! Mon Dieu!" a strong voice exclaimed from behind Elli. Although, she recognized Tante Izzy's voice right away, she hadn't heard the woman approach. "Garde voir le beau la galerie?"

Elli shifted her weight on the ladder to look at Tante Izzy, whose eyes were as wide as silver dollars. She held a paper plate covered with aluminum foil in her hand. "Do I want to know what you said or is it better that I remain in ignorant bliss?"

Tante Izzy snorted and waved the hand holding a royal purple and kelly green, shiny patent leather purse. "I was sayin' how beautiful the galerie is. 'Bout time somebody painted it a nice color."

Tante Izzy would be the one person who approved of the color, considering it was the only color she wore, other than her Mardi Gras colored clothes. Right now, she wore both. Besides the large purple, gold, and green purse, she had matching painted Keds on her feet and green bobby socks. Her dress, however, was a cool, cotton crayon-pink shift.

"It's called pink popsicle," Elli sighed, climbing down the ladder. "Ben will hate it."

"What does he know?" After Elli set the paint roller down, Tante Izzy handed her the paper plate. "It's pain perdu. You need to eat more."

Elli lifted the foil and looked at the golden strips sprinkled with confectioner's sugar. The faint scent of cinnamon and the sweet dark syrup pooled on the sides of the strips made her stomach growl. She laughed. "What is 'pan per do'?"

"Lost bread." Tante Izzy smiled and took one off the plate, dipped it into the syrup, and took a bite. "It's good. You take your old bread, dip it in an egg batter, and cook it in a black skillet."

"Like French toast."

"Mon Dieu. It's pain perdu. Lost bread. Don't youz Texians listen?" She gestured for Elli to take a strip.

"Mmm. Yummy," she said after taking her first bite. "It's really good."

Tante Izzy rolled her eyes. "Of course, it'z good. I wouldn't feed it to youz if'n it wasn't."

"Thank you." She took a second strip and slid it into the syrup. "You know, Ben will really be upset when he sees this pink color."

"So you only paint your half." She nodded. "Cain't say nothin' if'n that's all you do."

Elli smiled, wishing it were that simple. "I am only painting this side of the building. It's only temporary."

Tante Izzy opened her purse and started digging inside of it. "Why temporary?" she asked without looking up.

Elli hesitated in answering, knowing Tante Izzy might be too anxious to share the news of the movie shoot with her family and friends. She would probably find out anyway, though. It was better to include her and ask for her discretion than to leave Tante Izzy to her own wiles. "I'm going to tell you something only Ben knows, Tante Izzy. I want you to know and I want you to help us keep it a secret. It's important that it doesn't turn into a huge spectacle. We can't have crowds or fans or the curious."

"Spectacle? I'd never do dat," she said, bending over to adjust one of her bright green socks that had slipped down.

"I know you wouldn't." Elli smiled. "That's why I'm bringing you into my confidence. Into the inner circle—like in the movie Meet the Fockers."

"I saw dat movie with Bobby De Niro," she said, pointing to her eyes then to Elli, as De Niro had done in the movie to indicate he was watching his future son-in-law.

Elli laughed. "Well, you are in the inner circle of trust. There is a movie crew coming here for a couple of days. They'll be shooting some exterior scenes here at the plantation house and on the grounds."

"C'est si bon!" she clapped her hands. "Me, I can be an extra if dey need one."

"If they do, I'll tell them you are available."

Tante Izzy nodded and her eyes sparkled. "I can sing a little if dey need, and I can still dance the two-step."

"That's good, but I don't think they will be doing anything that requires extras. They plan to shoot exterior shots of the main characters coming in and out of the house and walking on the property. They'll also be getting long shots to set place and time."

"I think a nice fais do-do would make da movie more interesting."

"Well, probably so, but it's not for us to decide. It's not our movie. Besides, it isn't set in a Cajun town. It's set in a country town in Georgia."

"Georgia? Why come to Louisiana then?"

"It's cheaper, available, and looks like the fictional country home they want."

"They payin'?"

"Yes, it's why we've agreed to let them shoot here. They pay very well."

"Hmmm." She nodded.

"And it's why the house is being painted pink popsicle." She shook her head. "The lead actress, Heather Harley, is playing an eccentric artist. It's her house."

"Heather Harley? I like her. She's pretty. Her fesse is kind of round like that Jenifer Lopez, and her tettons are big like dat Pamela Anderson, but she's got a nice smile. The mans in town will go crazy if they know she's here."

Elli sighed. Tante Izzy was right. Heather Harley was a sex icon. She was also a very sweet person. Elli had met her when she auditioned for the lead role in Newfie. She did a fantastic read but was too sexy for the heroine. Even if they covered up all her trademark parts, they wouldn't be able to hide her innate sexuality.

"I'll need your help keeping it a secret that she and Sam Cooper are here."

"Ruby will be wantin' to get her hands on him for her benefit." Tante Izzy pursed her lips together. "We cain't tell her. She'll be madder dan a teet-less nanny goat, but I'll handle her. And, I'll handle anybody else dat comes sniffin' around—I got my shotgun."

"No!" Elli shouted, then lowered her voice. "They'll have their own security. I'll need you to help keep it on the DL."

"Deal? Maybe Beau can help nego-tee-ate."

Elli laughed. "I'm sorry. DL. Meaning down-low. Secret. We need to keep it a secret. And if that isn't possible, we have to just keep everyone off the plantation. Including Ruby." She said. "I'm sorry to have to do this, but that's how it has to be. It's no different than an accountant or doctor not wanting to have a crowd around while they are working. Well-meaning, curious people just get in the way. It'll slow production and time means money."

"That's fer sure." Tante Izzy took another piece of the lost bread. "I'm kinda surprised Ben's letting dem come film a movie here."

"Yeah, me, too." Elli picked up her paint roller. "The money is really good."

"Not better than my oil well, I bet." Tante Izzy leaned against the balcony railing. "What iz it with you and money? Youz don't seem like da type to care so much about it. Youz ain't like Ben's momma, Helen."

"It's not that I care about the money, but I need the money for something important." Elli inhaled a deep breath. God, she'd love to be able to confide in at least one person here. A person she could trust. A person who knew all the players. A person who could give her advice or at least listen to her ideas and offer an informed opinion. She looked at Tante Izzy adjusting her bright green socks on her skinny legs again. She knew, without a doubt, that she could trust this amazing, clever lady even though she was Ben's aunt.

"It seems today is the day for me to confide in you about a number of things." She put the paint roller down. "What I'm about to discuss with you can't go any further than us. It's personal, but I need advice and counsel. I need a…friend." Elli realized she almost said family.

"What you need is family. Not a friend." Tante Izzy said as if she'd read Elli's mind. "Consider me youz aunt. Better yet, youz fairy godmother. I always wants to be a fairy godmother since I first saw Cinderella. I liked dat better dan being a princess. Youz has superpowers as a fairy godmother, and youz always has sparkling stars floatin' around you. Mais, we are now relations. Imagine that. I've adopted me a Texian godchild."

Elli smiled. "I like that very much. Thank you." She sniffed, fighting back tears, surprised how much she wanted to have an aunt. "You are my only living family. Adopted or otherwise."

"Cher," Tante Izzy cooed and gave Elli a big hug. She wasn't round or soft as you'd expect an old aunt to be, but she was warm and loving and wonderful.

"I'm in big trouble, Tante Izzy," Elli said, bent over into the older woman's embrace. Izzy eased back and looked up at her.

"Youz wit child?" she said, her face full of concern but absent of judgment and condemnation.

Elli burst into tears. Never had she felt that kind of unconditional love since her father died. Her heart ached. She sobbed, big gasping sobs that led into deep hiccups. All of which prevented her from speaking to tell Tante Izzy that she wasn't pregnant.

"I'll find youz a good man to marry you to raise your fatherless child," she offered. "Don't youz worry none. I'll pick a good one."

Elli started laughing now. The combination of hiccupping and laughing had her nearly wetting her pants. "No. No. Not pregnant." She gasped. "Broke. Need money. Stolen. Children and families counting on me."

"Slow down, Texian." Tante Izzy opened her purse and pulled out a small flask. "Medicinal spirits. Youz need this. Youz is hysterical."

Elli took a swig and started coughing. It tasted like what she imagined battery acid would taste and feel like going down her throat. "Burns."

"Take another swig, the first one numbs the way for the next few," Tante Izzy advised. Elli took a second drink and her insides immediately felt happy.

"Thank you," she croaked, handing the flask to Izzy. Elli told her how Abby and she had founded the Gene I.D. Foundation. She explained how the donations from the latest fundraiser were stolen along with the private identity information of her generous contributors. She told her how funds were also stolen from the foundation bank account. She didn't tell Izzy that she had personally funded that account with a personal loan she made using all of her sizable savings. She thought she would be able to pay herself back most of the money in a few years. Now she was broke with only an annual merchandising royalty check to keep her fed, clothed, and sheltered. Her next payment wasn't coming for another eight months. "We only have enough money to tide us over for another week or two, at most."

"Mon dieu." Tante Izzy scratched her head. "How youz plan to get more money?"

"I'm going to sell my car and..." She shrugged her shoulders, looked at the ground, and then took a drink from the flask again.

"Give me dat." Tante Izzy swiped it from her hand and shoved it into her purse. "The bottle don't solve no problem."

"You're going to hate me." She looked away. "I want to sell the plantation to a venture capitalist interested in building a Hollywood South in Louisiana. The state is offering really nice tax incentives for movie productions to come to Louisiana."

Tante Izzy didn't say anything. Her brows lifted and her lips sealed tight in a wrinkled line. She opened her purse and took a big swig from the flask.

"Sugar Mill Plantation is really a wonderful location for a movie studio. The plantation and land are well suited for a number of different scenes. Country. Westerns. Midwest. Rivers. Bayous. Forest."

"Harrumph."

"Oh, I don't want to take Joey and Ben's home away from them." She twisted her hands. "I know how terrible that would be for them, but they still would have each other. There are kids, like Rickey and Keisha and sweet, cherub Paulina who don't care about a house, they just want to have their momma—alive and with them as they grow up. I need to make sure their family has the best opportunity to survive—and other families, too. That means they need knowledge and hope. Finding out if the breast cancer gene is in these families and helping them get the right medical surveillance means they can catch the cancer early, if it rears its awful head. Early detection saves lives. We just need to give them a chance, Tante Izzy."

"Youz are between a rock and a hard place." She nodded, twisted her mouth, and narrowed her eyes. "I think it'z nice and honorable and all, but seems to me youz cares an awful lot for dem strangers. Maybe more dan what is right for dem and you. Why is dat?"

Elli looked into Tante Izzy's wise, old eyes. "Because I am just like them." Tears filled her eyes. "I was frightened and afraid I was going to die from cancer. Alone, with no help. My father died less than a year before my diagnosis. My mother had been long gone from the same disease I had. I had no sisters, no brothers, no aunts, no family."

Elli walked to the balcony railing and looked out onto the lawn, remembering. "There were these two amazing women getting chemo at the same time as me. Both of theirs was stage four. One had breast cancer and the other had Melanoma. They knew they were dying." Elli took in a deep breath. "They were single mothers with no family to speak of. God, they worried so much about their beautiful families. They spoke of them all of the time. Never in the woe-is-me kind of way, but with real love for the children…and with such concern. Oh, what would happen to their daughters and sons when they died? Who would look out for them to protect them from getting the disease or being able to fight it off earlier? Elli rested her hand over her heart. The pain and sadness felt like a crushing ache. There are great organizations to help them keep a roof over their heads, to help pay their medical bills, and to educate them. But, there was nothing that was truly proactive in fighting cancer early on another level. It's just so awful to have that kind of fear. You are afraid of dying and wonder if heaven will welcome you. But, most of all, you are so darn afraid of leaving your children behind." Elli swallowed past the heaviness in her throat. When she spoke again her voice was hoarse and strained. "I heard their cries," she whispered. "From the people who were dying and those who were being left behind. They both need to know that it will all be okay." She crossed her arms over her chest. "Starting the fight before the cells start dividing is just one more way to fight to win-to make it okay."

Elli looked over her shoulder at Tante Izzy, who was leaning against the window frame of Ben's bedroom. "Knowledge is power, right? If you know you have the cancer genes, you can do medical surveillance in a more aggressive way. Insurance companies and Medicaid can't discriminate against you if you test positive, but they don't support the every-six-month surveillance protocol. Our foundation does that as well. We save lives. We find a way to give families hope."

"Everyone needs hope…and a family."

"And joy and security."

"Youz a human guardian angel on earth." Tante Izzy joined Elli at the railing.

"Hardly." Elli smiled. "You know, our foundation office has even become a kind of gathering place for the families? We have toys and games for the kids. There's a stocked kitchen for hungry bellies. Veronica, our social worker, has impromptu counseling sessions. You can't imagine how much fear attaches itself to cancer."

"Goddaughter, dis is real special." Elli smiled. "So, youz had cancer?"

"I did. I was one of the blessed ones."

"Youz survived it."

"I didn't have to burden my family with worry and problems while I had cancer." Tante Izzy started to speak, but Elli raised her hand to stop her from saying something kind and meaningful because she thought Elli needed the encouragement. She didn't want that. She didn't want sympathy or the focus to be on her when there were so many who suffered far worse. "Now, you know everything. I just hope you don't hate me for wanting to sell the plantation. I have to do it. I'll make sure that I find a place just as wonderful for Joey and Ben to live. I'll also make sure they have full access to the plantation if they want to come and fish or picnic or connect with their history."

Tante Izzy worked her mouth a bit, then walked up to Elli and looked her straight in the eyes. She didn't say anything, she just extended the plate of pain perdu to her. Elli took one and her eyes filled with tears again. This woman, who had every reason to hate her for what she was about to do to her family, didn't reject her. In fact, while it was clear Tante Izzy didn't agree with what she had to do, she cared for her as a person.

Elli threw her arms around Tante Izzy and hugged her. "Thank you. Thank you."

"Mon Dieu," she gasped. "Be careful, now. I'm an old lady with dat osteo-bone thing. Youz is turnin' my bones to chalk."

Elli laughed. "I adore you."

"And I love you, child." She put the plate on the ground, wiped her hands on her dress, and looked at the painted wall. "Youz got another paint brush? I'm good at dis stuff, youz know." Elli handed her the trim brush, then walked inside and got a chair from her bedroom. She placed the chair near the wall for Tante Izzy to sit on while painting. She sat and pulled out her cell phone from colorful purse. "I'll get a few of my teenage nephews over here to help us paint," she said.

"I can't pay them," Elli said holding up her hand to stop Tante Izzy from making the call.

She rolled her eyes. "Youz don't know nothin'" She shook her head. "They'z will do it because I ask dem' to do it." She swatted Elli away as if she was a nuisance. "Now, When dis is done, I need to get me my hair fixed so I look sexy for Sam Cooper."

"Fairy godmother, you are irresistible just the way you are with all of those dazzling sparkles shimmering around you."

"Got dat right."

* * * *

"Did you encourage this, Tante Izzy?" Beau asked stepping onto the balcony at exactly six thirty. "This pink color has your name stamped all over it."

Tante Izzy stood from her chair and picked up the plate of pain perdu. She handed it to Beau. "It's pretty, huh?"

He took a bite of the sweet bread. "You, yes. The pink house, no." He grinned, looking much too happy about the awful color. "Ben is going to have a seizure."

"We're only painting this one side," Elli offered with a forced smile before climbing down from the ladder. "It's on my half of the house."

"Oh, well, that makes it better." He shook his head looking at the four empty boxes of pizza. "The Bienvenu teen terrors were here I see."

"They were," Elli laughed. "Thank God. They paint as fast as they eat. They knocked out most of the job before having to leave for the school dance. I couldn't have done it without them." Elli smiled. "Those boys are going to be lady killers when they grow up. They are so charming."

"I taught them everything I know."

Tante Izzy harrumphed. "I'ze hope not."

"Maybe they can charm Ben to ignore your half of the house that's painted princess pink."

"It looks good," Tante Izzy insisted. "And it'z fer a good cause..." She looked at Elli.

"Does he know?"

Elli shrugged. "Do you?" she asked Beau.

"Pardon me, but I didn't study the encrypted female language in law school." He smiled, leaning against the railing.

"He's a lawyer," Tante Izzy said to Elli. "He's like a priest."

"What?" Beau choked on the bread he had just shoved in his mouth. Tante Izzy stood on her toes and whacked him on the back and when he frowned at her, she whacked him on the back of his head. "Hey, what did I do?"

"It'z what youz think dat got youz the smack on da head," Tante Izzy snapped.

"He's right," Elli stated, ignoring their exchange. "You're here as my lawyer, right?"

"I sure as hell am not here as your priest!"

"Same thang when it comes to secret repeatin'." Tante Izzy nodded to Elli. "Tell him."

"You can't repeat what I'm going to tell you. I invoke client-counselor privilege.

"Yeah, just like a priest hearin' confession," Tante Izzy added.

"I don't want to hear your confession." He pulled out his phone from the finely tooled leather case clipped to his pressed jeans. "Do I?" He lifted a brow and grinned. "No, I think it's best if I call Father Étienne. He'll come over right away."

Elli laughed. "Don't be silly." Beau looked at her as if he was dead serious. "This information doesn't have to do with my soul. It's not that bad."

"Part of it is," Tante Izzy corrected.

"I'm not going to tell him that part. He represents Ben for that. I'm not stupid." Both Beau and Izzy looked at her with their brows lifted. "I'm not. I'll have you know, I graduated with honors in college and high school. I've managed multimillion-dollar movie productions, hundreds of employees…all with a great deal of success."

"Dere is book smart and life smart," Izzy insisted before rolling her eyes in a gesture of mutual agreement with Beau.

"Some movie scenes are being filmed here tomorrow," Elli told Beau without preamble. She was feeling too impatient and frustrated with the tone of the conversation for subtleties.

"Oh, that. I know that already. Ben told me."

"Mon Dieu, why didn' youz say somethin' and stop her from yappin' on like a plucked hen?"

Elli looked at Tante Izzy and shook her head. "We are painting the house because of the movie."

"I get why you are painting the plantation, but why in the hell are you painting it this girlie pink?"

"Heather Harley is an artist and dis here is her house."

Beau looked at Elli, eyes wide. "The Heather Harley?"

"If you help us with keeping Ben from going apocalyptic, I'll introduce you to Heather," Elli said immediately, thinking of making Beau her ally. "Maybe I can arrange for the two of you to have lunch."

Beau's eyes lit up. "Ben will be apocalyptic putty in my hands." He smiled and it was bright, white, and warm. "Tell Harley that I look forward to meeting her."

"She'll be here tomorrow." Elli sighed. "And this place needs to be finished painted before the crew arrives in the morning."

"I'll help once we are finished with the fire marshal."

"Mon Dieu," Tante Izzy exclaimed. "The Po-Po is comin' to arrest her?"

"I don't think so." Beau grinned. "He said he just wants to ask her a few questions." Beau looked at Elli, and she knew he could read the anxiety on her face. "Let's put the painting on hold for now. He'll be here in about fifteen minutes. I want to review some things with you." Elli hated having yet another delay but couldn't do anything about it.

After covering the paint supplies and convincing Tante Izzy that she shouldn't hang around for the fire marshal, Beau sat across the kitchen table from Elli. The scent of a pot of coffee brewing made the room feel cozy, but it didn't do much to ease her nerves.

"Should I be worried?" Elli asked. "I feel like I'm in a scene from a movie where the heroine is about to be wrongfully accused of something bad."

"Nah." Beau clasped her hand. It felt warm, comforting, and friendly. Her relationship with Beau was similar to her relationship with Doug, but his touch felt very different. "All you have to do is answer his questions. Don't volunteer anything. It's simple. Let him ask you a question. Then you pause a moment before answering. That hesitation will give me time to interject or redirect if need be. So you just have to take it slow and easy. Relax and be yourself. And remember: Only answer the question he asks. Nothing more."

"It sounds like I'm on trial."

"Not at all. It's just an inquiry. Procedure. No worries."

Elli wasn't convinced. She was a stranger in town and rumors were flying of how she had intentionally started a fire.

The coffeemaker beeped and she got up to pour a cup for Beau. "It's worrisome when all I can tell the marshal is that I had this feeling something was wrong, and I think I saw a pair of eyes staring at me."

"The truth is the truth." Beau took the coffee she handed him just as his cell phone began to buzz. "Excuse me." He leaned back in his chair and answered the phone. A smile lit his face. "Yeah, I'm here." He looked at Elli and winked. "No, the marshal hasn't gotten here, yet." He took a sip of his coffee. "Yes. Yes. I know. Who's the brilliant lawyer here anyway?" Beau laughed and winked at Elli again. What in the world, did he mean with all that winking? Who else knew, much less cared, about her interview with the fire marshal? Tante Izzy? "I know my job. You go on and do yours. Leave me alone." Beau hung up and took a sip of his coffee, his eyes crinkled and bright.

Elli waited for him to volunteer who was on the phone. When he didn't, she slapped her hand on the table. "Okay, I give up. Who was that asking about me?"

"Consider me like a priest," Beau smiled.

"Oh for God's sake." She got up and poured herself a cup of coffee she didn't want.

"It was Ben," he told her when she returned to the table. "He's concerned about you. Wants to make sure you get a fair shake."

Elli bit her lower lip to keep from smiling. It was ridiculous to feel so pleased that Ben called out of concern for her. "I guess he's worried about what all this fire business will mean to the plantation." She immediately shook her head, feeling like a silly schoolgirl checking to see if the boy tugging on her ponytail liked her. "Sorry. That's not fair. I sound so mean-spirited. I really appreciate everyone's concern."

Beau smiled a knowing smile, "Including Ben's. I probably wouldn't have been here if it wasn't for him. He's the one who insisted you should have representation during the inquiry."

Elli shook her head. "He acts like he hates me, then he does this."

"Hate? Nah." Beau got up and refilled his coffee cup. "Maybe uncertain, afraid."

"Afraid?" She sighed. "I don't mean him any harm. I want to resolve our differences amicably. I don't have the luxury of time, though. Amicable for us might mean time. We have to find a resolution quickly."

"You threaten him, dear Elli. That is for certain." He sat and looked into her eyes with a genuine affection. "And, it doesn't have anything to do with the plantation, the kennel, or even Joey." He tapped on his chest with his fist. "You threaten his heart."

"What?" She swallowed past the lump in her throat. Was Beau talking about Ben having feelings for her? "We only met a few days ago. I think you misunderstand our relationship. It's adversarial, at best, with just a little bit of male-female attraction thrown in."

Beau laughed. "A little bit? You two sizzle, crackle, and burn when y'all are around each other." He grabbed her hands and squeezed them. "Darlin', there is some serious chemistry between you two—the heat burning the beaker and smoking up the lab kind of combustion."

"I think you're mistaken," she stammered, but her words didn't sound true to her own ears. Yes, if she was truthful, there was something basic and real that happened when they were together. It had nothing to do with their hearts and minds but everything to do with what made them a man and a woman. "Nothing can happen between us in that way. Our relationship is already too complicated."

"And you only know your half of it." Beau shifted in his seat and looked over his shoulder. "I can't explain Ben to you without pissing him off. I ought to do it anyway, but he's like a brother to me and it wouldn't be right. I will tell you this. He's worth the trouble. He has a lot of wounds inflicted by his wife. He's got to stop licking them like an injured dog." He exhaled. "I've said enough."

"I'm not the right woman to heal him." That would take time and commitment. She couldn't promise that to anyone, even if she wanted to.

"No, don't misunderstand me. He has to heal himself. I think he has—only he's still in the cowering stage. You know. When you get kicked in the gut, you walk around with your arm over your midsection to protect it because you're anticipating another attack."

"Yeah. I get that, and especially if you are blindsided. It can be life-changing."

"Exactly." He stood, kissed her on top of the head, and walked to the back door. She realized she hadn't heard the knock, but apparently Beau had. He escorted a man into the kitchen. A man with a full head of thick, gray hair that didn't match his curly, black eyebrows and youthful face. He appeared to be in his mid-thirties. "Elli Morenelli, this is Frank Cammer. He's the state fire marshal for our area."

Elli shook his hand, realizing for the first time that she was still dressed in her oversized painting clothes. She felt her face heat with embarrassment. "Please forgive me for how I'm dressed," she offered, trying to sound confident. "I was painting."

"I never mind talking to someone wearing a Saints Championship shirt," he said, in a New Orleans accent as rich and interesting as the city itself. "Who Dat!"

Elli smiled and punched her fist in the air with subdued enthusiasm. "Who Dat." She gestured toward a chair at the kitchen table. "Please, have a seat. Can I offer you a cup of coffee?"

"Don't mind if I do." He pulled out a yellow legal tablet and flipped through about a dozen pages before finding a clean sheet. He pulled out a small, digital recorder and placed it on the table. "You don't mind if I record our conversation, do you? I find it improves the accuracy of my recollection when I'm writing my report."

Elli brought two cups of coffee to the table and placed them in front of Beau and the marshal. She looked at Beau, who nodded once. "I don't mind at all." She put the cream and sugar in the center of the table. Mr. Cammer took a sip of his cup without adding anything to it.

The fire marshal turned on the recorder and spoke in a normal tone, stating the date, time, and reason for the interview. He also mentioned that Beau Bienvenu was present. "For the record, please state your full legal name as it appears on your driver's license."

"Crocifissa Rosalie Morenelli."

"Um, can you spell that," he asked, his black eyebrows lifted. Elli couldn't stop fixing her gaze to them. Did he dye them that blue-black color or were they that way naturally?

"Miss Morenelli?"

"Oh, sorry." She glanced at Beau who was covering his smile. She spelled her name. "It's Italian."

"That's what I figured," he smiled. "I'm Frank Cammertoni, but when my people came to America, the immigration official checking them in changed it to Cammer. Go figure." He wrote her name on the tablet. "It's nice that you have your original family name. Did you know that a large number of Italian immigrants came to Louisiana directly from Sicily?"

"No. I didn't know that."

"Yeah. A lot of them settled in the river parishes and outside of New Orleans. There were so many immigrants coming in the early eighteen-eighties that many of the overflowing boats went upriver and off-loaded there. The Italians found great opportunities in Louisiana."

"When you think of Louisiana, you think of the French, the Spanish, and the Cajun cultures here. You don't think of the Italian influence."

"There's a lot. I have a book on it. I'll bring it back with me when I come back this way." He smiled a huge smile, filled with pleasure in their Italian bond. "Now. Let's get to the business at hand."

Beau leaned over and whispered into Elli's ear. "You have him wrapped around your little Italian digit. Remember, just answer what he asks, nothing more." She swatted him away as she heard the back door creak open. It was Ben. Elli's heart started firing like a machine gun fully engaged.

"I thought you were going to the ball," she called to him, as her breathing accelerated. He certainly was dressed for the ball, though, wearing a deep ebony tuxedo set against a crisp, bright white shirt that looked tailored just for him. His jacket fit snug against his wide shoulders before tapering past his narrow hips. He didn't wear a cummerbund, but he did have an elegant bow tie. It dangled around his neck waiting to be tied. He was gorgeous.

Elli bit her lip, hard. She gave herself a mental slap and thought of Cher's line in Moonstruck when Nicholas Cage told her that he loved her—"Snap out of it." Not that this heart-racing, body-heating reaction had anything to do with love, she reminded herself. It had everything to do with lust. Pure and simple.

Ben walked with casual ease from the ugly wallpapered hall into the outdated kitchen, looking current, expensive, and perfect. He glanced at her with darkened, searching eyes. Elli felt her face redden. God, please don't let him know how hot she thought he looked. She looked away from him and toward the fire marshal, who stood to introduce himself.

"Ben Bienvenu," he responded before nodding to Beau. His cousin immediately smiled and winked at Elli.

"Aren't you going to the Hyacinthians' ball?" Beau asked with a bit of mischief in his voice.

"In a little while." He looked at the fire marshal. "Don't let me stop your interview with Elli." He walked to the counter and poured himself a cup of coffee.

"Do you mind if he's present for the interview, Miss Morenelli?"

"Well, actually…" She glanced at Ben who was taking a sip of his coffee and looking at her over the rim of his mug. His brows lifted and his eyes challenged her. She looked at Beau, who still had that amused expression on his face. "No. Of course not. This affects him, too."

"Good," Mr. Cammer said, settling into his seat again. He checked his recorder and spoke into it. "Joining Miss Morenelli's attorney, Beau Bienvenu, for the interview is Ben Bienvenu, her..." He looked at Elli, waiting for her to finish his sentence.

"Her business partner," Beau interjected, causing Ben to blow out a heavy breath. He clearly didn't like the description, but he didn't say anything.

"From the police report, I see that you were jogging and just happened on the hunting cabin."

"Yes, that's right."

"Uh huh." Mr. Cammer wrote something down on the tablet in a slow, methodical way. She hadn't really said anything, so Elli couldn't imagine what it was. "And the dogs went rushing toward the cabin?"

"Yes, that's right."

He wrote again and her stomach knotted. This process was slow and unnerving. She saw Ben frowning where he stood, leaning against the kitchen cabinet.

"How many dogs?"

"Three."

"Uh huh." He wrote again. Elli sighed, and he stopped writing to look at her. When he was certain she wasn't going to say anything else, he continued writing in his tablet. Elli looked at Beau, who gave her the hand signal to settle down. She looked at Ben whose brows were furrowed. "Okay. The three dogs raced toward the cabin and you followed them?"

She inhaled a deep breath. "Yes, that's correct."

"Uh huh." He wrote something down for a few seconds and looked up at her. "Did you run or walk to the cabin?"

Elli suppressed a groan. "I ran and walked. The ground was uneven."

"Uh huh." He spent a minute writing, then looked at the tip of his pencil and shook his head. He opened the bag he had placed next to him and dug in it for a few seconds. "There it is." He pulled a sharpened pencil from the bag. "Now, you say you ran and walked. Is that correct?"

Elli fought back the urge to tell him to hurry up and get on with it. "Yes, that's correct."

As he wrote again, she sighed and shifted in her seat. She looked at Beau, who seemed annoyed with her. That irritated her, too. She wasn't the one conducting this snail's pace interview. She shifted in her seat again.

"Were you wearing running shoes?" Frank Cammer asked.

Elli rolled her eyes at Beau. "Yes, that's correct." She leaned forward in her seat, then reclined. Ben walked to the kitchen table and sat in the chair next to Elli. He smelled of herbal shampoo, old-fashioned soap, and a bit of masculine impatience.

The marshal looked at Elli and jotted a few sentences, then looked at her again. "You seem anxious. Is there something you want to say?"

Hurry up, she thought but was smart enough not to say. "No. Nothing." She shrugged her shoulders and looked at Ben. He shook his head and squeezed her hand. She knew he meant to reassure her and ease her frayed nerves, but it had the complete opposite effect.

Cammer stopped writing. Ben squeezed her hand tighter, almost to the point of pain. "You really do seem like you want to say something," Cammer offered, looking into Elli's eyes.

She sighed. "No. Not really." He began writing in his tablet again. Ben released her hand. "Well, actually," she began and both Ben and Beau groaned. She didn't look at either of them. "I just want to say that I didn't start the fire."

Frank put his pencil down and looked at her. "Do you know who did?"

"How could she possibly know that?" Ben snapped, looking at Beau. "Tell him."

Beau leaned back in his chair, appearing to be at ease but his eyes met Elli's in silent communication. She understood he wanted her take his advice to only answer the questions that were asked. Elli nodded once to acknowledge that she received his reminder.

The marshal picked up his pencil, and Elli all but leapt from her chair. The man was going to be interviewing her when the film crew arrived in the morning.

"I think it was probably the guy in the cabin who started the fire," she blurted, wanting it to be over. She had a house to finish painting. "I'm sure you concluded that, too, after reading the police report." When Frank Cammer looked at her, she rushed into her account of what had happened that day. The fire marshal listened to her but didn't write a single word as she told him about chasing after the dogs and coming up on the cabin's porch to pull one of the dogs away from the door it was scratching. When she got to the part of her story about seeing a pair of eyes staring at her through the window, she realized the marshal had primed her. He had played on her impatient nature. All his slow talking and writing had set her up to spew her story like a filled balloon spewed its air when pricked with a huge pin.

She paused for the first time in five minutes and looked at Frank Cammer's knowing eyes. Then she looked at Beau. He was frowning. He shook his head, and she knew he wasn't happy with the way she voluntarily told the story and didn't wait to have a calm Q and A as he had instructed her to do. Ben got up and poured himself another cup of coffee.

"Elli," a strong voice called from the back door. It was Doug carrying Donna. "Oh, I'm sorry. Am I interrupting something?"

"You're about thirty seconds too late for that," Ben said as Elli jumped up and swept Donna from Doug's arms. She hugged the soft bundle of fluff to her neck.

"I don't know why, but I've missed you, you prissy little girl." She kissed Donna on top of her head.

"Yeah, I figured you'd want her. So after Helen picked up Joey to keep him over night, I brought her to you. Oh, Ben, she wanted me to tell you that she took Lucky with them because Joey wanted him to tag along." He smiled. "Is that coffee I smell?" Doug walked to the counter and helped himself to a cup from the pot. He spotted the cream and sugar on the table and sat down to sweeten his coffee. Elli returned to her chair and settled Donna on her lap. Donna growled at the marshal for a few seconds, then went to sleep.

Elli introduced Doug to Cammer. After they shook hands, she looked at the stars twinkling in the early night sky out the window. "Let's continue, please," Elli said. "I have a house to paint and I don't want to be doing it when the bats come out." When he looked at Doug, she smiled. "It's okay if he's here. Might as well have the whole family, right Ben?"

The fire marshal continued asking Elli detailed questions about what happened, and she answered as best she could. Had she noticed there was a small generator on the porch? She had not. Did she see if lights were on inside the cabin? She didn't think so. Had she noticed a vehicle parked nearby? She had not. Did she smell anything unusual? She had not. Were there any unusual shrubs or bushes near the cabin? Nothing different than she had seen growing wild in the rows at the back of the cabin.

"Could you identify the wild vegetation around the cabin if I showed you a picture?" He dug into his bag and pulled out a few colored photographs. "Did it look like this?"

It was a long shot of a cultivated field with tall weeds growing in the rows. "Yes. That's it. It looked like that." She smiled, happy that they were making progress.

Beau took the photograph from Elli. "I'll be damned." He handed it to Ben. "Do you think that was growing out there?"

"What was growing out there?" Doug asked, craning his neck to look at the photo Ben handed to Frank.

"Yes, I know that was growing out there." He slipped the photograph into the bag and pulled out another one. "The charred remains of the marijuana plants covered a quarter acre of land around the cabin."

"Marijuana," Elli and Doug said at the same time.

"Damn kids," Doug added. Frank looked at him. "I've had to chase kids off the land now and again. I thought they were just out there to camp or find themselves a quiet make-out place." Elli noticed Ben frowning at Doug. Was he upset that his father-in-law never told him about the kids before or that he was telling the marshal about the kids being there?

"Can you identify any of those kids?"

"Can but won't." Doug stood. "I've known them since they were babies. I can't do it."

Elli and Beau looked at each other. Ben moved to stand behind Elli. This time, instead of smelling soap, she got a faint whiff of smooth cologne. He shifted, and she heard the rustle of his wool jacket as it brushed against his cotton shirt. She had to fight the ridiculous urge to lean back and be absorbed into his heat and strength. His support was what she wanted and exactly what she didn't need. Even reaching for it in the short term felt dangerous. Still, she was touched by how protected she felt by him standing so close to her. It would have been nice to share her burden with someone.

"It seems to me that someone or some ones were cultivating marijuana out there," Frank began, "and in large quantities. From what I gathered from my field investigation, the amount of marijuana I found is more than someone would grow to supply their habit or a make-out session."

Doug shook his head. He carried his cup to the sink before turning to face the marshal. "I can't rat on the kids." He began to pace.

"I found the remains of some plants inside the cabin, along with a few high intensity discharge lights used for growing indoors. I suspect our culprit had some experimental, high-potency crops inside. I'll know when I get the forensics back on the buds I found. I also suspect most of it was taken out of the cabin before the fire."

"He must've seen how frightened I was, figured I'd tell someone what I saw, and bring them back to the cabin right away." Elli frowned. "Why risk getting caught clearing the cabin?"

"Money," Frank said. "That equipment is expensive. He'd want to save his equipment. Especially if the culprit was using a hydroponic system of growing beds filled with nutrient solution. Judging by the extension cords I found in the charred remains and a few electrical components, I think that's what was being used. The culprit probably had small pumps set up on timers to feed and water the marijuana plants, too."

"Man, you are good," Elli said, wondering for a moment if he'd be that good at tracking down an identity theft fugitive.

Frank smiled. "I'm just thorough." He handed Elli another photograph. "Does this look familiar?"

"Yes. That looks like my camera lens. I can't believe it didn't burn in the fire." He handed her another picture of a partially burned piece of the body of the camera.

"I think we might be able to recover something off the memory card."

"That's amazing." She handed the photos to Ben.

"What photos did you take on the camera?" Frank asked.

Elli glanced over her shoulder at the man who literally had her back. She knew if she told Frank that she'd been taking photos of the plantation for a real estate brochure, Ben would shift back to being her adversary. She preferred him being her ally.

"Elli?" Beau prompted when she didn't answer right away.

Ben looked at Elli as he handed the photos to Beau. His expression was tight and angry, but it wasn't directed at her. She could tell he didn't like someone conducting illegal activities on his property. That was clear. She didn't want to add fuel to that fire by revealing she had been taking photos to use to help her sell the plantation. There would be time to do that when he saw how great it was to have the film crew around.

"I had taken some general shots of the land and the main house." She shrugged and felt Ben shift behind her. "It's really very pretty." She smiled. "There's nothing like it in California. So much old wood and ancient trees."

"Is that it? Landscape and buildings?" The fire marshal asked.

"Oh, and of my dogs." She shrugged again while scratching Donna behind the ears. Ben rested his hands on her shoulders and Elli stiffened.

"Were there any pictures of the cabin?" Frank asked, stuffing the photographs back into his bag.

"Yes. I had some pictures of it. Close-ups of the wood grain siding. Some medium shots of the old door. Long shots of the wharf. And when I was frightened by the dogs barking and howling, I switched the camera to video. I don't know what I filmed because I just let it run without looking through the viewfinder. I just wanted to document my demise if I was mauled to death by a feral animal."

Frank looked at her, then asked. "I don't quite understand."

Elli sighed. "I know it sounds silly, but I was a woman alone in the cane fields. If I was critically injured or killed, I wanted the authorities to know how it happened. It wasn't real logical or thought out. I was frightened and just did it. I don't even remember dropping the camera until much later."

"Well. I think we're done for now," Frank said, noticeably not turning his recorder off. He stuffed his legal pad into his bag and stood. "I will probably need to speak with you again once I have the photos from your camera, Miss Morenelli."

"You can call me to set that up," Beau said standing.

Frank nodded and looked at Beau. "Miss Morenelli isn't a suspect at this time, contrary to rumors circulating around town." He laughed a gentle laugh, then turned to Doug. His face turned serious. "And I'd like to speak with you, again, Mr. Leblanc. Will you be available tomorrow?"

Doug stuck his hands in his back pockets. "Yeah, I'll be around. I'm not going to rat out a friend's child because of a stupid thing he did."

"I'll agree with stupid," Frank said, standing. "But this isn't a silly kid's prank, like toilet-papering a house. This is growing illegal drugs for profit. It's a crime. And you if you withhold information, you could be charged with obstruction of justice."

Doug shook his head and walked out of the house without saying a word. Elli felt sorry for him. He was in a tough predicament.

Frank looked at Ben. "I recommend you convince him to give us the information we need."

Ben nodded and shook Frank's hand. Elli stood and shook his hand good-bye as Beau escorted him out.

"I get the feeling that Doug isn't the only one withholding information," Ben said, moving to stand in front of Elli. "Got anything to tell me?"

Elli put Donna on the floor. "No. You are so paranoid." She smiled at him, trying to play coy, but his impossible good looks were disarming. She reached up and touched his freshly shaven cheek. "Don't you have a date?"

Ben covered her hand with his. His eyes were dark, stormy, and so ridiculously sexy. He opened his mouth to speak, but immediately shut it. Without saying a word, he turned and left the house.

When Beau walked in a few minutes later, he was grinning.

"Your partner is late for the ball."

"I hope Camille isn't too angry with him."

"Nah. She wouldn't risk it. For a smart lady, she sure doesn't know how to play our Ben." He gave a playful tap on Elli's cheek. "You, my dear, know how to play him, but I think you don't even know you are."

Elli shook her head. "Change of subject." She grabbed water from the refrigerator. Beau reached over her shoulder for a bottle of water before she had a chance to offer him one. "Can Doug really be charged with obstruction if he doesn't tell the fire marshal what he knows?"

"Yes. Title Fourteen of the criminal codes addresses the cause of hindrance, delay, or prevention of the communication to a peace officer, of information relating to an arrest or potential arrest, or relating to the commission of or possible commission of a crime."

He took a drink of water. "If he knows something and doesn't tell the authorities, he could face criminal charges."

"Doug doesn't know for certain if these particular kids he saw on the property in the past set the fire, so he really doesn't know anything about this particular incident." Elli sat in the kitchen chair. "I don't know why he just doesn't give the fire marshal their names and let him sort it out."

"I agree. An obstruction of justice conviction could mean up to a ten-thousand-dollar fine and five years in prison."

"I guess I'd hate to point the finger at some reckless kids who had nothing to do with a crime." She sighed. "I guess he'll be visiting those kids pretty soon to get to the bottom of it."

"I suppose you're right." He tossed his empty water bottle in the garbage. "How about I order more pizza?" Elli stood and retrieved the water bottle from the garbage and put it in the recycling can. "We can start painting while we're waiting for it to be delivered."

"Sounds good to me. See if they have organic pizza."

Beau grabbed his cell phone, laughing. "Find another one of Ben's rag shirts for me to wear."

Chapter Seven

I am so very, very tired today. I wish you good health, E.

Bosom Blog Buddies Post

Ben climbed out of his truck, glad to be back home and so close to his bed. The Hyacinthians' Ball was torturous. He hated the monotonous presentation of the court. Watching people pretending to be royalty, prancing around the civic center auditorium, was enough to make a man want to hide in the mosquito-infested swamp behind it. He was glad Joey was sleeping at his grandmother's tonight. That meant he didn't have to deal with a sitter and delaying needed sleep.

Ben walked into his bedroom and didn't bother to turn on the light. The front galerie light was on and shone through the small slit in the curtain to provide enough illumination for him to get around. He tossed his jacket and tie onto the bed and unbuttoned the top three buttons of his shirt. As he kicked off his shoes, he noticed a shadow walk past his window. Ben waited a minute for it to reappear. When it didn't, he started unbuttoning his shirt again. The sound of something falling echoed outside. He rushed to the curtain and looked out. A pink hue cast onto the brightened galerie. Ben started to open the window when he heard a woman scream. It was Elli. She was staring right at him, not recognizing him, then turned and started to run.

"Shit." He shoved the window open. "Elli. Elli. It's me. Wait." She looked over her shoulder and climbed in through the spare bedroom window. Ben raced after her. The woman still didn't recognize him.

"Ben!" Elli shouted as soon as he climbed through the other window, into the house. She rushed into his arms and hugged him. "I thought it was happening again! I saw a figure in the window and…and…" She lifted her cell phone. She had called 9-1-1. "I was calling the fire department. I didn't want the plantation house to burn down."

"Nine-one-one operator, may I help you," a voice said distantly on the phone.

"False alarm," Ben said after grabbing the phone. He disconnected the call. The phone immediately rang.

"Ben? Is that you?" He recognized the voice of his cousin, Rachel, who worked at 9-1-1. "I know your voice, Ben, but this isn't your number on caller-ID."

"It's the Texian's cell phone. She called you by mistake."

"You know, I need to confirm that," Rachel said, a smile in her voice. "Procedure. If I don't hear it was a mistake from the person making the call, then I have to dispatch a deputy."

"For God's sake, Rachel." He ran his hands through his hair. "You don't even know where to send a deputy."

"I assume it's Sugar Mill."

Ben thrust the phone at Elli. "You have to talk to her. She was always a brat."

"Hello," Elli said, biting back a grin. She listened to Rachel a moment, then looked at him. "She said she heard what you said." Elli's eyes were round and bright. He was just too damn tired to be dealing with this bullshit. "He didn't answer," Elli said obviously responding to Rachel's question. "He just rolled his eyes." Had he done that? Hell, he probably had. Elli remained silent a few seconds more before speaking again. "Rachel said she already knew that without me telling her. She says you always do that eye-rolling thing." Ben heard Rachel laughing over the phone from where he stood a few feet away. Elli laughed, too.

"So glad I can entertain y'all," he grumbled, sarcasm as heavy as his Cajun accent. "Just tell her that you called nine-one-one by mistake."

"But I didn't call by mistake," Elli said talking into the phone but looking at him. "I meant to call it."

Rachel's voice was a little distorted over the phone, but it was clear what she was saying. "Unit Two-twenty-three, we have a Code Twenty-one. Nine-one-one call was made by a white female, age...how old are you, Elli?"

"Uh, I'm thirty-six. Why?" She looked at Ben. "I think she's sending the police here."

"Oh for God's sake, tell her you called by mistake."

"But I didn't." She shrugged her shoulders, and Ben wanted to toss her over his knee. Damn girl was a pain in the neck. "Rachel, I called you by mistake, sort of. I'm okay. Ben is a little grumpy, but not enough to send the police over."

* * * *

Elli looked at Ben, who was clearly unhappy that she had called 9-1-1. Rachel sighed. "I'm glad to hear there's no trouble. I was afraid it was starting again. I hate having to deal with domestic violence calls. Ben sure doesn't deserve that, again."

Ben reached for the phone, but Elli turned her back to him. "What are you talking about?" she whispered, making sure her voice was too low for Ben to hear. "He beat his wife? I find that hard to believe."

"Uh, I can't talk about it. He'll have to tell you about it. It's not for me to say. Besides, I can lose my job talking about it. Our conversation is being recorded. Ask Ben." Rachel sighed again. "I really want to meet you and talk." The phone went dead.

"That's odd. I think she hung up on me." Elli looked at phone's screen. It began to ring with Blocked Number on display. She answered. "Hi, it's me, Rachel. I'm calling on my cell phone. No one is recording me on this thing." She laughed a soft laugh. "As I was telling you, it's important for us girls to cultivate gal pals, you know.

We owe it to ourselves and to humanity. Our world will be better for it. Especially with the wisdom we women in our thirties can share. You said you were thirty-six, right?" Elli heard typing on the other end of the phone and knew Rachel was pulling up her personal info on the computer. "You're a Leo. I knew it. I'm a Cancer. We are compatible."

Elli's mind was still on the bombshell news Rachel had dropped about Ben being involved in domestic violence, so she hadn't been really listening to what she said afterward. The word cancer did manage to register. "Cancer? What did you say about cancer?"

Elli felt Ben's eyes on her again. He had looked annoyed before, now he looked concerned. Why was that? She reviewed what she had just said. Did he know that Rachel was talking to him about domestic violence? He took a step toward her and wrapped his arm around Elli's waist as he tried to take the phone away from her. Elli stepped away.

"Wait," she told him, not certain what in the world had him acting so weird. "I'm talking to Rachel."

"What the hell is going on, Elli?" He insisted, tightening his hold on her. "Who has cancer?"

"Hang on, Rachel." She turned to face Ben and placed her hand on his chest. She felt his heart pounding beneath her hand. The man had gotten really upset just hearing someone he might know had cancer. Elli smiled at him hoping to ease his worry. "No one is sick," she said, her voice gentle. Rachel is talking zodiac-cancer. You know, astrology?" Her smile widened and she felt his pulse slow.

Elli's eyes softened, and Ben knew she was asking him if he was okay. Damn it, she was. How in the hell had her smile and eyes settled him so fast? It didn't make any sense. In the next moment, he felt the room fade and leave only Elli's image there, crisp and clear. He moved closer to her and hear Rachel speaking over the phone.

"Elli, how about I come by tomorrow before the movie people get into town?"

"You know about the movie people?" Elli asked, her eyes wide.

"I do work at the sheriff's office. I'm privy to all sorts of things. I don't gossip, so you don't have to worry. I'm trustworthy."

"I'm glad to hear it."

"I get off at seven a.m. Let's meet for lunch…"

"Can we do this in a few days? I'm swamped."

"Hmmm. I don't think so. Tomorrow is best. I'll meet you at the plantation. I want to get to know you before we ride in the parade on Tuesday."

"Is that this Tuesday?" Elli sighed. "Make it breakfast, and please, whatever you do, don't tell anyone about the movie shoot, especially Ruby. I know the Bienvenues are a close clan, but Ruby is unable to contain herself. She might mean well, but she's overenthusiastic. It's best she doesn't know about the movie shoot." Elli hung up and turned to Ben. He was laughing. "Did I miss something?"

"Ruby is Rachel's mother."

Elli slapped her forehead. "Of course, she is."

* * * *

Ben now stood toe-to-toe with Elli. The woman threatened to crush his world, but he was drawn to her like a moth to a light. Why in the hell was that? Why in the hell did he feel out of sorts with her tonight? Things didn't feel…normal. It had to be because he was tired, he reminded himself.

Elli bit her lower lip, twisted her hands, and shuffled her feet. "Uh…how was the ball?"

"Like every other damn one." Somehow, he backed her against the wall.

"Is that good or bad?" she asked, sounding out of breath.

He pressed his hands against the wall, one on either side of her. "I don't want to talk about the ball." He leaned toward Elli, but she put her hands on his chest.

"Wait. Stop." She was breathing hard now. "I know what's happening. I just don't think it should."

"Damn straight, it shouldn't." He grabbed Elli's hands and put them on his shoulders. He moved in closer. "Get in your fancy California car and drive away now, Elli, or it will happen."

"But you don't even like me."

"Parts of my body do. In City Slickers, Billy Crystal said, 'Women need a reason to have sex. Men just need a place.'" Elli sighed and let her head fall back a moment. It was all the time he needed. He saw the long, white line of her narrow throat and pressed his lips to hers. It was sweet, hot, and soft. His mouth fell to the rough fabric of his Saints shirt that smelled of fresh paint and hot woman. "I think he might be wrong," she whispered. "I don't need a reason right now, Ben. I simply can't resist you."

"Then, don't. Just for tonight. This one night." Elli nodded yes. Ben lifted Elli into his arms and carried her to his bed in the next room. In the dim glow from the galerie light, he gazed at her lying on his old, faded brown sheets with her bright hair curled around her head and her long, smooth legs angled to the side. His heart pounded into overdrive in his chest. He'd never seen a more sexy sight...and she was fully clothed. Her eyes were blue, piercing, and aroused. Ben yanked his shirt over his head and tossed it to the ground. Elli lifted her arms for him to come to her. Ben thought he'd died and gone to heaven.

"Just for tonight," she said as he lay beside her. "I can't promise tomorrow."

"I don't want tomorrow. Let's live in this moment." He crushed his mouth to hers and found her tongue as she slid her body on top of his. Her weight was light, but the places that made them man and woman felt heavy and hot. With the way his heart pounded, he knew his blood had to be as thick as yesterday's gumbo.

Elli slid her hands over his shoulders, in that light and heavy way that pulsed against his skin. Ben made a sound he didn't know he could make. This woman was torturing him and he didn't want her to stop. He couldn't breathe...he was breathing too much. Elli sucked in a breath and deepened the kiss, telling him without words that she felt what he felt...and wanted to feel more.

Ben slid his hands around her waist and into the loose band of her shorts. He gripped her firm, round bottom and she shivered. Never had he wanted a woman more than he wanted Elli. It scared the shit out of him. He knew he should walk away from her…from this…right now, but he didn't have the damn willpower to do so.

Ben tugged his jersey off Elli, leaving her in the snug camisole she wore beneath. He pressed his lips along her collarbone.

"That feels good," she whispered, gripping his shoulders.

Ben twisted in an easy move and was now on top of her. She was just a shadow beneath his large body and he wanted to see her long, graceful body, her alluring eyes. He supported most of his weight as he reached for the bedside lamp.

"No." Elli grabbed his hand and brought it to her mouth and began kissing his fingers. "I like being in the dark. It heightens the senses." She kissed his chest and ran her tongue over his skin. "I can taste your masculinity. Smell that great scent you carry on your skin. It's very hot."

"That's gotta be a chick thing." Ben laughed, but his body betrayed how her words had affected him as his muscles bunched and vibrated. "This, cher, is a dude thing." He grabbed her bottom tighter in his hands as his mouth and tongue trailed a path down the center of Elli's body, to a point between her breasts. She stiffened and her hands flew to the sides of his face. He expected her to push him away, but she sucked in a breath and let her hands drop to the bed. He didn't understand the hesitation. His sex-drained brain wasn't exactly capable of many thoughts, but on some level he did know it was an important surrender. It was sexy as hell and sent a charge through his already lust-heavy body.

He pushed aside the camisole fabric, his mouth closed over her left breast. "I wish I could see you."

"Just feel me," she sighed and the world eased away. She unzipped his pants and gripped him. "I feel your heat."

"Damn woman, you are killing me." Elli shoved his pants down his legs and kicked them away with her feet. Ben growled. "Elli, I need you now, cher." His words were both a statement and a question. He pressed a condom into her hand. She fumbled with it in the dark and laughed a breathy laugh at her clumsiness as she slipped it onto him. Ben's heart skipped a beat. Damn. What in the hell was that about? He felt her smiling face looking at him and was damn glad the lamp was off.

He rose on his knees above her, suddenly wanting to torture her as much as she was tormenting him. With his teeth and hands he yanked her shorts down. He kissed her smooth inner thigh, her soft knees, and her tight calves. "Oh Ben," she cried, restless beneath him. He pressed his body harder against her as he slid lower on her body, feeling the need to dominate her, control her. He ran his fingers between her toes as he kissed the instep of her foot. Elli cried out again. "Ben, I can't..." she managed, with gasping breaths. He moved up her body but Elli shoved him with all her might until he was on his back. He smiled at her and pulled her down on him.

"Then take me, cher. Take me any way you want."

And she did. She climbed on top of him and he forgot about trying to make her want him as much as he wanted her when she slowly slid her body over his thick, long arousal. Ben gritted his teeth. In the deep purple light and charcoal shadows of the dark room, he saw her full lips fall open, her head fall back and her breasts sway. "That's it," he gripped her hips to keep them from falling off of the planet.

"Oh, Ben," she cried out as an orgasm, hard and huge, tore through her. Ben flipped her onto her back and drove harder into her. While she was still falling apart, he did, too.

"Forget this," he said, falling back onto the bed, pulling her on top of him and caressing her bottom. "This isn't just for tonight. This is until the day you drive away, headed back to California."

Chapter Eight

Have you ever considered just how outstanding the nurses, doctors and support staff are that work with us cancer patients? They love us and care for us in such an intimate way, not knowing if we will live or die. Their hearts must constantly be breaking, yet, they smile and laugh and make us feel special. Here is a shout out to my medical team...my friends! Thank you, Jenny, Doe, BJ, Donna, Sonya, Raul, Bob, Jeffery, Harry, and all the rest I couldn't name here, but whose names are forever written on my heart! I love you all! I wish you good health, E.

Bosom Blog Buddies Post

Elli's face pressed into Ben's pillow, only her left cheek and pouty lips showing. Her smooth, white, shapely, naked derriere peeked from his brown sheets. The woman could inspire artists, Ben thought, wishing he could paint or at least had a camera. Damn. If he didn't want her out of his life so much, he might consider letting her hang around for a while. Damn shame, life was so damn complicated.

The sun was just starting to come up, its dim light casting a pink glow through the split in his curtains. Ben slipped on his sweatpants and looked at his cell phone clock. Five thirty? It was too early for the sun to be that bright. Ben remembered not turning the light off on the galerie the night before and smiled. He had had other things on his mind. As he recalled, he had it on his mind three more times after that. Damn, what a night. He stretched his arms over his head, feeling the sweet ache of muscles used in good sex. Elli was a surprise there. The woman didn't hold back.

Ben walked into the hall and flicked off the light switch to the galerie. He returned to his bedroom and found the light through the curtain was dimmer, but there was still that odd pink glow. "What the hell is going on?" He walked to the window, opened it, and stepped outside. "Merde…Elli!" Several crows near the bayou squawked from his shouting and took flight. He poked his head through the open window. "Crocifissa," he called in a loud but controlled tone. Elli's head popped up. Her short hair was a mass of blond curls sticking out at odd angles on her head. She rubbed her eyes and looked at him. He crooked his finger to her. "Can you step outside?"

Elli sighed. "No. I know what you want, Ben." She dropped her head onto the pillow, tugged the sheet over her exposed bottom, and lifted her hand. "Talk to the hand."

Ben stepped into the room and plopped on the side of the bed. "Are you kidding me? Pink? Hot pink?"

"It's hideous. I know." She rolled onto her back, keeping the sheets covering her. "Tante Izzy thinks it's grand. Don't be surprised if she paints her house that awful color."

"Do you know how many coats of paint it'll take to cover that crap? It'll eat up all of your profits." He tugged on the sheet, but Elli tugged back.

"Mine? It's a fifty-fifty split, remember?"

"Extra expenses come out of your share. Remember?" He kissed her shoulder and drew a circle around the spot with the tip of his finger. Elli's eyes fluttered. His heart began to pound. Damn, the woman didn't know how powerful her surrender was. He sure as hell wasn't going to tell her. He kissed her right breast through the sheet and went to pull it away, but Elli held on tight to it. "What's wrong, cher? I've seen you naked already, why are you shy now?"

She smiled, but Ben could see the worry in her eyes. What was wrong? She didn't mind him touching her. She liked it and encouraged it during their lovemaking. He stroked her exposed arm as he would one of his nervous animals. She closed her eyes and sighed. The woman sure as hell liked it.

"I'm sorry," she began. "I have issues. They shouldn't be your issues. This," she circled her hand above her chest, "is my Kryptonite. We are going to be together such a short time; there isn't any need to waste our time with Kryptonite issues. It's way too heavy and not fun to deal with. Just accept this," she waved her hand over her chest again, "quirk of mine. We'll both be happier if you do."

"Hmm." He smiled. "A Superman reference. If I didn't want a superficial relationship, I know there would be something really interesting to explore." Elli shrugged and Ben knew he was right.

"Let's just be like our dogs and live in the moment."

"Will you wag your tail when I enter the room, cher?"

She laughed a full laugh that squeezed his chest so tight that Ben thought he might be having a heart attack. "Yes, at the end or beginning of the day, in a dark room, with no one around to discover us." Ben tucked a wild curl behind her ear. "That's what you want too, right?"

Of course, it was what he wanted. He nodded, but the tightness in his chest gripped him again.

"Good," she said, too brightly. "We'll be superficial, covert and…" she sat up holding the sheet against her Kryptonite, "hot."

As she moved closer to kiss him, the sheet slipped under her right breast. She didn't notice it but Ben did. As he kissed her, he saw a flash of her plump exposed breast. It had a light pink scar along the outer slope with a small indention beneath it. It looked like the same kind of injury he'd seen on his dogs that were in a fight and had healed after a piece of flesh had been removed. Was it a birth defect? From an accident? Surgery? Attack? What the hell happened to her, he wondered. He deepened the kiss and pressed her back into the mattress. This obviously was the Kryptonite she spoke of. He'd respect her request to not discuss it. Why would he want to anyway? It seemed like it held both physical and mental scars they had no business exploring together. That was reserved for long-term relationships, not a fling like theirs.

Elli grumbled and broke the kiss. "Donna's up."

Ben dropped his forehead to hers. He hadn't heard the tiny fur princess, but he heard her funny yap now. "Figures. Just when things were getting nice and superficial, covert and hot."

"You know, Donna's going to be furious with me," Elli said, standing. She was careful to keep the sheet wrapped around her body. "She's in love with you. If she knows what we did in here, she'll have her pound of flesh—mine, not yours."

"I'll take her out," Ben said, running his finger along the top edge of the sheet, over her round, perky breasts. "You know my mouth was on every inch of your body. I'm not afraid of your Kryptonite. It's yours, not mine. You can let that sheet drop."

"I like having you think of me the way I look in the dark. It's my best lighting."

He tapped her on the tip of her nose. "Before I walk out of here, I want to make sure you are clear on a couple of things. One." He lifted a finger. "Last night did not and will not sway me regarding our impasse with the plantation." He held up a second finger. "Two. I'm going back on my word." He stood. "And I'm not holding you to yours." He smiled. "Last night wasn't our only night together, cher. I'm not done with you."

"Oh no, Ben. We agreed." Her eyes were wide, worry brightening them.

Ben shrugged his shoulders and left, deciding he wasn't giving her a choice in the matter.

* * * *

The morning erupted into chaos early and Elli was grateful for it. She didn't have a chance to dwell on her amazing night with Ben and how she had let her guard down with him. She had thought about it long enough while showering and concluded that it began when she gained confidence knowing her scars were hidden in the darkness of the room, but it turned into something more when she allowed his mouth on her breasts. The surgeries had left the area numb, but having him in her personal space, in an intimate way, had her wanting to draw him nearer. The focus on her body had nothing to do with cancer, radiation, and medical concerns. Her body was being explored for pleasure between a man and woman. It felt so normal, so wonderful. . .so healthy. She had tested her sexuality since all the scars changed her body, but this was different. It was much more intense. Real. Ben wanted her in his bed. She wanted that, too. It was just a physical thing. Yet, somewhere in the recesses of her brain where she allowed the thought to flourish for five seconds, she wished it could be more. Stupid girl.

A horn blew and Elli jumped out of her thoughts and back to the busy day. She had managed to change her breakfast meeting with Rachel to a quick coffee after lunch. It was a good thing she had, because the first of the production crew arrived in an eighteen-wheeler at 8:00 a.m. sharp. Elli directed them to park on a side road in the cane field, on the northern side of the plantation. Ben had picked up Joey and Lucky from Helen's, and when they returned to the plantation, the sweet boy asked to hang out with Elli. Ben reluctantly agreed, giving Elli a stern warning to keep an eye on him. He had his loyal chaperone join them, trusting the quirky looking animal with the short legs to keep an eye on his son. Elli guessed she understood why he would trust his dog more than her.

She enjoyed Joey's company, and he seemed to enjoy himself in the ensuing chaos when two more eighteen-wheelers loaded with equipment arrived an hour later. Three motor homes for the actors and director arrived with them. Soon, Sugar Mill was buzzing with production staff and security. Elli was rushing around, directing everyone where to set up the backstage gear and where to set up security. At 10:45, her phone rang, and Joey pulled it from her back pocket to answer it.

"Hi, Dad," he said, his voice bright. "She's right here, telling the man where to put the port-a-potties." He laughed and tapped Elli on the arm. "My dad wants to talk to you."

Elli smiled. "Thanks. Hello Ben, what's up?"

"I want them all to stay the hell away from my dogs and my kennel. That's what's up. The Texians are disrupting our training session." His tone was back to the pre-fantastic sex anger. Elli didn't want to be hurt by it, but she was. Nothing had changed between them and it was crazy for her to think it had. They had made an agreement that they would have a superficial, one-night affair. It was unfair for her—and for him—to expect anything more. They had very different agendas, which was clear in Ben's tone. "The dogs are in a frenzy. Those movie people are sightseeing in my kennel. I have work to do. Get them out of here or I'll evict them."

"I will." Elli shoved the phone back into her pocket. She looked at Joey and shrugged her shoulders. He slipped his hand into hers, and her heart felt three sizes larger.

"He doesn't like anybody to bother him when he's training the dogs," Joey said. Elli was touched by his loyalty to his father and his concern for her feelings. She kissed him on the cheek.

"Thank you for explaining that to me. Let's see if we can make sure no one disturbs him."

Elli, Joey and Lucky met with the director. She explained, again, that there was a working kennel on the property and it had to remain off limits to the cast and crew, no matter how cute the dogs were. He agreed, but to make sure everyone listened, Elli and her small entourage drove to the kennel to talk to the security guards that were hired by the production company. They were stationed at the main gate. She gave them instructions to chase anyone other than Sugar Mill Kennel staff away from the kennel. Once they finished that task, they went to the kennel office to tell Ben. As soon as they entered the office, Lucky went straight for his bed near the desk. Camille was holding a large German Shepherd on the examining table as Ben was looking at a slide under a microscope. The dog looked at Elli and began to growl. Of course he did, she thought, feeling out of place. Joey walked to the dog in a smooth, easy gait. The animal didn't mind his approach. Joey smiled at Camille and Elli felt a tweak of jealousy.

"Hello, Doc," Elli said, walking into the medical room. It smelled like a dirty dog with digestive problems. Her eyes began to burn and water. She covered her hand over her mouth, but not before gagging. Camille looked at her with a satisfied smile, and Elli tried to pretend it didn't bother her. "Not enough sick humans in Cane to fill office hours?" So much for pretending.

"I took off this morning, knowing Ben and I would have a late night at the ball." She smiled possessively at Ben. "And I was right. My feet are still protesting all the dancing we did."

Elli gagged again, then pinched her nose. The dog was still growling at her, so she stayed near the door, not that she could get closer to the stinky animal if she wanted. She'd be sick for sure. "Ben,

I know you're busy but I wanted to discuss security with you for a minute."

He looked up from the slide, opened an upper cabinet, and retrieved a huge, brown tablet from a medicine bottle. He pried open the dog's mouth, shoved the tablet in, and lifted the dog into his arms. He carried the shepherd to a pen along the back wall. After securing the dog inside, he walked to the sink to wash his hands. Camille joined him at the sink to wash her hands.

"I'll wait for you in your office," Elli told him, fighting the urge to throw up. She walked away, grateful her weak stomach kept her from witnessing any possible tender exchange between the Doc and Ben. "Oh God," she whispered, suddenly realizing she had allowed herself to be the other woman last night. Ben and Camille were the perfect couple, and she had sex with another woman's man. Why hadn't she thought of that last night? How could she have been so selfish? So dishonorable?

Elli walked to the window near the front door and looked out. Her heart felt heavy but her head told her she hadn't done anything wrong. She didn't have to rush to church to try to save her soul, just yet. Ben and Camille might be perfectly matched for one another, but they weren't a committed couple. Hadn't Ruby and others indicated that? It was clear that was where they were headed, but they weren't there yet. Still, did that make it okay for her to have sex with Ben?

Camille walked out of the treatment room ahead of Ben. She smiled at him as she walked to the door to leave. "If you need any more help with the shepherd, call me." She waved a friendly good-bye to Elli, but her eyes didn't match the amicable gesture. They seemed almost sad as she closed the door behind her.

"Can I bring these to the Newfies?" Joey asked his father as he walked out of the treatment room with a handful of treats. When Ben told him yes, Joey rushed out of the office to the dogs across the street in the training yard.

"Ben, should I feel guilty about what happened last night because of you and Camille?" Elli began, once they were alone.

"Nope." He sat at his desk and typed something into his laptop computer before placing a sheet of paper into a file on his desk.

She walked to the desk to stand in front of him. "I don't want to be the other woman."

"Elli, I don't do other women. I'm a single guy, free to be with whom I choose." He rolled down the sleeves of his denim shirt. "I guess you have a right to know about Camille and me," he added, looking at her. "We are not lovers. Never were." Elli exhaled and relaxed in the chair near the desk. "What did you come here to talk to me about?

"I spoke to the head of security." She crossed her legs, then noticed Ben's eyes look down at them. She hated to admit it, but it pleased her that he seemed to like what he was looking at even though they were covered in denim. "He'll have the guard at the gate watch for any cast or crew wandering around the kennel. He'll also post keep out signs along the perimeter fence."

"Good."

"Did you change the gate code like I asked? We can't have any well-meaning family coming onto the property while the stars are here or while they are filming."

"I took care of it." At that moment, a loud truck came to a screeching halt in front of Ben's office. The door flew open seconds later and Tante Izzy walked in. Elli shot Ben a look. So much for changing the code and security.

"I hope I'm not late fer cast call," she said. Elli covered her grin. She was wearing tan face foundation, two shades too dark, that settled in the deep creases of her cheeks. Her eyes were bright and dramatic with pale blue eye shadow coloring her lids. Her lips would've been a perfect shade of pink pansy had it not been in high gloss. As anyone who knew Tante Izzy would expect, her clothes matched the drama of her makeup. She wore dark denim overalls with a red and white checkered blouse beneath it and the white rubber shrimp boots that Jenny liked so much.

"Ready to work in the cane fields?" Ben asked, getting up to kiss her hello.

She shook her head and waved her hand. "Mais non. Dis is cuz da movie is set on a Georgia farm. Dis is farm clothes."

Ben slapped his forehead. "Yes, of course. That is the official uniform of Georgians. I should've known as soon as you walked through the door. Pardon." Tante Izzy smiled.

"Hello, Tante Izzy," Elli said with a big smile. "If you don't mind me asking, how did you get through the security guards at the gate? They have instructions not to let anyone enter without my clearance."

"Dem guards?" She waved a dismissive hand in the air. "I gave dem some pain perdu. Dey were good and happy 'bout it, too. After dat, I just drove right in."

Elli laughed. "I bet they were. Do you have any for me?" Elli looked at Ben. "Us?"

Tante Izzy looked at Elli a moment, then at Ben. "Comment ça, 'us'?"

"There is no 'us,'" Ben told his aunt in a tone that said the subject was closed. He looked at Elli. "Doesn't look like your security is too efficient. I really don't give a damn about it, other than I want them to keep all those Texian movie people away from my dogs, my kennel, and me. I have work to do. Don't make me regret agreeing to let this movie thing come to Sugar Mill. I'm already mostly there."

"Mais, youz sound like a man with cock-a-burs caught between his toes." She looked at Elli. "When youz are goin' to stop dancin' round each other and do what's goin' to be done anyway?"

Ben walked to Tante Izzy and kissed her on top of her head. "Mind your own business." He walked to a coffeepot on a small cart near his desk.

"All da Bienvenues are my business. I'm da oldest, so dat makes me da matriarch."

"I thought that made you queen," Ben teased.

"I waz queen before I waz da oldest. I waz born dat way."

Elli laughed and looked at Ben, who was smiling. He glanced at her and something nice and friendly passed between them. Ben's eyes didn't look hostile, angry, or resigned. He looked at her like a man who liked the woman he saw. Elli's heart began to thud. If Tante Izzy hadn't been around, she would have kissed him soundly on his beautiful mouth and thanked him for it. The pressure of dealing with a man who hated her was very difficult. This was much better.

"Mon dieu. Youz two are circlin' the truth like buzzards spottin' road kill." Tante Izzy rolled her eyes and Ben frowned. Elli looked at her feet. "I'm goin' to a Traiteur and get some love juice to make youz stop fightin' what youz want."

"Traiteur?" Elli said, massacring the Cajun word by putting the accent on the beginning instead of at the end of the word.

"Witch doctor," Ben clarified.

"No. She's a Cajun healer." Tante Izzy looked at Elli. "Don't listen to him. Traiteurs are holy peoples. She gots rid of my coup de soleil 'bout four years ago."

"She had sunstroke," Ben translated for Elli.

"And she healed Ruby of da scars on her back from la mal anglais."

Elli looked at Ben waiting for the translation. "The shingles."

Elli nodded. "Impressive." She stood and walked to the door. She had a full day ahead, and she didn't have time for this interesting but useless conversation. "Thank you for your interest in Ben and me. We don't need a tray-tour. We aren't circling anything like buzzards. We are just trying to find a way to deal with an impossible will…Ben's and the one Rosa left us."

Tante Izzy snorted. "I'm no fool, but it sounds like youz are."

Elli turned to Ben and shrugged. He shrugged back at her. "I've got to get back to the film crew before they decide to paint something else pink. Call me if Joey wants to hang out with me again." She turned to Tante Izzy. "You can come with me now if you want. I'll drive my car. Leave your truck here."

"You'z so bossy sometime," Tante Izzy complained. "I don't know if I want to get you da love potion."

"Good. I don't want it."

* * * *

The day was fading, with only about forty-five minutes of daylight left when Ben, Joey and Lucky got out of the truck down the road from the plantation. There were two young men who wouldn't let them drive any closer, but Ben kept his annoyance over that to himself. Joey was bright-eyed and excited at seeing the cameramen perched twenty feet in the air behind huge cameras on narrow bucket lifts. It looked like they were filming something along the front side of the plantation house.

Instead of going into the kitchen through the rear entrance, Joey convinced Ben to walk around to the front to see what was going on there. As they got closer to the lifts, a young, college-age girl in pigtails, stringy jean shorts and UCLA sweatshirt raced toward them. She had her finger over her mouth. "We're filming talent on the upper balcony," she said, her voice low but not quite a whisper. "It's just for some cutaways, no audio. Still, the director likes things quiet so the talent can hear his directions."

Ben nodded, not really interested in what she was explaining. He just wanted to get inside his house and fix something to eat. He supposed if he was being honest, there was something exciting about having all of this commotion on the plantation and having a few megawatt stars there. That kind of excitement, he figured, would wear off in about twenty minutes. Maybe, a little longer for Joey, who was especially interested in the cameramen.

"You see how the camera on the right is following the man actor and the one on the left is following the girl actress?" Joey whispered to his father. Ben nodded, looking where his son was pointing. "The third camera must be getting both of them. It's cool how they are all crowded up there and they don't film the other cameraman. They know how to stay out of each other's way, huh?"

"I hadn't noticed," Ben told his son, meaning it. He had little interest in the making of a movie, but it was clear that Joey did.

Joey remained quiet, at Ben's side, but continued craning his neck to get a look at what was happening. Ben scanned the couple of dozen or so people scattered around the front lawn and spotted his cousin Rachel. He wasn't surprised to see her standing in her Saturday night best near one of the crew members. He was surprised to see that she was writing on a yellow tablet, as if she was his secretary taking dictation. Elli was responsible for that, no doubt.

"Look, there she is," Joey said, smiling. "There's Elli." He pointed to where she was taking a drink from a bottle of water under a tent. He ran toward her, and Ben was surprised his son was more interested in Elli than the moviemaking business. He probably had a crush on her. Ben supposed he didn't blame him, with the way she smiled at him all the time and the way she boosted his confidence by asking him for advice about her stubborn dogs. When Ben and Lucky reached his son, he was chattering away with Elli. Chattering. How crazy was that? Joey never chattered. He was quiet. Not much of a talker. Who was this child? Joey's enthusiasm even make Lucky excited. He wagged his tail and looked up at Joey with her tongue hanging to the side of mouth.

"And Coon, the Newfie with the raccoon face, tugged on Jenny's tail so hard he began to drag her backward," Joey said, laughing. "Jenny didn't try to stop him either. She just let him pull her backward until they both were in the bayou. Can you believe it?"

"Jenny is so nonconfrontational," Elli laughed. "And she probably wanted to be in the water anyway. I know now that's because, as you taught me, she is part Lab."

"Labrador retrievers love the water as much as Newfies." Joey reached for a doughnut on the table, and before Ben could stop him, Elli grabbed his hand, gently moved him away, and walked to an ice chest, opening it.

"Are you thirsty? We have water and juice in here." She grabbed a bottle of water and offered it to Ben as Joey dug in the ice chest.

"Thanks," Ben said.

Joey took a grape juice box and stabbed the straw into the top as he spoke. "And, oh, did you hear about Doe?"

"No. What about Doe?" Elli looked at Ben. "Is she okay?"

"Yeah, she's fine," Ben said. "Doug's got a little gash in his thigh, though."

"Doe bit him," Joey said, jumping up and down. "Grandpa said he just walked into his yard where she was penned, and she rushed up to him and bit him."

"Oh no." Elli looked at Ben again. "Doe's mischievous and awfully noisy with her funny howling, but she wouldn't harm a flea."

"Doug would differ," Ben said, although he had been surprised to hear she had bit Doug.

"Is he okay? Did the bite break the skin?" Elli asked and Ben was bothered by her concern for his father-in-law. The cozy scene in his office still didn't set well with him.

"Yeah, she broke the skin, but it wasn't deep. He's fine. Getting bitten is a professional hazard." Ben took a long sip of his water. Elli's eyes remained on his mouth a long time, and Ben's body responded immediately. Damn but the woman's eyes were easy to read.

Elli reached up and gently touched the two tiny scars bisecting his upper lip. "Is that what happened to your lips? Were you bitten?" She dropped her hand as if just realizing she was breaking the covert rule they established.

"That was when he was a little boy," Joey interjected. Ben mussed his son's hair. "Younger than me. Tell her how the wild swamp dogs attacked you in the woods on the other side of the bayou and how you had to fight them off with a piece of dead wood." Joey looked at Elli. "He was hurt and bleeding and had to spend the night in the woods, not knowing if the dogs would come back. They bit him like ten times. Tante Izzy thinks the Lutins kept the dogs away, even though they usually just cause trouble and don't help anyone."

"Lutins," Ben said, his voice even, "are the mischievous spirits of babies who have died before they were baptized."

Elli seemed to not have heard him. Her eyes didn't dance with humor at hearing supernatural babies protected him in the swamp. Her eyes were gentle and looking right into his. "You must have been frightened," she said in a voice so soft, it felt like a whisper intended only for him to hear.

"I was a child. Yeah, I was scared. I managed to find my way out in the morning." He tossed the empty water bottle into the recycling box. "My mom and dad hadn't realized I was missing. My mom was…unaware. My father wasn't home. It was Tante Izzy who actually found me on the back porch around lunchtime. She took me to the Traiteur to get stitched."

"I'm so sorry," she said, and her three words sent a rush of heat through him. He knew, deep in that place where you know things, that she really meant it and cared. He was beginning to think she might understand what it was like to be young, frightened, and alone. Before he said something stupid or acted on that odd feeling, they were interrupted.

"Elli," the girl with the pigtails began. "They are ready to shoot Izzy's scene with Sam. She asked me to make sure you were there to watch. She's coming out of makeup now."

Ben began to laugh. "I knew she'd get in the movie, and with the star, no less."

"Yeah, but did you know that she has a current SAG card?" Elli laughed when he just stared at her like a deer caught in the headlights. "It seems she has had one since she was an extra in the 1958 Elvis Presley movie, King Creole." Ben shook his head. "It is quite a story. You might want to hear it someday when you have time. A lot of time."

"Elvis Presley?" Ben laughed. "Figures." He looked to where the director was standing near a camera. "I'm surprised Rachel didn't talk you into being in the movie, too."

Elli smiled. "Actually, Rachel has a very important job. She's now the local location liaison. She showed up at just the right time to help the location director and scene director find some things they need locally."

"Well, Rachel knows just about everything there is to know about Cane."

"Look, there's Tante Izzy with Sam," Elli said as they walked toward the bayou where the scene was to be filmed. "She's playing his grandmother." Elli smiled. "She hands him a glass of lemonade while he's sitting on the wharf. He's just returned from war."

"She makes the best lemonade," Joey announced. "It's the really yellow kind."

Ben, Elli, Joey and Lucky stopped to stand behind the cameras set up near the wharf. One camera was out of the shot of the other two, on the other side of the bayou and to the left. Another camera, Joey pointed out, was on a track so it could move around the actors. A fourth was stationary and closest to the wharf.

"You've got to appreciate her tenacity," Ben said, looking at the woman who was more mother to him than his own mother was. She walked to the wharf, wearing a modest, old-fashioned, pale yellow, cotton dress. She had a white apron tied around what normally was a skinny waist. Today, she looked plumper.

"She looks fat," Joey said, loud enough for Tante Izzy to hear, and she gave him a narrow-eyed look.

"Dis here is a costume, young man," Tante Izzy said. "Youz best know the difference. I'z got the figure of a thirty-year-old." She then turned toward the megastar, Sam Cooper, with sweet, twinkling eyes. Ben heard her tell him that she had the same body as his last supermodel girlfriend, only in petite size. Elli heard her say it, too, and covered her laughter with her hand, turning away from Tante Izzy, trying not to offend her.

"She's something." Elli smiled as they settled a little distance away from the filming, near a huge oak tree. There, they could still see the action but be out of the way. "Was my Aunt Rosa like her? Funny, eccentric, endearing."

Ben leaned against the centuries-old oak planted by the first Bienvenu to settle in Louisiana after the journey from France. Joey sat with Lucky on the ground a few feet away, closer to the action. He was engrossed in what each crew member was doing.

"That's a tough one," Ben began, with a slight nod. "I'm not sure I can give you a fair assessment of your aunt. I'm still ticked off at what she did. Maybe there was a time I would've said she was fun and loyal and smart. She did me a favor by encouraging me to start the kennel business." He paused to gather his thoughts. "Rosa was devoted to my father, that's for sure. It wasn't easy for her to be labeled as my dad's mistress, especially when my mother was so good at playing the victim. Rosa didn't seem to let it bother her. She was a confident woman, happy with her role as the fallen woman. I think the bottom line was that Rosa did what Rosa wanted. She wasn't conventional and she wanted the life she had here."

"I'm unclear as to why Rosa lived on the plantation and not your mother. It seems odd since she was still married to your father."

"It's a twisted tale, Elli." He wasn't comfortable with exposing his parents' broken lives, despite the fact that all of Cane knew it.

"I could get Rachel to tell me." She smiled. "She likes to talk about family...and astrology. I'm not certain which she finds more interesting." She looked him directly in the eyes. "She will not, however, talk about you, Ben. Why is that?"

"She knows she'll be tortured if she breaks her oath of silence." He grinned, but Elli just stared at him with a tight, serious expression. The woman acted fearless around him, yet, right now, he thought he saw a hint of fear in her eyes.

"Unlike her mother," Elli continued, looking away, "Rachel has restraint. I guess that's why she works as a nine-one-one operator. She hears a lot of personal things about a lot of people." Elli paused, and Ben got the feeling she was waiting for him to say something. When he didn't, she continued. "I know Tante Izzy would tell me about your history if I asked. I'd rather hear your version."

Ben ran his hand through his hair again. "I don't think it's any of your business, but it's not a secret." He exhaled. "My mother married my father for his money, prominence, and family name. When she got all of what she thought she wanted, it wasn't enough. She wanted more. A fancier car, bigger jewelry, a higher social position. She was obsessed with it to the point that she forgot about everything else in her life, including her husband and only child. The plantation home was drafty and old, and she wanted new and shiny. My dad built her a fancy mansion near the country club she was so fond of. He used this plantation as a retreat house for him and, for a long time, me. We moved out when I was twelve, so I was a teenager when we'd come here to hunt and fish and have what he liked to call testosterone weekends. I loved it. I felt like a big man. Even though my mom was getting everything she thought she wanted, she started to drink...a lot. My dad, miserable, lonely, and unable to satisfy his wife, turned to another woman. Was it right? Hell no. Why in the hell they didn't divorce beats me. I think it was because my mom didn't want to give up on the dream. I think divorce seemed too much trouble for my father. I guess being Catholic when divorce was taboo for their generation played into it, too. One thing led to another, and soon, Rosa was living on the plantation. She encouraged me to open the kennel on the property. I did. My father seemed the happiest I'd ever seen him and my mother seemed...well, relieved." He nodded. "She preferred to be left alone, to be a quiet drunk and the richest woman in three parishes. We all learned to not talk about the dysfunction stuff and just move on."

"That's so sad. You were lost in the void between your parents' self-centered lives. That was unfair to you." Elli touched his hand, but he pulled away. He didn't want her pity or empathy. He sat on the ground and she sat next to him.

"Greed, lack of discipline, and selfishness are not in short supply in this world," Ben said, his voice was even but the intensity of his eyes matched the power of his words. "You have to stay focused on what's important to you and work to get it; otherwise, you'll get sucked up by the bad stuff."

"I think we share the same philosophy, despite having completely opposite upbringings. I think we just have to do what Will Smith said in Hitch—'Begin each day like it was on purpose.' That way, we don't forget and we don't fail."

Ben could see she wanted to say more. She probably wanted to tell him something personal about herself to make her point, but he didn't want to hear it. He already knew too much about her. He didn't need to know anything more. Especially if it was something that would make him like her a little bit more. He already liked her too much. He liked her and he hated her. He didn't need to have either feeling as far as he was concerned. They had been strangers a week ago, and they would be strangers again. They didn't need a relationship other than the physical one they captured in private hours. Elli had a natural charm, and his family seemed to really like her. Joey was crazy about her. Hell, he knew why she was such a successful producer. He'd be damned if she used her skills to tug at his emotions to try to manipulate him.

"Elli, I've grown weary of this conversation. If you want to talk all this chick stuff, find some woman who gives a shit." His words were said in even tones but meant to offend her so she'd leave him the hell alone. When he looked at her to see if he'd hit the mark, her eyes crinkled, and she had a Mona Lisa smile on her flushed face. "You don't have the good sense to know when you've been insulted." More to the truth, the woman saw right through him. That was far worse and it made him damn uncomfortable.

"Grrr," she said wrinkling her mouth. "All bark and no bite. You're like Jenny. You make a big fuss when you're scared. And Ben Bienvenu, you are scared."

"I'll show you my bite if you keep trying to corner me, cher. Then we'll see who's scared." He flicked a fly off his knee before crossing his arms over his chest, over the heart he'd never admit was pounding hard against his ribs. Elli sighed and leaned back against the old oak. "I don't think we are communicating."

"'What we have here is a failure to communicate,'" she said smiling. "That's my favorite line from Cool Hand Luke." She sighed. "Look Ben, we are communicating just fine. We both just don't like what the other is saying about what to do with the plantation." Ben knew she was right. "There's got to be a compromise we can reach, an escape clause to find, a…something to get us out of the ridiculous terms of the will." Elli looked heavenward. "Why did you do this to us, Aunt Rosa?" She turned to face Ben. "Do you have any idea?"

"Hell if I know. It's damn frustrating to have the money to buy you out, but not be able to do it." He stood. "I shouldn't have to share my family home and family legacy with a stranger."

"Hmm." She sighed. "Aunt Rosa had to know you felt that way." She looked away. "And she hardly knew me or made an attempt to have a relationship with me. So why involve me in your life? Why give me such a complicated gift?" She stood. "I know this was done with intent, but I wonder if it's something I'll ever figure out, since I hardly knew her. She's a mystery to me." She looked away. "All I do know is what I want and need."

Ben looked at her. He didn't have to ask her what she wanted. That was clear. She had made it clear. She wanted to sell the plantation and make it a freakin' movie studio. She had already begun that process by getting the movie crew there less than a week after arriving. Damn, but she was good at manipulating things. How in the hell had he let her do that? She made a logical pitch and the money was good. Hell, it had made sense at the time. Selling the plantation never made sense to him. Never would.

"You know, Elli." He looked her dead in the eyes. "You can't have what you want. I won't let you. I don't care how good the sex is, it ain't happening."

Elli stared right back at him. "You have no idea what I want or what I'm willing to do to get it or why I'm willing to fight for it." She poked him in the chest. "So, back off. I'm not like your momma or Rosa or anyone else that skewed your image of women. I have my own history and experiences that bring me to the point I am in my life. I don't want your money—"

"Just my plantation," he interrupted. "Same thing."

"Quiet on the set," a deep, masculine voice shouted, ending their conversation. It was perfect timing as far as Ben was concerned. He had said enough. Now, Miss Movie Producer understood he would never change his mind. What she didn't know was that another woman had nearly succeeded in taking away what was his. His wife, Sarah. He had thought he loved her, and that she loved him, and he fell into her manipulative plot. She was like his mother, only worse. He had made the same mistake his father had. Never again would that happen. Lesson learned. He and Elli would be physical and have their fling, but never would he allow her to get close enough to him to wreck his life as his deceased wife had.

Chapter Nine

In response to the post from —JerseyGirlHairless55…Mourn the loss of your hair for an hour or two or three. Then, shave what wisps are hanging on and be done with it. It's time to adjust your perspective on going bald. Losing your hair is a positive, visible sign the meds are actually running through your body doing their job! If it is destroying your beautiful robust Jersey girl hair follicle cells, then why can't it be doing the same to the nasty cancer cells?!!! It's only hair—the baldness is a temporary thing…and you are here to fight another day!! Redefine the Jersey-girl big-hair cliché'…Maybe you will have Snookie considering a new-do when she sees how fab you look…Bald is beautiful! And, if you hate it, there are amazing wigs that will make your Jersey Girl soul happy. I wish you good health, E.

Bosom Blog Buddies Post

Elli parked her car in front of Doug's cottage, anxious to get her dogs and head back to the house to go to sleep. The argument with Ben weighed heavily on her mind all evening, and she had a headache from trying to think of a way out of their impasse. On top of that, the director worked everyone until eight thirty. She met with the location producer for about fifteen minutes after they called it a wrap for the night and discussed what Sugar Mill needed to do to make the second and final shoot-day run smoothly for both the movie crew and Ben. He told Elli there was a 5:00 a.m. call and 6:00 a.m. start. She had to be there before that to make sure Sugar Mill's interests were looked after.

Jenny, Doe, and BJ started barking as soon as she got out of her car. A few other dogs barked in the distance. Instead of going straight to Doug in the cottage, she walked around the side to greet her dogs.

They were in the larger of the two fenced yards, turning in circles, jumping and nipping excitedly at each other.

"My, aren't you girls happy to see me." Elli laughed, spotted their leashes hanging on the fence, and grabbed one of them. "Who wants to be first?" Doe pushed forward ahead of the others as Elli nudged past the gate without fully opening it. She knew from experience that would be a mistake. Doe and Jenny were in a cooperative mood and she leashed them without a fuss. BJ wasn't as willing. She darted away to the back of the yard where it angled behind the cottage. She slid behind a large water trough. "I'm not in the mood for this, BJ. Please have mercy on me."

BJ put her front paws on the trough and sat. When Elli approached her, she darted to the corner and went beneath a blue tarp.

"Don't think I won't climb under there to get you." She hooked Jenny and Doe's leashes to the water spigot before dropping to her knees. She lifted the edge of the tarp and nearly fell back. There was a powerful odor under there that struck with such force, her eyes began to water and her throat seized into coughs. "Oh my God. Get out of there. BJ come here now." Elli patted the ground next to her. Come on, girl." BJ sat next to a pallet of two hip-high stacks of bags, her nose continued to twitch in the air. Elli covered her own nose and mouth with the collar of her shirt as she kept the edge of the tarp lifted. From the illumination of the flood light nearby, she was able to read the tops of some of the stacked bags—perlite soil and humus. She doubted those were what smelled so badly. She suspected it was either something else stacked nearby or what was in the large, rectangular, plastic container with a round cylinder duct-taped to its side. "BJ, out," she said in her firmest voice. Jenny and Doe started barking and howling, and Elli stood, dropping the tarp back into place. "What are you girls' problem?"

"Elli? Is that you?" Doug walked from around the corner of the house. He had a pistol in his hand but immediately tucked it into his waistband.

"You have my permission to shoot these noisy dogs, especially the one under there." Elli pointed to the tarp. "Why do these three dogs insist on making my life so difficult? I just want to take them home and go to sleep."

Doug smiled as he walked to the tarp, whistling once and calling BJ's name. The frustrating animal walked out as if she was the most well-mannered creature on earth. Elli latched the leash to her collar.

"Thank you." She untangled the leashes for the other two dogs who were still barking at Doug. "That's enough. Quiet. You know this man. He feeds you, for goodness' sake. Doug, I'm sorry."

"No problem." He touched the small of Elli's back and led her toward the gate. She didn't sense that he was making a pass with the gesture, but still felt uncomfortable. "You might want to let me know before you wander around on my property next time. I'm packing heat, you know."

"Sorry. It's late. I didn't want to bother you." Elli smiled, noticing Doug's slight limp. "Are you okay? I heard that Doe bit you. I wouldn't have ever expected it of her."

"I'm fine. Dogs can be like people and just have a bad day. Don't worry about it." He let her and the dogs move through the gate first and then, with his hand still on the small of Elli's back, led her to her car. He seemed to be in as much of a hurry for her to leave as she was to leave. Doug opened the car door and helped put the dogs into the backseat.

"Tomorrow is the last day for the shoot," she offered. "I'm sorry some of the crew has been so disruptive to the dogs at the kennel."

"I got a kick out of some of them. Reminded me of my hippie days." He nodded and blew out a breath. "The fire marshal stopped by today. He wanted me to tell him what kids I saw loitering on the property." He shook his head. "I just can't do it."

Elli stood next to the car. "It's a tough position to be in, Doug, but you don't want to go to jail because of it. If the kids are innocent, there won't be a problem. If they are guilty, then they need to face the consequences of their actions. Either way, you can't withhold information from the law. No one will think less of you for being a law-abiding citizen."

"Still feels wrong."

Elli heard faint voices in the distance and figured it was the guards stationed near the front gate. "I expect Mr. Cammer will contact me soon, too. He said it would only take a few days to get the pictures on my camera processed in the forensic lab. That is, if it's even retrievable."

Doug didn't respond. He just looked at her. Elli turned to her car. The sound of voices grew louder, but she still didn't see anyone. "Is that the guards I hear?"

He shook his head as if he didn't know. He opened her car door and Doe began to bark. "You better go before they eat the interior of your car."

"Shh. Quiet Doe." Elli closed the door. She lowered the window to talk to Doug. "Thanks for your help with them, and Doug, I'm really sorry about Doe biting you."

"Don't you know I'd do anything for you, Elli?" Doug leaned into the open window. Doe continued barking. BJ climbed into the front seat, knocking Elli with her hind quarter as she got situated in the passenger seat. "I worry about you," he continued, trying too hard to sound sincere. Elli had dealt with enough people who wanted something from her to recognize someone sucking-up to her. What in the world could he want from her? "I'm not blind. I can see you and Ben are attracted to one another, but I know that will never work. He's not an easy man to get along with. He's self-centered and single-minded. Ben does what Ben wants—without regard for others."

Elli was insulted on Ben's behalf. How could this man be so disloyal when not only did Ben employ him, but he also lived on Ben's property? "I can take care of myself," she said, feeling her face heat. "Not that it is any of your concern, but I'm not planning to stick around to have a relationship with Ben. We are forced business partners. And, for the record, Doug, I think you're wrong about him." She wanted to tell him ways Ben wasn't single-minded and self-centered, but she couldn't think of any. He'd actually been just that way in his dealings with her for the plantation. Of course, she had been, too. And as far as the kennel was concerned, Elli understood that in order to have a successful business, you had to be driven. Single-minded or dedicated and focused? He was that way with Joey, too. He was focused on raising his son, right? Being single-minded for that definitely wasn't wrong. Was it?

"You don't really know him." Doug persisted. "Ask him how he drove his wife away. Ask him how he took her credit cards and told her all of their money had to go to the kennel. He wouldn't let her spend it on food or clothes or a little bit of fun. It was all about the kennel. Always has been. The man has the money of Midas, but do you think he could've let his wife spend a little of it?"

"Quiet, Doe," she scolded. When Doe stopped barking and sat on the edge of the rear seat whining, Elli turned her attention back to Doug. She wasn't comfortable with his anger or what he was saying. She wanted to defend Ben but could only speak of her gut feelings. She had no history or experiences to counter his accusations. "Doug, I would prefer we not speak of this. I like Ben. I think he is a good person. I like how he treats Joey and Tante Izzy and his family. What happened between him and his wife really isn't my business."

"It's more your business than you realize," Doug stated, his tone even but angry. "He didn't crash her car into the tree, but he may as well have. She was running from him when she died."

Dear Lord, what did she tell a grieving father who wanted to blame someone for his daughter's death? She didn't doubt that Ben had been a difficult man to be married to. He, no doubt, was hyper-focused on his business and making it succeed. He was probably even protective of his money and paranoid that his wife was after it, considering what he had told her about his mother. But had he driven his wife to her death? No. She couldn't believe it.

"I'm so sorry for your loss," Elli managed to say. "So very sorry." She couldn't think of another thing to add. This grieving for someone who died was exactly the reason she didn't want to ever marry, have children, or have a serious relationship. It was so damn hard on the survivors.

Doug stood straight and took in a deep breath. He reached into his front shirt pocket and pulled out a pack of cigarettes. Doe began to growl, again. "Bad habit," he said.

"I didn't know you smoked." Elli watched as he lit a cigarette and took a long drag with his eyes closed, exhaling slowly. He looked like a man crawling through a desert then taking his first drink. Doe didn't appreciate his need to smoke and lunged over Elli's shoulder to snap at the cigarette in Doug's hand. "Down, girl." Doe sat but continued growling.

"You go on home. Get your rest. The girls will be up early, demanding your attention."

"Not as early as the director's call." Before she started the car, she listened for the voices she had heard earlier, but it was quiet now. Maybe it was time for the change of guards and they were talking excitedly. She started the car engine as Doe and Jenny both tried to climb into the front seat at the same time. Jenny's wet snout bumped against Elli's neck, her heavy paw imbedded in her thigh. Doe's tail swiped Elli in the face as she shoved her way onto the seat with BJ. Jenny settled on the center console and knocked the car into gear. The Mercedes jerked forward, but Elli was able to slam on the brakes before they hit the wooden fence. "Sorry," she told Doug. "I'd back away from us if I were you…no telling what mayhem they will get me into."

Doug stepped back. "Good night, Elli."

"Good night." With great effort, she shoved Jenny aside to engage reverse.

Elli drove down the long shell road toward the plantation house. She thought about the anger in Doug's voice and eyes when he spoke of Ben. If he felt so negatively about Ben, why did he work and live beside him? Was it because of Joey? Did being close to Joey make him feel closer to his daughter? Elli wasn't sure. She didn't really know anything about Ben's wife, just her name, Sarah Leblanc. Did she have any siblings? Did Doug have any other children? Where was her mother? Was she still alive? If she was, why didn't she live with Doug? Elli shook her head. This was not something she needed to worry about. She had to stay focused on the one thing that had brought her to Sugar Mill Plantation. Worrying about the people who lived there just complicated things. She needed to sell the plantation. Tomorrow, she would talk to the producer and director to let them know that Sugar Mill was for sale and present them with the brochure she had completed at four in morning with photographs she found on line and taken with her new camera. Abby was happy with the way it turned out and was already sending it to a few potential buyers. With any luck, the plantation would have a serious buyer soon. With any luck, she could convince Ben to sell.

Elli saw the lights of the plantation ahead of her, around the last curve. She had to relax and get some sleep tonight. She glanced at BJ and Doe, happily hanging their heads out the window, enjoying the cool, moist night air blowing on their faces. Jenny yawned next to Elli and eased down further onto the console. Her heavy body knocked the gear shifter again, shoving it into reverse. Elli's car made an awful grinding sound and flew backward, right into the ditch running alongside the road. The tires continued to spin as Doe and BJ righted themselves from where they flew on top of one another on the front seat. Jenny was in Elli's lap, and it took a moment for Elli to realize what happened. When she saw the smoke billowing around her, she threw the car into park and turned off the engine. She looked outside the window and saw a small fire crackling in dry grass near where her tires had been spinning.

She grabbed her cell phone and rushed out of the car. It was a small fire, but her car's back end was close to it. "Oh God! She rushed back into the car, yanked the dogs out by their leashes, and let them go. "Don't get in my way," she shouted, racing to the trunk. Jenny and Doe were circling her feet, barking and howling. BJ had taken off down the road. "BJ, come back here," she shouted, opening the trunk and grabbing the blanket she kept inside.

Elli glanced in the direction in which BJ had run, but couldn't see her in the darkness. The fire doubled in size, and Elli raced to it, beating it with the blanket. "I've gotta call nine-one-one. Ugh. I wish you dogs could use my cell phone." She didn't want to stop battling the small blaze to make the call, but fumbled to punch 9-1-1 with one hand while beating the blanket on the fire. The number was probably still on the phone from the last time she called. At least Rachel was off, she thought—like that would stop the Bienvenues from descending on her again. They'd say she set two *forest fires*!

Just as she was about to make the call, the edge of the blanket caught fire. Elli stomped it out then, continued to beat the blanket on the three-foot section of weeds still burning. Jenny thought it was a game and started to leap after the blanket. "Stop, Jenny. No." Jenny got a good hold on a piece of blanket and started to tug. She growled and shook her head. "Stop." Elli used the other part of the blanket to hit the fire, giving Jenny even more encouragement. She thought Elli was playing with her and tugged harder, yanking the blanket from Elli's hand. "No."

Elli looked at the small fire and was out of options. She had nothing to stamp it out with…unless she used her shirt. Without a second thought, she yanked her shirt off of her body and started beating the fire with it. Swoosh. The top went up in flames.

"What the hell is going on?"

"Ben! Help!" Elli started stomping on a low section of the fire, wearing only a black bra and jeans. She looked at him as he rushed to her side, pulling off his shirt. He stomped and beat down the fire.

Elli fell against her car and fought back tears. "Oh my God. I don't know what I would've done if you hadn't come when you did." Jenny walked up to her with the charred blanket and dropped it at her feet.

"We could've used that a few minutes ago," he said, scratching Jenny behind the ear. He put his arm around Elli's shoulder and hugged her against him. She lost her battle with the tears and they slid quietly down her cheeks.

"She stole it from me. You little beast. I should have let Doug shoot you."

Ben leaned back and looked at her. "What? Doug wanted to shoot Jenny?"

"Bad joke." She wiped away the tears. "I hate crying. I'm just so tired. I was scared. I thought I'd have to face the Bienvenu firing squad with accusations of starting another fire." She sniffed. "I don't know how in the world it started. The exhaust and spinning tires and…oh, I don't know. There was probably some trash on the side of the road."

"Probably one of those signs." Ben pointed to a line of paper signs stuck in the ground along the roadside. "No parking."

Elli started to laugh, and Ben hugged her tighter to his naked chest. She turned and faced him. "Thank you." She smiled. "How did you know I was out here?"

"BJ told me you were in trouble." He motioned with his head to the car. Elli looked inside and saw BJ sitting in the driver's seat with her paws on the steering wheel. "You should've let her drive."

Elli smiled. "Look at us, Ben. We're practically naked in the middle of the road."

"Not naked enough." Ben's eyes darkened and he spread his legs enough to pull Elli tighter against him. He lifted her chin toward him. His hand smelled of smoke and man.

Elli sighed. "Just a look from you and I go to places that are naughty and unsafe. Why do I do that when I know you don't like me?" He rubbed her back, then slid his fingers under the strap of her bra. She shivered when he trailed a line of kisses along the side of her neck.

"Tell me about those naughty places, cher. In detail." Elli threw her head back and laughed. Ben seized the moment and with tongue and teeth, feasted his way down her neck to the middle of her cleavage. Elli shivered. This man knew how to pleasure a woman and here, on the side of the road next to a car stuck in the ditch where anyone could see them, she was going to let him.

"I can only think of one naughty place," she whispered in his ear. "It's on a dark road on Sugar Mill Plantation." She nibbled on his ear a moment in the way she had learned he liked, and Ben smiled.

"Tell me more about this dark, naughty place on Sugar Mill Plantation." He pressed himself against her center, and Elli arched her back to move in tighter.

"This place," she said, in a raspy voice she barely recognized as her own. "It's a cool night at this place and our exposed flesh is chilled from the air at the same time it's heated from wanting each other."

"Mm, you got that right, cher." He dropped to his knees and began to kiss her abdomen and navel. He slid his finger beneath the waistband of her jeans and played a while before unbuttoning them.

His mouth, sweet and wet, kissed each inch of flesh he exposed as he unzipped her jeans. Elli groaned. "Tell me more about what we do at this naughty place," he said, his voice deep and breathy on her abdomen.

"I…can't…talk." He slid her pants to her ankles, and Elli slipped off her running shoes to step out of them. Ben grabbed her bottom and pressed his mouth against her center.

"Try or I'll stop," he growled. "Tell me what you are feeling in this naughty place."

"Heat." She moved with him as he used his tongue over her panties, exciting her. "Desire. Wanting."

"What do you want, cher?" He slid her panties down her legs in a slow, seductive motion. Elli felt the silky fabric brush against every inch of flesh down her legs. Then, his mouth was on her.

"This. I want this," she managed in a hushed voice. She gripped his shoulders to try to remain upright on boneless legs.

Ben growled again and it vibrated through her core. Elli felt the beginning of an orgasm deep inside her and let her entire body flow into it. Ben slipped his finger inside of her and bright light exploded in front of her. She screamed out and the dogs began to bark. She and Ben ignored them as he stood and pressed against her. Elli moved against him to continue the rhythm he started. Ben gripped her hips tighter, sliding his body against hers in an erotic dance. He was so hard. His breathing heavy. Elli slid down his body, unzipped his jeans and took him as he had taken her. She hadn't noticed, but the dogs stopped barking and lay on the ground.

"You are killing me." He ran his hands over her head and let her do the pleasuring. She could feel his restraint and wanted him to let go. She slowed the rhythm, explored, tasted, enjoyed, until the muscles in Ben's legs started shaking. He pulled her up and kissed her deeply. Elli wrapped her legs around him as he drove into her. He looked into her eyes and her heart fluttered. Something unguarded and important was shared in the moment, that one look, but Elli didn't know what. If she had to give it a word, it would be trust, but she was too much awash in the passion to think of that now. They shattered in each other's arms seconds later.

Elli and Ben remained leaning against the cold metal of the car, now heated by their bodies. Neither spoke nor moved for a long time. They were still breathing hard as Ben hugged Elli tighter against his warmth. She rested her head on his chest and her palms on his shoulders.

Ben spoke first. "Should I be worried that we didn't use protection?"

"No. I don't have any communicable diseases and I'm good on the birth control front. No worries. Should I be worried?"

"Nope. I'm good." He yawned. "If I had any strength or sense, I'd get us off the road where someone might happen by."

Elli smiled. "By someone, I know you are referring to a Bienvenu."

"Yeah. I am." He patted her on her naked bottom and moved her an arm's length away. His eyes slid down her body, and he grinned his sexy crooked grin. "Why don't you slip that bra off, cher, and be naked all the way for me, to complete my fantasy." He ran his finger down the side of her waist, and then he surprised her by tracing the faded scar running from hip-to-hip. Elli stepped away and reached for her panties. "You sensitive about that scar?"

"Yes. I am." She slipped on her bright purple panties. "More Kryptonite."

"It's not mine," He stepped on her jeans and stopped her from putting them on. "What is the scar from?"

"You are so frustrating, you know?" He smiled, obviously enjoying her calling him that. "You send mixed signals, Ben. When you are like this, you are so ridiculously charming, when we are together..." She sighed deciding not to identify what their lovemaking meant to her. "Then, at the bayou side today, I felt you pushing me away. You were trying to corral me in that imagined fence you have to keep me locked in and distant."

"I can't disagree with that." He blew out a breath. "This is different. This is just wanting to know why you have the scar across your hip. It's not about relationship building." He tugged her into his arms again and ran his hand over her head, tucking a curl behind her ear. His actions didn't embody his words. His gentleness and affection touched her, and Elli felt vulnerable. Oh my God. This man could steal her heart.

"It's just a surgery scar, Ben." She shrugged her shoulders and looked away. "I have a few of them. Most everyone who knows me in LA knows about it. It's not a secret." She cleared her throat. "I was sick just over three years ago and had four surgeries as a result."

He turned her face to look at her. Elli saw the genuine concern in his eyes. Her heart constricted. This was what the cold and distant Ben looked like when he let his guard down. "How sick?"

Yes, she felt vulnerable, but telling him the truth would give her strength and resolve. It would protect her heart. It would make him want to stay at arm's length from her.

"I had stage three breast cancer."

She kept her eyes locked on his, wanting to see the moment he put up the shield to protect himself from that kind of harsh reality. She'd seen it before in others whose personal fears didn't allow them to be too empathetic or be near it for long.

Elli didn't wait for him to speak. "I don't mind talking about having cancer with you, it's just we aren't supposed to have this kind of personal conversation."

His eyebrows furrowed, then he nodded.

"Talking about my cancer is...intimate." Elli blew out a breath. "We said we would keep our relationship superficial. I'm not sure it's good for us to do otherwise."

He nodded, again. "Agreed." He handed Elli her jeans. "Tell me about it anyway. I promise to not care."

"Very funny." She slipped into her jeans. "I was diagnosed with invasive ductal carcinoma. My first line of treatment was a lumpectomy, then chemo and radiation. After I finished treatment, the doctors said they didn't see any NED—new evidence of disease."

"What does that mean?"

Elli shrugged. "They think I am progression-free. Another term doctors toss around. They used to call it remission. Now they attach percentages to the possibility of recurrence. They gave me a twenty-percent chance of recurrence because of the stage of my cancer and the fact that it infiltrated three lymph nodes." Ben opened the car door and motioned for her to sit inside. He stood just outside the car as she continued.

"About a year and a half ago, I attended a lecture about genetic breast cancer testing on the advice of a friend who was going. Afterward, I decided to have the simple blood test to determine if the cancer I had was genetic." She cleared her throat again, for it felt tight and raw. "My mother and her mother died of breast cancer." He squatted to be eye level with her but didn't say a word. "Well, I tested positive. The geneticist I consulted with recommended I take preemptive measures before I got a new cancer. He said I had an eighty-seven-percent chance of getting a new breast cancer. My chances of ovarian cancer were really high too, since the same gene mutation is blamed for both cancers. If I was proactive, I could reduce my chance of a new breast cancer to four percent. I liked those odds better. I didn't want to have to go through chemotherapy and radiation again. I would, if I had to, but I didn't want to."

Ben took both of her hands into his. "So what were the preemptive measures?"

"Prophylactic nipple sparing double mastectomy and surgery to remove my ovaries, fallopian tubes, and uterus," she said in a detached voice void of the emotion that went along with all that she had been through. For some reason, it was important to her to declare the information without emotion. She stared at him for a long moment, wanting to catch every nuance of his reaction. Did he think she had been overzealous with her medical treatment? Did he think she was reasonable and correct? She wasn't sure why his opinion mattered so much to her, but it did. "Ben, do you understand what I'm saying?" she asked, when he just stared at her with no telling grimace or frown or arched brow. "I had both surgeries, Ben."

"You had reconstruction?" He lifted his hands and gently touched her breasts. His eyes softened. "Must've been really talented doctors."

"They were all amazing. The doctors spent nearly seven hours performing the mastectomy and DIEP flap reconstruction. They used my stomach fat and microsurgically transplanted it to make breasts."

He winced. "Ouch. Sounds painful."

"It was, but only for a few weeks."

"And hard," he whispered.

"Yes, it was. But not as hard as you'd think and not as hard as having cancer. Fighting it, even with painful surgeries and debilitating chemo, is the easy part. You are engaged in doing something to get rid of the invader threatening your life—it gives you a sense of control. Having treatment is hopeful." She bit her lower lip. "Ending your treatment is both a joy that you are well enough to end it and a dread that the beast that could be hiding in your body is not being hunted. You can believe the cancer has been wiped out, but there is always the knowledge that it can return." She rubbed her chilled arms, and BJ climbed from the driver's seat where she had been sleeping, to snuggle at Elli's hip. "Sweet girl." She began petting BJ as she continued. "You know a lot of people think the nauseating side effects of the chemo or the burns from the radiation are the hardest part. For me, it was hearing the doctor tell me that I had cancer and I could die despite all efforts to fight it. No matter what I did, I could fail. I never failed. I was a damn overachiever who succeeded at everything I did."

"I'm sorry. You are a brave woman to keep pushing forward."

"People always tell me how brave and courageous I am to go through what I have, but the truth is, you go through it because you don't have a choice. That doesn't make you a brave person. All I did was fight for my life. At the end of the day, it was God who decided to let me stay on earth for a while longer. He makes that decision. Not me."

"Yes, He does." Ben stood, walked around the car to the driver's side, and climbed in. "Well, I'm glad you're alive and well."

"Thank you." She smiled at how sweet he was to say that. "Me, too." She closed her door. "You know, there are times I can actually appreciate having gone through all that I have in the last few years. My amazing, loving father died a few months before my diagnosis, but it wasn't until I, first-person, stared death in its ugly face that I learned to appreciate life. I realized that almost everything that I thought was important was just—stuff." She smiled and Ben nodded.

"Dogs are born knowing that. They are so damn uncomplicated. The best things I learned about life are from my dogs."

"They live in the moment and that was what I set out to do, not knowing dogs had invented it." She laughed. "I gave up on a movie producing career I loved so I could live like there was no tomorrow. I traveled the world, climbed the Himalayas and the Rockies. I hiked rainforests in Brazil. I tasted strange, exotic foods in towns I can't even pronounce in tiny countries I hadn't known existed. I slept on the ground under the stars and enjoyed my own company. I woke up every day and quoted William Wallace, aka Mel Gibson, in *Braveheart*—'Every man dies. Not every man really lives.'" She shook her head. "If I hadn't had cancer, I wouldn't have had that grand adventure."

"Especially not in just three short years." Ben looked out the window and whistled. Jenny and Doe came bouncing toward the car. He opened the door and let them inside. It took a few minutes before they settled in the backseat and went to sleep.

Elli looked at her dogs and smiled. "I can't believe I'm going to say this, but I like my three crazy dogs."

"Four. You are forgetting Donna."

"Donna, I'm not so sure about." She laughed. "Of course, I like that prissy girl. These three are eager and clumsy and lovable. They don't have an agenda. Donna, on the other hand, is manipulative, selfish, and sneaky."

"Sounds like the woman I married."

Elli shivered and rubbed her arms. She wasn't sure she wanted to talk about Sarah Leblanc. Something told her that they had shared enough for one evening. Besides, what she really needed to talk about was selling Sugar Mill Plantation. She needed to get funding for the foundation, soon. Ben seemed to be in a malleable mood.

She took in a deep breath. "Ben, do you think we can ever sit down with a willingness to resolve our differences over what to do with Sugar Mill?" Ben's posture immediately changed. He now sat rigid.

"No," he said simply. "I don't want to do anything with the plantation. I'm not willing to compromise on that point."

"So, let me be clear on what you are saying." She knew she was raising her voice but couldn't stop it. "You want to keep the status quo. No change. You want to pretend I have no claim to the kennel, the land, and the house. Is that right?"

"Don't forget, I also want you to go back to California."

That hurt, but Elli would never let him know it did. If he knew, then he would also know that she cared about him enough that he could hurt her. The people the foundation helped needed her not to get emotional. "So you think it's fair that I just walk away from here even though I own as much of this place as you do?

"Yes. I think that's fair." He looked at Elli. "You managed fine before you knew you owned half of Sugar Mill. You will manage fine when you walk away from it."

"Maybe," she admitted. "Maybe not. I do know that walking away right now isn't possible." Elli paused to consider if she should tell him about the important work of the foundation and how the money that funded it was stolen. Would he care? Was it fair to tell him about it? Did she have the right to try to guilt him into action, because her skills of persuasion were sub-par? Should there be full disclosure? "Ben…"

"Elli, let me be clear," he interrupted, keeping her from deciding if she should tell him now. "I don't want to change the way things are for Joey and me." He turned in his seat to look at her. "That's it. No further discussion. Time to go home. It's late. The temperature is dropping. Tante Izzy is spending the night at the house because she didn't want to miss anything with the filming. And you know she'll be waiting up to get the news on why BJ was so upset."

Elli nodded. "For the record, the subject is not closed. There must be further discussion." She pulled Jenny's leash from under her leg. "We'll save that for another day." A day that had to be sooner rather than later. She didn't have the luxury of putting it off. "For now," she continued, turning to untangle the leash, "you have to tell me how in the world are we going to explain why we are coming into the house shirtless?"

"You'll just walk in and pretend you are clothed like the Emperor in his new robes. She won't notice you aren't."

"Yeah, right. That'll fly with Tante Izzy." Elli turned to face him. "Hey, what about you?"

"I'll be pulling your car out of the ditch with my truck."

"I'll be helping you. I'll call her cell and tell her what happened, minus the wildfire."

She climbed out of the car, and Ben stood. He pulled her tight against him. "You really piss me off, you know." Then, he kissed her with so much passion she thought they would strip off what little clothes they wore and make love on the hood of her Mercedes. But he ended the kiss, tracing her lips with his tongue before pressing his forehead to hers. "Cher, for the record. I really am glad you beat breast cancer. I'm happy you are alive in this world. I just the hell wish you had never come into mine."

"Agreed."

Chapter Ten

Did you know that you would be graffitied when you were being prepped for radiation treatment? I'm told some centers use small dots, but my rad techs used red and blue permanent markers to trace the lines cast by the radiation machine across my chest and up my neck to mark the treatment field. It was surreal. I hardly felt the warm friction of ink gliding over my clean skin nor smelled the sharp, distinctive scent of ink drying. It was as if someone else was having a strange man draw on her chest with markers much like a recalcitrant three-year-old might draw on a bedroom wall. It was too impersonal, too lacking in humanity to be real. This wasn't supposed to be happening to me. I wasn't supposed to be here. Other people got cancer. They had surgery, chemotherapy, and radiation...not me. Why in the heck didn't they use GPS? I wish you good health, E.

Bosom Blog Buddies Post

The next day of filming got off to an early start, just as the director wanted. Sam Cooper and Heather Harley arrived on time in a limo from the Ritz-Carlton Hotel, which was an hour away in New Orleans. Crew members, who stayed in a more economical hotel near the New Orleans Airport, arrived an hour ahead of them to set up for the day's work. Even though they had worked twelve hours the day before and had gotten little sleep, Sam and Heather looked beautiful, alert, and perfect. He was a chiseled, masculine version of Ken, and she was a pinup-girl version of Barbie.

At seven a.m., Heather had a break from filming and sat on the back steps of the plantation house to smoke a cigarette. She was in costume—paint-splattered jeans, shredded at the knees, and indigo, tie-dyed T-shirt. She looked like the eccentric artist she played, but in a way that would not disappoint her fans. Her jeans were like a second skin over her trademark bottom and long dancer's legs. Her T-shirt's neckline was scooped low to highlight her pin-up girl breasts. Heather's bright blond hair was restrained in a single braid that hung down her back to her hips. The costume designer had nailed it down to her bare feet.

Elli looked at the pressed jeans, cornflower blue cashmere cardigan over a crisp white T-shirt that she wore. She, too had nailed her costume down to her Stuart Weitzman loafers. She looked like the character she played—the practical, sophisticated businesswoman working on a movie set. However, it lacked any of Elli's personality and essence. It was one-dimensional, she thought, looking at Heather. Was that because she was a one-dimensional woman?

Elli shook her head. Why in the world was she thinking such things? She should be thinking of this golden opportunity to speak to Heather casually about investing in Sugar Mill. She started walking toward the starlet when the back door opened and Ben walked out. His smile was big, warm, and immediate. He said something to Heather, making her laugh, and she patted the concrete step next to her for Ben to sit. She tilted her head and gave him one of the smoky looks that made her the favorite arm candy for dozens of Hollywood's A-listers. Elli stopped in her tracks, looking down at her shoes. Why in the world had she worn boring loafers?

"Elli?" She felt a tap on her shoulder before her brain registered that someone had said her name. "You look a million miles away."

"Hi, Rachel." She turned her back to Heather and Ben. Rachel obviously noticed them and raised her eyebrows.

"OMG. What's up with that?"

Elli shrugged. "You needed me?"

"Yes. I thought I'd warn you. My mom is on her way over here. She's with Tante Izzy. She made gumbo and potato salad and they are bringing it over." Rachel frowned. "I tried to stop them, but, well…you know how they are."

Elli glanced over her shoulder and was sorry she had. Heather had just handed Ben her lighter and was now leaning into him so he could light the cigarette cinched between her perfect collagen lips.

Elli's heart constricted and her stomach fisted. She swallowed past the tightness in her throat and looked at Rachel. "Well, it is what it is," she said, thinking about the Cajun Dog Whisperer and Goddess Queen, but intending for Rachel to think she was talking about the Cajun Fireball and Relentless Redhead. She forced a smile. "Can you help keep them under control?"

"Ben and Harley?" She grunted. "I don't think that'll be necessary. They look cozy on the stoop, but I don't see any sparks sizzling off of them."

Elli smiled and looked at the scene on the steps. Maybe, Rachel was right about the sizzle, but to her, they looked happy to share the same space. "Uh, I was talking about keeping Tante Izzy and Ruby under control," she said when she felt Rachel staring at her.

"I doubt it." Rachel sighed. "I'll give it the ole college try." Elli gave her a quick hug. "Don't look now, but here they come. Mom and Tante Izzy have two of the runners carrying the food for them."

"Elli. Elli. Allons." Tante Izzy shouted. "I got you somethin' from the Traiteur."

Elli and Rachel headed toward Tante Izzy, moving away from where Ben was sitting with Heather. Elli made sure she didn't look at them, but Tante Izzy had and jabbed her hands onto her hips.

"Harrumph. What's up with dat?" she asked when they reached her. "I don't like it one bit."

"Don't like what?" Ruby asked, walking up to join them. "Oh," she said, following the direction Tante Izzy was looking. Heather and Ben were laughing as they sat in a wraithlike cloud of cigarette smoke. They could've been on a fog-covered runway in Casablanca with how dramatic the scene looked.

"I'm sure it's nothing," Rachel said in a rush.

"Youz call smoking cigarettes 'nothin'?" Tante Izzy frowned. "It's bad for youz health." She pointed her crooked finger at Rachel. "I better never catch youz smokin', young lady."

"Yes, ma'am."

"Wow," Ruby said, her hand over her mouth, obviously star struck. "She's a little thing. She's every bit as gorgeous as she appears in the tabloids, but half the size I thought she'd be. Hmmm," she said, craning her neck. "Do you think she's approachable? By the way she's smiling at Ben, I bet she is."

"Mom, I warned you to stay away from the stars." Rachel narrowed her eyes. "You mustn't be disruptive. This is a job site. People work here."

"It don't look like Heather is working to me." She reached into her vinyl red purse hanging over her shoulder. "Here. Autograph this before I forget for a third time." She handed Elli the People magazine. "Right there, under your picture, which is really pretty by the way. I like that sparkly headband you are wearing. Is it real diamonds?" She handed Elli a felt pen and didn't wait for her to answer. "You know, all I want to do is ask Heather one question. It will take no more than two minutes."

Elli quickly signed the magazine and handed it back to Ruby. She was glad the attention was off of her again and wanted to keep it that way. "I'll introduce you to her."

"I'm comin', too." Tante Izzy said, sounding angry. She sure hoped it was over Ruby's insisting on meeting Heather and not the star's smoking habit. If it was the latter, this meeting could get ugly. She'd bet no one ever told Heather Harley what to do.

The four of them marched over. As soon as Ben spotted them, he rested his elbows on his knees and shook his head. "Prepare yourself, Heather."

"What?" she asked, turning to look at the four ladies approaching.

All four of them spoke at the same time.

"Heather, I'd like to introduce you to Ruby…"

"Heather, I'm Ruby Bienvenu. Do you want to be our guest of honor for our Prevent Forest Fires fundraiser?"

"Oh my God, Heather, please excuse my rude mother."

"Don't youz know smokin' will turn youz teeth yellow, youz face gray, and youz lungs black?"

Heather just stared at the women as their simultaneous chattering turned into a heated discussion with one another over who should talk to her first. Ben leaned back, and smiled.

"Do something," Elli shouted to him. "They're your relatives."

Rachel grabbed her mother's arm, but she would have had to clamp her hand over her mouth to stop her from talking. "Heather," Ruby said with a huge force of breath. She paused to paste a forced smile on her face. "Hi. I'm Ruby Bienvenu." She extended her hand and Heather shook it. "I made potato salad."

Heather looked at Elli to explain what that meant.

"For lunch. I think that was an invitation for lunch." Elli shrugged. "There's also gumbo."

"She made dat with two chickens from my yard." Tante Izzy nodded, then looked at the cigarette nestled between Heather's fingers. "It turns youz fingernails brown, too."

"I'm having a fundraiser," Ruby rushed on. "We'd like you to be guest of honor." Heather continued to stare at her. "We'll have it as soon as Lent is over. We wanted to have it before, but Ash Wednesday is in a couple of days and there's no time to get everything ready." She took a step closer to Heather, and the buxom star sat up, looking like she wanted to bolt. "Can you come to the fundraiser?"

"Elli, is this for your foundation?" she asked, looking at her with suspicion. "You know, I was advised by my accountants to stay away from your foundation for a couple of years or"—she lowered her voice—"or forever."

"That's terrible," Rachel gushed. "I'm sure she has a wonderful foundation."

Heather raised a brow and looked at Elli. She was allowing her to tell them about its troubles. Elli didn't want to. She didn't want it said by anyone. She didn't want to hear the truth spoken aloud. She didn't want these people she liked to know she had bungled taking care of people she promised to help. She didn't want Ben to think she was a bad businesswoman. She prayed for the dark Louisiana earth to grab her Stuart Weitzman loafers and suck her into the muddy abyss.

"I don't need you for her foundation," Ruby said, moving closer to Elli. "We'll be working to help her fix that later. Your accountants will be changing their mind about that forever comment." Ruby slid her arm through Elli's, and Elli's throat tightened with tears at this woman's show of support. She hadn't expected it. Rachel sidled up on the other side of Elli and locked arms with her, too.

"What do accountants know," Tante Izzy said with a nod. Elli felt the tears burn her eyes and fought not to cry.

"I'm paying them a lot to know a lot," Heather said, taking a drag from her cigarette. "Dealing with my credit card companies and the bank since Elli's Griffith Park fiasco has been a nightmare for them and my assistant."

"Ms. Harley, my fundraiser is to raise money for education to prevent forest fires." Ruby's voice was clear, and she was carefully speaking slowly to temper her rhythmic Cajun accent. "Forest fires are a recent problem here in Cane. In fact, we saw evidence of a fire right on the road leading to the plantation house. It was so close to this beautiful home. Can you imagine if it had reached this historical place?" She shook her head. "We want to nip it in the butt before it is out of control."

Heather looked at Elli as if she wanted to say something mean about preventing forest fires in wet, swampy, rainy Louisiana. They were saved from that when the back door flew open and hit Ben in the back. Loud barking ensued in every tone imaginable and Elli saw that her dogs had arrived right on cue.

"Sorry, Dad," Joey said with a giggle. The dogs wedged their way through the door, knocking into Heather. Doe stood at the threshold and growled. It was a serious, scary growl. It was how she had growled at Doug the night before and at the cottage before it went up in flames. It was a growl with a purpose. Then, she started barking a vicious, angry bark.

Heather jumped up, took a drag of her cigarette, and shouted at Joey as she exhaled a puff of smoke. "Control that animal."

Doe lunged toward Heather in a blur of teeth and fur, but Ben grabbed the possessed animal by its collar and turned her away from one of Hollywood's most flawless faces. Elli's reaction was a beat behind Ben's. She threw herself between Doe and Heather, making herself a human shield. It had been unnecessary, she realized as her hip slammed hard into the steps just as the door slammed behind Ben, who secured Doe inside the house.

"Ouch," Heather cried as Elli's elbow stabbed her in the back from her ungraceful dive. "What the hell are you doing?"

"Fracturing my hip," Elli said as she watched her saner dogs turn away from the drama on the stairs, running in circles, sniffing the ground, and doing happy dog things. Donna, however, high-stepped over to where Heather was sitting on the steps doing back stretching things to alleviate the blow from Elli. With a gentle whimper, the doggie diva sat at the starlet's feet and looked up at her in what Elli could only describe as admiration. No doubt about it, Donna considered Heather a goddess like herself.

Heather spotted Donna and tossed her cigarette off to the side in the grass. Ruby rushed to stamp it out as Heather kneeled next to Donna. The cute ball of fluff raised a tiny, perfect paw with designer nail polish and tapped the megawatt star her on the thigh. Heather ran her finger under Donna's collar. "Is that Gucci?" Donna barked a happy bark. Jenny and BJ rushed over to Donna, sniffed her, and finding nothing interesting, ran toward the food tent.

"I'll get them," Joey shouted, running after the dogs.

"I almost wish your dog would have bitten Heather," Rachel whispered to Elli as she helped her off the steps. "She's annoying."

Ruby looked at Elli. "I have some ideas how to save your foundation," she said, folding her arms over her chest, the magazine wedged beneath them.

"I didn't know you knew."

"I am a subscriber of the National Enquirer and People. I read it cover to cover," she huffed and sidled next to Heather. She spoke to the star a moment, then Ruby called to Elli. "You don't mind if we borrow your dog for a while? The nice one here, not the other demon dog."

"Her name is Donna. Bella Donna." Elli nodded. She was so grateful Ruby and the world wouldn't be reading an article in the National Enquirer about how the producer of the sweet dog movie, Newfie, had a pet dog that ripped the face off of Hollywood Beauty, Heather Harley. "Keep Donna as long as you want."

"We will." Ruby waved her fingers in farewell. "See you tomorrow for the parade."

"That's tomorrow?" Elli asked Ruby.

"Yep. Get a good night's sleep, it'll be a long fun day."

Tante Izzy continued to watch Ruby and Heather's departing backs when she spoke. "I'm so confused. I don't know what just happened." She frowned. "From nowheres, youz dog went rabid, youz throwed youzself in the air like youz were divin' into a swimmin' pool...only there wasn't any water around. Then, Ruby walks off with dat movie star and your fancy dog." She twisted her thin lips and narrowed her eyes. "Yep. I'm definitely confused. I jest know one thing. I didn't tell Ruby about dat man stealing all da money youz raised to help those families fight cancer."

Elli leaned in and kissed Tante Izzy's lined cheek. She tasted like old-fashioned cold cream and smelled like Ivory soap. "I was the featured story on page 36 of People Magazine and in the National Enquirer on pages three, four, and twenty-seven the week after the huge Griffith Park fundraiser. Ruby reads both."

"I only have time to look at da pictures in da magazine when I wait in da checkout line."

"I love you, Tante Izzy." Elli laughed.

"Oh, Mon Dieu. I forget." The old lady reached into the purple, pink, and green daisy purse hanging from her arm. "I've got somethin' fer youz." She handed Elli an amber bottle of liquid. "Da Traiteur fixed youz a love potion."

Elli immediately tried to hand the bottle back to Tante Izzy. "I don't want or need this."

She stepped back. "Now, youz be careful when youz drink it. It's mighty potent. Youz and Ben need to drink it at da same time and kiss immediately after. If'n he won't drink it, sneak it in his coffee, then plant a kiss on his lips."

Elli knew arguing with Tante Izzy was a waste of time. It was best for her to keep the potion and throw it in the garbage later. She shoved it into the back pocket of her jeans.

"Heed my words, now, youz hear?"

"Yes, ma'am." Elli really did love this crazy lady. "Is it too early for gumbo?"

"Not when youz as skinny as a worn shoe sole."

Elli laughed. "I'm skinny, but you have the body of a supermodel."

"Youz got dat right." Instead of heading to the tent, Tante Izzy climbed the steps and opened the back door. "Ben. Allons manger."

Ben came to the screen door and looked at Tante Izzy. "I'm not hungry. I'll eat later." Through the screen, he looked at Elli and pointed a stern finger at her. "You. Inside."

Elli sighed. "Tante Izzy, I need to see a man about a dog."

"Remember what I told youz bout da potion." She turned and walked away. Elli noticed that she was wearing popsicle pink sneakers that lighted with every step she took.

"How's Doe?" she asked when she stepped inside the house.

"I fed her and put her in the kennel in the spare bedroom." He walked into the kitchen and Elli followed. "The smaller kennel space will help calm her." He poured a cup of coffee and Elli remembered the amber bottle in her pocket. She pulled it out, thought about throwing it in garbage, but decided to wait until later. She stuffed it in her front pocket and sat at the kitchen table.

"Thank you for taking care of her." Elli stood and got a bottle of vitamin water from the refrigerator, not noticing how she opened the crazy, off-kilter door without a thought. "I don't know why she flies off the handle like that."

"I do." They sat across from one another at the table. "I made a few calls and found out that Doe was abused." When Elli gasped, Ben grabbed her hand and rubbed the top of it with his thumb. "It's bad. Her previous owner was a cruel son of a bitch. He burned Doe with cigarettes for kicks."

"I saw some raised circles on her belly. I felt some beneath her fur, too. I thought it was some sort of birthmark. It must be scars from the burns. Oh, poor baby." Elli's throat tightened with emotion. "Thank God, Aunt Rosa rescued her and gave her a loving home."

Ben let go of her hand and looked away. "Elli, I…"

"Her reaction to cigarettes makes sense," she interrupted. "Last night, with Doug, she went ballistic. He was smoking at the time. He was probably smoking a cigarette when she bit him."

"You were with Doug last night?" He ran his hand through his hair. "You don't need to answer that."

"Okay. I won't." It offended her that he would think she was with his father-in-law just before they had been together on the side of the road. Did he really think she was that lacking in morals?

"Good," he said, his lips moving over clenched teeth. Then he grabbed her by her arm. "No. Not good. If I don't do other women when I'm with you, I expect the same in return."

"Do you really think I was with Doug?" Elli narrowed her eyes, not wanting to miss a single shift in his expression.

Ben returned the stare; his eyes revealed nothing of what he was thinking, then his shoulders dropped and he shook his head. "No, cher. I don't think you were with Doug." He shook his head again and released her arm. "That's not to say I don't think Doug is making a play for you."

"Like Heather is with you."

Ben smiled and leaned back in his chair. Elli's heart began to pound. The man looked so crazy-sexy sitting there in arrogant splendor. "Are you jealous, cher?"

She snorted again. "Get over yourself."

He stood, walked around the table, and squatted next to her. He touched her chin and turned her to face him. Elli sighed. "I like the fire in your eyes when you're jealous. It makes me want to throw out my chest and beat on it."

Elli leaned closer to him, and the amber bottle weighed heavy in her pocket. She wanted to deny being jealous, but that seemed stupid and foolish. She was, and proclaiming anything else would be a lie. Still, she didn't have to give it voice. Instead, she kissed him. A kiss that started sweet and gentle, then fired into something spicy and wild. When she leaned away from Ben, he looked as surprised as she felt as to how fast things heated between them.

"C'est si bon." He squeezed her thighs, then stood. "With you, I expect one thing and get another, with lagniappe." He hadn't said it with heat, but when he began to pace, he looked angry. Elli wasn't sure how to respond to what he said. Heck, she wasn't exactly sure what he meant. She did know if she asked him to clarify what he said, he would snap at her and an argument would ignite. The dogs were a safer topic.

"I'm going to ask Doug to not smoke around Doe," she began. "And maybe you can ask your staff to do the same."

Ben stopped pacing and looked at Elli as if she'd grown two heads and a snout. "Doug doesn't smoke."

"Yes, he does. I told you, I saw him smoking last night. Doe immediately started growling and lunging at him."

"Doug is smoking? I've never seen him smoke before."

"You two probably don't spend much downtime together." Elli sighed. "Ben, I'm surprised you hadn't noticed Doe's reaction to cigarettes before. You've been around her for years." Ben stood and began to pace. "What can I do to help her?"

He looked at her. "We'll have to work on some behavior modification. I'll…"

Suddenly, there was a banging at the door. It sounded frantic. "Daddy. Hurry!"

Ben and Elli rushed to the door. "Are you okay, Joey?" his father asked.

"Yeah. I'm fine, but I just heard two movie guys talking about seeing some beagles near the road. One of them said they almost hit one of the dogs with his truck. Dad, do you think those are the hunting dogs you're training?"

Ben ran out of the house and Elli followed. When he jumped into his truck, Elli, Joey, Jenny, and BJ joined him. "If those dumb, carnie movie people let my dogs out, I'll have my pound of flesh."

Elli bit her lower lip. She said a quick prayer that the dogs were okay and the movie crew had nothing to do with them getting loose. They hadn't gotten very far down the road when Ben slammed on the brakes, jerked the truck into park, and raced out of the truck. He left the door open as he ran after a dark brown and black beagle running along the bayou's edge on short, muscular legs. Legs that looked exactly like Lucky's. "Wow." She leaned across the seat and closed the door before opening hers.

"Joey, stay right here. Keep Jenny and BJ in the truck with you."

"I will. I won't cause you any trouble. I promise."

"Of course, you won't." Elli thought about what the child had said as she ran toward the bayou. It was an overstatement for the situation. She wondered why.

By the time she got to Ben, he had the young chocolate brown and black beagle in his arms.

"Oh my God, Ben, he doesn't look like he's more than a few months old. He's a baby!"

"If this one is out, I'd bet my ass that there are five others running around somewhere."

Elli started slapping her thigh, making smacking noises. "Here doggie, doggie."

Ben rolled his eyes. "Let me call the dogs. You'll scare them away with all those kissing sounds."

She sighed. "I'm here to help. Tell me what to do."

"I think you've done enough."

Elli knew better than to argue with an angry, worried man. "Tell me what to do to help, Ben," she said with more force.

"Here." She wasn't expecting him to shove the beagle into her arms, so when he did, she was off balance and fell backward to the ground. Ben exhaled hard and helped her up. "Take him to Joey in the truck."

The dog barked at Elli, then licked her right on the mouth. "That's disgusting. I don't even want to think about what you have been licking or putting in your mouth during your grand escape." The dog licked her again. Elli started running to the truck with the dog's smooth, brown ears and head bouncing with each stride.

She and Ben repeated the dog capturing and her running to the truck with two more dogs. The last two were resting under a big oak tree near the kennel, looking ridiculously content and adorable. They could have been posing for one of those doggie calendars. Ben swooped them up into his arms and handed them to Joey who was now in the truck bed with one of the other dogs. Four dogs remained in the cab of the truck with Elli and Ben. Her two dogs and the two energetic young beagles were happily wrestling and nipping at each other in the backseat.

"Do you think the Newfies got out too?" she asked, worried about the cute little puppies.

"I don't know." His jaws tightened and his hands gripped the steering wheel. "They should be in the training barn, where I put them. I locked the building."

"I'm sure they will be there." She looked out the window, knowing she would only relax when she saw the puppies at the kennel.

"We'll see." He spoke through clenched teeth. "The beagles got out, and Doug was supposed to be there watching things at the kennel."

She and Ben didn't say a word until they settled the beagles in the outside pen and rushed inside the training barn to check on the Newfies. As soon as they stepped into the back room, the Newfies' heads popped up from where they were napping and instantly began their happy puppy dance. Elli laughed aloud in relief, but Ben still seemed as upset as he did in the truck. He gave the puppies a treat, and in less than two minutes, they were back outside where Joey was sitting in the truck with her dogs.

"The Newfies are okay," she told Joey with a smile.

"Phew. I was afraid they got stolen."

Ben parked the truck in front of the office and spoke to Joey when he got out. "Grab a snack in the office. I need to talk to your grandpa."

"Okay, Dad." He smiled at Elli. "You want me to get you a snack, Elli?"

She touched the child's sweet face. "No thanks. I'm saving my appetite for Tante Izzy's gumbo." Joey ran to the office with Jenny and BJ.

"Where is Doug?" she asked. "Where's the rest of your staff?"

"I gave the staff the day off with all the movie commotion going on around here. I figured with the security you had hired, Doug was all I needed to keep an eye on our interest here at the kennel." They started to walk toward Doug's cottage. "Besides, no one wants to work the day before Mardi Gras." He knocked at Doug's door. "If Doug was doing his job, the beagles shouldn't have gotten out." When Doug didn't answer after the second knock, Ben opened the door and stepped inside. The cottage smelled of stale beer, cigarettes, and excessive partying. Ben cursed.

"Someone had a party," she said, stating the obvious. Elli pushed one beer bottle to the side with her foot and then another.

"No kidding." Ben walked into what Elli figured was the bedroom and came out shaking his head. "The party made it in there, too."

"What about Doug? Did he make it in there?"

Ben shook his head and started to walk to the kitchen but stopped near the kitchen table; a body curled in a fetal position was beneath it. "Not Doug," Ben said after kneeling next to the young man with a bright purple streak down the center of his head.

"He's one of the best boy grips. I recognize his stripe. Why isn't he at work on the set? God, there's going to be trouble."

"And this one? Is he supposed to be working too?" Ben asked after walking into the next room. Elli stepped into the bright black and white, recently remodeled kitchen.

"He's one of the prop guys, I think." The mid-twenties guy rolled onto his back and looked at Ben.

"Dude."

"Should we be worried about Doug?" Elli asked Ben.

"Probably not." The words no sooner left his mouth than the rear door flew open. Doug walked in bare-chested, jeans hung low on his hips, and a beer bottle in his hand. His belt was unbuckled.

"Trespassing," he managed in a voice sounding as coarse as lava rock. "Out." He wobbled a bit as he pointed to the front door.

"The beagles got loose," Ben told him, his voice clearly restrained. "How in the hell did that happen?"

"They were set free to dance and howl at the full moon with us last night," a light female voice said as she walked into the kitchen through the rear door. She hugged Doug around the waist, but he shoved her aside. "Honey, what's wrong?"

Ben sucked in a deep breath and balled his hands in fists but didn't move. It was clear he wanted to clobber Doug, but showed remarkable restraint, considering what the girl had just said. Heck, Elli wanted to punch Doug. "How in God's creation did you ever think that was a good idea?" she snapped at Doug. "How could you endanger those vulnerable animals like that? They are babies. An alligator could have eaten them!"

Ben gripped her arm to silence her. She jerked out of his hold. "I'll handle this, Elli." His voice was tight. His body was as rigid as a wooden post. He was visibly upset and she could see Doug saw it, too.

"We'll let you two talk alone." Elli looked at the pretty, brown-eyed brunette with tangled hair and crooked her finger. "Come with me. Let's go wash up." She led the girl, probably just a year past legal, into the bathroom.

Ten minutes later, she came out of the small, mostly clean bathroom with the girl. Her face had been scrubbed, her hair combed, and her teeth washed with a face cloth. Elli tried to keep the conversation light, but the girl wanted to bare her soul on how she'd fallen in love with Doug. She went into great detail, to Elli's dismay, about how they ran naked in the cane field and made love behind a small wooden shack in the middle of nowhere.

"Ready?" Ben asked, walking away from Doug, who was washing dishes in the kitchen. Elli nodded and Ben grabbed her hand and led her outside. "I don't know what to do with him," he confessed as they walked toward the office. "He's been a loose cannon for some time, but it seems to be getting worse."

"It's tough to be employer to Joey's grandfather."

"Joey is his only connection to Sarah." Ben stopped before climbing the couple of steps to the office porch. "I can't let him be around Joey alone anymore. The man is irrational and bitter. Until a few minutes ago, I hadn't realized how deep his resentment for me ran." He looked at Elli. "He blames me for Sarah's death." He closed his eyes. "I think he's an alcoholic."

"Oh, Ben." She hugged him and rested her head against his chest.

"It can be genetic, you know." He sighed. "I worry about Joey having an alcoholic grandfather and mother, and"—he cleared his throat—"a grandmother. My mother."

"Joey will be fine." She looked at Ben. "He knows you love him. You are involved in his life, and you respect him enough to have him involved in yours. He's smart and willful and good. You are doing a great job raising him, Ben."

Ben pressed his lips to hers for a tender, chaste kiss. "Thank you. I wonder how much of his mother he remembers. He was only three when she died, but she did things with such drama that I wonder if he has memories of it."

"Have you asked him?"

"No." He looked at her. "I don't want to stir the pot." Elli thought about Joey saying he wouldn't cause her any trouble and knew the child probably did have bad memories of his mother. "Sarah did some crazy things with Joey at her side. She drank, smoked pot, and dragged him into dance clubs with her. She'd fly off the handle if he cried in front of her friends or didn't behave like she thought a perfect child should." Ben bunched Elli's shirt into his fists. "She'd verbally abuse him, then she would hug him and sing to him and be so sweet Joey would look at her like she hung the moon. She did the same with me. She knew the right things to say to make me believe the rumors were lies. She manipulated me and I let her. I should have protected Joey better."

"I haven't known you long, Ben, but I know you are a good man who loves his son. It sounds like you did the best you could in a difficult situation. You can only act on what you know."

"I loved her, or least the woman I thought she was—the woman she wanted me to think she was." He shook his head. "We were married for five years. Two of those years were good and fun and easy. When I started seeing people whisper when I walked into a room or stop talking altogether, I knew something was wrong. People did that when I was a child and walked into a public place with my mother or father. It didn't take me long to figure out they were gossiping about us and shut up when we got close enough to hear them."

"That couldn't have been easy for you. It must have brought back your childhood pain."

He looked at Elli and his eyes softened. He didn't say the words, but she saw them in his eyes. You understand.

"She manipulated me like my mother did my father. She did all the things to make me fall in love with her. Then, when Joey was born and she had the heir, she changed." He looked over his shoulder, probably wanting to make sure Joey wasn't listening. "I tried to make it work. I tried to get her to go to marriage counseling, private counseling. I researched how to make a problem marriage work. I even spent hours on the Internet trying to figure out what the hell was wrong with her...with me. I think she was textbook narcissistic."

"You and Joey didn't deserve that life."

"No, we didn't and I tried to change it. I tried to set boundaries for her. Nothing worked. She spent every dime we had in the checking account. I had to block her from our savings. She stole from the kennel's petty cash. She treated her friends to lunch, dinner, and cocktails when we didn't have any money left to buy formula for Joey." He looked over his shoulder again. "She bought lovers, Elli. She paid for male prostitutes, and she had the friggin' nerve to bring them into our home."

Sarah had been like his mother on steroids. If she was narcissistic, she wanted to be queen. Ben must have seemed like a king suited for her queendom. He was handsome, wealthy, and respected. Elli imagined she'd want to be the center of attention all the time. She'd seek that to feed her narcissism. The story Doug had told Elli about Ben cutting off Sarah's money was true, but he had gotten the version Sarah wanted her father to have. He may have even given her some money because of it. It was no wonder Ben had trust issues now and thought she was trying to manipulate him.

Elli closed her eyes and sighed. He was right. She had tried to manipulate him. Her heart weighed heavy in her chest. How could she have done that to him? He didn't deserve it. It was worse than talking a blind man over a cliff.

"Doug is grieving," Elli said, turning the conversation back to where it began.

"He blames me for making Sarah crazy the day she crashed the car into a tree." He sighed. "Shit, Elli. Maybe, I did. We had fought right before. She had been drinking all day at a dog show in Lafayette and was putting Joey in her car to take him home. I wouldn't let her." He gripped both of Elli's arms and held her at arm's length from him. "I took Joey from her and I told her to get the hell out of our lives. She did. She took off and crashed the car forty minutes later."

"Oh, Ben." Tears flowed down Elli's cheek. She hated seeing guilt and sadness in his eyes.

"Elli, I have gone over that afternoon in my head a thousand times. I should have taken the car keys away from her. I shouldn't have let her drive." He swallowed hard. "I just wanted to get Joey the hell away from her. I wanted her the hell away from me. I wanted a different life." He turned and walked onto the porch and peered through the window into the office.

"Just wishing for something doesn't make it happen. Trust me, I know this is true." Elli walked to stand near Ben, but didn't touch him. "You don't have that kind of power. No one does." She wiped away the tears burning her cheeks. "Your first responsibility was to make sure Joey was safe. You did that. I know that if you could have kept her from driving drunk, you would have. I know this, Ben." She beat her chest with her fist. "I believe you handled the situation exactly as you had to handle it." She sniffed and wiped new tears off her face. "Could you really have stopped her from driving off without endangering Joey?"

Ben turned and looked at Elli. There was so much pain in his eyes, her heart ached for him. "No." His voice was low, even. "I barely had Joey out of his car seat when she gunned the engine and took off. I had to tuck Joey into my body and dive out of the way to keep from getting hit with the open door. She didn't care if she hit her baby with the damn car, Elli. She didn't care if she hit me."

"Don't let Doug rewrite your history. You know the truth."

"I don't care what he says. I just can't let him hurt Joey, unintentionally or negligently with his behavior."

Joey opened the door and stepped outside. He had a milk moustache and there was peanut butter smeared at the corner of his mouth. He was adorable. "Hey there, you are way too young to be growing a moustache."

"What?" Joey laughed.

Elli ran her finger over her mouth. "I know it's a milk moustache, young man, but don't you try to shave it."

"Oh, Elli. That's silly."

Jenny walked out onto the porch with her snout stuck inside a plastic jar of peanut butter. Her tail was wagging in fast swipes.

"No. That's silly," she said. They laughed as Jenny shook her head and sent the peanut butter jar flying across the porch. BJ raced after it, and after a few licks inside with her long, pink tongue, she had the jar stuck on her snout.

"Why don't Joey and I hike back to the house and see what's happening on the movie set." Elli smiled at Ben. "You stay here and get some work done. Sort things out."

"Can I go with her, Dad?" Joey tugged on his father's hand. "It's the last day of filming."

"Sure." He kissed his son on top of the head, lingering a moment to give him a tight hug. "For the life of me, I don't understand what you find so fascinating with that circus."

"It's a movie, Dad." He laughed, moving like he had springs in his ankles. "Not a circus."

"Same thing." He smiled.

Elli grabbed her dogs' leashes, hanging on a hook on the porch, and latched them to their collars. Joey jumped off the porch. BJ and Jenny rushed after him, not bothering with the stairs. Elli screeched and was forced to jump off the porch into a run. "See you later," she shouted to Ben. "Whoa, girls. Whoa. Joey, help." She laughed and soon got another lesson on how to control her dogs from a very expert six-year-old boy.

* * * *

Ben settled his scuffed boots on top of his desk, clasped his hands behind his head, and eased back into his big leather desk chair.

Elli was right. He needed to be alone to sort things out. She had known that. She seemed to know a lot of things about him. Ben wasn't sure how he felt about that. Women with that kind of instinct about people were dangerous. Elli was dangerous, there was no doubt about it. There was another side of her that Ben couldn't deny either. She was caring. Ben wasn't sure he could trust his assessment of her in that category, though. As genuine as her affection seemed toward Joey, his family, the dogs, and even him, it could be manufactured.

Ben closed his eyes and breathed deeply. He hadn't been breathing right since Elli arrived. The air seemed to be sucked out of the room when she was around, especially when she was wrapped around him bare skin to bare skin. "Don't go there." Thinking of her in a carnal way clogged his brain and achieved nothing except getting him aroused. He had to put Elli on the back burner for now and figure out what do with Doug. That situation was more pressing.

Ben heard a car pull up outside and recognized the quiet purr of the engine. It was Beau. His cousin walked through the door, dressed in dark, pressed jeans and a crisp, light purple, tailored shirt. He wore a few strands of fancy Mardi Gras beads around his neck. One of the necklaces was made of thick black plastic beads, with three twisted straw voodoo dolls wrapped in purple canvas dresses. There were straight pins slipped into their dresses. Too bad there were only three voodoo dolls, he thought, thinking of the movie people who kept coming around his dogs. Might not be a bad idea to have one for Elli, too.

"Coming from a parade?" Ben asked his cousin, who had dropped into the worn leather chair across from the desk.

"No, these beads came from my private stash of parade throws." He had a mischievous grin. "These are some of my titty beads, cuz. I thought I'd see if the voluptuous Heather Harley likes them."

Ben laughed. "My guess is she will, especially if you give them to her. I had about a ten-minute conversation with her this morning and nine and a half minutes of it was her asking me about you. You made quite an impression over dinner last night. I think she might be sweet on you."

"No might about it. I'm driving into New Orleans to have dinner with her again tonight." He winked at Ben. "When you've got it, you've got it. I've got it." He crossed his ankle over his knee. "You don't."

"Did you come here to brag on yourself and dis me?"

"Yep." Beau walked to the refrigerator and got a bottle of water. "The third reason I'm here is to get you to help with loading the family float. Tante Izzy asked me to meet the delivery man who's bringing her and Elli's throws to the float. She wants me to set up their throws and organize everything. She said she was too busy starring in a movie to do it."

"You should've seen her in costume." Ben laughed. "Never thought I'd see the day that Tante Izzy would look like an average all-American grandmother."

"Yeah, no kidding?"

A loud vehicle with a busted muffler drove past the office and stopped nearby. When its engine went silent, Ben got up and pushed aside the blinds to look outside. He hoped it wasn't one of the movie crew people returning to hassle his dogs. Beau came over to look out the window, too. They watched as Doug rushed out of his cottage, waving his arms and pointing in anger at the young man Ben recognized as the guy who had passed out under Doug's table.

"What the hell is going on?" Beau asked.

"Hell if I know, but my guess is that it's carried over from the wild party Doug had at his place last night."

"He had a wild party and didn't invite us?" Beau asked but Ben knew there was no way in hell Beau would party with Doug.

The young man stayed in his car, as Doug continued shouting at him and walked to the passenger side of the car. He climbed in and slammed the door closed. The young driver's eyes were wide as he drove off with Doug toward the main highway.

"I sure wouldn't let him in my car," Beau said, moving away from the window.

"Doug's been acting more hotheaded than usual. Angry. Different." Ben shook his head and walked to his desk and leaned against it. "I'm worried about him." Ben fisted his hands, feeling anger bubbling inside of his stomach. "Do you know that the young Biloxi Police search beagles we're training got loose? It was his fault that they did. He was supposed to be watching the place. Instead, he not only invited the people who let them loose, he was partying with them."

Beau and Ben didn't speak for a moment, both assessing the situation. Beau spoke first. "I wouldn't have figured he'd associate with someone that kid's age. Mid-twenties, right?"

"That's what I'd figure." Ben walked around and sat in the desk chair. "Besides that guy, there were two others partying with him, including a barely eighteen-year-old girl he'd been messing around with."

"Doug is nearly sixty." Beau shook his head. "You know, come to think of it, I was coming out of the movie palace a week ago and saw Doug pull up in front in his truck. Two guys I didn't recognize walked up to him and talked to him through his open window. I didn't pay any attention to it. The guys looked to be college age, I guess."

Ben wasn't sure what the hell was going on. He just knew in his gut that something was wrong. "I'm not going to leave Joey alone with him. I'm glad he's going to Mardi Gras with Camille and her family tomorrow. Otherwise, I'd break the no-kids-ride rule and bring him on our float."

"It's probably midlife crisis," Beau said, standing. "You know, feeling his mortality. Trying to regain his youth."

Ben laughed. "Midlife? That would mean he'd live to be one hundred and twenty."

"As interesting as this conversation is—I am no psychologist. I am at this moment in time a roustabout. Time for me to roust myself and do a bout of labor for Tante Izzy."

Ben stood. "Let's swing by the barn and get my beads on the way out."

Chapter Eleven

Today is my first radiation treatment and I would like to tell you I am feeling brave as I lay on the cold, hard, narrow table, wearing only a plain, pale blue, cotton panty—the kind I only wear for doctor visits, or when I am too sick to care. I know I was prepared for how this would look and sound, but it feels so foreign. All I can do is take deep breaths, inhaling the sterile scents of alcohol and heated hospital equipment. It is a smell I haven't gotten used to in the six months since my diagnosis, it's a scent I'll never forget. Oh God, my body is vibrating now with shivers that started from somewhere deep within my soul. This feeling has nothing to do with the chillingly low thermostat setting that pampers the sensitive radiation equipment above my naked torso. It comes from that fearful place I can't control…my epicenter, where the solid, constant earth shifted. Funny, but someone once described falling in love as feeling the same way—like the earth shifts under your feet. All I can say is…been there, done that…No thanks. I wish you good health, E.

Bosom Blog Buddies Post

Fat Tuesday

It was ten in the morning when the Party Express bus ended its two-hour ride through the streets of Vacherie Parish. The tour included a lot of loud music, loose-hipped dancing, liberal drinking, cautious feasting and uninterrupted laughing from the Bienvenu clan aboard the bus. There were about twenty of them and they all wore similar costumes of plantation-era style clothes, but in the flamboyant colors and bling of Mardi Gras. And, to Elli's surprise, the costumes only covered the top half of their bodies. Shorts or sweat pants were worn on the parts of the body that would be hidden behind the walls of the floats. Since it was a warm day, Elli and Rachel wore shorts and rainbow-striped leggings beneath them.

Elli still couldn't believe she was on the Party Express bus. It was the same purple, green, and gold converted school bus that had carried Ben and his fellow neon pirates onto Sugar Mill Plantation the day she met him. Never in all of her wild imaginings had she thought she would be on that same gyrating, decapitated vehicle singing and having the time of her life. She wished Ben had been there with her. It was ridiculous, but she missed him. She hadn't seen him since the evening before, when he and Joey left the plantation house to stay at the kennel so he could keep an eye on things there. He didn't join the pre-parade party because he had to bring Joey to Camille's place along the parade route to make sure his son was settled before heading to the float. He had also volunteered to give Tante Izzy a ride to the float since she had given up on the early morning partying long ago.

"Come on, Elli," Rachel shouted over the blaring lyrics of *Mardi Gras Mambo*. "Time to load our float. Did anyone tell you the title of our float is the Krewe du Bienvenu? Don't you love the double entendre? The Welcome Krewe and it's our name, too! It's tradition that we're the first float, the welcoming float, right after the Krewe of Cajuns royal court." She waved her arm for Elli to follow, sloshing a generous splash of the spiked lemonade in her hand. Elli lifted her plastic cup of the sweet drink and took a healthy sip to keep hers from doing the same when she climbed off the bus with her cumbersome plastic bag. As soon as Elli's feet hit the parking lot pavement, Ruby handed her a decorated sports bottle with more of the spiked lemonade inside.

"This is better for the float," Ruby explained adjusting her bright orange and purple costume that had twisted during her last dance on the bus. "You won't spill your drink on the parade-goers. They don't like getting soaked with our drinks." She laughed and looked at her husband, John, who was stumbling off the bus. "And try not to toss it with the beads like my darling husband does every year."

"We won't, Mom," Rachel said, looping her arm through Elli's and tugging her toward the two-story float that was decorated with thick metallic tinsel and bright paint, depicting a cartoon-like scene of Sugar Mill Plantation, sugarcane fields and cypress swamps. "Come on, almost everyone from the bus is on the float already. This is it here."

"It's beautiful," Elli said, looking at the tall, moss-draped oak trees arched over the top of the float. There was even a wide plank swing hanging from one of the trees, high above the front of the float. An adorable eight-foot, tan, papier-mâché Labrador with his pink tongue hanging out of its mouth sat perched on the swing. This float and the others around it were a far cry from the homemade floats built on a trailer that she expected to see. "It's just like you see in the movies and the TV coverage of Mardi Gras in New Orleans. It's so colorful and fun."

Elli approached the rear of the float to follow Rachel up the steps and spotted Ben. Her heart started kicking in her chest as she watched him help Rachel, Ruby, and John on the float first. She was last. "Hello, there," she said smiling up at Ben. He returned the smile with such warmth and sincerity that she paused on the middle step and just let it soak into her skin. "Your smile is better than the sunshine on this beautiful blue sky day."

"Rachel," Ben shouted over his shoulder. "What have you given Elli to drink?"

"Lemonade." Elli lifted her sports bottle. "And vodka."

He tugged on her arm to get her up the last two steps. "You might want to slow down or you won't make the start of the parade at noon."

Elli threw her arms around Ben's neck, knocking him in the head with the huge plastic bag she carried. "Sorry." She kissed him on the mouth.

"It worked," Tante Izzy shouted with a happy hoot from behind Ben. "I tole youz the potion would work."

Elli released Ben. "I'm sorry. I shouldn't have kissed you. That wasn't very covert."

Ben tucked his hands into his pockets and gave her a half smile, but said nothing.

"We didn't drink it," Elli said, looking past Ben to Tante Izzy. "It probably has something weird in it like spider spit."

Tante Izzy laughed. "What youz worried 'bout? Spider spit is organic."

"What are y'all conniving about?" Ben asked, but both women just waved their hands at him as if he were a bothersome fly.

"You don't know nothin'," Tante Izzy told him from where she sat on her tall, gold lamé, cushioned stool. Her half gold, half purple lamé hoop dress encircled her like the petals of a flower. With the tall bins of beads covering every inch of space around her and the beads hanging on hooks behind her, she looked like she was floating in a sea of color. Elli grabbed her cell phone from her back pocket and snapped a picture of Tante Izzy. "Moodee, rascal. Take another picture. I wasn't givin' you my Greta Garbo smile."

Elli snapped another picture, then took a quick photo of Ben, who was just staring at her in that dark, sexy way that made her insides melt. After what seemed like a half hour but was probably only seconds, he pointed to Tante Izzy. "Your spot is next to her," he began, then burst out laughing when Elli turned to look at where he wanted her to go. "What is that on your backside, cher?"

Elli wagged her hips and the big, bulbous, naked plastic butt danced. "It's my backside. One of the riders at the very first parade I went to had it. I thought it was hilarious." She smiled. "I have one for you, too, Ben."

"She got me one." Rachel and Ruby shouted in tandem, bouncing their huge fannies to the beat of the music.

She reached into the bag and handed Ben and Tante Izzy each a two-foot fanny. "Where's your costume, Ben?" she asked, looking at his black T-shirt and jeans.

"Right here." He pointed to a southern gentleman's white jacket, purple shirt, and green-striped ribbon tie hanging on a hook with the beads. "And here." He shoved an obnoxiously tall top hat on his head. It was made to look even more ridiculous because there was a huge green rubber alligator perched on top of it. "I added the alligator for you, cher, since you seem to be so fond of them."

Elli and Ben laughed and continued teasing one another as he helped her climb over dozens of large potato sacks of beads to wedge into a spot that just fit her plastic butt. It was then that she spotted Beau on the other side of Tante Izzy. A woman was standing close to him. Her face was hidden behind a big feather mask, but Elli knew instantly who it was. There wasn't much that could camouflage her iconic body. Except, maybe, a huge, plastic fanny.

"Hey, Heather and Beau," she called out to them. Beau returned her greeting with a warm smile and big wave. Heather said hello. Then, without preamble, she offered to buy Donna from her. "Sorry. As much of a pain in the tush as she is, she's not for sale. Speaking of tushes…" Elli handed Heather the fake fanny she had originally given to Ben. She turned in a circle to show her the one she wore. "It's part of our costumes." Tante Izzy held up her fanny, too.

"Thank you," she laughed, hugging the fanny to her chest.

"Here, let me help you tie it on," Beau offered with a mischievous grin.

"You have just made Beau's day," Ben said, laughing. He patted the top of the sack of beads between them. "Just sit on the sacks of beads if you are tired of standing." He plopped onto the pile of beads closest to her. A high-school marching band started warming up nearby. He reached in the bin full of ice in front of her and dragged out a bottle of water. There were four more tucked inside. "Drink this for a while."

Elli had that warm sensation again. She knew he had put the water in the bin for her. It was very sweet and made her feel special. She took a sip and handed the water to Ben. "You should hydrate, too." He took a swig. "Tante Izzy told me you set up my beads for me." She smiled. "This must have taken awhile. Thank you."

Ben took another drink and handed the water back to her. "No problem." She wrapped her hand around the bottle, but Ben didn't let her have it. He twisted and grabbed her other wrist and pulled her down onto the beads next to him. Her face was inches from his. He stared at her a long time and Elli was helpless to do anything but stare back at him. Her heart hammered hard in her chest. She ached to just touch him but didn't dare in front of his family. He slid his finger to the thin flesh on Elli's wrist. "I feel your pulse, cher," he whispered so she was the only one who could hear him. "It's pounding like mine. Why is that? What's going on between us?" His eyes held hers a moment in an intense gaze. "Is this some kind of California voodoo?"

"I don't know, Ben. I don't know." Elli knew her voice was no more than a whisper, but that was all she could manage.

Ben let go of her wrist and blew out a heavy breath. "This is bullshit." He shook his head. "I know this spark we fire between us doesn't mean anything. So why can't we just enjoy it? Have fun with it today. I just want to be free to act and respond and do what the hell I want. Mardi Gras is a day for indulgences. I want to indulge. Just for today. Agreed?"

"Well, I..." This conversation with Ben was odd. It seemed out of character to Elli. He hadn't issued her any warnings or mentioned that this attraction between them had no bearing on their differences with the plantation. She supposed he didn't have to; she knew the truth of their situation. She understood he knew that she knew, too. Maybe the spiked lemonade just made this whole thing seem confusing to her muddled brain.

Ben stood, looked at her a long minute like he was trying to analyze something. Then he shook his head. "Screw it." He turned toward his family who were busy eating, organizing their throws, and chatting. He belted out a loud whistle, drawing their attention. "Listen up. I want all of y'all to know that I intend on enjoying my day. I want to have fun and not worry that you crazy people will read more into me hanging out with Elli than you should. So don't. We're going to enjoy each other today and tomorrow we are going our separate ways. It's that simple. So I don't want to hear any snickering or see anybody tripping over their tongues if we act like we like each other. We don't. I want you all to know, Elli and I will not be the butt of your gossip." Elli turned in a circle waving her big fanny, breaking the tension and making everyone laugh. Ben smiled. "Enough said. Laisser les bon temps rouler." A chorus of celebratory shouts went up.

"Now, why'd youz go and stand on youz soapbox like dat." Tante Izzy shook her head. "Now I won't have nothin' to talk 'bout with the family at the crawfish boil tomorrow."

Elli smiled at Tante Izzy, but she knew it was that kind of gossip Ben was trying to avoid. He hated it. He had been the topic of useless conversation his whole life because of his mother, father, and his wife. Whether it was good-natured or not, he was trying to prevent it from happening again. Elli understood now that he just wanted to have a carefree day and not be the center of gossip because of it. She intended to see that he got that. He deserved it. He had never done anything wrong to warrant being the talk of the town. Elli's heart squeezed in her chest. It wasn't fair and she hated that he had felt bad when people talked about his awful situation as a child of a dysfunctional marriage and as a married man with a crazy, cheating wife.

"I have a good idea, Tante Izzy," Elli began, her throat tight with emotion. "How about instead of gossiping about Ben, you talk about being in a big budget movie, with Sam Cooper and Heather Harley. I think everyone has plenty of things they can talk about other than something that is none of their business."

"I can do dat." She looked at Elli and winked. Oh, the old woman was a sly one, Elli realized. She was testing Elli to see if she cared about Ben, too. Her defense of him must have satisfied Izzy, for she started talking to Beau and Heather.

Elli looked at Ben, who was repositioning a few sacks of beads to open the space near her. She tapped him on the shoulder. When he turned to face him, she gave him a quick peck on his cheek. "I want you to know I think the declaration you gave to your family was awesome. It was brave and smart. You were proactive and defused anything awful that may have come from family gossip. You know, Dumbledore was right when he was awarding the House Cup he said , 'It takes a great deal of bravery to stand up to your enemies, but a great deal more to stand up to your friends.'" She smiled. "It was meant to recognize what Neville Longbottom did, but the same is true for standing up to your family, too."

Ben gave Elli a sweet hug and kiss on the top of her head. "You can be way too insightful sometimes, Texian."

"Hungry?" Rachel asked, as she extended a box of fried chicken to Ben and Elli. She smiled at Ben. "Nice speech."

Ben took a couple of legs and patted Rachel on her phony fanny. "Get along, little doggie."

She laughed. "You have always been my favorite cousin."

"Hey, I heard that," Beau said walking up. "I know that is only because you have never forgiven me for telling Johnny Breaux that you wanted to marry him and have his babies."

"Well, yeah." Rachel snorted. "I was twelve and totally mortified that you did that. Worse than that, after he heard I was in love with him, all he wanted to do was touch my tiny little preteen boobs."

"If I had known, I would've kicked his ass," Beau said.

"You didn't have to. Ben did. That's why he's my favorite." She pranced away.

"Brat," Beau shouted to her departing back.

"Didn't I teach you better manners than to call a pretty female names?" a male voice said from behind Beau. It was Sheriff Ronald Bienvenu. He was dressed in his dark blue and gray uniform. The row of tiny stars on both of his shoulders and the big one over his chest were shining like a set of new dimes. Beau pretended remorse and the men teased one another for a time, with Elli included in their sparring. After about twenty minutes, the sheriff's radio, which was clipped to his shirt, crackled. Ronald answered the call that no one except him had heard. "Okay. Let's get everyone lined up. Roll in ten minutes," he said into the radio. He patted Elli on the shoulder. "Ready for your first ride, rookie?"

"I never imagined I'd get to ride in a Mardi Gras parade. It's an unexpected gift. "She smiled at Tante Izzy. "Thank you. Thank you all—Bienvenu clan." She clapped her hands. "When I get excited, or nervous or scared, movie quotes just pop into my head and this one from The Notebook just did. I guess that's because being part of the Krewe du Bienvenu is a little miracle for me. The quote is this: 'Miracles, no matter how inexplicable or unbelievable, are real and can occur without regard to the natural order of things.'" She laughed. "And Mardi Gras is definitely not in the natural order of things."

"It sure isn't," Sheriff Bienvenu said. "Enjoy the ride."

Elli watched as he left the float and climbed into a red BMW convertible that had stickers along the side announcing that the vehicle had been seized during a drug arrest. He sped off toward the front of the parade. Sirens howled on the lead fire trucks, marching bands played happy tunes as they fell into precision lines, tractor engines warmed as each one prepared to pull the float hooked behind it, and people on the street jumped to their feet. Elli turned to Ben, who had not only changed into his costume, but managed to move the beads so she was standing right next to him. "My heart is going to shoot out of my chest, Ben." She grabbed his hand and placed it on her chest. "Feel it?"

His eyes crinkled with his smile. "Yeah, cher." He leaned into her, his lips only a whisper from hers. "Happy Mardi Gras." He kissed her full and wet and without restraint right there in front of his family and all of Cane, Louisiana. Elli was honored that he trusted her to show him respect and mutual esteem in front of his people. He had figuratively walked out naked and exposed himself to his family, not really knowing if she would point a finger at him and shout that he didn't have any clothes on. Had the people that he grew up with known what a huge thing had just happened when he asked them not to gossip about him? By their playful, good natured smiles she suspected they missed the real point of his actions. Elli didn't and her heart nearly burst knowing it. Her admiration had grown for Ben that day.

The float jerked forward as it began to roll and Elli fell back onto a sack of beads. "Tell me what to do, Ben," she shouted over the blare of the music on their float. "I don't know how this works." Rachel handed her a cold sports bottle filled with the spiked lemonade concoction she had earlier. Elli took a big sip and shoved it in the middle of the stack of beads to her left.

"Just grab a string of beads and toss it to the people lined up along the side of the road. If someone draws your attention, throw them a few extra. We have plenty." The float turned the corner and a sea of people, ten to twenty deep, fanned out before them. The float moved slowly enough for Elli to see happy faces, bright smiles, and dancing eyes. She grabbed a necklace and a dozen came with it as she tossed it over the side. Two men grabbed for it, but she wasn't able to see who got it. There were more people screaming for her to throw them something, so Elli looked at Ben to see how he was keeping up with the demands. She decided she was overthinking the whole process. Mimicking Ben and Tante Izzy, she fell into the same easy, but not so graceful dance of grab, separate, and toss. It was fun and physical to dole out the prizes. Elli had no idea how people got drunk on the float. There just wasn't any time to imbibe. There wasn't even time to snack on a MoonPie or two. Instead, she was tossing them to the children in the crowd.

"Ben, look." She pointed to a person in the crowd who was wearing a gorilla costume and eating a banana.

He immediately pointed to the woman in a safari costume next to him, holding a leash that was attached to a collar around the gorilla's neck. They laughed and continued that game of spotting something funny and trying to one-up it immediately afterward. They did a lot of laughing that day. When the parade stopped for the first time to give the bands a chance to rest for a few minutes, Ben helped her and Tante Izzy reposition their throws for easier access. He tossed the empty sacks behind them, offered Elli and Tante Izzy a sandwich from the float's community ice chest, and handed a stuffed animal to a precious toddler who was being lifted up to the float by her father. She blew Ben a kiss with her chubby little hands and he pretended to catch it. Elli's heart melted.

"You are such a chick-magnet," Elli said as she tossed a giant toothbrush to a young boy about Joey's age. On second glance at the child, Elli realized, it was Joey. "Hey there!" she shouted to him. He came racing up to the float, shouting her name. It surprised Elli that he was calling for her and not his father or Tante Izzy or another family member. It warmed her insides and she wished she could just reach down and scoop him up into a giant hug.

"I was down the street a few blocks and came running here to see y'all when the parade stopped," he explained. Camille stood next to Joey, the smile on her face from a second before wilted as she spotted Elli. Camille took a step back and nodded once to Elli. Elli understood she was giving up on the hope of a romantic relationship with Ben. How awful, she thought, looking at Ben who was completely oblivious that he had just broken a woman's heart along the parade route. Elli mouthed the words, "I'm sorry," to Camille and meant it. She never wanted to hurt anyone. Camille smiled a weak smile and answered, "It's fine. I never had him."

Ben, still blind to what was going on around him, reached into a small box off to the side of him and without warning, jumped up, making battle sounds and squirted Joey with a water grenade. "Dad!" He laughed and ducked behind Camille, who got squirted with water intended for Joey. She looked stunned and amused at the same time.

"That's not fair," Elli shouted, reaching into the box, grabbing a couple of water grenades, and squirting Ben with them. Ben retaliated. He reached into a bag behind him and drenched Elli with a huge super-soaker gun he had in the box. When Joey howled with laughter, he turned the water cannon on his son. The float jerked forward, and as the tractor began moving, Ben started dumping the plastic necklaces she now knew that the locals called beads, over the side to Joey. Elli and Tante Izzy did the same. Camille and Joey scooped as much as they could carry in their arms as a dozen people nearby dove into the fray to get their share. Others who had witnessed the ridiculous amount of beads being tossed off the float started shouting for Ben and Elli to give them a ton of beads, too. Elli grabbed a dozen beads at a time and threw them into the crowd in rapid-fire succession. She even tossed a few stuffed animals into the air over their heads for fun. The crowd went wild.

"We're having fun, now," Ben shouted to her, tossing Frisbees into the crowd.

"'Happiness is only happiness if there is a violin-playing goat.' Hugh Grant, Notting Hill," Elli said and Ben turned to face her fully.

His eyes brightened, shinier than she had ever seen before. He laughed, hard and loud and unrestrained. She forgot about Camille and the entire population of parade goers around them. Ben consumed her whole. She felt him on her skin and in her heart. This happy, free, joyful Ben ignited a wanting so deep, she felt it burning in her toes. She leaned over the mound of beads between them and kissed him on the mouth. He sucked in a breath and deepened the kiss. Somewhere from the crowd on the street someone shouted, "Get a hotel room." Elli broke the kiss and smiled at him.

"This," she began, pointing in a big, dramatic gesture to the crowd and to Ben, "is a violin-playing goat." It was in that lightning bolt moment that Elli realized she was in love with Ben.

Chapter Twelve

Every day I have to go into the radiation clinic and go through the same thing. Day after day after day. And, each time the radiation treatment doesn't get any easier. I shouldn't complain, and most days I don't feel compelled to. In fact, normally, I feel terribly guilty when I complain...there are so many others whose journeys are more difficult than mine. Yet, today, I'm feeling overwhelmed...I was told to expect it. Expecting and experiencing it doesn't make it easier. Today, as I did yesterday and the days before, I lay on a cold hard table with my breasts exposed and my torso squeezed into a tight foam form. I lay there so cold. So damn cold and oddly, grateful for it. The physical discomfort gives me something to focus on that is real, tangible, and immediate. Radiation is invisible...intangible, except for the burns it leaves behind on my flesh. With the chemo infusion I could see the medicine flow from the IV bag through the clear plastic tubing into the port in my body. Radiation is so different. Yes, the cold temperature of the room is tangible. It serves a practical purpose of keeping the machines with the invisible rays happy. The cold also gives me the distraction I need to stop my stampeding mind from jumping into an abyss of paralyzing fear where the only thoughts are of what is happening to me and why. If I close my eyes I can actually see the icy air blowing against my exposed flesh. It is there in thin, blue swirls. When I focus on the cold, I don't think of the breast cancer trying to eat my insides, or of how much I don't want to die...E.

Bosom Blog Buddies Post

Ash Wednesday

I'm in love with Ben.

Elli woke up with the revelation of the day before on her mind. The fact that she was able to sleep at all knowing that, surprised her. Mardi Gras had depleted all of her energy and rendered her brain nonfunctioning. It had been an amazing day. Now, with the hint of dawn approaching, the free spirit of Mardi Gras was gone. Elli understood that today would be no different than the day before she'd learned of her true feelings for Ben. It would remain her secret and she would never do anything about it.

Elli rolled over onto her side, careful to not disturb Donna on her pillow. Doe, who was crowded with the other dogs at her feet, looked at her with tired eyes. Jenny and BJ just continued sleeping. Elli reached for her cell phone on the nightstand to see what time it was and spotted the amber bottle with Tante Izzy's love potion. She smiled. Wouldn't Tante Izzy be pleased to know she had fallen for Ben? Too bad there wasn't a healing potion to cure cancer.

There was a creaking sound in the hall and the doorknob turned on her bedroom door. Elli sat up in bed. Ben wouldn't be sneaking into her room with his son in the room next door, would he? Her heart gave a quick start as the door flew open and a bleary-eyed Joey, tears on his cheeks, ran into her room and onto her bed. He hugged Elli, pressing his tiny fingers hard into her arms. "I had a bad dream."

Doe yawned a noisy yawn and jumped off the bed, turning in two circles before going to sleep on the floor. "Oh, sweet boy, I'm sorry." She shifted to the side, picked up Donna and pulled back her blanket for him to climb in. "Tell me about it."

Joey scooted under the covers and shook his head. "Don't want to."

Elli settled Donna on his lap. Jenny and BJ didn't like all the movement and jumped off the bed to cuddle with Doe. "You know, sometimes when we talk about the bad dreams, it helps us to realize that it can't be true."

Joey shivered and looked up at Elli. Tears filled his eyes. "This is true." Elli hugged him to her side. "My mommy was yelling at me and she had mean, red eyes. Then she laughed like a scary witch and kissed me on the forehead. There were other witches and warlocks there, too. They all were laughing and flying around the room making really, really, scary noises."

Elli smoothed his silky dark hair with gentle strokes. The dream probably was true in the sense that he got horrible mixed signals from his mother. Hadn't Ben said that she had yelled at him for not being the perfect baby in front of her friends, but continued to drag him into bars and parties with her? Had Joey dreamed of a memory of his mother? "That dream must have frightened you something awful. I know it would have scared me." He rested his head on her chest and for the second time in as many days, Elli fell in love.

"I hate witches and warlocks."

"Me, too." Donna looked at Elli and then Joey. She sneezed and went back to sleep. "But you know, don't you, that they aren't real." He looked up at her with big, bright green, trusting eyes—hanging on every word she spoke as if it were gospel. "I've been living a long time and I know I have never seen a witch or warlock or even a werewolf or monster under my bed. I think those things don't exist or I would have seen one by now, don't you think?"

Joey nodded and rested his head on Elli's chest again. His breath was even and steady as he petted Donna. His body was warm and relaxed against hers. It felt like heaven and she closed her eyes to burn the memory into her soul. "I love you, Elli," he said. "I wish you were my mommy." Right or wrong, in that quiet moment wrapped in the warm cocoon of blanket and child, she wished for that, too.

"I love you, Joey." They both fell back asleep.

* * * *

Ben woke and reached for Elli's soft warm body next to him. He felt only cool sheets and empty space. He wasn't fully awake, but disappointment lodged in his chest. He propped himself up on his elbows. "What in the hell is wrong with me?" He was okay with lusting for Elli, but missing her after spending an entire day with her was just plain nuts. He climbed out of bed and scratched his bare chest as he walked into the bathroom. Maybe if he had sneaked into her room in the middle of the night, he wouldn't be wishing she was in bed with him now. Maybe he would have gotten her out of his system. He looked at himself in the mirror. "Who are you kidding? You want her just as much today as you did the first time you had her." He splashed water on his face, brushed his teeth, and threw on athletic shorts and a clean undershirt. "Well, life is full of disappointments," he mumbled, leaving his room and heading to Joey to check on him as he did every morning. "I might not have the girl, but at least I'll still have Sugar Mill Plantation when she heads back to California."

Ben opened his son's bedroom door and saw that he wasn't in his room. It was early, but he figured Joey was still charged from the excitement of Mardi Gras and couldn't sleep. He was probably watching cartoons downstairs. He started to head in that direction when he noticed Elli's door was slightly ajar. He pushed it open, and felt like he had been struck with a bat in his gut. There in Elli's narrow single bed, his son was wrapped in her arms. His relaxed face was nestled against her chest; his pink lips were parted in that same sweet way they had when he was an infant. He looked so peaceful...and content. Ben's heart pinched. His son must have missed Elli, too.

He moved on stealth feet over the old creaky wooden floor toward them. Jenny, Doe, and BJ lifted their heads. A second later, when they recognized him, their tails began to wag. Ben pointed to the door and the dogs got up and walked out of the room. Donna looked up at him from the bed, then rested her head on her crossed paws. She didn't move, but she continued to look at him.

Ben nodded to her, acknowledging her silent communication that she wouldn't wake Elli and Joey. He moved another step closer to watch Elli sleep. Her face was smoothed of all expression as her head was sunken in a cloud of pillows. She looked ethereal as her thick, dark eyelashes cast a shadow on her porcelain cheeks. She looked so angelic that if it wasn't for the worn, fuzzy blue knit cap on her head, he would have searched for her halo. Ben smiled. They both looked so damn comfortable that he wanted to pull back the sheets and slip into the tiny single bed with them. If it wasn't for his impressionable six-year-old boy, he would have. Instead, he just stared at them a few minutes longer, than exited the room as quietly as he had entered.

Ben leaned against the closed door. "What am I supposed to do about this?" He looked heavenward. "The woman tries to take my son's home from him and coddles him with affection. It's a friggin' dichotomy. What is the truth, here? Does she care or not?" He shook his headed and started for the stairs. "She's freakin' Sybil. That's what she is."

Ben was halfway down the stairs when the aroma of coffee brewing hit him. The sound of dishes rattling had him running down the rest of the way into the kitchen. He doubted that the dogs were fixing breakfast, although those dogs did act more human than canine.

"Good morning. Glad to see you're up early."

"Uncle Ronald." Ben took the cup he was offered and sat at the kitchen table. "What are you doing here so early? We're not boiling the crawfish until ten-thirty." Ben started to get up to find the dogs to put them out, but Ronald stopped him.

"Elli's dogs are outside. Lucky is, too." Ronald, who was not in uniform, just a pair of jeans and red golf shirt, sat across from Ben. He pushed a manila folder on the table toward him. "I thought you'd want to look at this, before all hell breaks loose in a few hours. The fire marshal e-mailed me the photos from Elli's camera last night. That included the video that's been converted into stills."

Ben opened the folder and the photo on top was a picture of Elli's shoes in midstride as she walked in a cane field. The next picture was of Jenny's ear. The next two were of her knee and Doe's snout and of the dogs running ahead of her. "So, I see she is not much of a photographer," Ben said flipping to the next picture. "But at least the lab was able to retrieve the…" Ben's mouth snapped shut. He lifted the photograph of the front of the cabin that was on top of the stack. "Is this a face?"

Ronald looked to where Ben was pointing. "I think it is. It's hard to say. The dogs are reacting to something, that's for sure." He pointed to where they were standing on their hind legs and barking at the door. "Take a look at the next photo. It's zoomed in."

Ben lifted the next picture. "Yeah. That definitely looks like a face. It's too blurry to make out the details, though."

"This is the one I thought you'd especially want to see." He tapped on the next photo in the pile. Ben picked it up. "The state lab zoomed in on the southeast quadrant."

"Shit." Ben looked at Ronald and then at the photo again. "What the hell is my truck doing there."

"It's definitely yours." Ronald tapped the photo. "No mistaken that piece of crap you drive."

Ben felt his ears burn with anger. "Yeah, but I didn't drive it there before the fire."

"If you say you didn't, I believe you," Ronald said, his voice even. "I don't care if you have a strong motive. It doesn't matter to me that you wanted Elli to leave Sugar Mill more than anyone else." He shook his head and when all Ben could do was look at him because words didn't pop into his head, he continued. "Trying to scare her, might accomplish that. Not that I think you did that."

"I didn't." Ben slammed his fist on the table.

Ronald nodded. "Who has access to your truck?"

"Any one of my employees. Anyone who walked into my office. I keep the keys on the desk in an old chipped dog food bowl." Ben quickly looked through the rest of the photos. They were well-framed photos of the house, the bayou, and the sugarcane fields. There were even a few of Elli's dogs. "Are these the only photos the state got?"

"There were some others I didn't want to waste the ink to print. It was of her approach to the cabin and you don't see anything of use." He took a sip of coffee. "The fire marshal is coming today to talk to you."

"I don't know what I can tell him that will help." Ben stood and refilled his coffee cup. "Uncle Ronald, this makes me sick. How in the hell didn't I see someone take my truck? And why didn't I hear it being returned?" He shook his head and lowered his voice, like he was talking to himself. Ronald watched him as he paced while sorting his thoughts. "I was working some noisy k-9 Shepherds in the training field. Considering I was on the opposite side of where the truck was parked, I guess it is plausible that I couldn't see or hear the truck being driven away from the kennel."

"I was thinking, Ben, since you probably haven't cleaned it lately, we could try to lift prints off your truck. We can see who has been in it recently. Maybe we can figure out if there were prints left behind by someone who shouldn't have been in your truck."

"I guess that means you'll have to get my fingerprints and those of my workers to see if they match."

"Unless we have them in our files."

"You don't have mine." He shrugged his shoulders. "I don't know about Elli. The background checks I did on my employees all came up clean. No convictions. I didn't do a check on Doug."

"I'll dust your truck at the kennel." Ronald said. He carried his cup to the sink and washed it. "Park it out of view of the family. We know how they are if they get wind something is brewing. Especially, Tante Izzy." He laughed. "I'll print you and Elli when I'm finished with the truck. We'll be able to tell which are Joey's because they'll be child-sized. Let's see if any others show up. If they do, we'll run them in the computer. If we don't get a match, then we can come back to print your staff."

"I really hate this, you know." Ben leaned against the cabinet. "When do you expect the marshal?"

"He didn't say. I suspect at the most inconvenient time. That's when an investigator likes to show up. Then and when he thinks he can get a free meal."

Ben smiled. "The free meal will be at the most inconvenient time. During the crawfish boil."

"You got that right." The sheriff laughed. "I've got the fingerprint kit in my car. How about you drive the truck to the kennel now so we can get this thing done."

"Let me tell Elli I'm leaving for a while." Uncle Ronald lifted a brow. "Don't read anything into that. I just want her to keep an eye on Joey while I'm gone."

Ronald patted Ben on the back. "It's none of my business."

"Damn straight, it isn't." He frowned. "I'll meet you at the kennel."

* * * *

Ben was still not back from the kennel when Elli heard the first of the Bienvenues arrive. He had wakened her about three hours earlier to ask her to watch Joey, who was still sleeping beside her. He said he had business to take care of and wouldn't be long. Joey had slept for another hour before wandering into the kitchen where she was fixing organic, gluten-free pancakes. He ate them without complaint once she scooped homemade, chemical-free whipped cream on top of them. Afterward, they straightened the house in preparation for company, although Joey told her the family only came into the house to use the restroom or if it rained. Everything was set up outside under the huge oak tree.

"Hello. Hello," Ruby called from the back door. Doe, Jenny, BJ, and Donna started barking and ran to greet her. She stepped inside and closed the screened door behind her. "Hush, now. It's cousin Ruby. Y'all know me." She petted Doe on the head in an awkward pat. "My John and I are here with the tables. He's setting them up now. Cousin T-Boy is coming with the crawfish and boiling pots. And everyone else will come when they come. Except Rachel. She's at work. Y'all come on out when you want."

"Ben is at the kennel. It's just Joey and me." She looked at where Ruby's husband was setting up the tables under the huge canopy of the old oak tree. "What can I do to help?"

"You can spread the newspapers on the table. I remember Ben had the old papers stacked by the door, right here." Ruby looked around the space where coats and shoes and newspapers were usually piled. Elli bit her lip. She had picked up the clutter and thrown the newspaper into a recycling bucket she set up outside. "Mon Dieu. Call him to see where he put it. I know he must have it somewhere. He always saves it for the tables."

Elli nodded, but didn't tell her she had tossed it only a few minutes before. When Ruby left, she ran outside, gathered it from the shed next to the garbage cans, and carried it to the tables. It was still tied in a bundle with string. "What do I do with this now?" she asked Joey, who had followed her with the dogs outside. John walked over, took a pocket knife from his overalls, and cut the string around the newspaper.

"It's good to have one of these with you all the time," he said, showing her his sharpened knife. "I gave Ruby a brand new Boker single-blade pocket knife for Mother's Day last year. I even got her a fancy, tooled red case for it."

"I would have preferred pearl earrings," she said, walking up to them. "I can't wear a pocket knife to the garden club luncheons," she added, sounding amused.

"Bebe, you know you like it better than pearls." John pulled Ruby against his big grizzly body and hugged her. Ruby didn't push him away as Elli thought she would. Instead, she hugged him right back. "You love dat knife."

"I guess I couldn't open my QVC boxes with pearl earrings," she laughed.

"Isn't he the sweetest man? Taking care of me like that? Just this past Christmas he gave me Mace and a Taser. I keep them in my car. You never know when you might need them."

Elli wasn't sure she'd describe a man who bought a knife, Mace, and a Taser as sweet, but she supposed the man was just trying to protect the woman he loved. "Have you ever stunned anyone?" she asked Ruby.

"No, but I keep it fully charged and ready." She laughed and waved to the latest Bienvenu driving up with a flat-bed trailer loaded with two big pots and boiling equipment. Tante Izzy drove up in her bright pink truck soon afterward. More Bienvenues followed. Soon, the dogs were bouncing from one person to another, including Donna, who ended up in the arms of one of the pretty teenage girls. Music began to play from speakers that two college-aged men installed. Tante Izzy didn't like the music and yelled at the boys.

"Dis is Ash Wednesday," she shouted, pointing to the smear of ashes on her forehead. The boys smiled and pointed to the ashes on their foreheads. "The beginnin' of Lent. We cover da mirrors and there is no loud music. It'z a day of penance. We'z don't eat meat today, so it'z okay for da crawfish boil. It'z not a party." The boys complained but lowered the music and changed it to a slow Cajun fiddle instrumental. "Dat's better."

Elli looked around her. She had met most of the people there the day before either on the float, at breakfast, or along the parade route. She walked to the back steps and sat a moment, alone, needing to separate herself from the Bienvenues. They had made her feel part of their clan, but she knew she wasn't and never would be. If she was to do what she came here to do, she had to keep her spirit and heart separated from them. She had to separate herself emotionally from Joey and Ben, too.

Tears sprang to Elli's eyes as she gazed at the scene under the oak tree as she would a movie. The moss that was draped like thick ribbons on the full, dark branches swayed in a graceful dance above the tables in the light breeze. She saw the bright, happy eyes of the family members sitting at the tables, sharing stories. Clumsy dogs played in the dull green grass. It was something that she knew must have gone on for generations. If she managed to convince Ben to sell the plantation to a venture capitalist, this family tradition would be lost. She imagined there were other huge oak trees with gunmetal gray moss swaying in the breeze where they could eat crawfish on Ash Wednesday. It would be different for them, though, because it wouldn't be this tree that they had come to as toddlers, teenagers, young married couples, and parents. Would a change in location break the links in that chain?

The first steaming batch of bright red, boiled crawfish was spread across the center of the tables with bright yellow boiled corn on the cob. Bienvenues reached in and began eating. Tante Izzy waved for Elli to join them. She just couldn't enter this scene. She was the villain, the evil stranger who planned to destroy this happy world. She was nauseated knowing how wretched she was to continue with the plan to sell the plantation. Elli signaled to Tante Izzy that she had to make a phone call. She needed to talk to Abby. She also had to check her computer to see if any potential investors had responded to her e-mails. Elli wanted to throw up.

"Abby, I'm such a rat," she said to her friend on the phone once she explained what was happening under the beautiful oak tree.

"You care about them," Abby said, getting right to the heart of the problem. "You care about them as individuals and as a family."

Elli plopped on her bed with her laptop and downloaded her e-mails. "I care about the foundation, too."

"I don't know what to tell you, Elli. This is way too emotional for me. You know, I like to deal with the facts. With a linear thought process." She sighed. "You have always challenged my orderly processing."

The e-mails flashed onto the screen and Elli saw that one was from Online Auto Sales. She clicked on it. "Well, I sold my car."

"Okay." Abby's tone was even. "I can't tell if you are happy about that or not."

"Happy? That's a strong word." She sighed and forwarded the e-mail to Abby with the amount she got for her prized car that once signaled she had made it as a movie producer. "Considering the wild week I've had here, including a slide into a ditch, I'm just glad the car escaped damage." She smiled thinking of what else happened after the crash that night. It was a memory she would always enjoy thinking about when she left the plantation and Ben. "Well, the car is in the same condition that it was in when I drove onto Sugar Mill. I can't say the same for myself."

"Oh, Elli," Abby said, sympathy in her voice.

"I don't want to talk about me. I want to talk about the car." She closed her eyes to better focus on business. "I'm donating the money from the car sale to the foundation. It would've been nice to get a little more, but I think it's fair considering how fast I sold it." Elli's fingers tapped along the keyboard. "Can you help me do the title transfer?"

"I'll take care of it. Where should I have the buyer pick up the car? He's in Atlanta."

"Can you see if he'll come to Cane to get it? I expect I'll be here another week."

"Done."

Elli looked at the other e-mails with Sugar Mill Plantation in the subject line. "Well, two investors are going to review the packet I sent to them and get back to me in a couple of days. Sam Cooper's business manager e-mailed me that he wants to evaluate the property for investment, too."

"That's great. Three potential investors." Elli's stomach knotted as Abby got excited. "For the first time in a few months, I feel really hopeful."

"Well, one side is falling into place." Elli sighed. "I'm not sure Ben will."

Joey walked into Elli's room holding a live brown crawfish in his hand. He smiled at Elli and made monster sounds as he bounced the crawfish in the air. Its long claws waved in protest. "Tante Izzy sent me in to get you. She said the crawfish are better hot than cold, so you had better come now." Joey laughed. "And she said she didn't want to wait all day for you to come. She's almost ready for her nap."

"I wouldn't interfere with Tante Izzy's nap if I were you," Ben said, walking up behind Joey and mussing his son's hair. "Hey, what you got there?" He took the crawfish from his son and walked over to Elli. She shuffled off the bed.

"I have to go, Abby. I'm about to mauled by a mini lobster." She hung up and threw her fists onto her hips. "If you think that little urchin scares me, then…" Elli screamed as Ben placed the crawfish on her arm. He snatched it back and started laughing. Joey was laughing, too. Her heart grew three sizes seeing them so happy. She was so in love with them. There was no doubt about it: the sooner she got out of Cane, the better.

"Come on," Ben said, grabbing her hand and tugging her to the door. He handed Joey the crawfish. "I'm hungry."

Soon, Elli was settled at the table, sitting next to Ben and across from Tante Izzy. Ben placed a few dozen crawfish in front of her. "What am I supposed to do with that?" she asked.

Tante Izzy snorted. "Mais, she'z a Texian for sure."

Joey handed Elli a paper bowl with some sort of pale orange-colored sauce. "Uncle Beau said to tell you the sauce was made with organic mayonnaise and ketchup and some other stuff."

Elli dipped her finger into the sauce and tasted it. "Yum. I taste a little horseradish, too. It's almost like a remoulade sauce."

"Youz don't dip youz finger in it, Texian. Youz dip the crawfish." Tante Izzy rolled her eyes.

"Well, okay. I didn't know." Elli grabbed a boiled crawfish between her finger and thumb and carefully dunked the whole thing into the sauce. Joey started laughing so hard that Ruby walked up to see what was going on. When she spotted the hard-shell crawfish in Elli's hand, she started laughing.

Ruby smacked Ben at the back of his head. "Teach this girl how to eat crawfish right or we'll be hauling her to the hospital to get shells and claws out of her intestines."

Ben lifted Elli's hand with the crawfish in it. He put the sauce-covered crawfish on the table and stuck her sauce-covered fingers into his mouth. Elli felt her face heat with embarrassment and something more. "Now, cher," he began with mischief in his eyes. "You pinch the tail and suck the head."

Ruby started fanning her face as Tante Izzy started chattering in Cajun French. The only word Elli understood was Rascal.

Chapter Thirteen

Has this ever happened to you, my Bosom Blog Buddies? I lay beneath the radiation machine, stuck, uncomfortably, in my form with my arm bent in a V over my head…my upper torso bare. The white machine hisses and its gears whir in the soft way a well-engineered sports car does. Smooth. Powerful. Efficient. As it began its graceful dance over me, I find myself watching it as I might watch a documentary about someone else receiving radiation treatment—distant, impersonal, and detached. I know this is just a coping mechanism for people under severe stress because I read about it long ago in my college Psych 101 textbook. I never would have thought back then this would happen to me. Other people detached themselves from reality and watched their lives play out in a real-time movie. Not me! I had thought I was braver than that. I'm not. Oddly, I'm still able to joke and speak in a normal tone while all of these thoughts are racing through my mind and these crazy emotions are twisting in my body. If it wasn't for this blog, I would probably never have given a voice to these inner thoughts and feelings. Do you have these same thoughts? Do you think of other things? I want to hear from you. I wish you good health, E.

Bosom Blog Buddies Post

Elli was helping Ben and Beau clean the tables when Ben's phone rang. He stepped away to answer it. When he finished the call, he asked Elli if she'd watch Joey until he got back. When she said yes, he turned to Beau and asked him to take a ride to the kennel with him. Elli could tell by the way Ben's eyes narrowed that something was wrong.

"Is everything okay?" she asked, following him to his truck.

He turned and swept her into his arms. "Do you know how sexy you look eating crawfish?" He gave her the half grin that melted her insides.

"It must be the way that I sent the shell soaring into Ruby's husband's beard when I pinched the tail a little too tightly." She laughed. Ben tucked a curl behind her ear and kissed her very tenderly on the lips.

"I think it has more to do with the way your lips got all shiny and slick from the crawfish juice and the way you licked your lips to not miss the sweet taste." He kissed her again, and Elli's body tingled in sweet anticipation.

"Man, you two are really hot together," Beau said walking up to them. "Why don't you kiss her again, Ben, let me see if I can give you some pointers." Ben punched Beau in the shoulder. Hard. Beau rubbed his arm and frowned. "I was trying to share a little of my extensive knowledge with you, cuz. That's a hell of way to show your appreciation."

Elli laughed. "I thank you, Beau, but..." She gave Ben a quick kiss on the lips. "...I think Ben has figured things out just fine."

Ben threw his head back and laughed. He gave Elli a deep, long, passionate kiss, then turned her toward the oak tree and patted her on the fanny to move her along. Elli knew the benefit of a good scene exit, so she looked over her shoulder and winked at Ben. She heard Ben and Beau laughing and joking with one another through their open windows as they drove away.

"I think that man is sweet on you," Ruby said, walking up to Elli. "Tante Izzy told me she got you some love potion from the Traiteur. She got me some when I was dating John. He took one sip and couldn't get me to the altar fast enough."

"Ben hasn't taken it," Elli said. "I don't want him to fall in love with me. I'll be leaving in a week."

"Too bad." Ruby linked her arm through Elli's. "I think he could use an intimate confidant. Especially, with the fire marshal hanging around and all the trouble brewing with that."

"Fire marshal?" Elli stopped and looked at Ruby. "Okay. Tell me what you know."

"Well, I only overheard." She looked around to see if anyone else was listening. Her eyes twinkled as she looked back at Elli. The woman loved to gossip. "I heard Ben tell Beau that the fire marshal was at the kennel to talk to his employees about the fire. He also said something about searching Ben's truck and the kennel, too."

"Searching for what?"

"Fire-making stuff." She shook her head. "I guess that means you're off the hook."

Elli wondered what new evidence the fire marshal had found to have him searching the kennel. She also wondered if the marshal would be there alone if he thought the fire was related to a drug operation. Would there be other investigators?

"Did you hear anything else?"

Ruby thought about it a moment. "No. I think that's it."

Elli wasn't sure what to do with the information. She didn't want to rush over to the kennel and impede an investigation, but she wanted to know what was going on. She had a right to know since she owned half of Sugar Mill, didn't she?

"Would you keep an eye on Joey?" Elli asked Ruby.

"Sure. Are you going to the kennel?"

"I think so." She didn't have a plan, but she figured by the time she drove to the kennel she might have one. When Elli neared her car, she saw that it was blocked in by Beau's BMW. She found Ruby and asked to borrow her car. The animated redhead was more than happy to lend it to her. If she couldn't be a busybody in the middle of a drama, then having something she owned there was pretty darn exciting to her.

Elli arrived at the kennel in the big Cadillac, still without a plan. There was a marked sheriff's car and two other cars with government license plates parked in front of the office. Elli sat in the car a moment, hoping a plan would pop into her head. When it didn't, she just marched inside the office.

"Hello, Elli," Sheriff Ronald said, greeting her first. She nodded to him. He was standing near Ben's desk next to a uniformed policeman who was fingerprinting one of Ben's employees.

"Miss Morenelli. I was hoping to have a chance to speak to you." The fire marshal, Frank Cammer, smiled and stood from the chair he was sitting in. "I was just telling Ben that."

Elli looked at Ben, who was sitting on the sofa. He had his arms folded over his chest, his eyebrows were furrowed, and he was frowning. Beau, who was pouring himself a cup of coffee, just looked at her like he was disappointed that she was there.

"What's going on?" She hadn't directed the question to anyone in particular, but it was Ben who answered.

"The sheriff's office is getting everyone's fingerprints as part of the investigation."

"It hasn't been court ordered," Beau interjected. "Nothing has." He looked at Ben and frowned. "In the spirit of cooperation, and without the recommendation of legal counsel, just about everyone has agreed to be fingerprinted."

"Everyone, except you, Elli," Frank said. "Will you allow us to fingerprint you?"

"I don't know," Elli said, looking at Ben. "Should I?"

He stood, grabbed her hand, and led her outside. When the office door closed behind them, she realized maybe she should have asked Beau-the lawyer what to do, not Ben-the dog-trainer. They walked across the street near the training field before he spoke. "What the hell are you doing here? You should stay out of this."

"I heard there were lawmen snooping around. I wanted to know why."

The muscle in Ben's jaw twitched. "I know you have a lot of questions. I was going to tell you everything later. I don't want you dragged in the middle of this."

"I already am. You know that."

"I didn't see a need to have you involved right now. It's that simple." He shoved his hands in his jeans pockets.

"Well, I'm here now and the po-po wants to fingerprint me." She sighed. "Should I let them?"

"Beau says, no."

"What does Ben say?"

He shrugged. "I say it doesn't matter. I googled it and confirmed it with Uncle Ronald. Fingerprints are only taken and placed into the national databases when you are arrested." He looked toward the office. Beau had just walked out and was headed in their direction. "They only need a copy of your prints to figure out who has been in my truck. We already know you've been in it. They are just trying to figure out whose prints shouldn't be in my truck."

"Did you get fingerprinted?"

"Yes."

"Then I will, too." She didn't see any problem with it, since they already knew she was in his truck. "You didn't tell me why seeing who has been in your truck is so important."

He looked at her. "My truck was at the cottage just before the fire. One of your pictures showed it parked alongside the cottage."

"The police were able to get the photos from the charred camera?"

"Yes," Ben answered, but looked at Beau who was near them, now.

"I don't remember seeing your truck there," she told the men. "You'd think I would have noticed it."

Beau described exactly where the truck was parked and he and Ben discussed the angle at which Elli had to shoot the photograph to capture the picture and still not see it. After a five-minute discussion, Elli interrupted them.

"I was snapping pictures with the camera dangling from my hands. I didn't have it raised to my eyes like you would normally expect." She smiled. "I was scared out of my skin and only wanted the photos to document my death."

"We're ready for you, Elli," Sheriff Ronald called to her from the office porch.

Beau held Elli's arm and kept her from leaving until he explained all of the reasons he thought voluntarily giving her fingerprints to a criminal investigation was a bad idea. When he finished his attorney's legal lecture, Elli stared into his eyes. "You rode in Ben's truck. Did you allow them to fingerprint you?"

"Yes."

Elli was fingerprinted. Afterward, she washed her hands of the ink residue before joining Ben and Beau on the sofa.

"I was just telling Ben and Beau that I got the lab reports on the type of marijuana being grown inside the cottage," Frank Cammer said, sitting in the chair across from the sofa. "My hypothesis was right. It was a high-potency variety. That means our grower did have the indoor hydroponic system I suspected."

"That must have been a costly operation, then," Elli said.

"Yes and no," Frank said. "Hydroponics isn't that expensive to set up. What was costly to the grower was his loss of revenue when he burned the cottage."

"The sheriff had every inch of the Sugar Mill property searched by helicopter and by foot with drug dogs looking for evidence of other illegal crops," Frank told them. "He didn't find any. I think we're dealing with a small-time operator. That's not to say he didn't produce a lot of buds in and around that cottage."

"He must have left some behind. Can you trace where the grow lights came from?" Ben leaned forward, resting his elbows on his knees. "What does a marijuana farmer need to grow and harvest his crops?"

"Not a lot," Ronald said, joining the conversation. "The most important thing he needs is good soil. He may have had manure, top soil, fertilizer, or things like that."

"The lab found evidence of nonorganic plant nutrients," Frank told the sheriff. "I thought I sent that report to you." He walked to where he had left his briefcase near the front door. He retrieved a folder from it and handed it to Ronald. "Nothing unusual in the report. There's NPK."

"Nitrogen, phosphorous, and potassium," Ronald said, reading the report.

"It's been a lot of years since college chemistry, but I think I remember that phosphorous is flammable," Ben said.

"It's used to make matches, right?" Elli said.

"Yes and yes," Frank said with a nod. "Phosphorous is very flammable and according to the report, it was burned in the cottage. An accelerant was found, too. It looks like our suspect used gasoline to ignite the fire."

Elli turned to face Ben. "You remember how we smelled gas in your truck when we got in to head to the cabin? We couldn't find the source of it anywhere." Her heart began to pound in her chest. "He had probably just gotten back from setting the fire right before we hopped in your truck, Ben."

Frank and Ronald looked at Elli and Ben. "I hadn't thought about the gas smell," Ben said.

"Maybe there are other things you two haven't realized are important," Frank offered, sitting in the chair again.

Elli looked at Ben, but he looked away. She wanted him to tell them about Doug's irrational behavior and him smoking pot with some of the movie crew, but he said nothing. Had he considered that Doug's drug and alcohol use might be linked to this? Elli remained quiet. She needed to talk to Ben first about this. He knew Doug better than she did. She might just be making a big circumstantial leap and that wasn't fair to Doug.

When the subject shifted to the crawfish boil, Elli stood. She wanted to stay, but she had to get back to her computer to see if the e-mail arrived so she could finish the transaction for the sale of her car. "I have to get back to the house. I have some business to attend to. I wish I could help you more," she told Frank. "I wish I had been more observant at the cabin before it caught fire. If you have any questions for me or need anything, just call me."

"We will," Frank said before turning to Ben. "Now, let's talk about your employees."

Elli walked out the office and went straight to Ruby's car. She sat inside without starting the engine, sifting through everything that had been said. Something was niggling at her memory, but she didn't know what. She thought about the fingerprints, the gasoline, and the phosphorous. She thought about the nitrogen and potassium. Would she even know what those chemicals looked like if she saw them? She closed her eyes, wondering what was just out of her grasp that her brain couldn't capture.

She rubbed her hands over her face and shook her head. "I don't know." She slid the key into the ignition. Before she started the engine, the passenger door opened and Doug climbed in. He smiled at her.

"Hi, Elli." He closed the door. His eyes were bloodshot, his fingernails dirty. His clothes were neat, but he looked a mess. "Ruby let you borrow her car, huh?"

"Mine was blocked in," she told him.

"Quite the commotion around here." He blew out a heavy breath. "Did you get fingerprinted, too?" Elli nodded. "I never dreamed in all the years of working here, that Ben would have the police fingerprint me."

Elli wanted to defend Ben, but something in his demeanor said it wasn't a good idea. "How's your leg from the bite?" she asked, looking for a safer topic to talk about.

"It's fine. Ben told me that Doe has a problem with cigarettes." He shook his head. "Sorry to hear it."

Elli thought about how hysterical Doe had gotten the night she came to get him at Doug's cottage. Come to think about it, she remembered how odd BJ had acted too, hiding under the tarp on the side of his cottage. A flash went off in Elli's head. The tarp. The smelly thing beneath it. Did it smell like phosphorous? Nitrogen? Potassium? All three? What did those things smell like? She looked at Doug and his expression shifted. His eyes grew wilder, his face more strained.

"What are you thinking?" he asked, his voice low and deep. "I can see you are thinking about something. Something about me? You think I set the fire? You think it was me, don't you?"

She shook her head, not sure how to answer him.

"You do. You think I set the fire." He grabbed her arm. "Why Elli? Did the fire marshal say something about me?" He shook her. "Tell me."

"Doug, you're hurting me." She tried twisting her arm free. His grip tightened. "Please. Let me go."

"Why do you think I burned the cabin?"

Elli looked at him straight in the eyes and decided in that instant that she needed to talk to him honestly. He was a streetwise man who knew how to read people. She was a naïve, sheltered, daddy's girl, who had always been a terrible liar. "I don't know who set the fire, Doug. I was just wondering about that terrible smelling thing you keep under the tarp on side of your cottage."

He cursed and shoved her against the door. "You bitch. You told the law about that, didn't you?" His lips curled into a fierce growl, like the German Shepherd had when she got too close to him in the examining room. He punched the glove compartment, and then kicked it. It popped open. Elli spotted Ruby's Taser. Doug turned to her and grabbed her thigh. He squeezed her so hard she knew she would bruise. "Start the car and drive to the main highway."

Not a good idea, Elli thought, her heart racing and her head pounding. "Let's talk this through, Doug. I didn't tell them about the stuff under the tarp." His grip tightened on her thigh as he turned the key in the ignition and started the engine. "Doug, you're hurting me. Please stop." She tried to shove his hand away, but he gripped her leg tighter.

"I don't give a damn about you, lady. I just want to save my ass." He shifted the car into reverse. "Drive."

Elli had seen enough movies and heard enough about abductions to know you never got in a car with the bad guy. Too late for that. At least she was in the driver's seat, she thought, wondering just how far Doug would go to save his hide. His crazed eyes told her she didn't want to find out. She stomped both feet onto the brake. "Doug, you can't get away with this. Right now, all they have you on is a drug charge. It's only one strike. There are laws that give you three. If you kidnap me or hurt me, it'll be bad, Doug."

She eased her hands up to the steering wheel. If she could just blow the horn, Ben and the sheriff would hear it and come out to check on the commotion. Her fingers inched along the steering wheel toward the horn. "What the hell are you doing?" Doug slapped her across the face and captured both of her hands. Her cheek stung, her eyes watered, and her nose began to bleed. Elli had never been struck before. She was hurting and shocked by his violence but her instincts kicked in. She lunged at Doug, slapping, punching, and scratching him in the face, the arm, the stomach. She flailed her arms and hands and didn't stop.

"This isn't the first time I've had to fight for my life, you bastard," she screamed. Doug slapped her again, harder. Her feet slipped off the brake and the car started backing into the road. She dove at him, punching and biting. He hit her in the stomach and she fell back against the dashboard, her hand slamming against the open glove compartment. Elli felt the Taser. . .cold, hard against her hand. She grabbed it and felt for the Mace that she knew was there, too. The car kept rolling backward until it crashed into the fence on the training field. Doug shoved her again, and Elli took the Taser and slammed it into Doug's head.

"You bitch," he screamed, crushing her throat with one hand and capturing her hands with the other. She tried to raise her knee to kick him, but he had her pinned. Black spots started floating before her eyes. Dear God, this was it. After all she had been through fighting cancer, she had never thought she was going to die this dreadful way. Tears burned her cheek as she tried to shake her head free. He squeezed tighter, pressing his body heavier against her. Elli closed her eyes and saw the face of the man she loved. The man who would never know how much she cared for him. Oh God, this was so unfair. She prayed he wouldn't be the one to find her body.

Suddenly, the passenger side door flew open and Doug was yanked from the car. He didn't release Elli and she fell out with him.

"Let her go you son of a bitch." It was Ben and he was trying to pull Doug off of Elli. Ben drew back his fist and slammed it into Doug's face, again and again. He fought with him to get his hand off her throat. Elli looked at the Taser, tried to turn it on, but couldn't figure it out fast enough, so she began to hit Doug in the head with it over and over again. The black metal of the Taser tore into his forehead as Ben's fists tore into his body. Doug shifted, let go of her throat, kicked Elli in the chest, and sent her falling backward. Pain from her chest and back took her breath away and thickened the sounds in her ear. She knew the Sheriff was running toward them, knew he was shouting, but she had no idea what he was saying. The only thing she could hear from under the cloud of pain was Ben's voice. It was deep, feral and angry.

"I'm going to kill you," Ben shouted, diving on top of Doug, pummeling him with his fists. Elli didn't know how Doug could fight back. Ben was stronger, madder. But he did. Elli's nose was running, tears poured from her eyes as she crawled to the car and found the Mace in the glove compartment. She knew how this worked. She opened the top and turned to the men rolling in on the shell road. She aimed the Mace at Doug's eyes and when she had a clear shot, she sprayed it at him.

"Move away from him, Ben," she shouted. "Or you'll get Mace on you, too." Ben rolled away as Doug curled into a ball and howled. The sheriff and the fire marshal were on top of Doug a second later, handcuffing him. Ben rushed to Elli and lifted her in his arms.

"Are you okay?" Ben asked, looking at her face. It ached and she knew it was already swollen and discolored.

"I'm fine." She began to shiver. She looked at a small cut on his forehead; some tiny pieces of shells and rocks stuck to the blood around it. She shivered harder. She wanted to ask him if he was okay, but the words caught in her head.

"Somebody get her a blanket," Ben shouted and she didn't know who brought it to her, but a blanket was draped over her shoulders.

"You need to take her to the hospital," Beau told Ben. "Doug might've broken something."

Ben's arms tightened on her, his back stiffened. He lifted her to carry her to his truck. "Let's go in my car," Ronald said.

Ben held Elli as they drove to the hospital, breaking all the speed limits to get there. On the way, she found her voice and told Ronald about the tarp and the smelly sacks beneath it. She told them how Doug climbed into Ruby's car and how she fought to defend herself. "I didn't know how to turn on Ruby's Taser, so I just hit him with it."

"That's one way to use it," Ben said, through clenched teeth. "You fight like a girl on steroids, cher, you know that?" He stroked her hair and back and kissed her on the top of the head. "Thank God." His voice was low, unsteady. "I heard the car crash into the fence and came out of the office." He sucked in a breath. "I saw him hit you and my blood turned to ice. I wanted to kill him."

Elli rested her head on his shoulder. "Thank you for rescuing me."

Chapter Fourteen

My very dear friend, Abby, threw me a surprise party last night. What fun! It was a Radiation Liberation Party!! I'm finished! The seven week, daily dose of radiation to kill possible rogue cancer cells in my body is over! My Bosom Blog Buddies, I want this over for you, too! E.

Bosom Blog Buddies Post

Ben returned from the hospital and settled Elli into his bedroom to rest. His bed was bigger and more comfortable so he thought it was better for her to recuperate there. Ruby and Tante Izzy had stayed at the house with Joey and now were in the kitchen making soup and arguing over what they could and could not put in it to make it organic. Joey was upstairs reading one of his favorite bedtime books to Elli. Beau was on the phone with Abby, taking care of the details for the sale of her car. His family had rallied around Elli and Ben was damn grateful for it. His stomach was still tied in knots and he felt pretty damn useless every time he looked at Elli's black eyes and swollen cheeks. He hated seeing her hurt. All he could think about was how he wanted to break into the jail and beat Doug until he was limp and moaning on the hard concrete jailhouse floor.

"Allons," Tante Izzy said, handing him a cup of warm tea. "Bring dat to Elli. It's made with her funny lookin' tea twigs and leaves." He smiled and gave her a peck on the cheek.

"Thank you." He looked at Ruby. "Thank you, too."

Tante Izzy snorted and waved her hand to send him on his way. "Dis is what family is 'bout. Dat girl is family."

Ben entered his bedroom and Joey put his finger to his lips. "Don't make any noise," he whispered to his father. "She's sleeping. I read her Newfies Find the Pirate Treasure and she went right to sleep."

Ben gave him a thumbs-up. He placed the tea on the makeshift nightstand and sat on a folding chair next to his son. "You did well. She needs her rest to heal."

Joey stared at Elli and started to cry. Ben put his arm around his son's shoulder. "Is she going to die?"

"Nah. She's just got a few bruises and her hand has some cuts that the doctor glued with his special medical gunk." The knots in his stomach cinched tighter. He understood Joey's reaction. He cared about her, too.

"I heard somebody say Grandpa did that to her." He looked at his father for confirmation.

"Your grandpa is having some problems, Joey." How in the hell did he explain this to his son when he didn't fully understand it himself? "He's behaving badly. I don't excuse him for reacting the way he has to his problems. A man has to find a way to be a man and take care of problems without hurting others."

"Is he a drunk like Momma was?"

Where in the hell did his son hear these things? "He drank too much. Yes."

"I'm never going to drink." He wiped his nose with the back of his hand. "Just like you."

Ben nodded. "I choose not to drink because I never want to get into trouble when I have someone as special as you in my life."

"That's what a man is supposed to do, right?" Joey said with total conviction. Ben poked his son in his side.

"You are so smart," he told him with a smile. "How did you get so smart?"

Joey took his question literally. "I read a lot."

Ben's chest was so warm with love. How had he been so lucky to have him for a son?

Elli stirred in the bed and opened her battered blue eyes. "Look at my two favorite men," she said. Her eyes widened and Ben knew she was surprised she had said what she did.

"Do you want me to read to you again?" Joey offered, opening his book.

Elli smiled at him, but Ben didn't give her a chance to answer. "Later. Why don't you take the dogs out for a walk? They need exercise and Tante Izzy will appreciate you getting them out of the kitchen."

Joey jumped up and ran to the door, turned around, ran back, and after a few moments trying to figure where to kiss her, he gave Elli a tender peck on her hand. "I hope you feel better."

"I do already with that kiss," she told him, touching his face. He ran out of the room.

"He's in love with you, you know?" Ben said, hearing the words in his head—so are you. He looked at Elli, knowing his mouth had dropped open. Was that true? Was he in love with this pain-in-the-neck woman?

A tear slipped from Elli's eye. She sat up in bed. "He's the most wonderful boy in the world." She sniffed. Ben moved to sit on the bed next to her.

"Yeah, he is." He folded the edge of the knit cap that she wore to lift it off her swollen brow. He was having a hard time talking, with the idea of being in love with her still sloshing around his head.

"Is something wrong, Ben? You look pale."

He shook his head. "I'm good." He handed her the tea Tante Izzy brewed for her. His head was spinning. Was he in love with Elli? He knew he shouldn't be. Hell, their relationship was too damn complicated and they had different agendas in life. They had been fighting since their first meeting. But…he did love her. He loved this crazy, unpredictable Texian.

"Ben?" Elli touched his hand and electricity shot through him.

"Elli…" he began, but Tante Izzy walked into the room and stopped him from telling her what he had just discovered.

"Allons, Ruby, the girl will starve to death before you bring dat soup in here."

"It's sloshing all over the tray. I told you not to put so much in the bowl." Ruby walked into the room taking baby steps on four inch heels. She looked around the room. "There's no furniture in here. Where am I supposed to put the tray?"

"Mon Dieu, Ben. Don't youz know anythin' 'bout nursin' a sick person? Go get the TV tray in the livin' room."

"Yes, ma'am." He darted out of the room to get the TV tray.

"Hurry," Ruby shouted after him. "My arms are getting tired."

"That's because youz need to exercise more. Youz should do da Biggest Loser exercise video wit me in the morning." Tante Izzy lifted her arm and showed Ruby her biceps. Loose, wrinkled skin dangled beneath her arm. "See how good dey look?"

Ruby rolled her eyes. "Hurry up, Ben," she shouted.

Ben came in, set up the TV tray, and took the soup from Ruby. She immediately rubbed her arms. Now it was Tante Izzy who rolled her eyes. Ben sat on the side of the bed, unfolded the napkin, and awkwardly placed it on Elli's chest. He'd taken care of Joey when he had been sick with no problem. Why did taking care of Elli make him feel like he was all thumbs? He reached for the soup and spotted an amber vial on the tray.

"What's this?" he asked, lifting the bottle. Elli gasped behind him and frowned at Tante Izzy and Ruby.

"I'm leaving now," Ruby said, rushing out the door.

"Tante Izzy," Ben said, his voice firm.

She stepped closer to him and smacked him in the back of the head. "Don't worry what it is," she said. "Just drink it and give some to Elli, too. If she won't drink it, pour it down her throat."

"What?"

Tante Izzy started mumbling in Cajun French how he and Elli were as stubborn as a mule with a hoof ache. Then she pointed her crooked finger at him. "Don't be stupid and let this one get away." She left the room.

"You can drink that spider spit if you want, but I'm not doing it," Elli said, a smile on her face.

"What the hell is it anyway?"

"It's from a tray-tor." She shook her head. "A love potion."

"What a conniver." He laughed, putting the bottle back on the tray. His old aunt was too late. He didn't need this hocus-pocus potion. He was already in love with Elli.

He scooped up a spoonful of soup and lifted it to Elli's lips. She closed her hand around his wrist to guide the spoon to her mouth. "I can do this myself," she said after a second spoonful.

Ben blew out a breath. "Good." This all felt so weird to him. He wanted to make her well so badly that feeding her felt so damn important. This whole being in love with her thing was scary. He needed to think about it. Figure things out. Let it sit a while.

Elli ate in silence, sending him sidelong looks that stirred something powerful inside of him. When she finished, she handed him the bowl and the napkin. "You know, I'm not feeling that bad." Her eyes darkened and she touched him lightly on the hand. Every cell in his body went on alert. "In fact, I'm feeling pretty good."

He leaned in closer to her. He felt her warm breath on his lips. "How good?"

She rested her hands on his chest. "Real good." She touched her lips to his. They were soft and hot and delicious. Ben traced her plump lips with his tongue, careful to not hurt her battered mouth. He kissed the corners of her mouth, then the tip of her nose. Never had he wanted to be so tender with a woman as he did with Elli right now. He wanted to soothe her with his mouth and body. He wanted to comfort her with his hands on her skin. He wanted to take the pain away and replace it with pleasure.

Ben stood and locked the door, not giving a damn what anyone would think they were doing behind the closed doors. He eased into his bed, sliding his hand over her arms, down her hip. Elli moved closer to him, sharing her heat and desire. He slipped his hand between her thighs and she sighed, sinking deeper into the mattress, against him.

She gripped his shoulders, her fingers digging into his flesh. She held on to him like a woman afraid of falling off a high ledge. Her lips skimmed across his cheek, his chin, and down his neck. Her breath was heavy on his sensitive skin. Ben groaned. "That feels good, cher." He felt Elli's smile against his chest and he smiled, too.

He grabbed the end of her nightshirt and tugged it over her head, careful not to let the fabric rub against where the bruises were deeper, darker. Seeing the marks on her silky, beautiful skin, tore at his insides and Ben had to beat down the anger he felt towards Doug for doing this to her and at himself for not protecting her. "I'm okay," she said, lifting his chin to look in his eyes.

"I'm okay."

She took his hand and placed it over her right breast. Her lips lifted in a smile and Ben realized in that moment she was releasing herself to him. For the first time since they had made love, Elli didn't cover her body with her hands or with sheets or with darkness or with anything else. He understood that she was laying herself bare and vulnerable before him. Why was she doing this? Why now? Something different was happening with them. Something important.

He cupped her left breast with his other hand and slid down her body, leaving a trail of kisses until he was nestled between her breasts. He looked at them and touched the scars circling her nipples and curving under the slope of her breasts. He traced the new bruises and old scars along the side of her right breast and kissed where part of her flesh had been removed with the awful cancer. This battle she fought against the deadly disease had been part of what defined her today. It had been what made her such a fighter. It made her strong and sensitive and open.

"You are so beautiful," he whispered over her imperfect flesh and marveled at the perfection of her as a woman. Elli ran her hands through his hair and exhaled. He traced the scar that spread across her abdomen, hipbone to hipbone. He did the same with the scar near her collarbone, where her chemo-port had been. "So beautiful."

He grabbed the lace edges of her panties and slid them down her legs. "You are being so gentle, Ben. It fills me up inside until I want to burst with it. I want to cry. I want to laugh. I want to hold my breath. I want to breathe."

Ben stood, took off his clothes and slid back into bed with Elli. His skin felt sensitive as cool sheets and hot woman enveloped him. He lifted her on top of him and kissed her. Yes, he loved this woman. In this moment, he'd accept that, wallow in it. He'd leave logic and reality and everything else locked outside of the door with the rest of the world.

Elli reached between them and touched him in that way that drove all thought from his head. He restrained himself from tossing her beneath him and driving hard and fast into her. His muscles strained and ached as he stroked her derriere, and between her thighs. When she began making the soft sexy sounds of arousal, he slipped inside of her, taking her in slow, long strokes. Elli's body stiffened over him in a powerful orgasm that sent him joining her.

* * * *

Elli stepped into the shower and couldn't believe she and Ben had just made love with his family so close by. Never in her life had she lost every ounce of control like she just had. He had looked at her with such a deep, dark, desire that she wanted him. More than that, she had to be part of him—body and soul.

She closed her eyes and let the hot water flow over her head and down her aching body. Something had shifted with them and she was afraid to label what couldn't be. Yes, she loved him and in the tender play of their lovemaking, she could pretend he loved her, too.

Elli soaped a washcloth and ran it over her aching shoulders, arms, and legs. She took the soap as was her routine and lathered her hands and began to check her breasts for lumps. She had done it a thousand times and did it automatically and with precision. She started at twelve o'clock and worked her way in tiny circles around each breast. She had had a mastectomy, but she still had to search for tiny lumps that could form in the skin. Elli finished her left breast and began on her right. At three o'clock, she felt a small, hard bump. Her heart stopped. Her legs turned to liquid and she slithered to the floor of the shower. Water sprayed like tears over her.

"No. Dear God, no." She grabbed her breast, felt the lump again, and cried. "Please God. No. Not again."

Chapter Fifteen

Dear Bosom Blog Buddies, I thought I was finished with my cancer treatment…that the nightmare was over. Today I learned that it isn't. It is starting all over again. I discovered I have the BRCA inherited breast cancer genes. I have no evidence of active cancer now, but learning I have the inherited cancer genes feels as if I have been diagnosed with cancer again. My fight continues. It will NEVER end! I must hold on to the knowledge that on this day at this moment, I am winning. Right? I do not wish this kind of worry for you. I want you to have good health and good genes, E.

Bosom Blog Buddies Post

Elli did what she had always had done when her fear and anxiety were too much for her to endure. She crawled into her bed, in a dark room, and isolated herself from the world. She had done this every time she waited for the results of a PET scan, an MRI, or any news that might tell her the cancer had grown or it had returned.

Wet from her shower and shivering from terror, she lay naked in her narrow single bed behind locked doors. She didn't know what to do. Fear had paralyzed her. A tiny whine and dainty bark came from somewhere near her bed. Elli moved as if she was stuck in thick wet clay and looked over the side of the bed. It was Donna and she was up on her hind legs, wanting to come on the bed with her. Elli picked her up and placed her on the pillow. Donna high-stepped off the pillow and onto Elli's chest. She stood there, looking at her with her pretty button eyes.

"I can't try to read your mind right now, Donna." Elli wiped away a tear. "I can't think." Elli closed her eyes and tried to ignore her. Donna tapped Elli on the chin with her paw. "Please. Leave me alone. I can't do this with you."

Donna lay down and curved her body against Elli's neck. The small dog felt warm and soft and secure. She petted the fluffy animal that had always been so self-centered, prissy, and demanding. Now she was offering comfort. Elli was grateful for it.

There was a scratch at the door and whining from the other side. Elli recognized the sounds of her dogs. They wanted to come inside the room and she knew they wouldn't let her ignore them. She crawled out of the bed, picked up Donna, and went to the door. When she opened it, the three energetic animals raced in. They circled Elli, hitting her naked legs with their tails, nipping at her toes, and licking the moisture off her knees. She locked the door again and climbed back in bed under the sheets. Dear Jenny jumped into bed with her and stretched out along her side, resting her head on Elli's shoulder. Donna didn't complain from the position she reclaimed around Elli's neck as she usually did when Jenny came this close to her. Doe sneezed, put her paw on the edge of the bed, and waited for Elli to pat on the bed for her to join them. When she did, Doe jumped up and circled her body at Elli's feet. BJ leaped onto the bed and settled on the opposite side of Jenny. Elli looked around at the mass of fur and smiled.

"You don't like to see me sad, huh?" Donna whimpered in response. "I feel like you all are wrapping me up in a warm hug. Thank you."

Elli fell asleep like that and when she woke the next morning, she felt stronger. She had a lot to organize and made several calls before calling Abby. She told her that she had found a lump.

"Oh, Elli. I'm sorry." She understood how devastating this was better than anyone else Elli could have called. Very few words had to be spoken about it between them and there was a comfort in that unspoken insight. "Come home."

"I'm booked on a flight this evening. I have an oncology appointment tomorrow morning." Elli looked around the room at her dogs, which were lying on the faded wood floor in the slant of sunlight coming through the window. "I'm bringing the dogs home, too."

"Good. I'm anxious to meet them after the stories you've told." Abby's voice was even, but Elli heard the sadness in it. "Have you told Ben or anyone there about it?"

"No." Tears filled her eyes. "I care too much about them to drag them into my nightmare. And they would want to do exactly that. They are loving, caring people." She sniffed. "This is what I wanted to avoid in my life. I don't want to bring grief and sadness into someone's beautiful world." She sighed. "Oh Abby, I can't do it. I won't."

"Then don't. This is your life. Your choice. You need to write the script for your day because it's your day. It's all you can count on having." Abby said, echoing Elli's feelings.

They spoke a few more minutes before Abby told her about how the buyer of her car was coming to Cane to get it today. They both knew it wasn't important, but it was a detail that needed to be taken care of before she left Louisiana. They spoke a few minutes longer, saying a prayer together before ending the call.

Tears continued to flow as Elli packed her suitcases. She missed Tante Izzy and Rachel and Ruby already. Her heart ached knowing she'd never again have Joey read to her or Beau tease her. Most of all, her heart was bursting over knowing she'd never see Ben again.

Elli sat on the bed, powered up her laptop, and wrote a short note for Ben. Her heart was just too heavy to do the right thing and tell him in person that she was leaving. She also wrote a separate letter, telling him she would not execute any options to take possession of half of the plantation or kennel. She intended to have Abby draw up a will and bequeath her share of the plantation to him as it rightfully should have been since his father's death. She would sell her house in California and donate that money to the foundation and hope they could find another way to raise money to keep it operating.

She printed the letters, not noticing there were other documents in the printers' queue. She had one more thing to do. She intended to tell Joey she was leaving. It was too much to expect a six-year-old to understand why she was leaving in a note. Another woman had hurt him when he was just a little tyke; she didn't want to add more pain onto that. He had to know that she loved him but had to go back to California.

She found Joey in his bedroom, building a fort with his Legos. She sat on the floor across from him and asked questions about his fort. After a few minutes, she found the courage to address why she was there.

"Joey, I have something important I need to tell you." He snapped a piece onto an area he had designated as a dog kennel, but didn't look at her. The boy had good instincts and she would bet he was getting a strong vibe from her that he didn't want to face. "I have to go back to California." Elli had decided not to lie to the child, but she would talk around the truth. He snapped a bright yellow piece to the fort. She touched his hand to stop him from grabbing another Lego. "I have a big job to do and it's in Los Angeles."

"My daddy will give you a job," he said, his voice low, his face downcast.

"That is really kind for you to suggest that." She lifted his chin so he would look at her. The disappointment in his eyes broke her heart. "But I have to do a particular job and I can only do it in California. Can you understand that?"

Joey shrugged. "Can't somebody else do it?"

Elli fought not to cry. "I wish I could change the circumstances and stay here with you. I can't."

"I can come with you." He looked at her in that cool, calculating way his father did when he wanted something. "I'm a good worker. I can help you with the dogs."

"I would love that, but I think your dad would really be sad." She swallowed past the lump in her throat. "Tante Izzy would be upset and lonesome without you and Beau would miss his fishing buddy." She shook her head. "Your family is here. They love you and would miss you something terrible."

Joey started picking at the rubber on the side of his tennis shoes. "Can I come visit you?"

Elli scooped him in her arms, ignoring the pain it caused in her ribs and abdomen. "Yes. Absolutely. Come to visit me anytime." She prayed she would be well enough and that his father wouldn't be too angry for that to happen.

He touched her bruised cheek with his soft, plump fingers. "Does that hurt?"

"Not as much as my heart knowing how much I'll miss you." She squeezed him to her chest. "You are a good boy, Joey. The best. You are smart and kind and handsome and you will have a great life."

"I guess," He murmured into her ear. Elli leaned back to look at him.

"I know." She smiled but he was looking at the ground. "Look at me, Joey. I know things. I have a good intuition about people. My intuition is telling me that you will be a wonderful, happy man." She kissed him on the cheek. "I'm leaving this afternoon," she said, her voice catching as her heart tore in half. "I left your dad a note on the printer explaining things. Can you please tell him I left it there for him after I leave, not before? You understand?" He nodded. She sighed. "Will you give him a kiss for me?"

He nodded. "Elli," he began, his bottom lip quivering. "Before I knew you had to go," he looked up at her "I thought you might want to stay to be my mommy."

* * * *

A few hours later, Elli had her dogs kenneled in the back of the car service SUV that she had hired to drive her and the dogs to the airport. Then, she left Sugar Mill plantation.

Ben returned home a few hours early to check on Elli even though he knew she was well. She had looked luminous when he left her in his bed, but he hated not staying with her after she had been battered by Doug. It couldn't be helped. He had to go to work. The gossip had spread across several parishes about Doug's arrest and he had to answer his phone and reassure his customers that Doug's arrest would not affect the kennel and had never endangered the animals in his keeping.

Tante Izzy and Joey were sitting at the kitchen table eating cookies when he walked inside. Their movements seemed sluggish. Their eyes were sad and tired.

"What's wrong?"

"Youz didn't drink da potion, dats what's wrong," Tante Izzy snapped at him.

"Elli left," Joey said, his eyes filling with tears.

"Da Texian done gone back to Californ-i-ay."

"What?" Ben didn't wait for an answer and raced up the stairs. He shoved open her bedroom door and saw that all of her clutter was gone. He walked into the room, her scent wrapping around him like a feeble hug. He sat on her lumpy bed. "What in the hell happened?" When he left, she was soft and pliant and happy in his arms. How did she go from that to this?

Joey walked into the room and gave his dad a kiss. "She said to do that," he said, sitting on the bed next to Ben. "She said she left you a note on the printer."

He hurried to get the note, hoping to learn why she left so suddenly. Was there an emergency back in California and she hadn't been able to reach him to tell him she had to leave right away? Ben grabbed the stack of papers in the printer and read the one on top. With each word he read, his heart grew heavier and heavier. She wouldn't claim her half of the plantation. She would give him the power of attorney for her share to run the kennel and handle all Sugar Mill business. He was to use all the profits to reinvest in the kennel and plantation. He skimmed the rest of the sheet, knowing she had given him everything he had asked for. Why in the hell wasn't he happy about it?

The next note was a personal note for him. He read through it four times and still didn't understand why she left in such a hurry, without telling him good-bye in person. She said it couldn't be helped. That this was the best that she could do under the circumstances. He called bullshit on that. He had thought they had a different relationship than that. He thought she cared for him enough to not be so cold. He thought that maybe she loved him. What an idiot he'd been. He'd even thought that he might be in love with her.

Ben ripped the letter in half and crumpled it. He looked at the other papers in his hand and felt too sick to read them. What a fool he'd been. He tossed the letter into the trashcan near the printer and sat on the bed next to his son.

"She said I can visit her." Joey looked at his father. When Ben didn't answer, he didn't say anything further but looked at the papers in his father's hand. "Did Mr. Cooper write you a note, too?"

"Huh?" He looked down at the page in his hand and the two after it. He closed his eyes and sucked in a deep breath. Damn her. She was trying to sell the plantation to investors without his consent. Ben stood and walked to the window to look outside. According to the e-mails, she'd sent them brochures and photographs and every damn thing to make the sale happen—never telling him about it. Why was she letting him know about it this way, now? What was she trying to accomplish? Did she want to hurt him? Make him angry? Who was this woman that did this? It wasn't the Elli he thought he knew. Was this the real one?

Ben felt a deep ache in his chest. A heart attack couldn't hurt more. The woman had played him and he had let her. He couldn't believe it. He'd thought he was smart enough to never let that happen again after Sarah. He wasn't. He'd been played by a Texian.

"Dis house feels too hollow wit her gone," Tante Izzy said, standing in the doorway. "Go get her back."

Ben was about to tell her to mind her own business, but didn't when he noticed Joey sitting on the bed looking so forlorn. "Joey, we're going to get Rosa's dogs at the kennel and bring them here," he said, hoping the animals would put his son in a better mood. "Go downstairs and get the water bowls filled and ready." Joey did as his father asked.

"No dog will take her place," Tante Izzy told him.

"She's gone and that's the way it should be." Ben thought he had said enough and wanted to leave, but Tante Izzy stood in the doorway blocking his exit.

"Youz is a fool."

"No kidding."

"Youz don't know nothin', Ben."

"Did she tell you why she left?"

"No. I didn't even get me a note." Ben crossed his arms over his chest listening to every word his aunt said, hoping to learn something. . .anything. "I'm a little disappointed 'bout dat. It waz rude, but I trust her to have a good reason. I know her heart and a heart like hers don't run away like a crook unless somethin' is wrong."

"I don't buy it." The e-mails in his hand felt as heavy as the anchor around his heart. He took a step closer to his aunt. "Excuse me, I need to go." She didn't move.

"I guess youz need to let the shock wear off." She frowned. "She hurt youz pride. Dat's for sure. Tomorrow, youz will think right and go bring her back."

* * * *

Three weeks later, Ben had still not gone to get Elli and Tante Izzy wasn't happy about it. She kept blustering around the house, pointing out how miserable he was, like he didn't already know it. He hated himself for letting Elli manipulate him and he hated himself for trying to think of reasons to justify why she had. It was crazy and he had no time for crazy. He had a business to run and a son to raise.

The door to his office opened and Beau walked in. He tossed a folder on the desk where Ben was doing paperwork. "That's from Elli's attorney."

He opened the two-inch-thick folder. "Give me the abridged version."

"It's Elli's will." Beau stretched out on the sofa and put his hands behind his head. "In the event of Crocifissa Morenelli's death, you will inherit all of her interest in Sugar Mill Plantation and the kennel."

Ben looked at Beau. "This just dropped out of the blue sky." He was feeling like he'd been dropped in a blind-sided tackle, when another thought popped into his head. "Elli isn't sick or dying, is she?"

"I don't know." Beau sat up. "Abby never said anything about that. Maybe you should call Elli and ask her."

"Maybe I shouldn't." He looked at the folder, but the words just blurred in front of him. The idea that Elli might be really sick worried him. "Why did she send this to me? Why didn't she just let me find out in the event of her death?" There was that awful feeling in his stomach again. Ben got up and began to pace.

"The cover letter explains it."

Ben walked back to his desk and read the letter on top of all the documents. It was written to him by Abby, stating that her client wanted him to have peace of mind and assurance that the family home would remain in his care. It should be a Bienvenu legacy. "I'll be damned." Ben started to get a headache. What was she doing this for? She had already given him control of the plantation, although she retained half ownership. What scheme could she be cooking up with this? It just didn't jive with the way she conducted business behind his back and pretended to be someone else in front of his face. "This doesn't make sense."

"Yeah, right, huh?" Beau walked to the coffeepot, poured a cup, and took a sip. "Shit. This is cold." He shook his head and took the cup with him back to the sofa to finish it. "I think you read Elli wrong, couz. She's not the barracuda you thought she was. I think something else is going on. Unless you talk to her, you won't really know what she intended by leaving those e-mails."

"Talk to her? Do you think I can trust what she says?"

Beau shook his head. "For a man who has a crazy ability to read a dog's mind, you'd think you could figure out a little about a human's. Sarah really did a number on you. She messed with your confidence in your capacity to judge another person's character." He swigged the rest of the coffee and winced. "Maybe that's not true. She just destroyed your confidence in dealing with women."

Ben didn't like what Beau said, but he knew it might be right on target. Sarah had made him jaded. "You can't tell me that Elli's actions weren't deceitful."

"I feel like there are some missing pieces in this puzzle." Beau said, balancing the empty coffee cup on his knee. "Your girl is smart. Maybe things started changing faster than she could adapt. Call her and try to settle this. She just gave you a huge gift. At least you can tell her thank you."

Ben told him what he thought Beau could do with his advice as only close cousins could. But the truth of the matter was, he knew Beau was right.

"I liked you better when Elli was here." Beau put the mug on Ben's desk. "I bet you liked yourself better when she was here, too." He walked to the door. "Think about it, Ben. What did she do that was so horrible, anyway? She didn't bring a buyer here and try to sell it without your consent. She just solicited investors. Did she manipulate you to gain that end? What do you think? The girl didn't seem to have it in her to fake it." Beau laughed. "Unless she had to because you are a rotten lover."

"Ha, ha, ha." He leaned back in his chair.

"She is not Sarah." Beau looked at Ben and slapped himself on the forehead. "I'll be damned. You really are in love with her or you would have just called her to find out what in the hell is going on. You wouldn't be moping around like this if you didn't care a lot. I suspected you might be in love with her, but now I can see that you've got it bad. Well, cuz, I always thought you and I would be the level-headed ones in this world who wouldn't fall prey to society's dictates that a man had to settle on one woman." He laughed and came over to slap Ben on the back and laughed again. "Oh, how the mighty have fallen."

"You are too damn smug." He sneered at Beau. "I'm every bit as a confirmed bachelor as you."

Beau looked at his cousin for a moment and then let out a howl of laughter and left.

Ben opened the folder and re-read the cover letter. "What are you up to, Elli?" Part of him wanted to believe she had named him in her will because she meant what was written in the letter. The other part of him thought it might be another tool of manipulation. He just didn't know.

The door to the office flew open and Joey raced inside, dropping his school bag on the floor. His navy polo shirt, monogrammed with the school logo, was half tucked into his khaki uniform pants, which were stained green at the knees and skimmed the bottom of his ankles. His son was growing so fast. Time was racing by.

"Hi Dad." He walked into the kitchen and found a bag of cookies and box of juice. He sat on the chair across from Ben's desk and punched the straw into the juice box.

"How was school?"

"Good. Lucy Cheramie threw up on Tommy Simoneaux when he pretended to eat a lizard during recess."

"That's a new variation on scaring a girl with a lizard." The sound of someone slamming on their brakes in front of the office interrupted their conversation. Ben knew before she came barreling through the door, it was Tante Izzy.

"Moodee dis new phone." She handed her cell phone to Ben. "I can't get it to work."

Ben picked up the phone. "What do you want to do with it?"

"I want to do dat Face Time." She walked behind her nephew. "I have an appointment to talk to Elli. She keeps callin' me, but when I answer, we get disconnected. I knowz I need to press somethin' for it to work." On cue, the phone began to ring. "It's Elli, again."

Joey jumped off his chair and came around the desk. "You have to press this." He tapped the screen and shifted the phone's camera until it faced himself. Elli's face popped up. Her bright blue eyes were big and round and full of surprise to see his son. Ben's heart started to accelerate.

"Hi, Joey," she said, her voice cheerful. "I'm so happy to see you. How are you?"

"Good. Lucy Cheramie threw up on Tommy Simoneaux today."

Elli laughed and Ben's insides felt warm. "I bet that was something to see, huh?"

"Tommy threw up right back at her. It was really gross," he laughed making disgusted faces. He clearly enjoyed telling the story.

"No kidding. I'm glad I wasn't there to see that."

Elli and Joey continued to talk for a few minutes like old pals, laughing and telling each other stories. Ben forgot his anger for a time and just enjoyed watching their byplay.

"Okay, youz hogged the call long enough," Tante Izzy said, turning the phone until she was in the corner box on the screen. "I tole youz I'd get da fancy phone to talk to youz."

"You sure did." Ben could see Elli on the phone from where he sat. He watched her shrug her shoulders in that way that always made him smile. His heart pounded harder in his chest. His breathing grew heavier. His fingers tingled and he had a ridiculous urge to touch the screen, to touch Elli. How in the hell did that simple shoulder shrug get his insides stirring like that?

"Dis is somethin'." Tante Izzy smiled into the phone's camera. "Who would ever have thought dat one day I would be talkin' on a TV telephone? Me, who didn't have a phone until 1976 and it waz a party line at dat."

"What's a party line, Dad?" Joey asked Ben, and Elli's eyes widened. She seemed to back away from the phone a little.

"It's when da whole town shares da same phone line as you." Tante Izzy smiled. "Like when youz has extra phones in da house peoples can talk on at da same time. Except, da phones are in different houses. If youz call someone else, youz can bet someone on da party line will be listenin' to dat call, too. I miss those days. Youz got youz news by just pickin' up youz phone and listenin'."

Ben watched as Elli started fidgeting in her seat. She looked uncomfortable. Was it because she knew he was there? He asked Tante Izzy for her phone with a gesture. She handed it to him. "Hello, Elli," he said, when he knew she could see him. She tucked a curl behind her ear. Ben remembered doing that same thing. He remembered doing a lot of things to her. His muscles bunched in his legs and stomach. He sucked in a breath.

"Hi, Ben. How are you?"

"Comme ci, comme ça." He saw Tante Izzy and Joey staring at him, looking like they were afraid of what he might say. "How are the girls?"

"Oh, Ben, they're great. I thank Aunt Rosa every day for giving them to me."

Now it was his turn to shift uncomfortably in his seat. One day, he'd have to tell her where those dogs really came from and give her the three she was supposed to inherit. Ha; she could not possibly handle six dogs. He smiled, thinking of how she'd try to walk them all at the same time. They would be straining on their leashes as Elli raced after them, wearing her worn multicolored knit cap, body-hugging white T-shirt, and snug running shorts that exposed long, muscular legs. He shook his head. What in the hell was he doing thinking of that? "Look, I just wanted to thank you. I got a copy of the will today."

She shrugged and Ben's heart began to pound. What was it she wanted to say? She smoothed her hair behind her ear again. Desire flared hot and heavy in him. The woman made his body crazy just with two ridiculously simple gestures. Would time reduce his immense reaction to her? In that deep, crystal clear place where pride and hurt didn't cloud knowledge, Ben found his answer. No. Whether it was right or wrong, his feelings for Elli would never fade.

"It's your plantation, Ben. I just want to make sure you get what's yours." Elli stared at the phone a long time. Ben wondered if she was thinking about what he looked like naked, like he was thinking of her. After ten seconds of silence, she spoke. "I'm glad to have spoken to you. To all of you. I have to go now. Good-bye, Ben." Her voice broke for a moment. "Good-bye, Joey and Tante Izzy. We'll talk again soon." She hung up the phone.

"Mais, I dink dat girl was 'bout to cry," Tante Izzy said looking sad.

Ben thought so, too.

Tante Izzy tossed something on his desk that landed with a smack. He looked down at it. "People Magazine?"

"It's autographed. By Elli. There is an article inside youz should read. And, Ruby says Elli had a blog too that lets a person peer into her heart. Youz might be wantin' to read dat, too, is all I'm sayin'. Seems to me youz needs some serious learnin'. Youz been actin' real stupid."

* * * *

Elli hung up the phone and didn't move. Tears swept down her cheeks. God, she missed Ben. She missed them all. She looked at a sparrow that landed on the fence in the tiny backyard of her new apartment. She was right to let them all remain free, like the bird, she thought. She had no right to burden them with her reality.

She reached for the fresh carrot juice on the coffee table in front of her and flinched. The area where they had done a needle biopsy on her breast was still tender and slow to heal. The doctors said that was because the lump had been in the irradiated breast. Elli didn't care if it hurt like this the rest of her life. She was just so dang grateful the lump was benign.

Elli smiled, remembering the line from Deconstructing Harry. It had popped into her head a lot these past few weeks. "The most beautiful words in the English language are not 'I love you,' but 'it's benign.'"

"*I love you*" *seemed pretty darn good, too*, she thought. "*If it didn't hurt so much.*"

Chapter Sixteen

Did I tell you all how much I love my BFF, Abby? She hosted a wake to say farewell to my breasts on the eve of my double mastectomy. There was a memorial with gaudy funeral flowers and everyone in attendance wore funny wigs and colorful knit caps. Anatomically themed refreshments were served, too. If you want the recipes let me know. It may take a few weeks before I can respond with them, though. I will be recovering from my surgery and reconstruction. It's another step to try to keep the enemy away. I didn't choose this fight, just as my mother didn't and many of you reading this blog didn't…but I will not back down. That is my vow…til death do us part. E.

Bosom Blog Buddies Post

It had been two weeks since Ben had spoken to Elli on the phone. He thought of that call a lot, almost to the point of obsessing over it. He thought about what he should have said. He thought about what she wanted to say but didn't, as indicated by the ridiculously sexy shoulder shrugs. Most of all he thought about how he just wanted to talk to her again, especially after reading the magazine article and her blog posts online. Ruby had been right about the blog, it let him peer into her heart…but didn't he already know, on some level in his brain, what was there without reading it?

It was the article and the others he found online, though, that gave him the most pause. They all described the fiasco involving the foundation that Elli founded and the big fundraising event that had resulted in a few dozen celebrities and high rollers having their identities stolen. The articles stated that Elli had sold her house and donated the proceeds to the Gene I.D. Foundation to help keep it afloat. Ben thought that seemed like the actions of a noble woman. More than that, it was just one more thing that didn't logically paint the picture of the villain he had thought she was when she left Sugar Mill. It was time for him to get the answers to the jumbled mess Elli left in his head. It was way past time to speak to her face-to-face.

Ben sat in a nondescript rental car wearing a tuxedo. He had just parked in front the address Beau had given to him with stupid enthusiasm. He gripped the steering wheel, looking at the building in front of him, just breathing in and out...in and out. There was a neat but small apartment complex with a row of low-growing shrubs and a lot of bright pink and yellow flowers planted along the walkway. It didn't look like the fancy home he had originally thought Elli would own. It looked exactly like the home she could afford.

"Hello," Ben answered, when his phone rang. It was Tante Izzy, his second excuse for coming to California. They were there to attend a small but formal fundraiser for Elli's foundation. "Yes, I promise I won't be late. I know how important this event is and how worried Elli must be that no one will attend. I have something to take care of first." He wanted to talk to Elli alone, not in a crowded room.

He stepped out of the car. He brushed at the wrinkles in the black, formal trousers and looked at his reflection in the car window to straighten his bow tie. He had considered cutting his hair, but in the end just settled on wearing it in a stubby ponytail. Once, while they were settled naked and satisfied in his bed, Elli had told him that she liked when he wore his hair in a ponytail.

Ben took in a deep breath and walked toward the path leading to the complex. He hesitated when he reached the front of the car and saw a flash of baby blue. His body reacted physically before his mind fully understood what his eyes had seen. It was Elli. She was dressed in a flowing, glacier-blue strapless gown. She seemed to float around the corner onto his street as three happy dogs tugged on their leashes with joyful eagerness. She had never quite gotten that she was the pack leader, not BJ. It was the most beautiful sight he'd ever seen. His heart squeezed so tightly in his chest, he thought he might not be able to breathe. He managed to move forward to meet Elli on the path.

Ben usually would have greeted the dogs first, but this time, it was Elli he wanted to talk to most. "Surprise," he managed, turning his palms upward in a gesture of surrender.

She smiled a timid smile. "That it is." She bit her lower lip and shushed the dogs as they started whining about her stopping their walk. They sat with their tails sweeping the ground.

"I'm here for the fundraiser." He took a step closer to Elli and bumped into dogs. He instinctively bent and petted the dog closest to him, Jenny. "I'm here to get answers from you."

She lifted her chin and straightened her back. He really loved the way she got her hackles stirred when putting up her defenses. "Okay. I owe you answers." She looked at him, not backing away because it was tough. He'd learned that about her in the blogs- she didn't back down from a fight. "I should have spoken to you before I left. I was a coward. I'm sorry. So very, very, sorry."

"I don't buy the coward excuse." He shook his head. "You're not a coward. You are a tough lady who goes after what she wants with strength." He paused, steadied his voice. "I don't understand why you left the e-mails of your correspondences with investors interested in Sugar Mill. I could have lived my entire life not knowing about you going behind my back soliciting buyers, since you didn't continue pursuing that. Why did you want me to know? Did you want me to hate you?"

"What are you talking about? What e-mails?" Ben was surprised how genuinely shocked she looked.

"The ones you left on the printer." He stepped back a single pace. "Wait." He held up his hand. "You didn't know they were there." He reminded her what letters he was talking about.

"Oh God. No." Her eyes were bright. "I forgot I had printed them to review. So much had happened that day. I forgot they were there." She started to reach for his face, but pulled her hand back. "How awful for you to find them. I didn't want you to know about it. I had contacted the interested parties and told them the deal was off before I left Sugar Mill." She looked away. "What good would it have done if you knew that I was trying to find a solid buyer for Sugar Mill when that deal was over?"

Ben looked at her a long time. When he had read each and every blog, he had heard Elli's voice reading them to him in his head. He heard her fears, her worries, her triumphs and her loneliness. He not only heard it, he felt it heavy and real with every beat of his heart. He felt it now in her wide-bright eyed stare. On top of all that, he heard Beau's voice, too. He was telling him that he had lost confidence in his judgment of character. His cousin was right and he intended to regain that right now, right here. Like he did with his dogs, he looked for the subtle signs of what was really being said. The flutter of her eyes. The lift of her hand to her throat. The change in her breathing. "I believe you, Elli."

"Thank you." He saw her throat tighten as she swallowed. "I wanted to give you everything you wanted when I left. You deserved that. Joey deserved it. Your family deserved it."

"I didn't get everything I wanted." He pushed aside the dogs to stand closer to her. "How could I when I didn't know what the hell I really wanted? I know now, Elli."

She tilted her head and looked at him with the most hurt and confused look in her baby blues. His heart squeezed in his chest again when her bottom lip began to quiver.

"Please, Ben. You have the capacity to devastate me more than the cancer did." Tears pooled in her eyes. "I'm begging you to watch your words with me. I'm not as strong as you think."

"Ah, cher, I'm screwing this up." He ran a fingertip along her jaw. "My head turned to mush when I saw you come around that corner like a beautiful angel." He inhaled deeply, trying to gather his thoughts. "I'm not forgiving what you did, Elli, but I understand it. I know that you were trying to find a way to save your family, just like I was mine. I get it. I've been chasing that since Sarah started using me and destroying my trust in humanity." He folded his hand over hers. "If you hadn't chiseled away at the crap encasing my heart, I would have been…lost." Her tears began to flow now, and Ben didn't know what to do about them. "Don't cry, cher." She wiped her eyes and left a large smudge of black makeup under her right eye. He smiled. "You are so damn cute."

"Ben," she sighed. "I have to go. Thank you for being so kind and wonderful." She swallowed hard. "I hope we have everything cleared up." She turned in a hurry to leave him.

"Wait." He turned her to face him. "I'm not finished."

"Please Ben, don't," she said, swallowing back a sob.

"Elli, I didn't want to, but I do. I love you."

She swayed on her feet, and then locked her knees to stand steady. "No," she said, her voice just a whisper. "Love isn't ever going to be enough for us." Her voice was a sob. "I've known I'm in love with you from the first time we made love." Her voice lowered. "I knew you loved me on the side of the road when I started that second fire."

He laughed. "You knew before I did?" He grabbed her hands. "Of course, you did. Cher, you get me."

"I know how hard it was for you to come here and tell me…"

"Coming to accept it was hard, but telling you is easy. I love you. I want you to come back to Sugar Mill and marry me. I love you and Joey loves you."

"Oh, God." She grabbed her stomach; she looked miserable. "I don't want to hurt you. I know you are handing me your precious, dear heart. I can't take it. I wish I could. God knows, I wish I could, Ben. I can't."

Ben felt like he had been punched in the chest, then he remembered she had said she loved him. "Sorry, cher, but I won't accept 'I can't.'"

"Don't be stubborn. Don't dig your heels in."

"They're already dug, darling. I know what you are trying to do. I know why. You are afraid of tomorrows. I'm not asking for tomorrows. I want you for today. If we don't have a tomorrow, at least I've had you for today."

He pulled her against him and held her so tight he felt her heart pounding. "Ben, I found a lump."

He felt his heart stop. He eased back to look at her. "Are you okay?"

"That's not the point," she cried.

"Answer me, Elli. Are you okay?" His voice was full of concern and impatience.

"Tell me right now, when you are wondering if I have cancer, that you are also wondering if it was big mistake to ask me to marry you." She swiped at the tears. "I can't drag you and Joey into my world."

"Are you okay?" he asked more firmly.

"Yes. The lump was benign. It was probably a contusion from my battle with Doug, but the oncologists did a biopsy anyway."

Ben blew out a breath. His head felt lighter. Her hands felt warmer in his. "Is that why you left? You found the lump while you were at Sugar Mill?"

She nodded. "I was scared. I didn't want to drag you and your family into that dark, debilitating fear."

Ben hugged her again. "We are all afraid of things, cher. Fear drives us all. Even the dogs." He looked into her eyes. "How we deal with our fears is what determines our character, our mark on the world."

"I want to have thousands of todays with you, Ben, and with Joey." She stepped away from him. "But I can't do that to you two. What if the cancer returns? What if I die?"

"People die. No one leaves this world without dying. It's just how it is. Children die, old people die. My question to you is why in the hell aren't you living? Really living. Heart and soul and gusto living. Take chances. Let me take chances with you."

"Deep in the recesses of my heart and mind, I know you're right. I'm not sure I can let go of the fear, though."

"Take a chance with me, Elli." Ben stepped closer to her again. "I'm asking you to love me back, cher. My eyes are wide open and so is my heart. None of us knows when our time will come. All we have is this single moment. I want my moment. I want our moments." He went down on one knee.

"Oh, Ben." She didn't take her eyes off of him. "I want this moment and the next with you. I'm so blasted selfish to want it. Please let me be magnanimous. Let me do the right thing."

He shook his head. "The right thing is to say yes. I can't imagine how horrible the longing and loneliness will be if you say no. How much worse could losing you be than to never wake up with you in my arms, to never let Joey read bedtime stories to us together as the sun sets over the cane fields, to never play with our dogs along the banks of the bayou shouting at the gators to stay away?"

The dogs moved closer to where Ben remained on bended knee. BJ sniffed his neck. Jenny and Doe sat on either side of him and looked up at her. "This isn't fair. You are all ganging up on me."

"Dogs know instinctively what they want and go after it." He smiled. "They don't worry about anything else. They just live in the moment. Live in the moment with me, Elli. Marry me."

"Ben, are you sure you understand what you get with me?"

He smiled, hearing a bit of surrender in her question. "Darlin', I know exactly what I'm getting and I like it." Now, he knew it was time to hand Elli his heart. "I wanted to believe you were a deceiving, manipulative conniver because I was so battered by Sarah's deception, manipulation, and conniving. But you charmed me. You made me laugh. You made me want to believe you were just like the woman you presented to me. I didn't realize it at the time, but I wanted it so much that I risked gossip and ridicule by my family to see if you were really that person I liked being around." He inhaled like he had taken a blow to his gut. "Finding the e-mails was awful, Elli. I felt like I had been played a fool. It reinforced my original expectations of you. You were just like Sarah…only I couldn't believe that was true." He shook his head. "My heart said that wasn't right, but my head said it had to be. Head or heart?" He smiled. "Heart." He kissed her hand. "The character of the woman I saw working and playing on the plantation seemed real. The fact that Joey and Tante Izzy loved you also gave me pause. I came to California wanting answers, but the truth is, I knew here," he pressed his palm over his heart, "that I only came here to bring you home."

"Ben, I…"

"Let me finish, Elli." He smiled. "I worked on this part in case I would need it." He cleared his throat. "'I would rather have one breath of her hair, one kiss of her mouth, one touch of her hand than an eternity without it.'"

Elli sighed. "City of Angels." She sat on his bended knee.

"It's the most perfect thing you could have said at this moment." She smiled a tender smile. "I want to live each and every moment with you, Ben. I want whatever we can have together. Living without you hasn't been living. I love you so much." Her smile widened. "Yes, I'll marry you." She threw her arms around his neck and Ben felt her joy bolt through him. The dogs jumped on them, tails wagging. "I think the girls approve."

Epilogue

My dearest Bosom Blog buddies. Fear kept me from having real hope and real dreams for a future. I tried to label it as something else...being selfless, honorable, practical, even caring. The truth is, I was afraid to hope and to have that hope dashed away. I was afraid to dream of a wonderful tomorrow and to have that dream taken from me. I was so frightened of the emotional pain and heartache, that I thought avoiding the things that brought me joy would save me from it. It took a man and a small child and a pack of dogs to show me that fear is worse than death. We only have this moment, right now...shouldn't we live it with unconditional love and joy...like a child? Fear barricades us from that gift. When you see a puppy rolling in the grass or greeting you with its tail wagging and his tongue hanging to the side, think of that gift of living in the moment and thank God we have it. Dare to walk away from the fear.

I am living my dream. I want you that for you, too. You deserve it, E.

Bosom Blog Buddies Post

They were all dressed in red-carpet formals; Elli in a pale purple, low-back sequined gown, Ben and Joey in traditional black tuxedoes, Tante Izzy in a shocking pink chiffon with a chartreuse sash around her waist. While Elli was being escorted by who she dubbed the most handsome men there, Ben and Joey hadn't caused as much of a commotion as Tante Izzy's "dates"—the extraordinarily handsome Bienvenu brothers, Beau and Jackson. Beau looked expensive and classic in his tailored black Armani tux, crisp white shirt and black bow tie. Jackson, who just retired from the Navy JAG and moved back to Cane the week before, looked strong and sexy. He wore his formal dress white uniform waist jacket, evening blue trousers, dark bow tie, gold cummerbund, and gold Navy insignia cuff links. The paparazzi went mad with curiosity and intrigue over the gorgeous eligible bachelors, taking thousands of pictures of them and Tante Izzy, as they walked into the theater behind Sam Cooper and Heather Harley. The director had fallen in love with Tante Izzy and worked her into four more scenes in the movie. She was even featured in the trailer. Despite all the movie excitement, Tante Izzy claimed her biggest thrill was being named to the board of the Gene I.D. Foundation. The woman was full of surprises. As a wedding present to Elli and Ben, she donated two million dollars of her oil money to the foundation. With one million in an endowment and the other million available for their clients and operating costs, Elli was able to hire a wonderful director for the day-to-day operations in California and make time to share the responsibilities with Abby in dealing with the LAPD and their investigation. Most importantly, she could now be Joey's mommy, work at the kennel, and be a good wife to her dream man.

Ben kissed Elli on the cheek as they watched Tante Izzy being interviewed by Entertainment Tonight. "She's going to want to star in the next two films that are scheduled to come to Sugar Mill, you know?" He smiled. "You are responsible for this."

"Aunt Rosa is." She turned and moved into his arms. "You know I didn't quite understand why she gave us each half of the plantation. I get it now."

"Yeah? I'm still in the dark there, cher."

"From what I've discovered, she was an empathetic and intuitive woman. A good woman. She knew I was alone and you had boarded your heart up tight. She forced two lonely, damaged people together. She wanted to give me a family and dogs to love and to care for me. She wanted to give you a woman who would love you and not your status and wealth."

"Speaking of Rosa's dogs..." He smiled a mischievous smile. "I think it's a good time to tell you about them, considering we are in a crowded public event and you wouldn't want to make a scene to embarrass us in front of the paparazzi." He smiled again. "You know those really well-behaved, beautiful golden labs at the kennel? They are yours. They are the dogs Rosa really gave you. The girls crowding our bed every night came from the pound."

"What? Are you kidding me? I own six dogs. I think I'm going to faint." Elli turned, faced him, and lifted her shoulders in a big shrug. "Oh well."

"Uh-oh. What are you not telling me, cher?"

"You remember Donna?" He just looked at her. "Well," she batted her eyes at him and smiled. "I actually didn't sell her to a Hollywood dog handler, like I told you." She batted her eyes in false flirtation. "She was never really my dog. I rented her from that high-end dog handler to impress you when I first came to Sugar Mill. When he refused to sell Donna to me, I had to give her back to him."

He looked at Elli for a single beat then burst out laughing. "To impress me?" They both laughed, realizing they'd each used the dogs to fool the other. He hugged her. "Cher, you are as unpredictable as a surprise birthday party."

Elli looked up at him and kissed him on his chin. She softened her voice and leaned into him. "'Darling, the party is where you are.'" Elli kissed Ben on the cheek. "That was Lana Turner in The Bad and The Beautiful."

He leaned in and nibbled on Elli's ear. "I'll show you the bad and the beautiful at the party in our bedroom later." He reached into his pocket. "And to assure we have a good time, I have this." He handed her the amber vial with the love potion still inside.

Elli threw her head back and laughed.

Hope you enjoyed Elli's story. Please take a minute and leave a review at Goodreads, Amazon, or wherever you purchased this book. Tell your friends, family and co-workers, and then stay tuned for the next tale from Tina DeSalvo…

Jewel

A Second Chance Novel

When antiques' expert and picker, *Jewel Durand* arrives at Sugar Mill Plantation with her grandmother, Mignon, and turns *Beau Bienvenu's* nice tidy world upside down. Jewel is determined to help her grandmother find a lost twin sister that she mentioned having for the first time just a few weeks ago while they were watching a movie where the beautiful Sugar Mill Plantation appeared painted in a shocking pink color. Not only did Jewel's grandmother claim she had a twin sister, but she said she had lived on that plantation. Mignon's memory is far from reliable but Jewel can't just discount her insistent claims to her failing memory. She must do what she does best, research and investigate the past to find out if her grandmother's sibling exists before dementia takes Mignon away from her forever. She owes that to the woman who has been more mother to her than her real mother, the famous Bourbon Street stripper, *Miss Praline*.

Beau will always protect the Bienvenu family first and foremost. They had rescued him and his brother from a life of abuse and neglect when they were young boys. He is suspicious that the strangely behaving grandmother and gorgeous granddaughter may be a threat to his family because of the questions they are asking about the Bienvenu history. They could be con artists trying to stake a claim to a family trust that has been held in waiting for a missing heir that disappeared over eighty years ago. Beau will do anything to defend the people who gave him a Second Chance in life. Jewell will never stop until she has answers for the woman who gave her hers. Two people grateful to others for their Second Chance on life…but never really claiming it as their own.

About the Author and Your Donation

Tina DeSalvo was diagnosed with advanced Stage 3 Breast Cancer in 2008. She understands that when you are ill or the people around you are ill, finding *joy* in life can be *harder* and *easier*. Health battles have a way of making those on the front lines have a clairty that their busy lives had blurred before. At the same time, the financial worries and requirements that the illness creates can cast a haze over the celebration of being alive. In an effort to help lessen the financial burden for patients with Breast Cancer so they can get to the buisness of enjoying life, Tina is donating *all* of her share from the sale of this book. That means, with your purchase, you are fighting along side of the women, men and families who are living with Breast Cancer and who are celebrating being alive on this day. The money raised from **Elli, a Second Chance Novel** will help fund many *un-met needs* for patients fighting Breast Cancer.

Here are a few ways your support helps…

$25 Funds one gas card, which provides a patient in need of transportation a way to attend their scheduled cancer treatment

$35 Funds a post-surgery camisole for a breast cancer patient

$50 Provides one couseling session and supplementary materials for cancer survivors and their families to help them adjust to life after treatment

$100 Provides nutritional supplements or additional prothesis that isn't covered under health care

$250 Provides a lymphedema sleeve or a one-hour lympedema thereapy session for a breast cancer patient

…and there are so many more ways your donation helps.

To learn more about **Tina DeSalvo** *or how to help, visit* www.tinadesalvo.com or
www.MARYBIRD.ORG/GEAUXPINK

Made in the USA
Columbia, SC
05 June 2018